THE CROWNKILLER SAGA

I

HEIRS

OF

DESTRUCTION

T.N. VITUS

ISBN
Paperback: 979-8-9868415-2-6
E-book: 979-8-9868415-3-3

Cover art and design by: Sarah Lee
Printed in the United States of America

For those who prefer the quiet company of a book and a loud imagination. Who only come up for air after the final page is over. I see you, and I'm with you. Fantasy is real. You just have to keep reading.

Other books by T.N. Vitus

Sacrilege

Emelie has always known to stay away from the woods—the elders in her village won't let her forget it. No matter how the wind between the trees calls to her, she's to stay away.

When her exiled childhood best friend Halvar emerges from the woods unharmed, she begins to question the things she's been taught, and whether there is life outside of their village. But when Halvar's reappearance coincides with a series of murders, Emelie must decide if she prefers the safety of her puritanical people, or the chance to escape to a new life with him.

As Emelie explores who she really is and what she really wants, dark secrets of her village begin to come to light. As the bodies start piling up and lines are drawn, Emelie needs to decide which side she stands on, and she may just need to unleash her inner nature to survive the fallout.

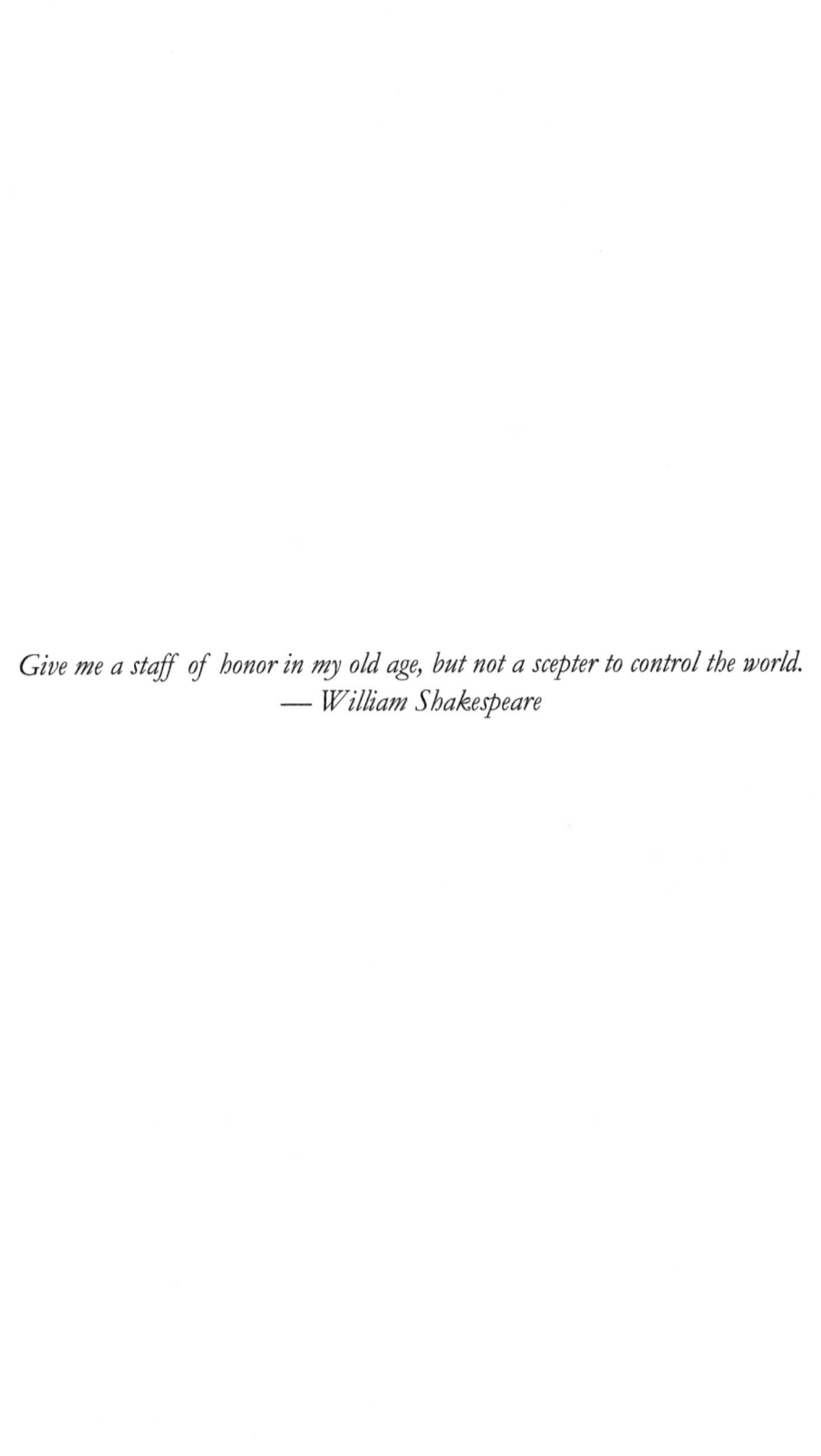

Give me a staff of honor in my old age, but not a scepter to control the world.
— William Shakespeare

THE GREAT HOUSES OF ADRISTAN

I. HOUSE LANCOR

Keeper of Amenities, Fashioner of All Furnishings, and the Strong Bones of Adristan

Ewan Lancor - High Lord of the First House
Laila Redspire - Lady Wife to the High Lord
Ezra Lancor - Heir Apparent to the High Lord, Prince of Segsiege
Freya Lancor - First daughter of the First House, Princess of Segsiege
Ledger Lancor - Second son of the First House, Prince of Segsiege
Doctrina Lucius - Servant of the Order of the Dux Doctrina

II. HOUSE OBERON

Keeper of Health, Healer of All Wounds, and the Rejuvenating Breath of Adristan

Isaiah Oberon - High Lord of the Second House
Sage Oberon - Heir Apparent to the High Lord, Prince of Scalesound
Doctrina Quentin - Servant of the Order of the Dux Doctrina

III. HOUSE VESERVUS

Keeper of Intelligence, Knower of All Events, and the Vast Brain of Adristan

Alden Veservus - High Lord of the Third House
Adria Erestine - The Late Lady Wife to the High Lord
Asriel Veservus - Heir Apparent to the High Lord, Prince of Isle Verdale
Rhaella - Daughter of the High Lord, Ward of House Veservus
Doctrina Dogan - Servant of the Order of the Dux Doctrina

IV. HOUSE REDSPIRE

Keeper of the Arts, Master of All Styles, and the Beating Heart of Adristan

Allison Redspire - High Lord of the Fourth House
Lilliana Ledova - Lady Wife to the High Lord
Aida Redspire - Heir Apparent to the High Lord, Princess of Sandorne
Asa Redspire - Princess of Sandorne
Alora Redspire - Princess of Sandorne
Adrianna Redspire - Princess of Sandorne
Doctrina Xanthe - Servant of the Order of the Dux Doctrina

V. HOUSE STILLGROVE

Keepers of Nourishment, Refiner of All Tastes, and the Full Belly of Adristan

Geralt Stillgrove - High Lord of the Fifth House
Regina Normora - Lady Wife to the High Lord
Gerard Stillgrove - Heir Apparent to the High Lord, Prince of the Mainland
Galilea Stillgrove - First Daughter of the Fifth House, Princess of the Mainland
Roman Stillgrove - Second Son of the Fifth House, Prince of the Mainland
Doctrina Ophelia - Servant of the Order of the Dux Doctrina

VI. HOUSE AVIATIS

Keeper of the Veil, Seer of All Things, and the Triumphant Spirit of Adristan.

Zerin Aviatis - High Lord of the Sixth House
Raven Aviatis - Heir Apparent to the High Lord, Princess of Pearlscape & High Priestess of the Tradition of Lucerianism
Doctrina Beatrix - Servant of the Order of the Dux Doctrina

VII. HOUSE LIGHTPIKE

Keeper of Wealth, Accountant of All Coins, and the Nimble Hands of Adristan.

Galahad Lightpike - High Lord of the Seventh House
Regis Aviatis - Lord Husband to the High Lord
Hiram Lightpike - Heir Apparent to the High Lord, Prince of Trimount
Ramsey Lightpike - Second Son of the Seventh House, Prince of Trimount
Doctrina Cadmus - Servant of the Order of the Dux Doctrina

IX. HOUSE MIDAR

Keeper of the Peace, Bringer of All Justice, and the Unrelenting Muscle of Adristan.

Vincent Midar - High Lord of the Eighth House
Madeline Salgrat - Lady Wife to the High Lord
Virgil Midar - Heir Apparent to the High Lord, Prince of Greenisle & Lord Commander of Adristan's Forces
Doctrina Nicholas - Servant of the Order of the Dux Doctrina

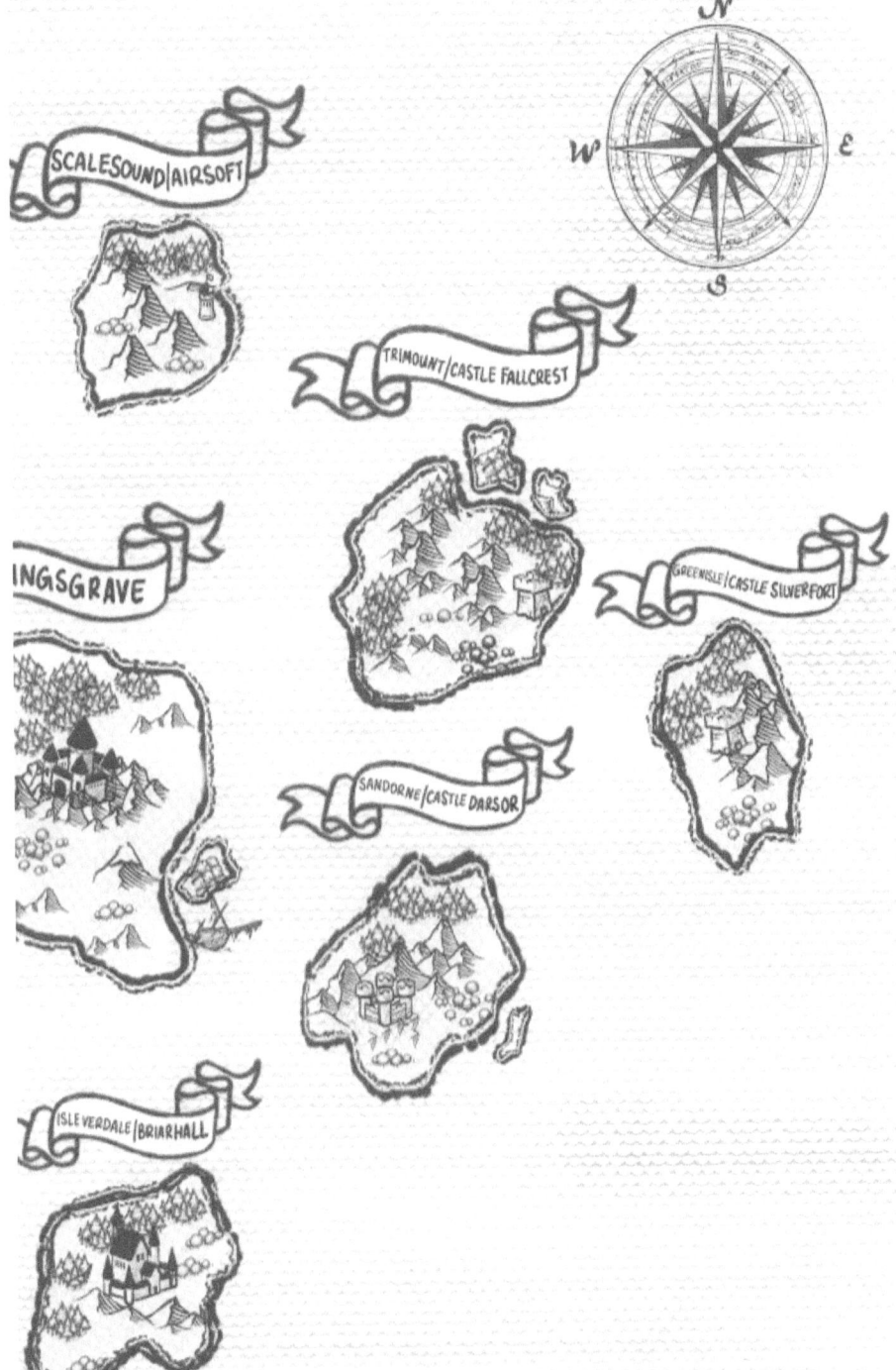

CALENDAR

MONTHS OF THE YEAR

LANCORUN	SPRING	NAMED FOR HOUSE LANCOR
OBERUN	SPRING	NAMED FOR HOUSE OBERON
VESERVARY	SPRING	NAMED FOR HOUSE VESERVUS
REDSPIRARY	SUMMER	NAMED FOR HOUSE REDSPIRE
STILLGREL	SUMMER	NAMED FOR HOUSE STILLGROVE
AVIATOUN	SUMMER	NAMED FOR HOUSE AVIATIS
LIGHTPEL	FALL	NAMED FOR HOUSE LIGHTPIKE
MIDANAE	FALL	NAMED FOR HOUSE MIDAR
LUCERIARY	FALL	HOLY MONTH OF LUCERIANISM
MORTENUARY	WINTER	HOLY MONTH TO HONOR THE DEAD
REQUERY	WINTER	MONTH OF REST
PONTIS	WINTER	BRIDGE INTO THE NEW YEAR

Days of the week

The Lucerian Calendar is inspired by the stages of stoking a fire. The days are as follows:

Fome	Tinder
Incen	Ignition
Auct	Growth
Increm	Flashover
Replet	Fully Developed
Cari	Decay
Frax	Ash

PROLOGUE

"And we name ourselves the governing force of Adristan. Always equals, never tyrants over one another. This power has been vested in us by our own self-determination, against the wishes of an oppressive monarch. Under this new system, eight houses split the responsibilities of ruling, and such a figure will never rise again."
—Treaty between the founding High Lords of Adristan

The girl did not go easily, and perhaps that was why they had to bind her. To avoid the thrashing and screaming. She was a hitter, which was unbecoming of a girl of her status, but she was young and uneducated in the ways of a Lady. That was why her family had sent her here, after all. Simply donning dresses and curtsying was not enough to qualify one as a Lady. They would know, for Ladies were plentiful after spending time under their guidance.

Something was noticeably different about this one, though. It had been many years since the nation had seen royal blood, but when it was seen, it was undeniable. And the royal blood in the girl standing before them was undeniable. Even as she threw her weight against the bindings, it was clear she was not to be taken for granted. It shone in her eyes and in each wild, commanding movement.

They could see it.

Those minute differences that called back to her predecessors were there and they were clear as day. The order of her birth did not matter, nor did the charge to prepare her for the lifestyle of a Lady.

She was not meant to be a Lady.

She was meant to be *queen*.

For so long, this day had seemed unreachable. Years passed—and continued to do so—and the royal line seemingly faded into history. Without a worthy heir, they had to wait in the shadows, biding their time with lesser matters. But they would not be swayed. Not when the fraudulent leaders of both the stronghold and the lesser houses insisted on sitting upon their thrones and hiding behind their parapets. Handing out decrees as though their word was law.

Their betters now sat in seats of power they did not deserve, inferior in every way to the king that had come before. They would not serve false prophets in earnest, but they had to pretend for the time being. They were not fit for war. Not now, at least.

It did not have to come to this. They could have had their needs met peacefully. Diplomatically, even. But the High Lords atop their unearned peaks were not to be reasoned with. Not on matters of ruling. They were convinced that their way was better, purposely ignoring the legacy of rightful heirs to the throne.

But they would be made to remember, even if by force. The girl's sharp cries rang out across the room as they molded her into the woman—into the rightful heir—she was always destined to be.

She didn't want to see at first, and perhaps she wouldn't for some time. But the truth needn't rear its ugly head so soon.

Kingdoms weren't built overnight, and neither were rulers.

They needed time to forge themselves into what their lands and people needed. They needed time to find the strong hand that would guide the future. And though the girl's hands were weak now, she could be trained. Her spindly, clumsy fingers could be trained into agile, nimble things. She could be taught to slip those deft hands between the cracks that the bloated, greedy ones could not reach through. And her desire to grasp that power would be different.

It would not be greed if it was her *right*.

The people wouldn't see it that way at first. Though, given the right amount of time and the girl's strengthened hand, anyone could be taught to see what was right. And there would be no alternative once the great houses bent the knee. They would be sure of it.

CHAPTER ONE

"Once the feigned retreat draws in the enemy forces, we will launch an attack from our hiding post beyond the trees. In order for this to work, we must make camp closer to the mountains to remain better hidden."
—Battle strategy, from the collected documents of *High Lord Alden Veservus*

3 Aviatoun, in the Benevolent year 112 A.E.

In the war tent crowded with voices fighting for dominance, Rhaella kept her head down and listened. Though her eyes were on the piece of parchment in front of her, her attention was focused on the rest of the room as she grasped each strand of conversation. There was little she didn't already know, however, and the men were mostly relaying information she had given them.

It wasn't so much that she needed to glean any more out of them. Instead, she was pointedly using them as a means to avoid drafting a response to the letter she had received that morning.

War is no time for children's games. I will speak with the true Hawk of Veservus and no one else.

Although it was only one sentence in a nearly page-long letter, the words jumped out at her. They demanded a response.

The High Lord had made a grand miscalculation when saddling her with the responsibility of impersonating her brother through correspondence, but she hadn't had the nerve to tell him so at the time. What weight did her opposition carry when she wasn't even in line to inherit her father's legacy? That was for Asriel. Her job had always been to be his shadow, never her own.

She told herself the other heirs likely wouldn't pay attention to *who* was sending out the strategies when they were winning nearly every battle, so long as they won.

Prince Virgil Midar, though, apparently *did* pay attention to who was sending him letters.

Rhaella briefly flirted with the idea of lying—of keeping up the ruse until the war was over—but House Veservus could not risk their alliance with House Midar. And they certainly couldn't risk the invaluable aid of the Midar army either, let alone the good will of their Prince. Her house owed his a great debt. The least she could afford him was some honesty—or at least an approximation of it.

She let her eyes glaze over as a voice on the other side of the tent caught her attention. From anyone else's perspective, her eyes and full attention remained fixed on the letter in her hands. Her ears, however, latched onto the sounds of one of her father's men—some Lord or young soldier—laughing too loudly. Too jovial for the grisly scene on the other side of the tent flaps.

Rhaella listened as he told jokes that were crude and ill-timed. She listened to the other men's responses, whether they encouraged him or told him to piss off. Whatever they said, she cataloged it in her mind. Neatly filing tidbits into categories of important or unimportant enough to relay to her father.

These men were entirely too comfortable around her, forgetting that she was the daughter of their High Lord. Though perhaps if she were legitimate like Asriel, they would remember. But her illegitimacy afforded her the words of loose-lipped men.

Being invisible was her greatest gift, and remaining unseen and unheard was easy enough when those around her assumed she was of no consequence. In fact, they thought her inconsequential enough that, even in her presence, they spoke freely. So she listened.

And so the High Lord Alden Veservus had given his bastard daughter a place at court.

She'd heard enough inside this cloistered tent. Rhaella rose from the corner stool she'd been sulking on and hurried out into the fresh air of the afternoon. None of the soldiers or Lords called out to her. She pocketed their remarks, sorting through which jokes would be worth retelling to Asriel when she saw him. As she crossed the expanse of the camp, she observed the soldiers running drills and formations. There was something so earnest in what they were doing, and the thought drove Rhaella to attempt to ignore how few of them were left.

Virgil had been correct when he said that this was no time for games. Rhaella hated the sounds and smells of war. If she believed in the cause any less, it would be unbearable. But it was only that frail belief in what was to come—that belief as threadbare as spidersilk—that kept her sane.

The presence of her dragon at the edge of the clearing teased her, and she wanted nothing more than to go to him. She saw his scales slinking between the trunks and heard the whisper of his growl as it rustled the leaves. Better to leave Egorion alone, though. If she got too close, she wouldn't be able to resist taking him to the skies. And since she couldn't do that, she chose to do nothing at all.

It didn't take her long to reach her father's tent, which sat atop a small hill under a couple of trees. She breezed past the guards who stood at the entrance, and she felt the weight of a legacy that was not technically her own as she walked beneath the family crest that was emblazoned on the front. And when she pushed back the tent flap, her eyes immediately adjusted to the shade as she found her father, High Lord Alden Veservus. True to form, he was bent over a pile of letters, furiously transcribing something.

The first words out of her mouth were, "Where's Asriel?"

"Training with his guard," her father said without looking up. His pen moved ceaselessly across the page. "Which is where you should be as well."

"I'm busy. Doing what you always ask me to do."

He peered up at her. "And have you heard anything?"

She shook her head. "Nothing of value. But if I stop, I'll miss something that *is*."

"Fair enough," her father said, collecting his pages. And before she could let out a breath, he continued. "But you will make up any missed training after dinner."

"Yes, because your men won't admit to treason after their bellies are full."

Her father sighed wearily. "Did you only come to jest? I'm in no mood, Rhaella."

Wordlessly, she handed Virgil's letter to him. His eyes scanned the page quickly the first time, and then she watched as he read it twice more. Once to get a basic understanding, twice to glean the important details, and thrice to gather any hidden meaning the Prince hadn't said outright.

She fidgeted while she waited, feeling strangely vulnerable with her father's eyes on her correspondence.

He coughed. "How do you intend to respond to this?"

It was startling, the way he shifted between the roles of her father and of the High Lord of one of the great houses. The muscles in his face contracted differently, his eyes either sharp or soft depending on the situation. And she had learned long ago to discern the subtle nuances in each.

Right now, she was speaking with the High Lord.

"At your discretion," she answered smoothly. "Although I would suggest that we not continue lying to him. It's not worth putting our alliance at risk."

"House Midar would not break our alliance over something as trivial as you concealing your identity."

"No, but they might stop sending their men to our aid." She paused. "And we are very in need of men. It simply isn't worth the risk."

Casting aside the pile of papers, he looked up at her with a guarded fondness. "Go find Asriel so we can discuss how to proceed."

Rhaella dipped into a half-bow and exited the tent. She found Asriel several yards east, sparring with his guard, Barrett. As she watched them fight for a moment, she found herself fascinated by how slowly her brother's form was improving. It was no wonder their father kept him off the battlefield; Asriel would be skewered before he could even manage to grip his handle properly.

"Your elbows, Asriel," Barrett scolded. "You have to *use* them."

Asriel's face twisted into a scowl, but he peered over the guard's shoulder to meet Rhaella's eyes as he threw down his sword. In a matter of seconds, he had effectively ended his and Barrett's lesson as though it hadn't mattered in the first place.

"We can reconvene later," he said. Then, just before he passed the guard, Asriel threw his arm around Barrett's neck and trapped him in a headlock. The two men laughed, wrestling until Asriel let up. Her brother jogged to close the distance between them, and there was an easy smile on his face as he caught up to her. "All's well, Rhae?"

"Not sure yet," she shrugged. "I got a letter from the Midar heir."

"That's nothing new," he said, wiping his face with his discarded shirt. "What did he say?"

Holding out the letter, she said, "See for yourself."

His smile faded as he read. Once he was finished with it, he blew out a whistle, handing the page back to her. "What are you going to do?"

"Father wants to discuss that with *both* of us," she said sternly. "That's why I came and got you."

"Joy," Asriel said drily, finally pulling the shirt over his head.

Back in the High Lord's tent, the three of them gathered around her father's war table. A map of the surrounding area had been burnt onto the surface and figures were placed around the landscape. Each one marked where another house's camp stood. Over the past few weeks, they had fought their way across the mainland, which was beholden to no nation, and they were currently nearing the border of Steephelm. As it stood, the houses of Adristan were on good terms with Steephelm. Good enough terms, at least, that they did not contest the presence of several war camps on their doorstep.

The High Lord tapped his finger next to one of the figures. "The Midar camp has moved about a half day's journey away. We only have to decide which of you is going."

"There's nothing to decide," Rhaella said firmly. "If we keep up the lie and send Asriel, Virgil—" *A slip of the tongue.* "Excuse me, *Prince* Virgil might take offense. We are reliant on his house's forces. We'd be remiss to treat him as a fool."

"I don't take him for a fool," her father said. "But it is imperative that Asriel is seen as the Master of Strategy."

"It's a bit late for that, isn't it?" Rhaella bit out. It was a rare show of temper from her, but it was an impulse she'd need to keep in check nonetheless.

"She's right, Father," Asriel said. "I don't know the battle plans as well as Rhaella does. My presence will raise more questions than I'll be able to answer."

"So we admit that we've been lying to a house heir, further souring our good name?"

Rhaella shook her head. "Prince Virgil needs my strategy. And he's a man of politics, just as you are. He'll understand the need for discretion."

Unconvinced, her father said, "You're sure of that?"

"Not entirely," she admitted. "But enough to convince him."

Finally, her father nodded. Rhaella couldn't help the cool rush of relief that ran through her. More often than not, it was her ideas that they followed through with. But that moment of hesitation always made her stomach tie itself in knots. Just once, it would be nice if her father gave her the benefit of the doubt.

"Gather your things," her father said. "You'll leave at once—*on foot*—and you'll extend our house's sincerest apologies for the dishonesty."

"I won't have to travel through enemy territory to get to their camp," Rhaella argued. "If I stick to the clouds, I don't see why I can't take Egorion."

"Because," her father said, his tone measured. "Riding your dragon across an active war zone puts a target on your back. Even if you think you won't be seen, our enemies have eyes everywhere. You're stealthy, so you'll trek through the thickest trees as soon as you pack a bag. We can't spare the men, so you'll have to go without a guard. Make sure to arm yourself."

Rhaella flinched. "Why can't I take Barrett?"

"Ser Barrett needs to stay with Asriel," her father said dismissively.

"What about one of your guards?" Her voice pitched as she argued. "You have two!"

"As I said," her father began, offering her no more than a glance, "we cannot spare the men. And you are the acting Master of Strategy, are you not? You can manage to keep yourself hidden for half a day's trek. And if you cannot manage that, then you will have earned whatever consequences come your way. Now, have you planned what to say, or must I send you with a script?"

Rhaella swallowed down her rising emotions. "I'm going to tell him the truth. A version of it, at least. I'll tell him that my brother, Asriel, has busied himself with the war effort. And then I will tell him that I, a strategist of equal measure, took up his correspondence instead."

"And if he argues with you?" Her father wasn't even looking at her now, able to spare only a fraction of his attention. As though this conversation no longer merited his focus.

"I will remind him," she paused to take a breath, "that it is our strategies currently winning him the battles. Not his own."

The conversation grated against her the longer it went on, and Rhaella found herself counting the seconds until it was over. Until she was dismissed to gather her things and go. *Unguarded.*

Asriel was still learning to do all of the things she already knew how to do. If he was going to successfully Ascend as High Lord someday, Asriel *needed* to know how to sword fight and strategize and collect information in the Veservus tradition. His entire life had been devoted to that very training. And, graciously, their father decided to include Rhaella in that training as well, but only when it seemed convenient for him to do so. The moment it benefitted him more to send her to be useful somewhere else, he never hesitated. But it had long ago stopped bothering her that she picked up the material more quickly than her brother, or that—in any other circumstances—she would have been the more deserving heir. No, that wound no longer stung her pride.

Asriel hadn't done anything wrong by being born legitimately. From birth, Rhaella had been aware that this was her lot in life. That she would always be rewarded less, even when her cup of abilities ran over. She could be twice as gifted as Asriel, and in many aspects she *was*, but her greatness did not legitimize her. She was lucky their father allowed her a seat at his table at all.

"Make haste," the High Lord finally said, effectively dismissing her. "I'll be waiting for you at the edge of camp."

Rhaella and her brother bowed at the waist, departing without protest. Once they were out of earshot—which was a greater distance for a man like their father—Asriel huffed out a laugh.

"I can't believe we were bested by the Midar heir, of all people," he said. "He paints a worrying picture for the future of his house."

Rhaella hummed. "Is that your scholarly deduction, or simply your opinion?"

"A bit of both," Asriel shrugged. "You've heard the rumors. Several failed abdication attempts, fighting in the seedy pits of his cities, a reputation for blood and brutality... I'll be surprised if he lasts long enough to Ascend from heir to High Lord."

Asriel followed her into her tent and watched as she stuffed necessities into a knapsack. A few days worth of clothes, some items for personal grooming, nothing superfluous or unnecessary. She donned a breastplate and vambraces before harnessing an extra dagger to her waist, but nothing more. She couldn't afford the weight a sword would add.

"Nervous about going into the wolves' den?"

"Not since I'm going to show them my teeth," she quipped as she secured a quiver of arrows across her back. The bow, she'd have to carry. She was afraid, but admitting that to Asriel wouldn't change anything.

Asriel snorted, but then his face hardened a fraction. "Be careful, ðoz." *Sister*. He must have truly sensed her fear, to try and offer comfort by referring to her with the Vessial moniker. The family tongue, a now-revived, once-dead language was one known only to them. It was a language they avoided using frivolously. Rhaella shuddered to think of what was written on her face to push him to do that.

Rhaella rolled her eyes, feigning disinterest. "I'm not afraid of Virgil."

"You're on a first-name basis with the Midar heir?" Asriel raised a brow.

"We built a rapport while I was pretending to be you," she said cooly, ignoring how her stomach tightened.

"Well," he said, "I still worry."

Something in her softened at that. For all of her brother's flaws, Rhaella couldn't bring herself to be angry with him for getting them into this situation. For her brother, there was little she wouldn't do. And writing letters was far from the worst she'd already done. It had always been this way, and she had settled into too much of a chafing comfort to want to change that now. And being one of her only allies at court, she needed him as much as he needed her.

They were two sides of the same coin, her and her brother. The only difference was how valuable each of them was to their father's schemes.

"You ready to go?"

Rhaella nodded wordlessly, hefting the sack onto her shoulder. She followed Asriel out of her tent and into the mid-morning sun. In the distance, their father waited with his hands folded behind his back. As they approached, Rhaella noted how tense his posture was. He stared at her for a long, quiet moment before clearing his throat and speaking in Vessial.

"Siu, ŭ afnaw swa zyisha." *Remember, you are a hawk.*

A reply rolled off her tongue effortlessly. "Ep, mìn." *Yes, Father.*

———◆———

The unclaimed terrain of the mainland was less familiar to Rhaella, and yet a vision of the map of the realm was crisp in her mind. She remained off the trodden pathway, cutting close to the mountainside to avoid travelers. The midday sun bore down on her, unforgiving in its heat. It was the thick of summer and the worst possible time of day to be out. Here, they felt the full extent of each of the seasons, each one's weather more extreme than on her island home. Which meant that by the time the camp was in sight, the back of Rhaella's neck was coated in a thin sheen of sweat.

Two guards waited at the fringes of the camp, a longsword at each of their hips. The guards couldn't have been much older than her, but the attentiveness in their stance spoke of experience. House Midar started them young.

"Greetings," one of them called out. "If you wouldn't mind disarming yourself, my partner will take your weapons."

They were expecting her, it seemed. Her father must have sent word ahead to the High Lord. Or maybe he had even alerted Virgil himself. She hadn't expected any less of him, truthfully. Rhaella made a show of removing the dagger at her waist before placing it in the waiting guard's hands. Carelessly, she tossed her quiver and bow onto the flattened grass before unlacing her vambraces and depositing the matching breastplate onto the ground beside everything else.

"Prince Midar is down this way," the taller one said. "You can get settled after meeting with him."

Again, Rhaella stayed quiet, following behind the men. They brought her to a large tent in the center of camp. Even from this distance, she could hear the cacophony of voices coming from inside. *Wolves' den, indeed*, she thought to herself. The shorter guard pulled back the tent flap and gave a small, almost mocking bow.

"My Lady," he said, gesturing inside with a flourish.

Rhaella ducked her head and slipped inside. There were few candles lit, which was no problem for her preternatural sight. Her eyes quickly adjusted to see the men gathered around a table, arguing and pointing at various spots on the map atop it. Most of them stood hunched over the wooden surface with tension written into every line of their bodies. But there was one man seated, legs spread languidly beneath the table. One elbow was perched on the arm of his chair, his hand switching between gestures in the air and holding up his chin.

As she approached the table, Prince Virgil Midar looked up from his seat and grinned.

"So, the Hawk decides to grace us with her presence."

He motioned for the others to clear the room, and they did so without protest. But she didn't miss how reluctant some of them looked. A few stared at her openly, looking her over with the same consideration she was giving to them. Though it was with far less discretion than she used.

"If any of those were your spymasters," she said once the room had emptied, "you should dismiss them from their position."

"You'll have to forgive their boldness. They don't often get the pleasure of meeting vampires," Virgil said. He gestured to a chair across from him. "Please, sit. I called for dinner, but it's not here yet."

"Thank you, though you should know that I am only part-vampire. The Veservus bloodline is just as diluted as that of any other house." Taking the offered chair, she stared at the Prince for a moment before deciding to cut to the heart of her summons. "You were insistent in your letter that I come. Now that I'm here, what can I say that wouldn't have sufficed through correspondence?"

His fingers toyed with a pen on the table. "I wanted to know if my guess was correct, and it seems it was. *You're* the Master of Spies, not your half-brother."

"Brother," she corrected. "And the title is Master of *Strategy*."

Virgil waved a careless hand. "Verbiage."

Rhaella's temper soured. "For weeks now, you and I have corresponded just fine under the pretense that my identity was a ruse. You understand the need for a good reputation just as well as I do, and yet, you were willing to risk yours on, what? A guess?" She paused, waiting for him to deny any of what she had just said, but he just stared back at her with the same easy confidence he had commanded when he cleared out the tent with nothing more than a wave of his hand.

"You can't change the subject so easily," he challenged her without missing a beat. "Sure, you and your brother are both hawks of House Veservus, but you're *The* Hawk. What does your brother do? Preen through court meetings while you do the heavy lifting in the dark?"

"He sits on our house's council and attends to his duties as the heir to my father's title," she corrected him with a barely-checked temper.

"And those duties are…?" Virgil trailed off, waiting for her to fill in the blanks for him.

She raised a brow instead. "Being an heir yourself, I would assume you'd know."

Virgil chuckled. "Do they teach you to sharpen your wit in that house of yours, or does it come naturally?"

"Both." She adjusted in her seat, avoiding the urge to squirm under his brazen observation. "Now that you've proven your point, what can I do for you?"

"You create the battle strategies, and I apply them," he said, clearing his throat. "With the tide of war turning in our favor, I wanted to cut out the middleman of having to send letters." He took a breath, seeming to center himself while he talked. "I want you to strategize what I believe will be the final few battles."

"And I couldn't do that from my camp?"

"But then I wouldn't have the pleasure of watching that mind of yours work." She arched a brow at him. "Plus, by doing so here, in *my* camp, we can get word out to my men much faster."

"I've given you months worth of battle strategy for dozens of possible scenarios. Plus, with the tide *turning in our favor*, as you said, I haven't found it necessary to create more."

"No, but the end of war makes men desperate," he said. There was a haunted look in his eyes, but she glimpsed it for only a moment before he blinked it away. "Our enemies aren't going to go down quietly. They're going to attack wildly and without thought. I'm a fine fighter, but I don't want to become desperate to match them, and that's where you come in."

Virgil was more than a fine fighter. Their combined armies could have been cut in half and he would still manage to win them the war. Stories of his heroism had already begun to spread throughout the nation. Which meant that he was either being modest or foolish, and she had already decided that he wasn't a fool.

The political script came to her easily. "What will House Veservus have to gain from my involvement with you?"

"It could earn you back the trust of the other houses," Virgil said, quirking a brow. "And it's no secret you're in need of some help in that area, given your house's current reputation."

She soured. "There are traitors from every house."

"But none so many as yours," he said pointedly. "This is a chance to affirm your loyalty to the nation."

"So your house gains my knowledge and intelligence while my house gains respect," she said. "Does that seem equal to you?"

"It's *fair*," he replied. "And that's what matters."

Rhaella resisted the urge to roll her eyes. "Fine. Though, if we're making a deal, you should know that House Veservus draws deals in blood. If you'd like my word, we'll honor that tradition. That way, I know you'll uphold your end of the bargain as well."

His eyes flashed with something like excitement. "I'd ask you to draw your dagger but I'm sure my men disarmed you before coming in here."

"They did," she said as she reached a hand down her shirt, tossing one final dagger onto the table with a clatter.

That confident grin returned to his face in full force. "My guards could storm in and seize you for that."

"They could, but they're about..." She paused, listening. "...Ten paces too far away to have heard anything."

"Oh, you're good," he said, laughing as he took the dagger. He unsheathed the blade and held it up to the light, examining it with a careful eye. "Your house custom demands that I cut my palm, correct? That's a difficult place to heal."

"Ensuring that you won't make promises you don't intend to keep," she finished for him.

Without another word, Virgil sliced open his palm, and bright vermillion blood welled to the surface of his skin. When he handed the knife back to her, the handle was covered in droplets of his blood as well. Rhaella cut open her own palm before holding out her hand to him to shake. Virgil took it without hesitation, gripping her hand firmly in his.

"You know I have to record everything I see and hear," she said, cleaning her palm with a handkerchief.

"I'd expect nothing less from a Veservus. Especially as we're living through history in the making."

"All time is history in the making," she pointed out. "We just feel it cut deeper right now."

He waved his clean hand. "Figures of speech."

One of the guards poked his head into the tent. "Dinner, Virgil."

"Send it in," Virgil said. "And bring a carafe while you're at it."

Once they were alone, Rhaella said, "I'm not much of a drinker."

"I am," he replied, setting aside the maps and figures strewn across the table. "The hours blur together between battles, and it makes the food go down easier. I feel as though I have to warn you, House Midar isn't much known for its cooking."

She snorted. Just then, a few men came in and set the table with a multitude of dishes. Rhaella thanked each of them. Sitting back, she waited for them to depart and for Virgil to begin the meal.

He must have noticed, because he said, "You don't have to wait."

"House customs," she said, removing the lid from the dish nearest her.

"Impeccable manners," he said, and she thought there was a tinge of sarcasm to it. "How does a member of House Veservus let loose?"

She pretended to think. "Studying the histories, saying our prayers, and reading poetry by the fire after the sun goes down."

"Such things are foreign to people of my house. All we know is wrestling in the dirt and drinking ourselves into oblivion."

They began eating, the silence interrupted by the sound of utensils scraping against plates. He'd spoken true—it wasn't the best meal she'd ever had. But it was warm and flavorful, and that was enough.

"Does it make you nervous," he asked, "being away from your house?"

"It can't," she answered honestly. "I've traveled between houses since before the war. It's part of my duties."

"Never to mine. I've hardly been off Greenisle, except to go sailing," Virgil said. He paused while he chewed, humming thoughtfully. After a long moment, he spoke again. "One would think High Lord Veservus would be more protective of his offspring."

"My father knows I can take care of myself. I don't even need a sworn sword. It seems the case is the same for you, if the rumors are to be believed," she said, deflecting with ease.

"I'm Lord Commander of the most powerful army in the nation," he said without an inch of pride. If anything, Rhaella could have sworn that was *resentment* she heard in his voice. "Every soldier is my sworn sword. You, however... Your father must consider your skills of great use if he places so much trust in you."

"My *skills* are that of a busybody," she said, feigning disinterest with a wave of her hand. "Anyone with the proper attention span can do what I do."

"If that were the case, you wouldn't be the Hawk," he said, his eyes on her as he drank from his cup. "Yet here you are."

If she wasn't on her guard to glean information out of him, she would be flattered. Virgil was just as pleasant in person as he was in his letters. Somehow, in person, he brought out that same urge to confide in him as she felt every time she put pen to page. There was just something about the warmth in his demeanor despite the shadows beneath his eyes.

It was earnestness, she decided. A fine trait for a future High Lord.

"Do you fight, Princess?" After the silence, the timbre of his voice startled her fractionally.

"Had I been straightforward about my identity in our letters," she covered, "I would have explained to you that I'm not a Princess by law. Being the illegitimate daughter of a High Lord, I'm afforded the privileges I have by being a ward of House Veservus. And I do fight, on occasion. Though my father mostly just keeps me with his advisors so I can monitor things as they happen."

"Had you been straightforward," he said, pulling a pitcher of water to him, "I would have said that semantics are pointless. You're treated like a Princess, which would imply you should be referred to as such. Did you bring armor?"

"Some. Not a full suit," she said, fighting to keep the bitterness out of her voice. "I wanted to travel light."

He poured them each a glass without asking, sobering as he spoke his next words. "You should never be without armor. My men in the armory can have you fitted as this is a long time to be without it."

"Do you expect me to fight?"

"Expect?" He asked, eyes flitting up to hers. "No. This is an invitation."

"I should warn you I'm not the strongest fighter," she said, her face warming. "I can hold my own in one-on-one combat, but I usually relegate myself to the back corners of formations."

"Would it sweeten our deal if I offered you combat lessons as well?"

She barked out a laugh. Composing herself, she said, "I'll only embarrass myself."

"I wasn't born with a sword in my hand, unbelievable as that might be," Virgil said. "I know what it is to learn."

Rhaella took a long drink of her water. "If it wouldn't inconvenience you, I would appreciate that."

"Of course," Virgil said, wiping his mouth with a napkin before rising to his feet. "If you're finished, you can follow me while I set up your tent."

He led her outside, passing soldiers who were training under the direction of watchful superiors. Rhaella figured that it was usually Virgil leading these sessions, and she could only assume that he was shirking those duties on his insistence to meet with her.

"You'll be camped here," he said, pointing to a bare patch of grass some paces away from the riverbank. "I share the tent we were just in with my father. Should you need anything, I wouldn't go there first. My father might not be the most welcoming."

"How shall I call on you, then?"

Virgil thought for a moment, and then Rhaella watched a smirk bloom across his face. "You're a hawk, aren't you? Do you know any bird calls?"

"A hawk's call isn't very discreet," she pointed out.

"What other songs can you sing then, little bird?"

Bringing her hands to her mouth, Rhaella imitated a perfect mourning dove call. She did it once, twice, before dropping her hands and raising a brow in silent question to Virgil. He stared at her for a moment, frozen in consideration, before he mimicked the call just as well.

"Doves it is," he said.

As Virgil set up her tent, Rhaella tried to help where she could, but he waved her away. He worked quickly and efficiently, bringing her a cot and two blankets. When she asked for a table and writing supplies, he brought those as well. And when she asked for privacy, he gave her that, too.

She set about writing notice of her safe arrival to her family, meanwhile thoughts of war, obligation, and deception swam about in her mind.

CHAPTER TWO

"We hold steady the hand that wields the reins."
—*Motto of the Order of the Dux Doctrina*

17 Aviatoun, in the Benevolent year 112 A.E.

There was little more Asriel hated than listening to the Dux Doctrina preen at his father.

Doctrina Dogan was a silly man with a silly name, but he had served House Veservus faithfully for over two decades. In his full regalia, the man was the living definition of somber and solemn, with the appearance to match. Over his buzzed hair, he wore a black veil and spiked halo crown. When he moved, the chains decorating it made a soft tinkling sound as they dangled in his face. His eyes were shadowed in shades of gray and black, and there was a cunning gleam in them that the bumbling of his words overrode.

If it weren't for that slight stutter that softened Dogan's edges, Asriel might think him fearsome.

For the time being, Dogan's position on the political ladder was higher than Asriel's, but that would change when he Ascended to High Lord. Until then, Dogan had his father's ear, which gave the Doctrina enough sway to guide the High Lord's hand. Asriel's place as his father's heir may have set him to inherit power, but it did not make him powerful. That simple fact would remain true until he Ascended. For now, all he could do was sit quietly and listen to Dogan ramble on to a visibly annoyed High Lord Alden.

It was crowded in the war tent. The air was stuffy and lacking—not suited to fit one grown adult, let alone three. But his father insisted on having dinner together every night when the fighting didn't call them away, and

Asriel wasn't in a position to refuse his father anything.

"I simply wonder if two weeks is too long enough for Rhaella to have been away." Even listening to Dogan speak made Asriel daydream of violence.

"Rhaella wouldn't have gone if she didn't trust she'd return safely," Asriel said, barely dulling the edge in his voice. He didn't appreciate the condescension in the Doctrina's tone.

"House Midar is full of reasonable men with good heads on their shoulders," the High Lord said levelly. "And according to her latest letter, the Eighth House's Prince thinks we've avoided the worst-case scenario in battle."

"We're already *in* the worst-case scenario," Dogan argued. "More than a third of our people wish to return to the old ways of a tyrant king. Flying *our* banners into battle."

"And yet we retain two-thirds of our population," Alden said with some measure of finality. "The rest of the High Lords will come to recognize our loyalty despite the traitors they see on the battlefield. We've kept our lives through all of this, now we must restore our livelihoods. If we want to enter a time of peace—*true* peace—we will have to make compromises."

"It would help," Dogan said slowly, "if Rhaella would agree to an advantageous marriage. One of the heirs, or one or their siblings. Even the niece or nephew of a lesser house would offer House Veservus considerable leverage toward restoring our reputation."

"That sounds like a power grab," the High Lord said, rubbing his temple. "And I do not want for power, Dogan." He paused briefly before speaking again. Whether it was to think his words over or for dramatic effect, Asriel wasn't quite sure. "I want for *peace*."

"Rhaella is no peacemaker," Asriel said darkly. "Nor is she a bargaining chip."

"No," Alden said. "She is my daughter, and she has not been served any suitable proposals. Arguing over that fact will not change it."

"It's no matter," Asriel said. "It's more important that we retain my betrothal, seeing as I'll be the one to carry on the family name."

With trained patience, and a barely leashed temper, his father said, "Your betrothal is no true contract. It is merely a verbal bargain the First High

Lord and I made decades ago. He'll be more willing to marry his daughter to you once we've proven it will be good for the nation in the long-run. At the very least, I need you to begin the process of courting her. It will settle my nerves." This time, the pause in his speech weighed heavily on Asriel's shoulders. "I have other paths in mind for Rhaella."

Asriel's father outstretched his hand to pass him the letter Rhaella had sent. It had come in just before dinner, the ashes shifting in the High Lord's brazier until the parchment manifested. That strange magic unsettled Asriel. Their family lacked the mystical powers bestowed upon the fae or elven families, and sorcery such as this was still foreign to him.

As for the letter, it stated that Rhaella intended to extend her stay at the Eighth House's camp. She wanted to stay with their heir as long as it took to strategize the final few battles of the war. Whether it took them mere weeks or if they would need the rest of the summer season, Asriel was uncertain. Regardless, his sister insisted that she and the Midar Prince could practically taste victory, and that their combined talents would be necessary in securing it.

Their father couldn't deny that even if he wanted to. Adristan had been winning the war before, surely if not unbearably slowly. In the two weeks since Rhaella had gone to stay in House Midar's camp, that truth became undeniable as they waited for the enemy's surrender. Although it felt drastic at home on Isle Verdale, the majority of House Veservus had withstood its cleaving. The distance afforded to them on the mainland showed them that.

The High Lord leaned back in his seat. "Dogan, I understand that a fortnight is a long time for Rhaella to have been gone. But we have other important matters to focus on in the meanwhile. Asriel is right. His insecure betrothal requires attention. When you court Princess Freya, you need to do your best to appeal to her and her Lord father. You must appear exactly as a Veservus heir should."

"Which version?" Asriel asked cooly, his lips pulling back in a smile wide enough to show his fangs.

His father's stare hardened. "The put-together heir of one of the stronghold houses of our nation. I need you to *behave*."

"And if she shows herself to be lax, shouldn't I? To appeal to her?"

Sighing, his father rolled his eyes. "Do what you must. If you have to act like some common gentleman, so be it. But remember that you are not one of them. You know what you are."

"A hawk," Asriel answered solemnly.

"That's right," he said. "We cannot afford so much as a misstep, especially after so few of our people have shown their support."

Beneath the table, Asriel fidgeted with his hands. The lectures always started this way. His father's lectures about the fate of their family's name and legacy were painful enough to endure on a normal day. But here, now, with Dogan watching, Asriel found it humiliating. The familiar shame tasted sour in the back of his throat as it crept up. But still, even through that, he recognized this as the show of trust it was. Serious tasks were usually relegated to his sister, as she was the more capable of the two, and yet here they were. It was unnerving still how easily she excelled at the things she did. How quickly it seemed to come to her. How she instinctively knew the things she did.

No matter what skill Asriel managed to pick up, Rhaella had learned it first. There was an air of preternatural anticipation that rolled off of her at all times, and, try as he might, Asriel could never quite shake the small tug of jealousy that nagged at the farthest corners of his mind when he watched her in her element.

It always seemed as though she could predict the very flow of any given chain of events. She absorbed their father's teachings like it was nothing, easily mastering the things Asriel still had to work at. The way it seemed to him, Rhaella enjoyed being ahead of everyone else. Even if it only served him or their father, she was always so eager to put her talents to use. It never seemed to gain her much other than the mere acceptance of her presence, and he could never quite understand her desperation just to be merely tolerated, but there was nothing he could do. Not until he was High Lord.

Because Asriel knew with a certainty afforded by years of watching Rhaella be put second that he was the heir solely due to the legitimacy of his birth. It didn't matter that he was older; the measly nine months he had on her would have meant nothing had she been born legitimately. And it certainly didn't matter that he was a man, seeing as there were women and genderless folk among the nobility. High Lord Alden Veservus was far from the first High Lord in history to father a bastard, and he would not be the first to legitimize one either. Yet he'd had Rhaella's entire life to do so and he hadn't.

Whether his father held some sort of lingering love for his mother, Asriel wasn't sure. For all he knew, the High Lord could just be scheming as he always did. But one thing Asriel did know for certain was that it was a conscious choice to keep Rhaella illegitimate. And it was a choice both he and Rhaella paid the price for.

Asriel might have been able to bear the crushing responsibility, the weight of his own inadequacy, and even the ire of their father were it not for the fact that it ate away at his sister every day. How it consumed her. How she tried to pretend it didn't.

The weight of that guilt bore down on Asriel, pushing him to include Rhaella in every meeting. To insist that she have a seat at the table. It was the least he could do when he had been handed everything that she had worked so hard for her whole life. Everything that she deserved.

Asriel might have been the heir, but Rhaella was the eyes and ears of House Veservus.

Dogan cleared his throat. "Might you share some of these potential plans for the girl's future?"

Being out of the loop was not unusual for the members of his father's court. The High Lord of House Veservus rarely revealed any piece of information to his advisors before he absolutely had to, and his own children were no exception to this rule.

Asriel's father hummed softly. "A politically-motivated marriage does offer considerable benefits. But I think Rhaella's talents would be best suited within the Dux Doctrina."

Asriel stiffened. The Order of the Dux Doctrina had branches that extended into many parts of Adristan, but they all shared one thing in common. Every branch of the Dux was devoted to clearing the path for ongoing improvement. Each of the eight High Lords operated with a Dux Doctrina at their side, and these advisors functioned as the silent guides shaping the inner-workings of Adristan.

They helped mitigate the murky waters of politics, but their duties were not so easily defined. They were also genealogists, keeping extensive records of family bloodlines to ensure the most prestigious matches, and they oversaw the etiquette schools for the noble children who had not been chosen as heir. During their childhood, even Rhaella had spent a summer or two in such a program. Forced to learn such things as manners and dancing and penmanship.

"You're sending her for another season in their etiquette program?" Asriel asked his father slowly. "But she aged out of such things long ago…" He trailed off at his father's hard stare.

Over the rim of his glass, the High Lord said, "As a Doctrina."

Asriel said, "You can't," at the same time Dogan said, "An excellent plan, my Lord."

"Rhaella isn't going to want to do that," Asriel spoke up, leaning over the table. Her talent for spying and compiling evidence into strategy would make her a formidable Doctrina, but he knew his sister. If she had desired to be a Dux Doctrina, she would have said as much by now. At the very least, she would have confided as much to *him*.

"We all have to make sacrifices," his father said with measured finality. "We've been fighting fanatical commoners and disillusioned Lords for months on end. If we don't want to repeat history in the near-future, Adristan will need great minds at the helm to support the High Lords of every house. Your sister is brilliant and calculating, and her talents are wasted here, picking up your slack."

"If you're sending her away to teach me a lesson on responsibility, it's an unnecessary one. I'm perfectly capable of learning such things with her *here*."

"Show me, then," his father said, and there was a weighted pause that followed. Both of them knew Asriel was bluffing but neither one was willing to admit as much out loud. "Nevertheless, intentions still have little to do with you. Offering you the opportunity to prove your worthiness is simply a benefit."

Dogan spoke up then. "I can send word to my brothers and sisters in the Order. They will be ready for her as soon as you are prepared to send her."

Asriel couldn't imagine his sister being sent to the tower where the Order trained new initiates. He couldn't imagine her *gone*.

Over the years, their father had sent her on missions that required she travel between islands and the mainland, but she had never been away for more than a few days at a time. Training with the Dux Doctrina would take months, maybe even a year. And even after that training, she would stay with the Order until she was chosen to serve a High Lord. And there was no guarantee that it was *their* house she would be serving.

"I won't be the one sending her anywhere," Asriel's father said to Dogan before turning to him. "This decision falls on you, my son."

Asriel's voice was quiet. "Why?"

"Your opportunity doesn't simply begin once your sister is gone, should that time come. It begins now. Decide what you think is best for Adristan: The advancement of our house through a political marriage, or Rhaella at your side as a trained scholar and warrior. Should we marry her off for the sake of an alliance, or could she become someone able to advise a future High Lord?"

Asriel bit his lip, the tip of his fang digging into the flesh. "Can you at least give me some time to consider things?"

His father started to respond but was interrupted by the sound of yelling from outside the tent. Pushing up from his seat, the High Lord barked out a clipped, "What's going on?" More command than question.

Captain Rune pushed his way inside with guards at his back, Asriel's sworn sword among them. Urgently, he said, "There's been an attack out west. They're calling for all hands."

Asriel's father moved into action at once, tugging on his armor as he walked, followed by a frenetic Dogan.

"Asriel, stay with your guard. I'm keeping one of mine here to watch over you as well."

He chased his father out of the tent. "If it's all hands, Father, I can go."

"No." The finality in that single word chafed at him immensely. "You'll stay here with your guards." His father turned on his heel as he spoke, this time to the Doctrina. "Dogan, find the Lord Commander."

"Father," Asriel insisted. "I've been training. Throw me in one of the back units where I'll be safe."

"You'll be safest in camp, surrounded by your guards." He put his hands on Asriel's shoulders, looking grave as ever. "You are the future of our house. Of our *family*. I won't put your life on the line."

"What sort of leader will they see me as if they believe me afraid of combat?"

"A living one," his father said, squeezing his shoulder. Then, he snapped his fingers at Barrett. "Make sure he stays put."

Barrett came to Asriel's side. "As you say."

Asriel wanted to protest. He wanted to rage at his father. But he only watched the High Lord's back as he walked away. Hot tears sprung to Asriel's eyes as he stormed into his own tent. The lavishness of it only made him angrier. What good were the furnishings of an heir if he couldn't act like one?

He could at least get drunk like one. From the makeshift bar, Asriel poured himself a generous portion. He held out a glass to Barrett. "You want one?"

His guard looked conflicted for a brief moment before accepting. "Just one," he said aloud to no one in particular. "Have to keep steady."

"That's a crock of shit," Asriel snapped. He laid back on the pile of pillows next to the cart that held the carafes and glasses. "You won't have to guard me from anything and we both know it. The enemy stands no chance of getting through to assassinate me, or whatever it is my father's afraid of."

"It's a precaution," Barrett said, sitting next to him.

"It's as planned," Asriel said, taking a long drink. "Everything is happening according to Rhaella's strategy. She might as well be a child of the gods considering how well she's predicted the outcome of this war. Maybe then, her parentage wouldn't be up for debate," he added miserably.

"Your sister's done her best with her lot in life. I want to say you've done the same."

"You want to," Asriel said, knocking his knee against Barrett's. "But you won't."

Barrett smiled. "You can have my praise, or you can have my honesty."

"I'd rather have another drink," Asriel said, clumsily refilling his glass before raising it to his lips. "A toast, to my utter uselessness."

"Hear, hear," Barrett said, clinking his glass against his.

His guard's presence was a comfort. An unearned one, seeing as

Barrett *had* to stay with him. Though he was still glad to have it. Having only been an anointed member of the guard for a handful of years, he was as devoted to keeping Asriel safe as he was to helping him unwind. The fact that they could share a drink together over conversation was something he had never experienced with the older guards. The ones that had already spent years guarding his father never seemed to meet Asriel on the same level that Barret could.

After gulping down half of the glass in one go, Asriel groaned and threw an arm over his eyes. "I don't want to send my sister to the Dux."

"So don't," Barrett replied.

"You and I both know it's not that simple." Asriel moved his arm behind his head. "My father wouldn't have mentioned it at all unless he was seriously considering it. Which means it's the decision he favors. My choices are either to disappoint him, or to essentially exile Rhaella."

"Well," his sworn sword mused, "what if Rhaella *wants* to become a Doctrina?"

"She doesn't."

"You're certain?"

Asriel frowned at the guard. "Why are you questioning me? If she wanted to go into the Order, she would have said so by now."

"Have you ever considered that your sister may not feel as though she can express her deepest wishes to you? Because of your positions? Your obligations?"

"Rhaella and I don't keep secrets from each other."

"I'm only suggesting that Rhaella may have ambitions that go beyond assisting in your Ascension to lordship," Barrett said, holding his hands up. "Maybe she doesn't want to speak out of turn. You know she *wants* to help you, and this could allow her to help both you *and* herself."

Asriel hummed and sat back on the cushions, chewing on the words. He was afraid to verbalize just how deeply the Order both frightened and vexed him. Dogan was a loyal advisor to his father, but he was also pushy and overbearing. When he wasn't giving advice to the High Lord, he was skulking around corners and downing potions that kept his powers in check.

He tried to picture Rhaella in the Order's classic black robes, stalking the halls and listening to every word. It wasn't entirely dissimilar to how she behaved now. Only, as a trained Doctrina, she'd have a year's worth of training dedicated to honing her skills. Not to mention, she'd have access to the magic of their concoctions. If she was this gifted at spying and secret-keeping now, she'd be unstoppable with the Order's resources close at hand.

But the Dux Doctrina required so much beyond a particular set of skills. They demanded that their Doctrinas remain celibate, unbiased, and, in many cases, voiceless. Doctrinas were not to speak unless spoken to. Not to give advice unless asked.

Dogan failed at this regularly.

Then again, Asriel was certain Rhaella desired marriage even less than she desired the life of a Doctrina. As his father said, no worthwhile proposals had ever been sent to his brazier. On the occasion that his sister joined him in sneaking out of the high walls of Briarhall, she flirted with commoners. But she had never shown express interest in finding a suitable match to present to their father. If Asriel could just delay the topic of Rhaella's future until he Ascended to his place as High Lord, he would be able to keep everything as it was.

Barrett said, "Rhaella really is incredible. It's going to be a shame when your father gives her away. To the Order, or to another house, it doesn't much matter."

"He's not going to," Asriel replied firmly. "I will ensure as much."

"And what if she found someone worthy of falling madly in love with? Would you deprive her of as much?"

He shook his head. "I'm the one with an obligation to marry, not her. The First's High Lord and my father have been speaking of our eventual betrothal since before I could walk."

"Which you're not displeased by," Barrett pointed out.

Asriel shrugged. "I've only met Freya in passing, and we were much younger then. And even in those times, there were a thousand eyes on us. Neither of those options are the circumstances I wish to get to know my future wife under."

"So you admit you want to get to know her." The smug look on Barrett's face was enough to set Asriel on edge.

He shoved Barrett's shoulder with a laugh. "If I'm going to share my life and title with her, of course I want to get to know her. I just don't want it to be so... *public*."

"I think that comes with the territory," Barrett said, reaching over Asriel to the bar cart. He refilled his glass conservatively and took a slow, measured sip. "You know, being heir and all."

Asriel huffed out a breath. "Do you remember that fortune teller I told you about? The one that came through for the spring festival when I was younger? She told me I was going to become something that no one anticipated. I've spent years unraveling what that could possibly mean."

"You're going to become High Lord, no matter what you do," Barrett spoke plainly. "How you go about such a thing is what will both surprise people, and determine what kind of ruler *you* will be. For all his efforts, you are not your father. It's as simple as that."

"You sound so certain that I want to believe you," he said. "Though I'm afraid it could be more than that. Prophecies are rarely so straightforward."

"I think they're simpler than you want to believe."

For a few breaths, Asriel stared at the ceiling of the tent, mulling over the plain truth Barrett had just laid out. He would be content to spend the rest of the night there, talking and drinking with Barrett, but it wasn't contentment Asriel wished for.

Pushing to his feet, he said, "Follow me."

"Where are we going?"

Asriel heard Barrett rise from the pile of pillows and set his glass back on the makeshift bar. He didn't wait for his sworn sword to follow, knowing that it was Barrett's duty, after all.

The two of them pushed out of the tent and into the quiet of the night. The lack of sound was more unnerving than the sounds of battle would have been, and Asriel found himself a little bit off-kilter. The noises of battle were too far away, swallowed up by the thick trees surrounding their camp, but he knew they should be there. He might have been comforted by the clanging of swords and furious yelling if only for the fact that it meant that his men were fighting for something. That they were succeeding thus far.

Barrett began dragging his feet with every step that brought them closer to the High Lord's tent. "Asriel. What are we doing?"

"I want to see Rhaella's strategy," he said. One of his father's swords stood at attention, but he did not protest as Asriel pushed his way inside. "I may not be good at coming up with such things myself, but I *can* follow along. I want to get an idea of how the battle's going."

"So let's look for it in her tent," Barrett argued, lingering by the open flap.

"He has to have left a copy lying around here somewhere. Father always demands he has one for his records," Asriel said distantly. His focus was on the piles of papers littered around the space. "Help me look." There was more command in Asriel's tone than he cared to admit, but Barrett ultimately gave in.

Begrudgingly, Barrett began sorting through the mess alongside Asriel. There was much of the expected paperwork. There were *weeks'* worth of battle plans and detailed lists of the advantages of each maneuver. Everything a High Lord would need to execute an effective war-campaign was here. Even his sister's correspondence—even though it had grown far more sporadic as the strategy grew stronger and more effective—was here. She had begun planting the seeds of long-term growth, all the while, their enemy grew weaker with each passing battle.

Picking up another pile of papers to sort through, Asriel cursed his father for letting things get this messy. It was a wonder he was able to find anything at all. Why would the newest plans not be readily accessible?

"Is this something important?" The sound of Barrett's voice pulled him away from his search, and Asriel looked up to see his sworn sword holding a yellowing piece of parchment.

Asriel took the paper from Barrett's hand, scanning it for anything important. "No it's just..."

But he realized quickly that he was staring at a list of every influential political figure in the nation. Every High Lord, their Dux Doctrina, their council of advisors, and even their heirs. The other children of the High Lords were there as well. And next to each of the names, in the High Lord's shorthand, were letters of the Vessial alphabet.

"All these years," Barrett muttered, "and I still can't read your language."

There was a symbol for *yes*, *no*, and *maybe*. With a start, he realized there was a NO next to his and Rhaella's names.

"It's a checklist," Asriel said with sudden certainty. "Though I'm not sure what for."

"Perhaps attendance for an upcoming meeting?"

"My father doesn't often write in Vessial," Asriel said, shaking his head. "He speaks it better than he writes it, and Dogan doesn't know it at all. This isn't for convenience."

"What do you make of it?"

Asriel turned the paper over in his hands. "Whatever this is for, he doesn't want just anyone to see, let alone comprehend. It's likely one of his schemes. I can't imagine it'd be anything else."

He set the page down on the desk and placed another one atop it. Then, taking a piece of charcoal, Asriel scribbled over the blank page so that it left an impression of the lettering beneath. When he finished, he folded his copy neatly and shoved it in his pocket for later.

"I want to keep tabs on this," he said, dusting off his hands.

The paper felt as heavy as a rock in his pocket, and his instinct was to ask Rhaella what she made of it. Though another, smaller, instinct warned him against such a thing. It warned him that maybe, this time, he should be the one to piece things together.

Once he had figured things out himself, then he could show her. But not until then. It would do her no good if he dropped a puzzle on her lap at the same time she was being optioned for her vocation.

It's for her own good, Asriel reasoned with himself. He couldn't decide if that was true, or if it was just wishful thinking, but he didn't have time to discern between the two.

"Come on," Asriel said, heading for the tent flap. "The strategy isn't here or we would have found it by now. My father probably has it with him. We'll await his return."

Waiting really just consisted of drinking themselves deeper and deeper into foolishness—playing dominoes, imitating the High Lord, and play-fighting. When he and Barrett eventually tired, Asriel sat with his back against Barrett's knees and let the guard plait his hair into something passable as a braid. Though, passable seemed a generous term, given how shaky Barrett's hands were when he was intoxicated.

Some time after dawn, Asriel heard voices in the distance as they approached—signaling the High Lord's return. Still awake, and not quite sober, Asriel and Barrett emerged from the tent and waited for their men in the center of camp. His father approached, looking haggard and weary, but he was alive nonetheless. Battle tended to have that effect on men, even if they weren't on the front lines.

High Lord Alden crossed the flat expanse of grass to close the distance between him and his son. His shoulders drooped, and he stopped a few paces away.

"Come," he said by way of greeting. "We're going to pray."

There was no room for argument in the statement. Asriel followed his father to the crudely assembled prayer tent at the far edge of camp, and he knelt beside his father, waiting for him to ask what he had decided to do with Rhaella's fate. But the question never came. High Lord Alden Veservus stayed on his knees with his hands clasped and eyes squeezed shut. It was clear that he was shaken. Asriel kept quiet, pretending to pray, as he willed the inevitable conversation to never come.

CHAPTER THREE

"Foolish is the man who runs into battle unarmed in weaponry or wits."
—*Proverb among the common people of Adristan*

20 Aviatoun, in the Benevolent year 112 A.E.

There was sun in Virgil's eyes. He put a hand up to block the glare as day broke across the sky. The fighting had lasted throughout the night, and now the cruel light of day made the carnage impossible to ignore. This was sure to be a historic battle. One that scholars would pass down through the generations to students in polished rooms. They would know nothing of the smell of death that clung to the air, only what their textbooks described to them. They would never hear the silence that swallowed everything after the clamoring ended.

Virgil was a lonely historian, looking down on the bodies scattered across the flattened grass. He committed the sight to memory, taking it all in with a heavy sigh.

Somewhere in the distance, shrikes chittered in the trees. Their calls echoed through the camp, reminding each of the soldiers that they were never far from the fate that could have been theirs.

Virgil didn't believe in gods, but he believed in death. It didn't have a face, or even a name, but it had the terribly sweet birdsong that met his ears now, and its singers were perched on so many trees.

"It's terrible, what we've done," Virgil said as his uncle came to stand by his side.

"It's necessary."

"I'm finding that hard to believe."

"You don't have to believe it," Uncle Nicholas said. "You just have to do it."

34

Virgil tried to walk away, shouldering past his uncle, but the man put out a hand to stop him.

"You're to come with me to your father's tent." Virgil began to speak, but Nicholas swiftly cut him off. "And don't say you don't want to. It's not a request."

"I want a bath," Virgil replied gruffly.

"We don't have time for that."

Virgil gave his uncle a hard stare, though it was hard to meet his eyes with the chains from his Doctrina headpiece hanging in his face. "I'll be more amenable to whatever it is my father has to say after I've had a bath."

"I look forward to that," his uncle said. And as Uncle Nicholas turned to walk toward the tent, he called over his shoulder. "I'll let your father know you're going to be late."

Virgil stared after his uncle for a moment, watching the black of his Doctrina robes disappear behind the tent flaps. Then, Virgil briskly turned on his heel and stormed toward the thick copse of trees where a river waited only a few paces deep. As he neared the water, Virgil discarded his bloodied armor and weapons in the grass on the bank. Once he had stripped bare, he wasted no time stepping into the water and submerging his body beneath the surface. The cold was a shock to his nerves, but he hardly felt the sting as he scrubbed at the crusted filth all over his skin. He needed to feel clean. The water could never wash away the things he'd done, but it could at least remove the appearance of them.

After taking a moment to come up for air, Virgil ducked back below the surface and began to scrub at his hair. When he resurfaced again, it clung to his cheeks and the back of his neck. It was getting too long, but the constant of battle did not afford him the luxury of routine maintenance. There'd been no downtime for so much as a shave as of late. He probably looked half-wild. Maybe he was.

Maybe the nobility were right to call him The Shrike behind his back when they thought he wasn't listening. He always heard, despite his efforts not to. His men tried to fight the first few who dared to grace him with the brutal nickname, but it was no use. Virgil was a butcher. A death-dealer and a killer. The Lords and advisors and emissaries trusted him to fight their battles for them, but they didn't respect him enough to call him by his name or the title he didn't even want.

Pulling himself out of the water, Virgil sat on the bank and bandaged the angriest cuts on his skin, leaving the minor ones to scar. The ritual of removing the old bandages, cleaning his cuts and scrapes, and putting fresh bandages back on called him back to his body. It made him feel less like a weapon. There was something grounding in the act of taking care of himself amidst all of the slaughter and brutality. It felt like bringing some sort of beginning back to his torn skin. He wanted to bottle up the feeling and drink it with the meal that was being prepared. Perhaps he'd sleep better if he could do such a thing.

Thankfully, he hadn't suffered any major injuries. There weren't gaping wounds, and he had nothing more than a few scratches to show for his efforts. None of them would scar too badly, which was a welcome change, but he couldn't help but wonder if the scars at least meant he had something to prove he was real. On the other hand, he was running out of fresh skin. His shoulder would require wrapping, as would his knuckles, but it was nothing he couldn't manage. The skin on his knees was torn to shreds too, but he didn't bother covering them. They would heal well enough on their own.

As he redressed in a simple undershirt and pants, Virgil's thoughts drifted to House Veservus and what made them decide to posture their Prince as the master strategist of this war over their Princess who clearly excelled in that regard.

All hands of the major houses were putting in an effort, so it wasn't strange that High Lord Veservus would task his daughter with such a thing, but something about such a calculated posturing didn't sit right with him. And Virgil might not have even picked up on the lie had she not put so much of herself into her letters.

Their correspondence had been militant at first, only concerning strategy and the necessary updates, but she had quickly grown careless. Or, at least, less careful. She had let details slip about her whereabouts that contradicted what the Midar spies knew about Prince Asriel's location. Which meant that, unless the Veservus family had been hiding a secret ability to teleport, Virgil was being lied to.

It should have concerned him more that the High Lord of the

house of historians was willing to lie about details at his convenience. But, fortunately for High Lord Veservus, Virgil couldn't bring himself to care. The discrepancies in the letters had seemed so trivial compared to the death that stained his hands.

It was that apathetic disregard for consequences that pushed him to demand a meeting with the Third House's spare—if she could even be called that. And it was that same impulse that drove him to offer her nothing but hospitality upon her arrival. He wanted to find an ending to this seemingly infinite conflict, and he knew from their letters that her keen eye for strategy would be the key to doing so. He'd also gone to great lengths to assure she never felt used the same way he might in her position.

In the weeks since Rhaella had been at camp, she had accepted every offer of combat training, joining in on daily practice with the rest of the soldiers as though she were one of their own. Plus, it didn't hurt that Virgil had an excuse to watch the way the muscles in her back flexed every time she drew her bow. He had to push her to train with the sword, which she griped about, but he refused to give her a choice. Should push come to shove—even though he didn't quite understand the instinct just yet—he wanted her capable of holding her own should she find herself backed into a corner. And yet, despite her initial reservations, her form had improved some. If nothing else, it offered him a strange comfort that at least one thing could still blossom while everything around it was being cut down.

He had fought with his father and uncle about whether to allow her into their camp, but the gamble of bringing a Veservus into their ranks was paying off thus far. In fact, the decision had proven itself fruitful almost immediately. Already, the battles were dwindling.

The enemy couldn't survive with the combined strength and strategy that Virgil and Rhaella brought to the fields. As a unit, their skills complemented each other quite nicely. He wanted to be glad for that—to know that someday soon, this could all stop—but he had a feeling that they were still to face down the bloodiest parts of this war. He wanted to believe that someday, he wouldn't wake with the knowledge that he had to end lives for the sake of saving others. That knowledge did nothing for him, though, when that day was still yet to come.

Virgil shoved his way into his father's tent, noting that the High Lord was still dressed in his armor. He stood before a basin of water, rinsing the blood and muck from his face and hands with a washcloth. Uncle Nicholas sat on one of the low stools, sorting through maps. Neither of them looked up as he walked in.

"That was more than a minute," High Lord Vincent Midar said tonelessly.

"Can't stand the smell," Virgil said, hunting through his things for a clean shirt and pair of pants. "Don't know how you can."

"Unlike you, I don't have the luxury of taking long baths as I please," his father quipped. "Perhaps when you inherit my title, you'll understand."

"I misunderstand nothing," Virgil muttered as he shucked off his dirty clothes. "We may be beasts of war, but we're not animals. You want me to act as heir to a High Lord, I can at least look like one."

"Iyd heke chai pcibe tuy kolt," Uncle Nicholas said in Menmal. *You need to act like it.*

"You have to show off the pride of House Midar," his father added.

"That's me, isn't it?" Virgil said darkly. "Isn't it enough that I'm commanding our armies in battle and leaving rivers of blood in our wake?"

"For the good of the nation, Virgil," his father said. "You're serving your purpose beyond what is expected of you. You alone have the highest headcount in all of our armies put together."

Uncle Nicholas cleared his throat. "But defending your people is not your only duty as heir to the mantle. You must ensure that you lay out a path for the Midar legacy to continue. Beyond war, beyond transfers of power, *that* is what is most important here, nephew." Virgil did not care for the measure of disgust his uncle threw into the last word.

"Say what you mean plainly, or do not speak at all," Virgil snapped.

Virgil's father held up a hand to silence his brother. "I know you don't want to, but once the dust settles, we must find you a bride. That way, you can produce an heir."

Virgil's hands curled into fists at his side. "I don't need to marry to name an heir. I can name a cousin, or one of your councilman's children for all our laws are concerned. They need not be my direct descendant."

"The laws are changing," Uncle Nicholas said. "The Concilium is in talks of sending out a mandate for each heir—all of you currently unmarried—to find spouses. We're at war. It is by the skin of our teeth alone that none of you have died yet." The longer he spoke, the more impassioned his uncle became. "We need to secure our future, and you have far too many resources at your disposal to waste them. Any eligible Lady would accept an offer of betrothal after all you've done for the nation. You could have anyone you want. That Veservus girl likely knows better than we do who the best choice would be. You could ask for her counsel!"

"The Concilium cannot *mandate* such a thing. It's simply something for us to consider more seriously," his father said, sighing heavily. He tilted his back to stare at the ceiling and took a deep breath. "Once I'm gone, my wants will no longer matter. But while I am still walking and breathing, I intend to carve out the future I want for our house."

"So I don't have a choice," Virgil said plainly.

"You must bear the responsibilities I have handed down to you, yes," his father replied. "I won't name another heir. Your naive plays at abdication are behind you. It's time to earn your birthright."

Virgil recalled those times he tried to run away from his destiny. From his duty. Abdicating his position as heir was not unheard of, and if House Midar held a fraction less power, it would hardly register with the rest of the nation. But they *did* hold considerable power, so it did matter. Those brief stints of freedom won him little more than drunken nights and sick mornings. Each time, his father's men dragged him back to camp like a puppy dragged by the scruff. They were wolves draped in his house colors, and they thought they were doing the honorable thing.

It left him feeling shackled to a destiny he never asked for.

Virgil didn't pray—he never had. But if he were a praying man, he would beg some higher power for this weight to pass over him in favor of someone else. "Let me win your war first," he said, his voice equal parts acidic and exhausted. "Then you can decide if I've earned anything."

Virgil's father stared at him for a moment before turning to Nicholas. "Give me a moment alone with my son."

The Dux Doctrina of House Midar hesitated for a moment, but eventually bowed to his High Lord. "As you say."

Once Uncle Nicholas had vacated the tent, Virgil's father turned a

39

tired eye on him. "I don't want these things for you for selfish reasons. I've lived the life you live now. I was heir during a tumultuous time too."

"You lived through *skirmishes*," Virgil spat. "This is *war*."

"And yet I knew days like this were ahead of us, even when I was a young Lord. How do you think we descended into the state we're in now?"

His father began to pace the length of the tent, then, and a familiar somberness crept over the space. Virgil sensed a lecture on its way, and though it irritated him, he bit his tongue.

"My fellow High Lords and I have not done our due diligence. We have let traditions and procedures slip through the cracks. Each of the houses are near strangers to one another, and that distance has allowed the royalists to slip into the cracks. They've convinced the people that a singular ruler—one who is susceptible to corruption and greed—would be a better alternative to the world we've built with our own hands. The world our ancestors fought tooth and nail for. Once this mantle passes to you, I don't want you to have to live your life in fear of another war the same way I have." Virgil's father thought his next words over carefully. "With the eight major houses sharing the duties of one government, you're going to have to do things you don't want to do, Virgil. You're going to have to compromise."

"Becoming Lord Commander was a compromise," Virgil nearly pleaded. "I do nothing *but* compromise. By your measure, I should get what I want at some point. Have I not earned that by now?"

"And you will," his father said. "But only after the unfortunate necessities are through with."

"Did you consider marrying my mother an unfortunate necessity?" Virgil felt cold. Hollow. He felt distant from his body. "Did you consider bearing me an unfortunate necessity?"

His father glared. "Don't be crude. You have been the great joy of my life. I don't take that for granted. But I will do what I must to protect and honor the compromises I've made to secure this life for you. Not just for you, but for the good of what we've built. I will not be made to feel shame over that."

"And what if I want to honor that sacrifice by crafting a life for myself that I'm proud to live?" He let the question hang in the air for a moment. "Or am I to be your shadow for the rest of my days?" Virgil couldn't stave off the bitterness that crept into his voice.

The High Lord's expression turned stony as he began to remove his armor. The belt around his father's hip held his famed sword, Veritas, and it was an impressive thing. That blade had taken the lives of more men than Virgil could conceive of. Some generations, and too many great-grandfathers ago, it had been the very blade to kill the tyrant King Edmund, which had established the new nation of Adristan.

This sword was the bringer of justice. The dealer of death. Not unlike the names they called him. His father unbuckled the blade from his side and unceremoniously unsheathed. And even though the light in the tent was dim at best, the sword's steel glimmered brightly. With carefully steady hands, Virgil's father held the sword out to him, and Virgil wasted no time taking the flat of the blade into his own.

"This will be yours someday," his father said, softer than before. "As long as you do what you must in the meantime."

Something in Virgil's chest fluttered. He told himself that he didn't want the responsibility of such a thing, but he knew he was lying to himself. It would be an honor to inherit his father's sword. Despite their differences, despite the expectations, there was still a part of him that desired his father's approval. And it was that piece of him that kept him in position as heir. That piece that prevented him from forsaking all of it in favor of a life of true freedom.

For better or worse, he was his father's son.

Taking a deep breath, Virgil said, "I am doing what I must."

He strode out of the tent and made his way to one of the circles of logs where people were eating. All around, each soldier's shoulders seemed to droop just a little bit lower than they had at the outset of the day. It was as though an invisible weight pushed down on each one who had seen battle. It had hardly been a fair fight; Virgil and his men had demolished their enemies despite being caught by surprise. They had fought members of every house, including family and friends, and they had a victory to show for it. They were fighting people who had been conditioned to think that a life under oppression was a life worth fighting for. Perhaps, centuries ago, monarchy had been the right idea. But their rulers had grown rotten with power, and their time had passed as the cool death of winter passed into rebirthing spring.

It had taken a long time to reestablish the nation as the powerhouse it had always been. Although the great houses had existed during the time of the monarchy, they had held much less influence than they did now. But their new, shared hold on power allowed for checks and balances to the *amount* of power each house held on to. Not to mention the Order and the councils that made up the other arms of the Concilium. Never again would a lone figure be allowed to rise above the rest, stomping on those less powerful to keep their grasp on power and influence.

Despite this distribution of power, however, love for the royalty had never fallen completely out of fashion. The common folk saw the monarchy as a romanticized ideal. Something to look up to. It gave their otherwise anonymous government a face to lay claim to. And it was that same sort of romanticized fondness that led the new generations to retain titles such as Prince and Princess. Titles like these allowed for distinctions as rulers without amassing enough power to decay away at their morals. It was an attempt to remember their past while ensuring they were not damning themselves to repeat it.

Virgil took a plate from one of the cooks and searched for a place to sit. Off to one side, his guest sat upright with a plate in her lap. She didn't seem comfortable, exactly, but this wasn't the rigidity of someone in unfamiliar territory. In fact, she looked quite at home doing what she was best at. *Listening.* And he knew, without having to ask, that she was aware of his approach. Those keen ears would never miss such a thing.

Rhaella was talking with his men, addressing each of them by name as she listened to their stories and laughed at their jokes. Virgil couldn't ignore how uncharacteristic that was of someone of her status; people like them were more likely to look down on foot soldiers.

As Virgil arrived at her log, the soldiers beside her made space for him to sit. He didn't intend to speak at first, he merely hoped to keep his head down and try to focus on chewing and swallowing. The mechanics of eating cleared his head, but he missed the pleasure that came with enjoying a good meal.

Around him, his soldiers started to crack jokes as they chatted, pushing past the impossible weight they all carried. He wondered what joke he had missed out on as he forced out a humorless chuckle. He replied when it was expected of him, and he gave his best attempts at wry humor, but it was all hollow. His mask was convincing enough for a disinterested audience, maybe, but his men knew him better than that. Eventually, they left him alone to his thoughts.

That humanness that he felt while tending to his wounds was slipping out of reach the longer he feigned normalcy. Every attempt at it felt like grasping at water in his cupped hands. The harder he tried to contain it, the less control he had. And the longer he felt it slipping away, the less he could ignore the growing fear that he would never catch that feeling again. Even more fearsome yet was the distinct worry that he wouldn't want it once he did.

Rhaella seemed to notice his distance—he imagined it would be impossible for her not to—and she took a moment to nudge his knee with hers. "Not hungry?"

Looking down, he'd been moving his food around more than he had been eating any of it. He shrugged. "It's hard after battle. I don't have much of an appetite, though I know I should probably eat *something*."

"I know the feeling," she said.

Virgil could tell that she meant it. She still wore the armor they had fitted her with. It was plain, but it suited her well. Though now it was covered in dirt, as were both her face and hair. Pieces of her braid had come loose and were hanging in her face, and her eyes looked so tired. She wasn't bowing her shoulders, though, and he saw a quiet strength that hovered just below the surface. He admired that.

"You know," he said, making an attempt at levity, "I was hoping I would've gotten to see your dragon."

She snorted, staring straight ahead. "I wanted to ride Egorion all the way here, but my father said no. He was afraid I would call too much attention to myself."

"But sending you on your own—unguarded and wearing only a breastplate—was fine with him?" He huffed, taking a bite as bland as sawdust.

"My father is complicated," she admitted. He noticed a barely-visible flash of regret before she shook her head. "I've developed a habit of telling you too much. I think all those months of letter-writing made me

43

too comfortable."

"I did the same. Though it was a welcome distraction to speak of things aside from strategy and war," he admitted, recalling the little truths he'd spilled as well. "And, if I may be so bold, your father seems to have a habit of limiting your potential with his rules. Granted, that's an assumption based on the contents of such letters, but your time here has proven me at least somewhat right."

"He's…" Rhaella sighed. "Yes." The admission seemed as though it cost her something on the way out. She continued on. "That is the case some of the time, though from what *I've* gathered—and from what Ser Declan and Ser Eric say—your father behaves much the same way."

He paused with his fork halfway to his mouth. "You learned their names."

"I made it a point to," she said, taking the moment to swallow down a spoonful of her own.

Virgil hummed. "Not many people in positions like ours take even a moment to see them as anything more than bodies."

She might have mimicked his humming, or the sound came naturally to her. "I'm hardly more than that myself."

He might not have noticed it, the way she imperceptibly stiffened before relaxing again. But it was that small tell that gave away the fact that her words were no calculated bit of politicking. No, her words revealed a certain amount of real, genuine vulnerability beneath her impenetrable exterior. Given her reputation, she didn't do that often. That was, unless she was writing her hundredth letter to him in the midst of battles and bloodshed. Or sitting beside him at breakfast after days of more of the same.

Perhaps it was only fair that he offered her some measure of that same vulnerability in return.

"If there's anyone who knows how that feels," he said, "it's me. I'm no son to my father anymore. Only a warmonger."

"They should call you war*ender* instead," she said blithely. "Though I'm afraid that doesn't quite roll off the tongue."

He couldn't help himself—he burst into laughter. Around them, heads turned in their direction, staring openly at their commander who had been somber and solemn only moments ago. Virgil didn't care; he couldn't remember the last time it had felt this good to laugh.

Rhaella poorly hid the way her mouth turned upward as she set her plate onto her lap. She tried to dust her hands off but immediately winced at the contact, opting instead to set them gently in her lap.

"Are you hurt?"

"My callouses burst," she said, holding up a palm. "I'm not used to holding a sword this frequently."

"Here," he said before he could think better of it. "Let me see." She tried to pull away for just a moment, some sort of refusal already ready on her lips, but he took her hand in his before she could stop him.

Torn, bloodied skin littered the palm of her hands, and when he picked up the other one he found it to be the first's twin. The bandage covering the slash along the center of her palm was stained; that wound was angry, too. Virgil sucked air through his teeth and pulled a roll of wrappings from one of his pockets.

"Oh," Rhaella said. "You really don't have to—"

"I don't mind," he replied.

Between polite words, he wrapped her hands with a gentleness that even he was surprised by. He was surprised that, even after everything, he still retained the capacity for gentleness. That he hadn't been robbed of it completely. It didn't take long to care for her wounds, and the moment was over before it truly began. But it had happened, and Virgil thought that meant something.

Once he was finished, Rhaella pulled her hands back into her lap. "Thank you," she said. This time, when she smiled, it was wide enough to show off the pretty fangs that Veservus were known for.

Without thinking, and before he could stop himself, Virgil said, "You have a very lovely smile."

Her entire face seemed to change after he said that, brightening somewhat. A slight flush bloomed across her cheeks, almost as though he had embarrassed her. It was something he hadn't thought her capable of previously.

In a breathier voice, she repeated, "Thank you."

Virgil nodded, a grin breaking out on his own face. Suddenly, out of nowhere, he felt like doing something foolish. He felt like complimenting her again just to try and earn another smile. Only, as he had the thought, he glanced up to see his father and uncle whispering from across the way, neither of them making any effort to hide the fact that they were watching their conversation.

He needed a distraction. Not only for his own sake, but to take the attention off of Rhaella. Muttering an excuse, he climbed to his feet and strode to one of the flattened circles of grass. Putting two fingers to his lips, Virgil let out a sharp whistle. Any of his soldiers who were still awake and trying to run off the leftover energy wasted no time circling up. So many of them were eager to be called upon and made an example out of. There was an aspect of pride to this for them, to fight the heir and commander and hold their own. He could respect that, though it didn't stop him from throwing punches with his full strength.

The soldiers needed this, he thought. It pained him to push them past their limits, but adrenaline lingered in the camp like dew clinging to the grass after an early rain. If he left them alone, fights were sure to break out. This, too, was a way to keep them in check.

Once he'd had enough of exerting himself, he called out, "Get into groups. Scrimmages. Go, hurry. Remind me why you're members of the Midar army."

The troops hollered as they sorted themselves into smaller circles. Virgil circled the perimeter, monitoring every fight. It was just as much his duty to observe them as it was to act.

His father and uncle were off on the sidelines, likely spitting useless political jargon as they gestured to the open air around them. But their eyes kept drifting over to Rhaella with an unwelcomed mix of wariness and calculation. It unnerved Virgil. House Veservus wasn't a house of traitors, despite their high number of defectors. Worse yet, their houses were meant to be allies; he would not risk burning this bridge. Crossing to the patch of grass where she sparred with another, Virgil blocked their line of sight with his body and continued calling out corrections.

He unsheathed his own sword, a respectable blade he'd named Airslinger. The feel of it in his hands centered him; it felt like a natural extension of his arm. He held it aloft, demonstrating a sequence for the soldiers to run through. They repeated the exercise, slowly at first, then at the speed of battle. When he was done demonstrating, Virgil ruthlessly watched for mistakes. There were few, but there was no margin for error on a battlefield.

Training concluded with striking and parrying while weights were attached to their backs. His men were strong, but they needed to be able to utilize that strength. Virgil watched as they grew more tired. He watched as they reached their limits and he pushed them to continue anyway. He wanted to give them a break, to allow them to sit around and drink as they ate, but he needed to be cautious of how much slack he allowed his men.

So they ran through everything again.

When the sun reached its highest point in the sky, Virgil let the soldiers go. They would be cranky and sore, of that there was no doubt, but they'd be stronger for it. They would be forged in fire, just as he had been.

He went into his own tent. His father had not yet retired, so he had the whole thing to himself. And as Virgil lay there in the quiet, he allowed his defenses to fall and for his body to start trembling. He was rarely given time to process the things he was made to see, but sometimes—in moments like these—those things caught up to him faster than he could fend them off. Comfort was rationed conservatively, and he simply could not afford it most of the time.

In the dark, though, he let tears fall as he recalled the hoarse screams of men and the squelching of flesh as they fell. Some of the others had gotten used to it, but Virgil abhorred even the idea of such a thing. He wanted the horrors of battle to haunt him until the end of his days. What kind of man—what kind of *leader*—would he be to remain uncalloused by the loss of life? Even the lives of his enemies?

Men weren't meant to witness death on such a scale. Squashing traitors who wanted to return to the days of old—to the days of monarchy and tyranny—wasn't an unworthy cause. But some days, that cause felt more like a vanity project the eight High Lords had dreamed up as opposed to genuine justice.

Sleep came for him like a fiend, and when he blinked back to consciousness, night had fully fallen. On the cot beside his, his father was fast asleep. But now that he was awake again, Virgil had a feeling rest would continue to evade him, so he quietly left the safety of his tent instead.

There were always soldiers milling about the camp. It was one of the few constants that came with this way of life. They kept such odd hours, unable to fully adopt a routine as long as threats were abound. A fire was going in the center of camp, and a few sleepless men were gathered around it. Some of them were eating, some of them were just watching. It was a warm summer night, no time for a fire, but Virgil was drawn to it all the same. He took a seat on a log and looked around. When he didn't see the Third's Princess anywhere, he kept to himself.

He wondered if he lived up to his sigil the way she did. She was clearly a gifted strategist and a burgeoning spymaster. They didn't call her the Hawk for nothing. Their house sigil would be little more than a vanity symbol if it weren't for her. The third house's High Lord was too reclusive, and their heir too passive. But if there was anyone who embodied what House Veservus stood for, it was Rhaella.

His father was a wolf; that was for certain. And on his good days, Uncle Nicholas could pass for a fierce representative. But Virgil himself had never felt particularly at home within his house's values. Where his father and his uncle represented the fierceness of that wolf who watched over their house, Virgil couldn't help but think of himself more like a pup that had wandered into the wrong den.

He had not been born for this life, nor these titles, but none of that mattered. He had to live it. Whether as a man or a weapon or a mistake, he just wanted to put an end to this. He was sick of the ongoing numbness of war, and so Virgil stared into the flames and let his mind empty of anything but its warmth.

CHAPTER FOUR

"We, the united banners under the Trueborn, offer our unconditional surrender to the opposing forces."
—*Unsigned notice of surrender from the Royalist Army*

23 Aviatoun, in the Benevolent year 112 A.E.

The sounds of whooping and hollering should have startled Rhaella as they woke her up, but somewhere deep in her bones she knew this was a good thing. And the sense of relief that slowly settled over her body only confirmed those suspicions. She knew better than to assume the war was over, but the excitement coming from outside the tent told her that things were slowing down. The gravelly voices shouting about good news only confirmed such suspicions that the worst of the fighting was over. Dormant, but not dead.

Rhaella roused herself, rising to her elbows as the last dregs of sleep faded away, and she took a sharp breath in as she did so. The smell of roasted meat and vegetables surrounded her, and she felt even more grateful yet for the presence of such a thing. If they were preparing a feast this early in the day, surely things must be looking up. In all likelihood, battles would continue popping up around the islands as word slowly trickled out to the farthest of their outposts, but things would begin to settle soon enough. And, someday after that, war would fizzle out entirely and the bloody conflict of the past months would be nothing but a horrendous, inescapable memory.

They were children of war, after all. They'd never be rid of such a thing entirely.

There was a noise at the front of the tent that brought her attention back to the present. "Rhaella?" Ser Eric's voice called. He was one of the more tolerable guards, devoted to Virgil in the way a sworn sword would be, though the title still did not belong to him. "There's breakfast."

"Thank you, Ser Eric," she said, flopping onto her back. If she could've delayed getting up any longer, she would've, but duty—and her stomach—called. Rhaella sat up once more and quickly plaited her hair. Without a mirror, she couldn't achieve the intricate designs she usually opted for, but the practiced motion of it worked just as well.

At the breakfast line, Virgil stood in a huddle of clearly intoxicated soldiers. He appeared as though he'd had a drink or two himself. He looked up as she approached, and, to her surprise, he pushed his way out of the crowd to walk towards her.

"Did you receive a notice of surrender?" She asked by way of greeting.

"Something like that. They sent a sacrificial messenger to tell us as much. I would have woken you, but it didn't seem necessary." A smirk bloomed on his face, and he chuckled to himself. "Besides, I trusted you could put things together on your own."

She smiled, but it felt forced. "Do you trust that this is over, however short lived it may be?"

"No," he answered swiftly. "But tensions have eased enough that we can afford to split our priorities."

"Back to the duties that bind us," she said, grasping her hands behind her back.

He nodded. "There's going to be a feast tonight. My uncle has already sent a letter to your Doctrina. Your house's camp should be arriving a little after midday."

"Oh," she said. "Wonderful."

Virgil frowned at her tone but didn't question her. Rhaella excused herself, muttering about needing to find something to eat. She took breakfast alone, needing the time and space to ready herself before facing her family again after so much time spent away. It wasn't that she didn't want to see them. Or maybe it was.

Distance had given her perspective, as it often did.

Her father had sent her on plenty of reconnaissance missions before, but he had rarely tolerated her absence for more than a few days at a time. These past weeks felt like a generous eternity. And she thought she had done well with it. But, having had a larger taste of freedom, Rhaella found herself craving more. Perhaps, if her father was pleased with her work here, she could bargain for a longer leash.

Retreating into her tent, Rhaella rifled through the few clothes she'd brought with her, and she tried to find something presentable for a feast. Of course, it wasn't going to be a glamorous affair. But she wanted to feel like something aside from a strategist or a soldier for one day. After a long moment, she found a passable blouse and a clean pair of pants at the bottom of her bag. She took a moment to redo her braid into something neater, and when Rhaella emerged from her tent again—as ready as she could be for her family's arrival—she found that their caravan was within sight.

The guards at the border of the camp shouted something, but Asriel ignored them as he sprinted past with his arms spread open. He crashed into Rhaella, enveloping her in a massive hug.

She laughed into his shoulder. "So you heard the good news."

"All thanks to you," Asriel said. "And your brilliant mind."

"It wasn't all me," she said. "It was Virgil, too."

Something sparked in her brother's eye at that, but he didn't get the chance to ask about it before their father was there, crushing Rhaella against his chest.

"Scì cìr," he murmured. *My daughter.* "Yo kù kì law ðeìb shlu." *We are all very proud of you.*

Rhaella forced a smile onto her face and tried to take the compliment for what it was. Somehow, though, it felt hollow. She stifled the feeling as the rest of their camp made their way in, soldiers immediately running to their comrades to take part in the drinking. Asriel stared after his guard, and she couldn't help but wonder if he was enamored by him or the drinks.

She looked around. "Where is my dragon?"

"Slinking between the trees somewhere," her father answered. "You can meet with him later. Right now I'm going to meet with the High Lord and both of you will accompany me."

That wasn't the answer she wanted to hear, but she followed orders regardless. Ducking into the High Lord's tent, Rhaella took a seat at the corner of the table. Asriel sat at their father's side while he and Doctrina Dogan spoke with High Lord Vincent and Doctrina Nicholas.

51

"Thank you for taking my daughter in and sheltering her," her father began. "Our house extends our most sincere gratitude for keeping her safe and sound."

"You need not thank us for that," High Lord Midar said dismissively. "We would not have dared to harm your ward."

Rhaella flinched as though she had been struck. There was a tone that many nobles took when referencing her that made her status sound like an insult and the High Lord of the Eighth House had done just that. When her eyes met Virgil's, he mouthed an apology.

Smoothing past the slight, her father continued on. "Your house received the benefit of my daughter's strategizing. In exchange, Prince Virgil has offered to vouch for us to any who ask about our loyalties. Can I trust that you will hold up this end of the deal as well?"

High Lord Midar crossed his arms over his chest. "Why should you doubt us?"

"It's not that I doubt," her father said, raising his hands placatingly. "I simply seek assurances wherever necessary."

"I'm not going to coddle you," High Lord Midar said. "You can trust us or you can choose otherwise. We'll hold up our end of the bargain either way, just as we'll expect you to maintain watch over the remaining members of your house. After all, it's crucial that we ensure no more traitors raise their heads out of the dirt."

"Of course," her father said, and it was impossible to miss the sharpness in his tone.

The High Lords continued to bicker, going over the minutiae of the costs of the feast and what House Veservus could supply as part of their gratitude. These discussions no longer hinged upon matters of life and death, and Rhaella found it impossible to connect with anymore. Instead, she tuned out of the conversation and played with the fraying edges of the bandages in her lap.

From across the table, her eyes kept snagging on Virgil's. She couldn't help that it made the corners of her mouth twitch every time he caught her staring. Even as she fought back a smile, she saw him doing the same. There was tension in the lines between his brows, but nothing that completely consumed him like it had the other night around the fire.

"Let's be done with this politicking," High Lord Vincent said. "Alden, you've done what you can. We're grateful for that. Why don't we indulge in the festivities our children have worked so hard to earn?"

Her father rose to his feet. "We can have a drink in their honor."

"Hear, hear," Virgil said, his eyes glued to Rhaella's despite the fact that he was replying directly to her father.

She liked how it felt to know he was staring. The weight of his gaze on her was a welcome one. As she made her way out of the tent, she cast a glance over her shoulder as she walked beside her brother toward the barrels of ale and wine. Someone was pouring them into cups and passing them around. Her and her brother each took a glass and clinked them together, content to enjoy each other's company.

The two of them stood on the fringes of the crowd and drank, which was typical for them. Asriel was more suited to parties than she was, but even he had the good sense to not throw himself into the mix just yet.

"Their camp is bigger than ours," Asriel remarked.

"Their army is bigger than ours."

"Right," Asriel said, taking a long sip of his drink.

For a while, the two of them watched everyone else celebrate. It was never easy to let loose with their father—or his watchful eyes—hovering in the background. But Rhaella had grown so comfortable amongst the Midar army that it felt disrespectful to not laugh with them as they engaged her in conversation. A few of them even hugged her. It was entirely unbecoming of her to act this way., but then again, she belonged with people like Virgil's foot soldiers. She had always been destined to fight for her place among a world that refused to accommodate her.

Virgil seemed to understand something about that, even though he had been afforded every luxury of a Prince, and she wondered what experience could have afforded him that insight. She knew he had had a hard time growing into his role, but she also thought that gave him a unique sense of empathy. Yet another fine trait among an ever-growing list.

When her eyes found him next, Virgil was playing a drinking game with his men. He looked more relaxed than he had in weeks, and there was an easy smile on his face. All of the tension of the past months had ebbed out of the lines of his body. She'd studied him long enough to recognize the signs when it was there. In another life, she might've marched right up to him and his men and thrown herself into the game. But her father was there. And so was his. And so were so many other eyes. So instead, Rhaella made herself content to simply watch, stubbornly refusing to shy away from the attraction that bloomed in her chest every time that pair of brown eyes caught hers.

The day grew long, and there was a never-ending supply of food and drink. There were toasts to various people and to battles and to the death of their enemies. And once the sunlight started to fade, they filled the patches of open field—the same ones that had been used for sparring only days ago—with dancing. That ache to join in filled Rhaella once more, and she allowed herself to join in only once Asriel had already done so.

At first, Rhaella kept close to her brother's side. As long as she was beside him, she didn't think her father would mind the occasional soldier that sidled up to her and danced. Asriel certainly busied himself becoming familiar with every attractive face that came their way, so why shouldn't she? These long, mirth-filled nights felt so utterly in line with the life they were living prior to the war that it sent chills down her spine. They had fought hard to regain such a freedom, and now it was close at hand again.

Thanks, in no small part, to *her*.

And also to Virgil.

Rhaella wanted to talk to him, to relish in their victory together. There hadn't been time earlier. Casting a cursory glance around the camp, she spotted both of their fathers sitting outside of the head tent as they shared a meal. Exhaustion sat heavy on both of their shoulders, and she thought that it might be time for them to retire soon.

Seeing that they were otherwise occupied, Rhaella made an excuse to her brother and slipped out of the cluster of bodies dancing in the setting sunlight. She didn't allow herself even a moment of unsurety as she walked towards Virgil, who stood on the opposite side of the crowd with a half-emptied cup in hand. He spoke to no one, and when she neared him, it was as though he turned to her on mere instinct alone. Naturally sensing her presence and adapting to it with ease.

"It's a bit crowded for me," she said. "Could we talk elsewhere?"

Virgil raised a brow. "I hear that dragon of yours is lurking around somewhere. May I meet him?"

She nodded and pointed toward the trees. "He should be somewhere in there."

Nodding, the Prince followed her out of the open clearing and into the security of the trees. At once, Rhaella felt less like she was being observed. It afforded her a deep breath she hadn't been able to take since the festivities had begun. Virgil kept pace with her as she followed the instinct pulling her to where Egorion waited. Soon enough, she heard the impatience of his breathing; he was so anxious every time she was away.

Jogging ahead to him, she wrapped her arms as far around his neck as she could manage, and she squeezed tightly.

"Scì af," she murmured affectionately. *My dragon.*

When she turned to look at Virgil, she saw him frozen a few paces away. He stared up at Egorion in awe, and it was then she realized that he had probably never been this close to a dragon before. She rubbed Egorion's snout and waved for Virgil to come closer.

"He's sweet," she said. "You don't have to be afraid."

"He's *big*," Virgil remarked.

"So are you," she countered, raising an eyebrow at the Butcher of Adristan. "You'll be fine."

Rhaella was viscerally aware of how close Virgil kept to her, using her as a barrier between him and the beast. She scoffed, taking him by the wrist and placing his hand on Egorion's snout. The sharp intake of Virgil's breath as he felt the scales was punctuated by the stiffening of his arm. But she held him there, letting him acclimate to the closeness. If he startled, Egorion might react in kind. She wanted to avoid that.

"He's softer than I imagined," Virgil said thoughtfully. "You said his name is Egorion?"

"Yes," she said, petting him affectionately. "He was hatched from the same family as my father's dragon. From the time my brother was born, they were promised to one another. But when it came time for them to bond at age twelve, Egorion chose me instead."

That had been a dark time in their relationship.

"How did your brother take that?"

She wiped dirt from beneath the dragon's eye. "He tried to be happy for me. But he's never been able to lie to me. I knew it was a mask to hide his hurt. It even shocked the nobles that such a venerable creature would bond itself to a bastard rather than the trueborn heir."

"The people of your house are wrong for dismissing you based on something as trivial as your father's indiscretion."

Rhaella shrugged. "I'm a bastard. It's not a dirty word."

"You're more than that," Virgil said. The warmth of his body felt closer, though his hand was still gently petting Egorion's snout, and his arm brushed against her shoulder.

"But still that," she pointed out.

"If anyone looks down on you, or speaks down to you," he said, "you should show them what they're missing."

She rested her hand on Egorion's temple. "It's better for me if I remain unseen."

Softly, Virgil said, "I see you."

Rhaella turned her head to look at him finally. He was so much closer than she'd anticipated, his body only a breath away; her back was nearly pressed to his chest. He had only an inch or two of height on her, and his face was so near to hers. He was looking at her with an intensity she couldn't put words to. But when he leaned down and pressed his lips to hers, she wasn't taken aback. No, she had been waiting for this very moment, and it had yet to disappoint her. Virgil's mouth was soft, and he didn't push for anything further than that, but she let the kiss linger anyways. Wishing desperately for this moment to stretch out into blissful perpetuity.

When he pulled away, Virgil whispered, "Was that alright?"

She nodded, fearing that if she spoke too loudly she'd scare him away. "Yes."

Virgil swallowed, and her eyes tracked the movement down the broad column of his throat. "Then I'd like to do it again."

Somewhere within her, she had words for him. But Rhaella found herself unable to speak them so instead she nodded her head again, tilting her face up to reach him. Virgil's hand went to her waist, and she turned to face him fully. Before they could do anything more, though, she heard cursing in the distance and the slight commotion of twigs snapping and leaves rustling.

Virgil moved immediately, his hand going to the pommel of his sword. Rhaella, however, recognized her brother's voice too crisply to be afraid.

"I'm sorry," Asriel called out from the trees. "I came out here to relieve myself and I... I'll leave. I didn't see anything. I'm going now."

Rhaella groaned, putting her face in her hands. "This is humiliating."

"It's alright," Virgil said. "Though perhaps we should get back."

Suddenly unsure of what to do with herself, Rhaella fidgeted with the hem of her shirt and kept to Virgil's side as they made their way back to the festivities. Just before they broke through the tree line, though, Virgil turned to her and said plainly, "I owe you one now."

Smiling, Rhaella instantly felt lighter as they walked back into the crowd. Already, she could see her brother back in the throng, seemingly unbothered by what he had or hadn't seen. He wouldn't meet her eye when she waved, though, which didn't ease her worries entirely. There was nothing scandalous about what she'd been doing, and he of all people was the last who could judge her, but the fear nagged at her regardless.

Her father found them shortly after they returned, cutting both of them off as they walked. He ignored Virgil's presence completely and said, "I need you to pick up a few things from my suite in the Palace."

"Alright," she said. "When?"

"Now."

"*Now?*" She barked out. "Father, I don't—"

"It can't wait," he said curtly. Casting a glance at Virgil, he said, "Zlaû yoûb dfuhj."

It is careful information. Which was her father's way of saying it was compromising. Likely, whatever it was regarded the war, or some other serious matter. She sighed and shot Virgil an apologetic look. They could resume the fun once she returned.

"Fine," she said. "Let me go on Egorion. A ship will take too long."

Her father nodded, and his acquiescence startled her. This would be her first flight in months after his continuous denials. Tentative excitement fluttered in her stomach, but it existed right alongside that speck of trepidation. She sped back into the trees and made quick work of saddling Egorion. It wouldn't take them long to get there and back as long as she hurried.

———◆◆◆———

The Palace of Many Rooms was housed squarely in the center of all of the islands. Even from miles away, its white stone walls rose above the vegetation and uneven terrain. Kingsgrave was a dangerous island, especially after dark. There were prowling beasts wandering the land, hungry for warm flesh. Egorion could, without a doubt, keep her safe, but it was better to stay inside and avoid the things that bit.

After a quick flight, Egorion landed right in front of the Palace. She trusted him to wait there and to take care of himself if needed, so she made her way to the open doors. A Mediator met her there, greeting her with all the respect afforded to a noble daughter as they led her inside to the heavily furnished foyer.

Once, the Palace of Many Rooms had been the King's Palace. The beautifully decadent, gluttonous finishings left no room to debate the power housed within its walls. Now, the Palace was more tasteful in its decoration. It was still beautiful, nonetheless, but it was far more utilitarian.

Despite not having visited in months, though, Rhaella did not linger on the finer details. Instead, she focused on the back of the Mediator's head as they led her down the halls and through archways until they reached the Veservus wing. They passed doors that led to the family library before reaching the suite.

Leaving the Mediator at the front door, Rhaella slipped into the shadows of her father's bedroom. She didn't bother lighting a lantern or throwing back the curtains, instead opting to let her preternatural eyes adjust to the darkness. When she did such a thing, the room was encased in a fuzzy sort of pseudo-light. Her father's directions had been vague, which was nothing new. Seeing as it had been so long since they'd been here, she assumed he wanted her to bring back everything that had been left in his desk.

Sorting through the mess of papers scattered amongst her father's things, Rhaella opened the drawer, hoping to find anything of importance. In that drawer, she had expected to find odds and ends of information scratched onto any piece of paper her father could find.

What she hadn't expected, however, was the *content* of those papers.

How many thwarted betrothal proposals were laid out in front of her? Half a dozen? Possibly more. All this time, Rhaella had thought she had never been properly courted because no respectable suitor wanted to align themselves with a bastard. But these pages told a different story. They painted a picture in which her father handed out refusals on her behalf without ever thinking to confer with her about such matters. As soon as she reached adulthood, she thought she would have to fight off expectations of marriage from her father and from Doctrina Dogan. She had been prepared for those battles.

This battle was something else entirely.

It gutted her that her father had orchestrated all of this right under her nose. It was one thing if he kept secrets. But seeking out information like this is what she had been raised to do since birth. This felt *personal*.

It felt like *failure*.

As she shoved denial after denial back into the drawer, a folded sheet caught her eye. Her hands shook as she raised the Dux Doctrina code of conduct to where she could see it. She knew enough about the Order to know that this was no ordinary list of rules that detailed their standards and expectations. This document contained explanations of procedure, what to expect when entering the Order, and so much more. And worse yet, her Vessial name was scribbled at the top of the page.

This wasn't just a handout about conduct. No, this was an *application*.

How long had it been since her father had been able to leave the mainland? Certainly, he couldn't have done so without her knowledge. Which meant that this document had been mixed in with her father's things for months. Maybe even *years*. He couldn't possibly expect her to go into the Order, could he?

Had he wanted her to find this? Or was she simply stumbling upon it by accident?

Rhaella felt dizzy. So rarely did she feel out of her depth, and yet this had thrown her so far into the ocean that she was losing sight of the surface. The crushing weight of her father's expectations bore down on her, and for a devastating breath, she felt as though she might understand what it was to be Asriel. To have such a constant and unyielding weight upon her shoulders.

She couldn't burden him with this, but she couldn't bear it on her own, either. It was too heavy. Already, she felt as though she might drown.

She had to leave. She needed air, and she needed to complain within earshot of someone who could help her carry this weight. Emptying the rest of the drawer into her bag without so much as a second glance, Rhaella stormed out of the suite and past the Mediator, heading all the way outside.

Egorion was already on his feet as though he had been expecting her. But of course he was; the bond linking them would have told him of her arrival the moment she decided to come. It had started to rain outside, and she thought she heard thunder in the distance. Egorion was a strong flier, and fearless at that. They could handle a little rain.

The moment she sat atop her dragon and took to the skies, Rhaella felt the weight on her chest begin to lift. Riding always made her feel better, even when things were dire. Which made her father's refusal to let her ride throughout the course of the war all the more painful. It seemed he found it easy to refuse her things that might bring her even a little bit of joy.

Even Egorion seemed more at ease in flight. Her dragon knew where to take her, but he still went out of his way to take the longer route, circling around the islands before heading in the direction she wanted. It was a short flight to Sandorne thanks to its proximity to Kingsgrave. In the old world of kings, House Redspire had managed an intimate relationship with the monarchy because of that closeness. And it was that very same closeness that had allowed House Redspire a hand in the tyrant king's downfall.

Rhaella steered Egorion toward a secluded beach at the very edge of Sandorne. Once she dismounted, he immediately took off to find shelter from the rain. She snorted before rushing to scale the mountainside. It was a lengthy trek up to the house proper. Even from a distance, it was clear that every inch of this castle was built to honor the arts—the house's specialty. House Redspire was a house of fae gifted with the ability to manipulate both the elements and the senses toward a deeper appreciation of beauty and pleasure.

There were few others in the nation that could create things as fine. Castle Darsor's exterior was covered with sprawling columns and high-mounted gargoyles. Metal and flora mixed in the trellis that led up to the heir apparent's bedroom, giving Rhaella plenty to grab onto as she climbed.

Princess Aida Redspire was seated on a plush velvet loveseat facing the window when Rhaella entered the room. She didn't look startled or even surprised. In fact, she almost looked bored.

"You're traveling late," Aida mused.

"I need to talk to you," Rhaella said, climbing all the way inside before sliding the window shut.

"What's wrong?" Aida clutched a hand to her swollen belly. She was wearing a remarkably revealing dress for someone who intended to keep their pregnancy a secret.

Rhaella crossed the room in a few steps and knelt before her friend, pressing a kiss to her bump. "Hello, little one," she said. Then, to Aida, "It's about my father."

"Is he well?" Aida asked, making room for Rhaella on the loveseat as though it was second nature.

"Is he well," Rhaella scoffed under her breath, collapsing beside her friend. "I went through his things at the Palace. He's thinking about sending me to the Dux Doctrina."

Aida burst out laughing. "That's ridiculous. I don't mean to offend. You'd make a fantastic Doctrina. But he has to know how much you'd hate that, right?"

"Apparently not," Rhaella grumbled. "He's collected all of the necessary paperwork. All he needs is my consent."

Just as quickly as she had brightened, Aida sobered. "He can't."

"It appears he already has," Rhaella said. "All that's left to figure out is what I can do to stop it."

"Well," Aida said, leaning her head on Rhaella's shoulder. "There are a few different ways you can navigate this."

"My jacket's wet," Rhaella said, making no move to push Aida away.

"Be silent," she said, squeezing Rhaella's arm. "You can tell your father you don't want to go and deal with his disappointment, which you'll inevitably make up for with your talent. Or, you can give into his demands and try out the Order." She paused. "I think we both know which path you'll choose."

"I don't want to be a Doctrina. I don't want to take a vow of celibacy, and I certainly don't want to spend my days telling some High Lord—most of whom barely tolerate me among their ranks on a good day—how best to rule their territories." It had come out of her in a rush, leaving Rhaella breathless for a moment, but that didn't make it any less true. Absently, she was braiding a few strands of Aida's curls, when she spoke again.

"But if I stay, I'll never break free of my brother's shadow. I'll be doomed to trail two steps behind him at all times. Or worse," she paused again, this time for dramatic effect, "they'll marry me off to some lesser Lord just to wash their hands of me."

"That last option might not be so terrible." But even Aida didn't sound as though she believed the words that came from her mouth.

Rhaella hummed, poking Aida's belly. "If you really thought that, you'd have married the moment this happened."

Aida swatted her hand away, snorting. "I have my reasons for not marrying, just as I have my reasons for keeping this a secret."

"You trusted me, of all people, to know it."

Aida looked up at her. "I haven't told you everything."

Rhaella held her stare. "You know if you told me who the father was, I would keep it to myself. I'm not the Hawk when it comes to my friends."

"You would if you had to, though," she replied sadly. "And I don't fault you for that. It just means I have to keep some things to myself."

Letting out a deeper breath than she felt capable of holding at the moment, Rhaella dropped her head onto the back of the couch. "I don't want to follow any of the paths laid out in front of me. I don't want anything to change. But also, I want *everything* to change."

"I think it would help if you clarified that for yourself," Aida said.

"I don't know how much time I have," she lamented, sinking deeper into the cushions. "If I could freeze time and think through every decision, that would make it easier."

"I've wanted that for myself plenty of times," Aida said. "But things can't always be easy."

"Are they ever?"

"I think so," she said. "It feels like it when I'm working on my art. Which, for the record, I haven't touched in days. I can barely keep on my feet now. Even on my good days."

"If I go," Rhaella said softly, "will you craft me something beautiful?"

Aida sat up and gave her a long, unbroken stare. Then, "For you, I'd try for my masterpiece. I can't promise it would be, though."

"That's alright," Rhaella said, brushing her wet hair back from her face. "I should go. I only came to commiserate, and you need your rest."

"You can stay."

She shook her head. "My father will be wondering where I went."

"I understand," Aida said. "Send word when you can."

"Of course." Rhaella rose to her feet and pressed her forehead against Aida's, a gesture of goodwill in the Fourth House. "You'll hear from me soon."

"Let's hope," Aida replied as Rhaella climbed back out the window.

The rain had stopped, but the ground was wet, making her journey down the mountain more treacherous than before. Egorion was waiting for her, and, noticing her struggle, he climbed up to meet her halfway.

"Good dragon," she murmured as she mounted him.

The wind whistled in her ears on the ride back to the mainland and she stayed quiet as she guided Egorion through the skies. Her hands gripped the reins tighter than was strictly necessary, and she fought to keep her composure. The ride no longer cleared her head. And so, as Rhaella rode, she did what she did best.

She thought.

CHAPTER FIVE

*"Though it is rare that my father allows me to attend, I do enjoy the symphony and
hearing the music."*
—*Letter from Rhaella Asriel Veservus to Virgil Midar*

24 Aviatoun, in the Benevolent year 112 A.E.

Oblivion was a wonderful feeling. So wonderful, in fact, that Virgil
thought he could drown in it. He took another swig from the glass bottle of
amber liquid, deeper than before. He groaned as the last drops slipped down
his chin and into his hair. Pressing his head against the wooden floorboard,
he blinked up at the ceiling and tried to find patterns in the painted mural.
Somewhere between images of trees and uniformed soldiers, he stopped
seeing the paint and felt transported back to the battlefield. The clanging of
swords echoed in his ears, backed by the squelching of flesh as it met their
sharpened blades. When he raised the bottle again, it was empty.

A shadow fell over him, and for a moment Virgil wasn't sure whether
he was still on the battlefield or if he was actually laying on the floor of his
mother's manor. But then his vision cleared and he realized his mother *was*
there, looming over him with her dark hair hanging in her face. The one
that his so clearly resembled. She was frowning, of course, but the softness
at the corners of her eyes spoke to the pity she must have felt as she looked
down at her son.

"Get up," she said, not harshly. "Your uncle awaits you."

"Why did you let him in?" Virgil slurred, his tone pitching up to
a whine.

"Because, although I may live here, this is still your father's home.
And Nicholas is your father's brother," his mother said bitterly. "Clean
yourself up."

The High Lord may have paid for this manor to be built in Steephelm and had it fully furnished to his Lady Wife's liking, but he did not approve of its existence and he *definitely* did not consider this his home. Not that it mattered much anymore, though. Virgil couldn't recall the last time his parents had stayed under the same roof. His mother was a Lady Wife by law alone.

Virgil forced himself up to his elbows in time to watch his mother steal out of the room just as his uncle stormed in. He watched as his mother hardly gave the Doctrina—her brother by law—the time of day. Uncle Nicholas's face was free of veils and chains and masks today. He was here as an uncle, not an advisor, though that didn't ease the sting as his uncle stared down at him with thinly-veiled disgust.

"Get up," he snarled. "We have too much to do for you to drink yourself into a piss puddle."

Despite himself, Virgil let out a laugh which quickly devolved into a hiccup. He pushed himself to sit up fully; he wouldn't stand, not yet. Instead of asking for direction, he stared up and waited for Uncle Nicholas to continue, which earned him a long-suffering sigh.

"We sail to Segsiege as soon as the captain gives the order. House Lancor is hosting us for dinner tonight. You are to get on the ship, bathe, and dress in your finest before we dock."

Virgil wanted to lay back down on the tile where it was cold and solid beneath his body. Where he wasn't expected to wear fine clothes and eat seasoned meats while there were still dead being carted out to burial. It wasn't fair—none of this was. He just wanted to be left alone. To rot, and, perhaps, to die.

Uncle Nicholas kicked his foot against Virgil's. "Get *up*. I'm not asking."

He reached out a hand and, reluctantly, Virgil took it. Nicholas all but yanked his nephew to his feet, and Virgil was reminded that although the Doctrina lacked the consistency of training, he still came from Midar blood. Meaning, his uncle possessed the very same inhuman strength that ran in their family. Men of their bloodline were meant for heavy things because they were strong enough to carry them. It might have felt like a privilege but for the fact that that strength had been historically used to hurt and maim and kill.

"You're lucky you started drinking so early in the day," his uncle said. "You'll have time to sober up."

"I'll just get drunk again at dinner," Virgil said pointedly.

"You'll drink an appropriate amount so that we don't look uptight," his uncle said. "But you will remain respectable and you will *behave*. It falls to me to ensure that. Perhaps if you weren't the heir, you could do what you pleased, but that's not the case. And it does no good to dwell on what might or might not be. Get it together. People are waiting to see you."

Confused, Virgil moved to follow his uncle out of the bare room he'd been stowed away in. Finding that he could keep his balance with some effort, Virgil kept pace with his uncle. There was commotion down the hall, far too jovial for his current mood. Coming down from battle was one thing. War had not fully left Virgil yet. He wasn't sure when it would. *If* it would.

As they walked, Virgil mentally prepared himself to face down overbearing Lords or opportunistic tradesmen. But when he and his family's Doctrina rounded the corner, Virgil couldn't help but to draw in a soft gasp.

The northern frontlines had robbed Bianca and Mila of the color in their cheeks; they looked paler than before, but no less joyful. As she saw her cousin approach, Bianca let out a sound and ran to him, embracing him in a fierce hold. She briefly stole the breath from his lungs with those arms that were more like lethal weapons, but he was glad for the embrace nonetheless. He laughed, leaning into his cousin. Only a few months separated them in age, and she had never let him forget those months she held over him. They'd both grown into their inherited muscles as of late, leaving her to look like the more feminine variant of him—if not a little taller and broader.

Mila patiently waited her turn before finally throwing her arms around Virgil's neck. She lacked the bulky muscles and considerable height that were typical of their family, but there was still remarkable strength in her lean figure. A whole three years younger than him and her sister, Mila held more lightness in her. There was a hope that hadn't yet been broken down. It inspired something much the same in Virgil.

"Hello, cousin," Mila whispered, months of separation filling her voice.

"We didn't send word," Bianca said. "After your father called us back from the front, we were supposed to tour the mainland and assist the nurses."

"We weren't about to do that," Mila said, shaking her head. "They can handle themselves. We wanted to see you."

Bianca was eyeing him warily. Knowingly. She reached a hand out and wiped sweat-slicked hair back from his forehead. "You look tired," she said, a sad smile playing on her face.

"I *am* tired," he admitted. "How did you fare in the north?"

"We got to see snow," Mila said. "That was nice."

It hardly snowed on Greenisle. The mainland was usually caught between an angry spring and a forgiving summer. Right now, it was the latter.

The sound of Uncle Nicholas's voice sobered Virgil. "You're all coming to dinner tonight. I hope that makes it easier for you."

It might have been kind, and Virgil thought it might be his uncle's best effort at such an emotion. But even still, it fell short.

Silence fell over the room, which was full of lingering soldiers, staff, and officials. And at the center of the room, Virgil's mother descended the grand staircase with practiced ease. She paused near the bottom step with her hands folded in front of her. Standing ramrod straight like that, she looked every part the Lady Wife of House Midar, even if she couldn't continue to act like one.

"Say goodbye to your mother, boy," Uncle Nicholas said. "Only the gods know when we might return to the mainland."

His mother's expression softened as Virgil approached, and she let her head tilt to one side. She made no move to touch him, though. Her hands remained clasped tightly in front of her.

"My son," she said with as much gentleness as a daughter of warriors could. "I'd fight your father for you, if only I could."

Virgil bit back the retort that, if she tried, she could likely win such a fight. His father had always been soft for her, in his own way. Virgil's mother had been born and raised on Greenisle, the daughter of another family of strongmen. Her family had served in the army beneath generations of Midar leaders. His parents had grown up childhood friends—something Virgil knew was a rare occurrence for a man like his father.

Sometimes it ached that his mother had given up on his father. That she knew what—and *who*—she was getting into bed with. But, just like his father, Virgil was soft when it came to his mother. Even as a child, he saw how hollow his mother grew in his father's presence. The distance she kept was for her own sanity.

If fate didn't have other plans for him, Virgil would want that distance for himself, too. The few times he had attempted to abdicate his position always led him to his mother's doorstep. She brought him in without argument each time, but the wolves always showed up at her doorstep to bring him back to Greenisle and Castle Silverfort. At some point, the allure of freedom lost its splendor. Acceptance was just another sacrifice. Another blade for Virgil to throw himself on.

"I'll visit when I can," was all he said.

"I'm sure you will," his mother said, somewhat sadly.

They both knew it was an empty promise. A reward dangled in front of an impossible task. Virgil had to go forth and be the heir. His mother would remain here and be the Lady Wife, if from a distance.

From the center of the foyer, Uncle Nicholas cleared his throat. Virgil followed the sound, a dog to a whistle. He cast only one more glance at his mother over his shoulder. She did not meet his eye.

The Midars were not sentimental people. Virgil told himself he was just like his parents in that sense.

He caught up to his cousins and walked with them toward the docks, listening to their stories from the past few months. He already knew some details, thanks to the few letters they'd sent back and forth. But his cousins had been as preoccupied with battle as he had been, so there was plenty to fill him in on during the walk there.

His mother's house had been strategically built deep inside the mainland, far from the borders of Adristan's politics. The ports that housed their ships, however, were in Stillgrove territory. Purple banners waved above every harbor, bearing their signature crest of a ram in front of stalks of wheat. Farmers could grow food just about anywhere, but it wouldn't taste as good as the food grown with Stillgrove hands.

Purple-clad guards greeted them as they made to board a ship. Virgil recognized a few of them—they had been trained at the school on

Greenisle. The Fifth house grew food, the Eighth grew fighters.

Virgil made a point of acknowledging them, shaking their hands, and thanking them for their service. The guard nearest him still looked fresh, not beaten down by battle. He must not have been sent to the frontlines, then. Good for him.

Once they boarded the ship, Virgil excused himself and kept to the bow where he could look out at the water and clear his head. He was still dizzy from the drinks; he wanted more, but water would have to do until dinner. Damn his uncle, he would drink himself back into the oblivion he had only just left behind.

But, sober or not, Virgil's thoughts drifted back to battle.

Almost a year ago now, seemingly random bouts of violence had begun to spring up from disgruntled field hands and craftsmen. Efforts at diplomacy from their respective High Lords went nowhere. Soon, self-proclaimed armies had popped up around the islands—and then on the mainland—and men were claiming to fight in the name of the rightful heir to the throne. The very same throne that Virgil's ancestor had slaughtered to free the nation. It had taken three months of casualties before Virgil finally pieced together the fact that they were all connected.

That was where Rhaella came in.

Rather, that was when Virgil had finally contacted House Veservus, asking for the aid of their expert strategy. His father had not approved of that decision, viewing the Third as a house of traitors. That was fair enough. A third of their population defected to fight for the idea of a Trueborn heir that the opposition held fast to. But the house itself had not fallen. And, loathe as they were to admit it, High Lord Veservus had a skill they needed. So when Prince Asriel, his son and heir, managed the missives between them, Virgil had thought little of it.

He had assumed that the Veservus heir was much like him, trained to do all of the things the High Lord could do. Never would he have assumed that someone else would handle the young Prince's missives for him. Though Asriel's reputation should have told Virgil otherwise. And so when those first missives turned out to be a ruse, Rhaella's existence as the Hawk came as a pleasant surprise. One that, in retrospect, he should have suspected from the beginning.

Though it concerned him that the Veservus family would allow such carelessness to slip through the cracks. Virgil tucked that piece of information into his arsenal, noting that it would be useful if brought to light at the right moment, but he hated doing so as much as he hated war. He did not wish to reduce himself to such a tactic unless explicitly necessary. Not when that very ruse was the thing that had won them the war. Not when it was the reason they no longer needed to call it war at all.

No matter how long Virgil Midar stood there and tried to puzzle things out, he just kept going in circles. Each time, coming back to the look in the Veservus girl's eyes as he wrapped the wounds on her palm. Each time, remembering that it was the mind behind those very same eyes that had put an end to things in the first place.

Frustrated, Virgil grumbled beneath his breath before running a hand through his hair in an attempt to clear his mind for good. Now came the tedious parts, he thought to himself. Though Virgil had to admit, he preferred paperwork and meetings with his father's committees over living in tents between carnage.

So why was he complaining now?

The buzz of liquor was quickly fading and logic slowly crept in at the edges of his thoughts. He wanted the war to end. He wanted to go back to pointless busywork. And yet, now that such a thing was possible again, he felt just as terrible as he did before. Even off the battlefield, Virgil couldn't help but feel like a beast of war.

He thought about the hero's welcome that would be waiting for them once they arrived at the Hutch. There would be plenty of drinks involved in such a celebration. And if he could manage to sneak out of the house, perhaps he could distract himself at a shitty tavern with a good fuck. On his better days, that worked well enough.

Segsiege was the island nearest to the mainland. Its docks were still shrouded in fog, which was not unusual for this time of year, and it looked foreboding in the distance. The Hutch—the Lancor family home—rose above it, sitting comfortably in a valley between two hills. The architecture was impressive, though understated. Tall, cream-colored towers of mixed stone burst from the rocky mountains, bold and unmoving as the land surrounding it.

"Virgil." Declan's voice came from a few steps behind where he stood.

Virgil turned to look at his guard. He stood a careful few feet away, likely sensing the tension radiating off of Virgil's body. When given the go-ahead to speak, Declan cleared his throat.

"We're docking soon. Your uncle charged me with watching you. I wanted to know what you'd prefer I do instead."

"Gods," Virgil groaned, dragging a hand down his face. "He's ridiculous if he thinks I need to be supervised like some child."

"Far be it from me to agree," Declan clarified for good measure. And Virgil thought there was a ghost of a smile pulling at his mouth.

He wanted to crack a joke. To encourage that hint of a smile to become full-grown. But he couldn't. He felt drained and empty of anything pleasant or conversational. He was barely going to make it through the greetings once they were ashore, let alone an entire dinner.

"See that my cousins are taken care of. They've only just gotten back from the north, and I'm sure they're exhausted."

"As you say."

Virgil nodded before turning to look out at the open sea once more. Once they were in the castle, he doubted he'd even be afforded the luxury of staring out a *window*. With a sigh, he ducked into the cabin. In his private chambers, Virgil stripped down to his skin and used the basin to wash. Minding the scrapes covering his body, he cleaned himself with methodical care. For the first time in too long, he trimmed his nails and shaved his chest. Then, using a small mirror balanced against the wall, he trimmed his hair and beard, and the sight of his chin after so many weeks made him want to laugh. The beard had aged him, making him look too much like his father. The long hair was a good look, but the feeling of the strands tickling the back of his neck and shoulders reminded him too much of the way it had clung there in the thick of battle.

After drying off, he dressed himself in Midar blue. The pants fit a tad too loose after weeks spent living off rations, and the shirt itched. The vest felt superfluous, and the necklace bearing the family crest weighed heavily where it rested at his breast.

Virgil allowed himself one last, long look in the mirror. He was the warbringer clothed to look like an heir. It fit him wrong, wronger still after all that he'd done. But for tonight, it would have to be right.

His father waited at the helm, looking more well-groomed than he had in weeks. High Lord Vincent Midar was a wolf in a well-made suit, but that hadn't dulled his teeth or his claws.

Giving Virgil a once-over, his father said, "This'll do."

Uncle Nicholas met them there, dressed in his full Doctrina regalia. His mask would stay on until it was time to eat. Technically, when he wasn't advising, he was welcome to remove it. But in his uncle's case, the advising never really ended.

Bianca and Mila stood side by side behind their uncles in fine gowns, one of pink and one of blue. The two of them were, for all intents and purposes, Princesses. Though they'd bash the teeth in of anyone who referred to them as such. Their mother, sister to the High Lord and Dux Doctrina, had raised them to be fierce; they were all gnashing teeth and spiteful smiles. Exactly the sort of women who could match seasoned soldiers beat for beat.

Virgil fell in line beside them like the good dog he was, and he linked his hands behind his back as they disembarked. The rest of the house officials trailed behind, conversing amongst themselves. Virgil scoffed at the amount of nobles who eagerly lapped up the opportunity to network with another house. No councilman's opinion carried the same weight as that of a Doctrina. Members of the Order had served as the head advisors to every house since before the downfall of the king. Even so, nobles still raised their children to be politically savvy enough to warrant a seat at the table. Which made it all the more ironic that High Lord Vincent Midar had appointed his own brother as his right hand.

A herald cleared his throat and announced them with vigor.

"High Lord Vincent Midar of House Midar, Keeper of the Peace, Bringer of All Justice, and the Unrelenting Muscle of Adristan. And his son and heir, Prince Virgil Midar. And his assembled court."

They approached the front steps of the Hutch, home to the First House. The Lancor family stood on the front steps of their home, staring down at them from their enormous height.

At Virgil's left side, Eric muttered, "Those are the tallest people I've ever seen."

That was hardly a fair observation, seeing as Eric wasn't very tall to begin with, and the Lancor family were descended from giants. The Lancor heir looked to be seven feet tall, easily. His father was even taller.

Doctrina Nicholas shot them a dirty look over his shoulder, warning them to remain silent. Virgil fixed his gaze ahead so he wouldn't laugh.

Their party stopped a few feet from the steps. High Lord Ewan Lancor stepped forward to meet them with his Lady Wife at his side. Bowing deeply at the waist, he righted himself to formally welcome them. Matching hand tattoos peeked out from beneath the First Lord and Lady's clothes, a symbol of their marriage bond.

"Vincent," High Lord Ewan said, "how long's it been?"

"Long enough for me to feel ancient. I trust everyone's in good health?"

In proper fashion, Virgil's father turned to the Lady Wife and bowed to her as well. She returned with a curtsy, smiling unabashedly.

"We're well enough," she said. "Just happy to hear that war is coming to an end."

Virgil's father nodded. "With no small thanks to your house's contribution." Turning around, he gestured for Virgil to come forward. "My son, and the commander of my armies, Virgil."

Lady Lancor pulled one of her sons forward. "Our son and heir, Ezra."

The boy was tall, to be certain. But this close, Virgil could see how *young* he was, too. It was one thing to read about his fellow heirs on paper; it was another experience to see all twenty years so clearly written on Ezra's face.

Red-faced in the cheeks, which were nearly as bright as his hair, Ezra bowed at the waist, practically folding himself in half. In a too-gentle voice, he said, "Thank you for your service."

Virgil's stomach turned over. He looked past the boy at his siblings. His brother was barely younger, though he was nearly as tall as Ezra was already. But his sister looked closer in age to Virgil and the rest of the heirs. She had taken after her mother, it seemed. Still tall, thanks to the fae blood of the Redspire line, but nowhere near the height of her brothers.

"Why don't we head inside?" High Lord Ewan said. "Dinner should be about ready."

They entered the castle and were led down the hallways until they reached an ornate dining room. The Lancors took their seats around the table with confidence, and the Midar party filled in where they could. Virgil ended up between the heir and his older sister with his cousins sitting across the table.

"So," High Lord Ewan said as they were seating themselves. "Why don't we cut right to the chase? We're all friends here, aren't we?"

"Agreed," High Lord Vincent responded instantly. Virgil swallowed his scoff.

"While I am very curious to hear the stories you have from the frontlines, it's your son I'm most interested in speaking to."

Virgil stiffened, and his father shot him a look before composing himself, saying, "My son is not much of a story teller, but he'd be happy to tell you anything you want to know."

"Virgil," High Lord Ewan said, turning to address him directly at last. "You haven't had the pleasure of meeting my daughter. My eldest, Princess Freya."

Freya Lancor straightened in her seat, nearly equaling him in height. She carried herself with a regality common among the nobles, and she flashed him a smile just as becoming. Her hair was a softer shade of red than her brothers, and her cheeks were lightly dusted by freckles. She was beautiful, and that beauty set Virgil on edge. He didn't dare to think that the High Lord was trying to steer this conversation in the direction of marriage.

"Freya was just as involved with the war effort, though her duties were relegated to the islands, away from the worst of the fighting. But I'll have you know that it's thanks to her efforts, alongside her brothers, that our enemies were unable to destroy most of the buildings made by Lancor hands."

Virgil nodded as he began filling his plate from the trays being laid out. "You have the gratitude of both myself and my house."

"We were hoping you would extend that gratitude to shed a little light on your experience," High Lord Ewan said. "Particularly regarding your interactions with House Veservus."

Virgil froze with a serving spoon midair. Coughing once, he carefully measured his tone as he spoke. "What about them?"

"Years ago—a lifetime ago now, it seems—High Lord Veservus and I agreed to a betrothal between his son and my daughter. An informal agreement, nothing set in stone. And, not to be crude, but..." The High Lord cleared his throat, looking to his own Doctrina for confirmation before continuing. "It's no secret that many from the Third House chose to fight for the enemy. We're aware that you were in communications with the Veservus heir, and that his contributions helped expedite the end of this conflict. We were hoping that, out of gratitude, you would tell us more about what he's like."

Virgil weighed the cost of lying further—of keeping up Rhaella's ruse—against the cost of dropping it entirely. He remembered the feeling of her knife against his palm, and it reminded him that he had made a deal. One he had no intention of breaking. He shot his father and uncle a glare, silently beseeching them to keep silent. And they would, if only to feel that they possessed even a grain of knowledge the other house did not.

"The Third House are good people who remained loyal to the nation. If it's treason you're worried about, you'll find none within the house itself. If it's kindness, I didn't find that in short supply either. Though our conversations mostly stuck to the business of war. The frontlines aren't exactly a breeding ground for much else."

Freya seemed to relax marginally. Her father, however, sat stiffly upright.

"I'm relieved to hear that," High Lord Ewan said. "I have no interest in arming our enemies with any kind of leverage. Which is exactly what a marriage with my daughter, Freya, would be."

"House Veservus is not our enemy," Virgil affirmed.

"Yet the Third House has not earned back the good graces of the other houses," Uncle Nicholas said, swirling his goblet. "My peers across the islands cannot speak to the achievements of Prince Asriel the way you are able to with your daughter."

"The conflict is newly ended," Virgil said through gritted teeth. "Give them time to prove themselves."

"And if we do not possess that kind of time?" Uncle Nicholas gestured around the table.

"Say your piece and be done with it, Nicholas," Virgil's father said, leaning back in his chair.

Uncle Nicholas pointed at his brother, his face triumphant. "Precisely my point. Be done with it. All of the houses should adhere to such an ideal. We need to move forward, as a *nation*. And there is no place for parasitic betrothals. What can House Veservus offer you that another house can't? Our house requires no leverage. Our reputation remains intact among the Concilium. There would be only mutual benefit if we were to unite our houses."

Silence fell across the table, meanwhile Virgil stared incredulously at his uncle, who pointedly avoided his gaze. He turned to each of his cousins and beseeched just *one* of them to intercede on his behalf. But what could either of them say as lesser noble daughters that would reach the ear of either of the High Lords?

High Lord Ewan's eyes were sparkling. He even seemed *pleased* at the suggestion. This was dangerous territory.

Virgil's father barked out a laugh. "Forgive me, my brother is very forward. We have no intention to interfere with plans already in the making."

"But your son is not attached to any marital agreements, is he?" The First House's Doctrina eyed Virgil with an too-hungry stare.

"He's tired from the war," High Lord Midar said swiftly, leaving no room for argument. "Once he's ready, then we can broach discussions of marriage. But for tonight, I propose we eat this delicious feast the cooks have prepared for us."

"I agree," Virgil said, pointedly digging into his food. After a long pause, the rest of the table joined in and Virgil felt his shoulders dip just slightly. He allowed himself a fraction of a moment's relief.

He felt his father eyeing him from across the table, and when Virgil finally found the courage to meet his eyes, he was surprised to see his father dip his chin in a subtle nod. His father had just done him a considerable kindness, and it was not one that would go unnoticed. His father had given him the space to breathe. The space to decide for himself. This was likely the last time he would urge away a house who was so eager for an alliance.

Virgil would not squander this gift.

In the seat beside him, Ezra Lancor sat stiffly, not engaging in conversation with anyone—even his siblings. His face remained flushed although he was not speaking or being spoken to. His eyes were turned down, only occasionally darting around the table. He fidgeted with his place setting, merely picking at his food. In that moment, Virgil decided Ezra must be quite the anxious young thing.

Meanwhile, his sister sat comfortably as she made conversation with Virgil's cousins and cleared her plate. Her bright laughter echoed around the room. She was a star that the other nobles flocked to stare at. Virgil could easily see the appeal of a woman like her, and yet, something deep in his spirit rejected the idea of a match with the Lancor daughter.

Politically speaking, however, Virgil couldn't fathom how she hadn't been named High Lord Ewan's heir. By all accounts, she was older, more sociable, and seemingly more accomplished regarding the war effort. If she were from any other house, the High Lord would have paraded her and her accomplishments for all to see.

Why would the High Lord wait for his middle son to come of age when he had a perfectly suitable eldest daughter?

Coming of age was a strange phenomenon by their standards. One wasn't considered an adult until they turned twenty. But looking at the First heir now, Virgil thought he needed a few more years to grow into a seasoned leader. So many years ago, when Virgil himself had turned that fateful age, he had made yet another attempt to abdicate his position. That one was more successful than his other attempts, seeing as there was little his father could outright order him to do as a legal adult. Even so, the wheels of fate caught up to him eventually.

And now, it seemed, Ezra Lancor was doomed to the same fate.

"Enjoying the meal, op?" Bianca asked. The hint of Menmal in her words told Virgil that there was more she actually wanted to say. More that she did not want overheard.

"Manw. Dawlch?" *Yes. Why?*

"That's such a unique accent," Freya noted. "What language is that?"

Bianca and Virgil locked eyes before she put on a courteous smile. "It's our family tongue."

"Gorgeous," the First Princess remarked. "I've never heard it translated."

She was leading this conversation somewhere they were forbidden to go. Virgil shook his head minutely at his cousin. Now was not the time.

They continued to speak in the common tongue for the remainder of dinner. Once he and his cousins were informally excused, they should have stuck around to mingle with the Lancor siblings. But none of them were in any mood to talk, so Virgil asked a servant clad in orange to show them to their rooms. Filing in with his cousins and his guards, Virgil shut and locked the door behind him. Leaning back against it, he closed his eyes and let out a sigh.

"I hate sitting through political dinners," he said.

"You seemed to like it with the Veservus girl," Eric chuckled.

Virgil went utterly still and silent, which was decidedly the wrong choice as the rest of the room busted out in laughter. He leaned forward and punched his guard in the arm.

Bianca continued giggling as she sprawled onto the lavish bed. "So your men aren't just spewing rumors. You *do* like the Veservus Princess!"

Staring at the floor, he said, "She isn't technically a Princess."

"How romantic!" Mila clapped. She tossed off her shawl and sat with her legs crossed beneath her. Grinning up at him, she said, "We had heard rumors, but we thought there was no way it could be true. I'm surprised you're going to be the first of us to break the no-marriage pact."

"Which means you're now free to explore *your* options, Mila," Bianca said.

"Shut up," she said to her sister. "I want to hear more about Virgil's love affair."

"It's not a love affair," Virgil said. "And don't think we won't be revisiting these *options* of yours, cousin. Rhaella and I were communicating about strategy before we ever met in person. We've been exchanging letters for months."

"She's the spymaster, isn't she?" Bianca asked. "Did you spill all of your secrets?"

"You're poking fun, but she's quite the genuine person. She didn't play games or posture with me. So much of duty tends to feel like a pointless game, and she was unwilling to play."

"Which is why you like her," Mila answered for him.

"It's a *friendship*," Virgil said. "I haven't pursued her."

"It would make sense if you did," Bianca pushed. "I'm sure your father would be thrilled if you finally settled down."

He had considered that. Several times, in fact. The prospect of marriage seemed less daunting when it was her face on the other side of it. Though ultimately, he resolved not to bring the idea to his father until he was sure it would go in his favor. Which meant acquiring the approval of the Third High Lord. A prospect that intimidated even Virgil himself.

But then again, didn't House Veservus owe him a favor? Virgil was doing his part to keep their reputation intact. If he asked permission to court Rhaella, he couldn't imagine the High Lord would refuse him.

In a moment of rare, unchecked impulse, Virgil decided it was at least worth the effort of writing a letter. Even if he never sent it, maybe just the act of doing so would bring him some much-needed clarity.

Surely, the desk drawer had to contain pens and parchment. And there was a brazier sitting atop it. He could send a letter to High Lord Veservus and receive a reply by the time they were back on Greenisle. He could get it over and done with before he could talk himself out of it.

As inconspicuous as he could, Virgil crossed the room to the desk and began looting through the contents before pulling a tablet onto his lap and composing a letter. Conversation buzzed around him. As he wrote, he caught flashes of jokes thrown his way, and he heard snippets of more serious topics as well. He ignored it all, though, focusing on wording this letter that could determine his future exactly right.

And when he finally finished with it and dropped the letter into the fire, a small part of him hoped that the Hawk would intercept it first. That it would make her smile in the way that had captured him so completely.

CHAPTER SIX

"The weight of lordship sits heavy on those who bear it. Though many of the High Lords have been devoted, true, and noble, they are reportedly unhappy creatures. The wretchedness of decision making—especially in matters of family—often caused bouts of depression."
—The High Lords of Adristan: A History, *by Gawain Redspire*

26 Aviatoun, in the Benevolent year 112 A.E.

With hands braced against the rim of the washbowl, Asriel tried and failed to maintain eye contact with his own reflection. A thin sheen of sweat had formed along his brow and he couldn't quite swallow past the lump in his throat. His head dropped back to the porcelain currently holding him up, and the emptiness of the basin allowed his mind to fill with visions of Rhaella's face. He could already picture the way her expression would shift when he told her how concretely he had fucked up.

He hadn't meant to tell their father what he'd seen that night on the mainland. It had just slipped out, a tumble of nonsensical words that should have meant nothing. And since his father hadn't brought it up the following day, Asriel foolishly assumed that the knowledge would fade into the background—as unimportant as anything else that happened that night.

But now, their father wanted to talk to them both at the same time. He wanted to make a decision about Rhaella's future, and he would force Asriel's hand while he did it. This would be a final decision, spurred into motion by the information he should never have let slip in the first place.

Taking a deep, shuddering breath, Asriel lifted his head and blotted the sweat from his brow. He slapped his own cheek once, and then twice, as he willed his pulse to slow. It would only take Rhaella one look at him to know that something was wrong if he showed up in this state. And, frankly, the cowardly part of his heart didn't want her to know until he was ready. Asriel wasn't sure how many courses of their meal that would take, but if it took him until dessert had been served for him to say it out loud, so be it.

Asriel pulled himself into the shape of a man worth his burdens—into the shape of an heir. Throwing the washroom door open, he strode through his room, throwing his clothes off as he went. His outfit for tonight was laid out across the unmade bed. He pulled on the blouse and tapered trousers, alongside the two draping belts and a brooch with the family crest. Then he layered on rings and necklaces, leaving his ears free of jewelry, and he left his white-blonde hair loose. His father wouldn't be pleased about that, but Asriel was already doing unsavory things to make his father happy. The braids, he could sacrifice.

Barrett was waiting in the sitting area, looking remarkably relaxed for being on duty. His feet rested on the table in front of him, one arm slung over the top of the sofa. Asriel wanted nothing more than to throw himself onto the sofa with him and forget about the mass and the dinner. But if they didn't show their faces, Asriel would hear about it from his father. Or, worse, Rhaella.

Neither option sounded pleasant.

Asriel's guard lifted his head, eyes bleary with exhaustion. They hadn't been able to let him off duty for more than a few hours at a time, recently, and the man deserved it. The house's lack of guards was becoming a pervasive problem.

"Ready?" Barrett asked.

"No," Asriel answered honestly.

Barrett nodded knowingly, expecting as much out of him. "Let's go."

The halls of the Veservus wing in the Palace of Many Rooms were ghostly. Walking through them felt like walking through a living museum of the way things used to be. Along the walls, ornate, lavish decorations covered every inch. But it felt hollow. All along these walls, reminders that their once-proud house had been abandoned by people of every rank were inescapable. The High Lord had always taken so much pride in their family name. Asriel wondered if that meant much of anything now that they couldn't prevent the masses from rallying around a dead king.

As they left the Veservus wing and re-emerged into the Palace proper, members of every house crossed their path. Some bowed respectfully, while others averted their eyes and quickened their steps. Asriel couldn't fault them for that.

The foyer splintered off into halls that led to each of the different wings. The left hand staircase opened onto a landing draped in the silver banners of House Aviatis. Asriel and Barrett went up the stairs and down the hall, eyeing all of the owl imagery with guarded interest. As the house of religion and spirituality, the sigils were not unfamiliar to him, though that didn't make them any less unsettling.

After rounding one final corner, Asriel and his guard arrived at the Aviatis chapel doors—large wooden arches crossed with black metal bars sealed away the supposed holiness inside. Asriel waited for Barrett to push open the doors before he stepped inside, but he halted in the threshold when he spotted Rhaella already seated in the front pew with her head down. She might have been praying; Asriel had ceased doing so years ago. Steeling himself, he went to sit beside her.

"You've been acting strangely," she said before he could fully sit down, eyes fixed firmly on her hands in her lap.

He hesitated above the pew before collapsing beside her. "Trouble follows me."

"Is it Father?"

"It's always Father," he replied, thankful for the excuse. "He and his thousand expectations. The older I get, the more of them he seems to have for me."

"You know I understand that," she pouted, still refusing to so much as lift her eyes.

Asriel let out a heavy sigh and looked around the chapel. Barrett waited along the far wall, as guards did. He and Rhaella were the only ones seated for mass so far, though their father was sure to join them shortly. They had arrived on Kingsgrave the morning after the celebratory feast on the mainland. Upon said arrival, Rhaella had become a shell, refusing to speak unless spoken to. She had even gone so far as to refuse to share meals with anyone. Impulsively, Asriel wanted to rip open the wound he was holding a tourniquet over, but he had to wait for his father. This, too, felt like a test.

"Everyone's late," Asriel remarked, keeping his gaze around the room.

"We're early," Rhaella corrected.

"Old habits don't die quite so easily," he said on an exhale. "I don't want to be here."

"Yet here you are," Rhaella said.

At last, she looked up. What took Asriel aback first was that her eyes were tinted red, as if she had been crying. That couldn't be right—Rhaella *never* cried. And the rest of her face was soft, almost pondering. It was rare that she wasn't thinking something through or turning it over to examine every angle. But right now she looked as though she was actively *avoiding* lingering on something.

When Asriel swallowed, it felt as though shards of glass were sliding down his throat, but he did it anyway. "You feel it too? The weight of his expectations?"

"I can't *not* feel it," she said shakily. There was a pause where his sister looked as though she might say more, but it was then that their father chose to make his appearance.

High Lord Alden Veservus stormed into the room, all quiet thunder and straight lines. He came down the aisle and slid into the pew beside his children, giving Asriel a hard stare.

"Your hair," was all he said.

Where Asriel's hair hung loosely, his father's was pulled away from his face in two intricate braids. Beside him, Rhaella's hair hung half-loose and half-braided, a sign of her own devotion to the family's tradition.

"We both know you're far too old to warrant a scolding," his father said under his breath, turning his head to the door a few seconds before it opened and people began filing in. "If you want to dishonor our history, that's your decision."

Too many listening ears were around for Asriel to respond the way he truly wanted to. Instead, he took the blow in silence, bowing his head and listening as the musicians began to sing a hymn. If nothing else, he never minded the music at mass.

Priestesses gathered on the altar and began to speak the holy words, and not a moment too soon. Lucerian masses were traditionally held late at night. Asriel neglected to check the time before he left the suite, but he thought it was nearing midnight. He felt a pang of guilt over Barrett having to stand on his feet against the wall, keeping watch over his pitiful self, when he was so clearly exhausted. He wanted to send his guard to bed, to permit him to get some much-needed rest.

Passionate verses from the Good Book spoke of the Martyr. A figure so selfless that their followers mourned for an entire month after political opponents assassinated them. Devoted as they were, the followers continued to offer up prayers to the Martyr. Once those prayers had been answered, they knew for certain that their leader had, in fact, been a god.

Asriel had always looked down upon devotees who were insistent upon following in the footsteps of the saints. For those who held firm to the Lucerian teachings, canonization and a place in the afterlife awaited them. Saints heard the prayers of the lowly people on the earth. And the saints who answered more prayers than others were bestowed with godhood in the eyes of the people. Asriel had never had a prayer answered that couldn't be explained by perfect timing and a little bit of luck, so he had ceased doing so entirely.

When the time came, the priestesses gestured for those gathered to begin lighting candles wherever they found they could around the perimeter of the room. Asriel's father wasted no time crossing to one of the many altars laid out. He knelt before it, praying with his hands clasped, before lighting several candles. Rhaella sighed heavily and rose to her feet, kneeling in front the empty altar nearest them. Asriel followed her on instinct, kneeling beside her.

With her eyes closed and hands grasping one another, she said against her own skin, "You need to at least look like you're trying."

Silently, Asriel mimicked her pose. With his body tensed as if intensely praying, he watched her. Although her eyes remained shut, he knew she could sense him. His gaze traveled over her face, a near-mirror image to his. For how much they had both grown up, he could still only see her as his baby sister. It didn't matter that they had different mothers. Rhaella was his sister, through and through. He tried to imagine her gone and tried to soften himself to the idea. But his heart clenched and he felt a sinking in his stomach. He thought that it must be nervousness for his own sake, or maybe that familiar selfishness rearing its head as it always did. He didn't want to think that it was anything else, like regret.

One way or another, though, tonight would determine that Rhaella was going to leave House Veservus. She could go into the Order. But he was beginning to suspect that the kiss she shared with Virgil Midar was more than just a kiss. He wondered if his sister could be happy with a man like that. If he would be a better alternative to the Order.

For so long, she had expressed nothing but explicit disinterest in getting married. *I am not cattle to be bartered with*, she would say. Though, how could she be content to know that her fate was in Asriel's shaking hands? That she didn't get to decide this on her own? Could she have grown used to such an idea after all these years? That sounded like a very sad existence, he thought to himself.

This wasn't fair to either of them.

Mass finished in a dreary haze, and their father led them back to the living quarters in the Veservus wing. He signaled to a passing Mediator to send for dinner, which they went for instantly. There was a perfectly fine dining room off of the great hall, and hardly any space to eat in their quarters, but their father insisted on privacy.

Rhaella floated into the room on light feet, settling on the sofa without a word. Though he could sense her building temper, Asriel sat next to his sister, praying that she couldn't smell the deceit on him. Of course, he couldn't be so lucky. She stole glances at him out of the corner of her eye, openly assessing him.

Her evaluation was cut off by a knock at the door followed by servants entering with trays of food. They laid the spread across the small table in front of the sofa, and it was quickly overfull. Asriel watched in frozen anticipation, reminding himself to say *thank you* at the appropriate times. And just when he thought he couldn't handle the rising tension any longer, Dogan entered the room. Asriel's father greeted the Doctrina in the same gruff manner he did his children, which made sense given the fact that the two had been at each other's sides since childhood.

"You've made yourself scarce," the High Lord said.

"I was handling affairs," the Doctrina replied smoothly.

If possible, Asriel's stomach sank even further. The affairs in question were about to be discussed. He wasn't ready to bring it up. He wanted to sink into the floor, all the way through the house and into the earth where he could rot for the rest of time.

His father and the Doctrina began serving themselves while Asriel and Rhaella sat stiffly. For a few weighted moments, the only audible sound was the clinking of silverware against dishes. Then, the shifting of fabric as Rhaella sat at the edge of the cushion and began putting together a plate. When Asriel's father shot him a glare, he picked up a serving spoon. He tried to keep the tremor out of his muscles, and managed through serving himself spiced meat, roasted potatoes, and leafy greens. But as he reached for the rice, his nerves took over and the spoon dropped back into the bowl with a clatter.

Rhaella dropped her plate back onto the table with a thud. "Why is everyone acting so odd?"

Asriel's father nodded his head, silently encouraging his son to give an answer. Helplessly, Asriel looked around the table. He was going to have to do this in front of Dogan. He couldn't do this in front of Dogan. Asriel looked to Barrett for some sort of comfort, but even he was poised at the front door with a stone face. He then turned toward his father, feeling his eyes bulge out in a desperate, flailing attempt to push the conversation forward.

Sighing, his father did not relent. "Asriel and I have been talking about your future. About your position within House Veservus."

Shoulders hunched, Rhaella slowly said, "Alright."

Between small bites, their father said, "Your brother tells me that you've grown familiar with the Midar Prince."

Blushing all the way to her ears, Rhaella's head snapped toward him. Her brow furrowed as she shot him a furious glare. Embarrassment was rife on her face, and she began to stammer. Another rarity for her.

"I-" She took a deep breath before trying again. "I wouldn't put it that way."

"I wouldn't think so, given how clear you've been with your feelings regarding marriage. You don't want to get married. Do you, Rhaella?" It was a leading question, trapping her in the middle of his web. Unable to untangle the threads without further exposing herself.

She stiffened, her eyes darting between their father and Asriel. "Where is this going?"

"I'm asking you, genuinely," their father said. "That's not what you want, is it?"

Hesitantly, she said, "If you want to argue about betrothals—"

"I don't want to argue about anything," their father interrupted. "I know you were prepared to fight me on that, and I admire your vehemence. But I don't want to use you as a bargaining chip for leverage and power. I do not want for such things."

Asriel was taken aback by the use of his own words out of his father's mouth. Even so, he kept his mouth shut and his focus off of his sister.

His father continued, "I do, however, want peace. I know you want the same, given everything that you saw on the fields of battle."

Rhaella nodded again. With a small voice, she said, "I do."

Asriel could practically feel the fear roiling off of her. He couldn't stand it. Their father needed to get this over with as quickly as possible. He halfway thought his father was dragging out with the sole purpose of making this as difficult as possible for Asriel. Some misguided attempt to teach him a lesson. To teach him what would happen when he delayed a decision for too long.

"Don't you think frolicking with Princes in the forest is an unproductive way to achieve that?" Their father took another bite of his dinner. There was a long, stretched-out silence before the High Lord spoke again. "Especially now that House Midar has already denied the proposal I sent their way."

Rhaella's eyes widened. "He *what?*"

"After your brother informed me of your interest in Prince Virgil, I sent the High Lord and his son a letter expressing my desire to formalize a union between the two of you. He declined."

She shook her head. "He wouldn't have—"

"He did," their father insisted. "And it is his loss. He would have been very lucky to have you. Everyone at this table knows how talented you are. Everyone in this *house* knows. By the gods, I'd be surprised if the whole of Adristan didn't know by now. And I have made the grave mistake of wasting your talents by keeping you here, at your brother's side, in an informal capacity. Or by seeking out matches with nobles who are simply not on your level. We want *more* for you, Rhaella."

"Who is we?"

It killed Asriel a little, in that moment, the way her eyes shot to Dogan. How she wanted to find anyone to blame besides her brother. But as their father stared at Asriel, waiting for him to pick up where he'd left off, Rhaella's face darkened.

Staring directly at him, her voice dripping with poison, his sister spoke. "Asriel, what has he been telling you?"

Asriel struggled to keep his head upright, dropping his chin to his chest before picking it up again. Lamely, he said, "We want what's best for you, Rhae."

"And what do you think that is?" The venom in her voice was enough to send Asriel's gaze straight back to the floor but Rhaella did not let up. She snapped her fingers in his face. "Look at me. Say what you mean to say, and *look* at me while you do."

He shrugged twice before running a hand through his loose hair. Eyes finding purchase anywhere that wasn't her face, he said, "I... I agree with Father. The Order could be a good fit for you—"

She barked out a harsh laugh. "The Order. You're serious? You think becoming a Doctrina will be good for me?"

Dogan cleared his throat. "The Dux Doctrina values all of the things that you are naturally gifted at, my dear. With them, you would blossom—"

"I don't recall asking for your input, Doctrina Dogan," Rhaella snapped. "Or am I remiss to think that Doctrinas are supposed to remain silent unless called upon?"

Dogan sat back in his chair and had the good sense to keep his mouth shut. The High Lord shot Rhaella a warning look. She, however, did not balk from it. She looked at their father with tears in her eyes and kept her chin high, even as her lower lip trembled.

"You don't have to be rude," their father said.

"And you don't have to suggest sending me away," she countered. Rhaella pressed her body into the arm of the sofa, creating as much distance between her and Asriel as possible.

"We aren't suggesting, vzoz cìr."

Rhaella pressed the heels of her hands into her eyes and when she pulled away, Asriel saw that she was fully crying now. "Stop saying *we*. Asriel, tell him this isn't what I want. You *know* this isn't what I want."

"I *don't* know what you want, Rhae." Asriel threw up his hands, frustration reaching its breaking point within him. "You never tell me! As far as I knew, you were only speaking to Virgil on a need-to-know basis. His father was rude from the moment we stepped foot in his camp, and his Doctrina looked like he wanted to have us taken away in chains. They think we're traitors! By the gods, *would* you marry him, knowing that about his family?"

"I don't know," Rhaella said, wiping her eyes. "I thought I would have time to think about it."

Now, he truly thought he was going to vomit. Asriel shriveled against the couch cushions, a burning in his throat that meant tears threatened. He couldn't find words to say that wouldn't sound utterly pathetic in the face of his sister's obvious upset. Had he truly been misled?

"If I may…" Dogan said leadingly.

"You may," the High Lord replied.

"The Order may seem overwhelming at first. Truly, it is not for everyone. But out of anyone else in the whole of Adristan, Rhaella, *you* would be the best fit for them. Putting your talents to use for the good of the nation is the next logical step for you."

Sniffling, Rhaella ignored the Doctrina and turned to their father. "Another house could take me in and make me work for them."

"They won't," their father said confidently. "It's not right, but the Order accepts… reservations… of Doctrinas in exchange for a small price. I would put down the necessary amount to secure your station within House Veservus. You won't have to worry about serving another house, I can promise you that."

"What if I marry someone else," she moaned, placing her palm against her forehead. "You can marry me off to whatever Lord or Lady you choose. Whoever will be the quickest means to your ends."

Gently, their father said, "That's simply not going to work."

"Because you turned down every eligible match before we could consider them," Rhaella said bitterly. "I saw your handiwork. It was very clever of you, too."

Asriel flinched. His father hadn't told him that. But he couldn't truly be surprised; more often than not, his father withheld the whole truth. Asriel was only the heir—the pretty, golden face to sit in the window and be admired rather than brought into serious conversations. As was the case with this one. And so Asriel sat and listened without argument. Just as the heir of House Veservus had been taught.

Their father took another bite of his dinner as though the conversation wasn't completely earth-shattering. As if it was completely normal for Rhaella to be crying while they discussed the details of her future. He wiped his mouth with a pristine white cloth napkin and took a sip of water from a crystalline glass.

At last, he said, "I don't recall authorizing you to read the documents I sent you to retrieve."

"Whatever I do," Rhaella said bitterly, "is what you taught me to."

Their father set his silverware down with a soft *plink*. "I can't make House Midar change their minds. Do you want me to apologize for thwarting other suitors over the years? Would you have preferred I married you off to the highest paying noble in exchange for the other houses to stop gossiping in front of our faces? It would have been very easy for me to do so, but I chose not to because I respect your skillset and the potential you have for great things."

"I suppose it's my gratitude you want, then. Well, thank you, Father," Rhaella said. In his periphery, Asriel could see her face turn toward him, but he couldn't make himself meet her eye. "And thank you, brother, for your consideration in these discussions behind my back. I bid you both goodnight."

"Rhaella," Asriel said miserably. She ignored him, storming off to the room they shared.

"Let her go," the High Lord said, digging into his dinner once more. He ignored the door slamming behind him. "Give her time to adjust to the idea. She'll be better by morning."

Asriel wanted to argue. He wanted to defend his sister. He wanted to scream in his father's face that this wasn't right and that he was making the wrong decision. But his nature proved too hardened to break, and so he sat in silence and finished his meal. He listened to his father and Dogan finalize plans to send Rhaella to the Order. He absorbed none of it.

Just as Asriel rose to his feet to retire for the night, his father spoke again.

"Oh, and Asriel? Since your sister has gone to bed, I'm going to need you to get her signature on the forms," he said. "This is *your* decision, after all."

Swallowing dust, Asriel said in a small voice, "Mìn." *Father.*

The High Lord's eyes glossed over Barrett, who had broken protocol by coming to stand directly at Asriel's side rather than clinging to the shadows of the room.

"Ser Barrett," he said, "go guard Rhaella's door."

"As you say," Barrett said, bowing.

His father stared hard. "Are you going to make me repeat myself? You said you were going to think over this decision, and you took too long. Either write a letter to House Midar that is convincing enough to make them change their minds, or get her to sign these papers. But since you prefer to let your sister handle all your correspondence for you lately, that might be inadvisable." His father paused for a long moment, letting the words wash over Asriel in full. When he spoke again, it was entirely the High Lord speaking and nothing of his father. "Make good on your word, and make it quick. Members of the Order are sailing to Kingsgrave as we speak. If we've wasted their time, *you* can explain to them why that is."

He shoved a stack of papers toward Asriel, along with a pen. It rolled across the table, practically begging him to pick it up. They both stared down at it, and Asriel had the distinct sense that the parchment was staring back. Judging him.

With a final pleading look at his father, Asriel said, "There's no one else Rhaella could potentially marry? No one that would be most beneficial to our house?"

"What will be most beneficial to our house is if Rhaella serves Adristan in this way," he said. "Service to the Order is something solid. Something tangible we can present and take credit for. Betrothals are fickle things. You, more than anyone, should know that. Or do you need another reminder?"

Choking on unshed tears, Asriel said, "You were never going to let me approve a marriage between Rhaella and another house, were you? It isn't just Virgil you disapprove of."

"At last, you've learned something," his father said coldly.

Resigned, and with a shaking hand, Asriel picked up the pen and papers, pocketing them to take to his sister.

The High Lord said, "You'll be staying here for the foreseeable future while you adjust to your duties as my heir. Every day, you'll study the histories in our family library and you'll interact with any other house members you come across. You will work to repair the relationship between our house and House Lancor, and you will help to salvage the betrothal that is hanging on by mere threads. Accomplish all of that and maybe, in a few months, you'll have proven your worth. Understood?"

"But I—"

"Am I understood?"

Caught in the web of duty—duty that belonged to both he and his father—Asriel nodded. Then, to his surprise, his father stepped around the table separating them and placed a hand on Asriel's shoulder. Asriel mastered himself enough to hold still. He kept his spine straight and his muscles locked. At his full height, Asriel stood a few inches taller than his father. Both he and Rhae had outgrown their father in at least one respect, it seemed.

With the eyes of the High Lord, his father said, "My father did not leave me with much instruction when I transitioned from Heir to Lordship. He left me with piles of books and the know-how to sort through them. The rest was up to me. However, he did leave me with this."

Nestled snugly in the palm of his father's hand was a key. It was an old-fashioned, brass thing with a red ribbon tied around its handle. At first glance, it was tarnished beyond repair. But a closer inspection revealed that it was due to the makeup of the metal itself. There were streaks of black and gray floating amidst the gold, leaving an almost marbled effect. At his father's insistence, Asriel took the key. It was heavier than it looked to be, forcing Asriel to wrap his fingers around it as he held it up to the light.

"What is this for?" Asriel asked, not taking his eyes off of it.

"Yo me frìsh vwen vya chtaì lyo," his father said. *We have more than one library.*

Asriel tore his eyes away from the key, furrowing his brow. "Do you mean the archives?"

"No," his father said. "There is another resource. One that I hope you will utilize rather than relying on me. Between the shelves of the Palace library, there is a study locked away. Once I leave you, it will be yours to take. It was mine to inherit not long before my father's title passed to me, and now it is yours to explore in kind. With any luck, the answers to any questions you might have can be found there."

To his surprise, Asriel thought he saw a faraway hint of fondness on his father's face. It was strange to see such softness on a face so hardened by time and effort, especially given how cold he had looked only moments ago.

Asriel looked a great deal like his father—more so than he looked like his mother—and he couldn't help but compare himself to the man that was both his father and his ruler The longer he looked, Asriel could hardly pick out his mother's features on his face, if there were any at all. He only knew her face from portraits, but he'd always half-assumed that his ability to smile as wide as he could was thanks to her. Seeing it mirrored on his father's face was disarming.

All Asriel could manage to say was, "Law shlu, mìn." *Thank you, Father.*

His father nodded thoughtfully. "One thing I've never had to explain to you is that discretion is one of our most powerful weapons. You must wield it carefully. Say nothing about the key, or the decision that's been made about your sister. Not until the time is right."

How would he know when the time was right? Asriel wanted to ask, but found the words lacking. When his father sent him to bed, he didn't push against it. He did, however, hesitate at the door.

It was no use; Rhaella would already know that he was there. Nudging it open, he slipped inside and shut the door with a soft *click*. Abandoning the papers on her desk, he climbed beneath the covers of the bed that had always been his but never truly felt like it. This room, which would be his home for the next few months at minimum.

When Rhaella's sniffling became unavoidable as it devolved into crying, he rolled over and pretended he didn't hear her. He ignored it, just as he ignored the smoke still rising out of the brazier on the dresser between them, and went to sleep.

CHAPTER SEVEN

"The gods have bestowed within all of us the strength we need to persist."
—Lucerian Proverb

27 Aviatoun, in the Benevolent year 112 A.E.

Rhaella wasn't averse to a darker color palette, but there was something about seeing herself draped in Doctrina Black that made her stomach turn over. The dress had belonged to her grandmother, and the veil was one of Dogan's spares. Her white-blond hair refused to hide completely underneath it, strands of her front pieces slipping out despite how she tried to pin them back. The Order was fond of jewelry—something about the craftsmanship and dedication, or so they claimed—so she donned a pair of teardrop earrings, a gold chain, and a matching gold bangle. All gifts from her Father.

Asriel had left her the room so she could get ready and make her peace with things in private. It was just as well. If he couldn't face her, he'd have plenty of time to reckon with his decisions while she was gone. On average, training with the Dux took a year. With her talents, though, perhaps she would manage to finish in eight or nine months. No more than a year of schooling.

Even so, she would remain in the Silent Keep with the rest of the "unclaimed" Doctrinas until Asriel took over as High Lord. Rhaella pointedly ignored the pit in her stomach that reminded her that, once her brother Ascended, it meant their father would be dead. She wasn't going to see Isle Verdale or Briarhall again for a very, very long time.

In the deepest recesses of her mind, where the logic fell away and her feelings took over, Rhaella wondered if everyone else was right. If she might benefit from becoming part of the Order. She knew that she was too good to be doing Asriel's dirty work from the shadows. The seat she held on her father's council only mattered so long as she contributed to her house's welfare. And yet her brother received the credit for her wins regardless. Perhaps at least with the cloak of a Doctrina surrounding her, she could do such work in the light.

Perhaps her father would take her seriously after all this was settled.

But was that really what lay at the heart of the issue? Was it that he didn't take her seriously now? He wouldn't trust her with as much as he did if he didn't believe her to be capable. She had always been a doer, even before she really understood what it meant to be second-born and a girl—let alone a bastard—and a Veservus. Her whole life, her father and brother tried to tell her that those things didn't matter, but their actions said differently. No matter how far she excelled or how competent she proved herself, neither one of them ever saw fit to legitimize or reward those efforts.

The truth of the matter was that those were the *only* things people saw about her. The gospel of her life had always remained unseen—just like she had been—watching and listening and learning. If she could fill herself up with everyone else's secrets, then those hidden pieces of herself never needed to see the light of day. They never needed to matter, and certainly not to her father.

Rhaella heard Barrett's footsteps shift in her direction a full five seconds before she could make out his footsteps, and there was another pause before he knocked on the door. She bid him entry, and he quietly shut the door behind him.

"Rhaella," he said, leaning his back against it. "You have to know your brother's a mess."

"He's always a mess," she said. "And my time cleaning up after him is through. He saw to that."

"He's not trying to be cruel, I hope you know that. He really does think this will be good for you. We all do."

"So you were privy to this discussion as well?" She scoffed, crossing her arms over her chest. "Was the whole of House Veservus involved in this decision making?"

"Rhaella," he said, helplessly throwing up his hands.

She stared at Asriel's guard, who had also become her guard in the last year thanks to the depletion of their forces. Even before that, he had served House Veservus from a much younger age than any guard should. Having been educated in both the Veservus and Midar schools, Barrett had had the unique opportunity to grow up at Asriel's side and to learn the histories at the same time he received world-class training with the rest of the nation's soldiers. If she wasn't in such a sour mood, she would feel more gutted about leaving him behind.

At her silence, he continued, "I felt the same when I went into the guard. New experiences can be terrifying. But I went in with an open mind and it turned out alright. I think it'll be that way for you, too, if you let it."

"You chose to go into the guard," she pointed out.

"There are only so many choices for a young boy in the countryside," he said. "We can't all be born noble."

Rhaella brushed a loose hair back into her veil. "I know. I'm sorry."

"I'm not. I've made do. That's all I want for you. I hope you can see that with time."

"I don't doubt you, Barrett," she said. And she meant it. The informality of his relationship with Asriel and his proximity to her as of late had turned him into something of a friend. "I doubt the political machinations at play."

"Well, once you're in it, you'll be the one making plays. You can turn the game in your favor if you want," he said.

"I'm not that ambitious," she said, brushing his words off as she leaned against the frame of her bed.

"I dare to disagree, and I'd wager that you don't even believe that either," he said.

Rhaella perked her head up, letting her eyes glaze over as she focused her attention toward the other side of the apartment. In the other room, Asriel was considering coming in here, his footsteps shuffling back and forth over the carpet. That was the last thing she wanted while her throat was still hot with the threat of tears. Last night had been humiliating enough. She'd always done her best to save her tears for when she was alone. But she simply couldn't hold it together in the face of exile. That was how she had been referring to this. A cleaving, a tearing, an incurable shattering.

"I need to show my face," she said, rubbing a knuckle beneath her eye.

Barrett nodded, opening the door for her. "As you say."

As Rhaella passed her desk, she picked up the stack of papers that had been left there. She came through the doorway and was immediately in view of the sitting room where her father and brother waited. The curse of these small quarters at the Palace. Both of their heads perked up at her entrance, although they definitely heard her coming the moment her footsteps headed for the bedroom door.

"Rhae," her brother said, taking a step toward her. He held out a hand pleadingly but his damned eyes still wouldn't meet hers.

"It's fine," she said swiftly. "I'll go, and you'll stay. We'll both be better for it."

She knew she was lying, and she knew that her father could hear it as well. Had he honed in on his listening, Asriel would have heard it, too. But even if he had, she could still outwit him. She was still the Hawk, despite all of their wishes.

And so when Asriel's shoulders sagged in visible relief, the cracks in her heart deepened ever so slightly. "Do you mean that?"

She swallowed bile. "I do."

He exhaled shakily—standing straighter as he did so—as though her weak assurances were all he needed to stay standing. As if she wasn't a hair's breadth from collapsing in front of him.

Rhaella pushed down the ache, forcing her spine to remain ramrod straight. She could not afford to show weakness. If she did now, Asriel would be left alone with their father to deal with the consequences. And, loathe as she was to admit it, she didn't want that for her brother.

Rhaella placed the paperwork on the low table and knelt beside it. With a steady hand, she placed her signature where it bid her, effectively signing herself away to the Dux Doctrina. Standing, she shoved the paperwork at her father.

"I need to stop at the dragon pit before the Order arrives," Rhaella said, keeping her tone placid.

Her father, lordlike even when the situation called for him to be a parent, nodded his head. "I can allow that."

Rhaella wasn't sure she would have listened had he not. Leaving without saying goodbye to Egorion would be like leaving one of her organs behind. It simply wasn't possible. She excused herself, ghosting out of the room on light feet as she felt her heart crawl into her throat.

The walk to the dragon pit felt endless, and when she reached the barred door she was half-certain she wouldn't make it back out once she'd said her farewells. It was one thing to be away from her family. But Egorion had *chosen* her, which was more than she could say of her father and brother. Rhaella and her dragon had been bound for over a decade. They had taken to the skies together. They felt one another's emotions. They were sacred beast and sacred rider. That bond was irreplaceable.

As she passed through the thick doors, she turned to the dragon masters lingering nearby. They bowed their heads and waved her through the next set of doors, where Egorion waited in the dark.

She heard the dragon's huff of breath before his scaly figure came fully into view. He was perched upright on his arms, staring directly at the doorway as she passed through. Even without words, though, she could see the pain on his face. The betrayal that mirrored her own. It was as if his downcast expression was saying, *Why must you leave?*

"I know," she said aloud. "I don't want to go either."

Rhaella strode over to her beast and laid her palm upon his snout. His scales were rough, but her hands were calloused from drawing her bow and so she hardly felt its harshness. She rested her forehead against her hand, forcing herself to take deep breaths.

"Scì yi vyuhs." *I feel fear,* she said, the words rising and swirling on her tongue. "I wouldn't go if it would only affect me. But I can't do that to my father and brother. Maybe if I were more like Asriel, I could. Shwosh kì slù pfa scì mìn." *But I'm too much like my father.*

Egorion exhaled, and she felt the heat of his breath ruffle her veil. Even so, she stayed like that, half-hugging her beast.

She continued in a messy mix of Vessial and the common tongue, uncaring if she was overheard by any of her father's prying ears. "I can imagine that this is hard on my brother, too." A choked cry slipped out and she swiped her hand beneath her nose. "Scì twu huht yap cheì." *I wish he told my father no.* "Swosh scì smoû mpùz twon a scì vyad eswiffong lav mìj." *But I don't know that I would've been able to do the same for him.*

A growl came from deep in Egorion's belly. Rhaella ran a hand down his snout to soothe him, softly shushing him. The gesture was as much a comfort to herself as it was to her dragon.

"Scì tha dled," she said at last. *I must go.*

She placed one kiss on his scaled snout before departing, careful not to turn around once she started to walk away. The dragon masters met her at the door. She looked between the two of them, men she'd known her entire life. They knew Egorion as well as she did, in their own way. She could trust them to care for him.

Even so, she found herself saying, "He needs to be taken to the skies as often as possible. Being grounded during the war weakened his wings. Have my brother write with updates on how he fares."

Bowing again, they said in unison, "Yes, my Lady."

With as much grace as she could muster, Rhaella ascended the steps out of the pit and back into the light of day. She walked with her chin held high all the way to the foyer of the Palace, where the members of her house were already waiting.

Rhaella had thought she might have another minute to speak with her family, to bid them a real goodbye. One where she might allow herself to break a little. But, to her dismay, her father said, "Let's welcome our guests."

She heard the Mediator coming before they pushed in from outside. They approached, bowing to the High Lord.

"The Reverend Mother has said the Order will not come inside," they said. "She instead wishes for you to meet them on the steps of the Palace."

"We will honor the Reverend Mother's wishes," Rhaella's father said smoothly, although she heard the growl forming at the back of his throat.

At her father's gesturing, Rhaella walked ahead of their party, breaking the typical protocol. If this were a political or social affair, she would be behind them, draped in house colors and jewels. But this was a presentation to the Order. She was primed and draped in black, ripe for the taking.

A small horde of guards—smaller than it had been in months—followed close behind. The honorable Dux Doctrina weren't to be feared or defended against, and it would appear an insult to suggest as much. But, in a way, it was just as insulting to show up unguarded. To think that Doctrinas were harmless was folly as well.

They stepped into the fresh air, only now there was a sea of black swimming toward them. Contrasted against the high noon sunlight, the Dux Doctrina were a sprawling expanse of darkness. In all these years, with how many people they had sent for training, Rhaella had never actually attended a ceremonial sendoff. She'd read enough to have an idea of what to expect, but the image was startling in reality. She didn't have to try to commit it to memory; it happened involuntarily, burning itself into her mind.

Her father and brother came to stand on either side of her, listening as a hark announced the Order. Rhaella wondered if they were as moved by the vision before them as she was, or if this ceremony would slip into vague memory as the rest of their lives wheeled on.

Distantly, Rhaella noted that no other nobles lingered on the steps of the Palace. There were no people strolling the grounds, either. And she couldn't help but wonder if this absence of an audience was by her father's design, or if it was mere coincidence. But then again, she was grateful for the absence of prying eyes.

The middle ranking Doctrinas—Brothers and Sisters who had completed their training but were not yet assigned to a house—filed in lines with their hands folded and heads bowed. Before them, in more ornate robes, were the higher ranking Doctrinas. The Fathers and Mothers Superior. Seasoned Doctrinas who led the Order after their partnerships with their High Lords fizzled out. Leading the charge, with a tall headdress atop her head like its own crown, was the Reverend Mother.

"Honorable Reverend Mother Locasta," the High Lord called out in a booming voice. "We are humbled by your acceptance of my daughter, Rhaella, into your ranks."

From this distance, Rhaella studied the Reverend Mother. She looked to be in her seventies, maybe older, if she was descended from an inhuman race. Her glittering veil obscured most of her face, she had old eyes that were washed out by age. Many were blessed with long life in Adristan, but those years weighed heavy.

"Enough formalities," the Reverend Mother said, her voice crackling and fierce. "Send forth the child."

No one else would have noticed how imperceptibly her father stiffened. But Rhaella had done the same too many times to count. Her father, the immovable Lord, was taken aback.

Breaking the silence, Asriel chuckled lightly. "A child of twenty-five, to be truthful."

The Reverend Mother's gaze shifted ever-so-slightly toward Asriel. "Hush, Lordling, and do as we say."

Now it was Asriel's turn to look taken aback. He cast a glance at Rhaella, nodding for her to step forward.

"Go on, Rhae," he muttered.

Her feet felt glued to the spot and yet, somehow, she picked them up one at a time and moved away from the safety of her family.

As she passed, her father leaned down and whispered, "The Order demands respect. They have earned it through everything they've done. *Jaw aw.*"

Be good.

Good. That's all she ever was. She had only ever been *good*. So much so that she wasn't screaming and tugging at her hair and hiding behind her father's legs. She was doing exactly as they asked of her and she had not resisted once.

Rhaella was good at listening and committing facts to memory. She was better at spying and handling correspondence than her brother. She was more fluent in Vessial, their mother tongue. She was the best in everything that embodied House Veservus. And yet here she was.

And yet she had no choice in the matter of her own life.

And yet.

Her head spun as she approached the sea of black robes and veils and masks. The Reverend Mother regarded her, and Rhaella regarded her right back. If she remembered correctly—which she knew she did—Locasta hailed from Sandorne, the daughter of a cousin's cousin of a Redspire nobleman. She had gone into the Order as soon as she came of age. At the fresh age of twenty, she worked her way through the ranks until she Ascended to Reverend Mother in her forties. She had been the Reverend

Mother for quite some time.

"This is acceptable," her harsh voice said, breaking through Rhaella's thoughts. "We'll be going now."

Rhaella had known it would be this way. She wasn't foolish enough to think the Dux were a sentimental people. Still, she yearned for her father to insist that the Order stay for dinner in the Palace. And perhaps after, the weather would be ghastly and they'd have to spend just one night here. Maybe the ship would be destroyed in the night during a horrible storm and they'd have to wait for reinforcements to take them to the mainland. Perhaps, by then, her father would have changed his mind and she wouldn't have to go away at all.

Perhaps, indeed.

But the organized lines of Doctrinas and Superiors simply turned in formation and began their long walk down to the docks, toward the ship that would take her so very far away.

She tried to be strong. She attempted to face forward and to keep her back straight. But she was weak—if only in matters regarding her family. And so she turned over her shoulder, only once.

Immediately, she wished she hadn't.

Which was worse, the fact that her brother was crying, or that her father wasn't?

As they approached the ship, the ranks of Doctrinas parted, leaving a clear path for the Reverend Mother. Once she was on the ship and still no one moved, Rhaella realized they were waiting for her to go, too. She went down the aisle they had cleared for her—the only one she would ever pass through in her lifetime—and she stepped onto the deck.

The rest of the Doctrinas filed onto the ship, and while Rhaella expected them to stay in orderly lines, they all seemed to relax and occupy themselves in different areas. Some went to sit on the chairs laid out in full view of the sunlight, but Rhaella sequestered herself at the bow, ready for a long and lonely journey.

In every direction, Rhaella could make out other islands in the distance. Isle Verdale, and her home of Briarhall, lay somewhere to the west when facing the mainland. She absently wondered when her family would return there. Whether her father would hold true to his word and force Asriel to remain living at the Palace. How her brother might react under the force of so much pressure.

As much as Rhaella had longed for her freedom, it felt strange whenever she was away from the house for too long. She imagined it was the same for her brother.

This wasn't the first time she'd had to watch her home fade into the distance from the bow of a ship, but right now it felt like the most permanent. Her father had always been generous with his punishments, never failing to remind her that while she was his daughter by blood, she was not a true Veservus. Her position as a ward was precarious enough, and he reminded her of as much every time he sent her to stay in other houses after disobeying direct orders. Her body shook at the memory of his callousness. It felt mirrored to the way he had let her go just now. And the similarity was strong enough that she couldn't help but wonder if she was being punished for a crime she had no memory of committing.

As she kept her eyes glued to the horizon, Rhaella wondered how many on board were like her. How many of these Dux Doctrina were unwilling trainees about to embark on a new path of their lives. Everyone wore black, and if they were new recruits like her, they were wearing handed-down fabrics. Doctrinas-in-training wore gray robes, which would be given to them upon arrival. She wouldn't have to cover her face and hair until she was a dedicated Doctrina. And even then, at least she'd have her jewelry and her cosmetics.

She'd never been opposed to making herself up with shimmer on her eyes and rouge on her cheeks. Most of all, Rhaella loved a dark lip color. She could express herself in that way. And when she wasn't advising, she could do what she pleased, for the most part. With her place in House Veservus secured, things could go back to mostly normal once she was officially a Doctrina. It would be fine; she just had to get through these next years.

Rhaella called on all the information she had collected on the Order of the Dux Doctrina, some of it from books or the experience of the Dux she had interacted with. Her father had been dutiful in his record-keeping, as his father before him had been. Despite this, there was little documentation of what the inner workings of the Order were actually like. As a whole, they were notoriously secretive, keeping the specifics of their processes to themselves. And, as good historians, House Veservus acknowledged that some things were better left alone.

What she knew was that the Order was older than Adristan, having existed in some slightly mismatched shape back when the tyrant King Edmund was still in power. In those times, the Doctrinas were advisors of lower rank, existing as agreeable faces to validate the king's decisions. When the houses overtook the monarchy, the Order had gone quiet for some time before re-emerging. This new iteration had proven itself more powerful, as well as more diplomatic, and so they had remained a fixture of Adristanian politics ever since.

When men were given power, they were so easily corrupted by it. The Order's position in all of this was to level the heads of those wielding such power by working in tandem with the councils to keep the High Lords in check. They also helped to distribute the duties that came with running a nation by lifting some of the weight off of the High Lords' backs.

Their proximity to magic was what captivated the masses. It was an open secret that the Dux mixed herbs to brew potions which were consumed as part of their routine. Those potions had a euphoric sort of effect, and that was why they had trickled down into the cities for recreational use. But for practicing Doctrinas, the potions allowed them to develop an extra sense; an intuition unmatched in their field. One that ranked above even House Veservus's affinity for such things. It improved their hearing, strengthened their eyesight, and it even went so far as to open their minds to all routes of possibility in a situation. Rhaella wasn't so humble as to ignore that she had been born with such a gift, or that it was one she dedicated her life to honing.

Yet, even with that in mind, she couldn't quite wrap her head around things. Who was she to keep the heads of powerful men balanced? Rhaella had been born into a unique slot, both powerful and not. The daughter of a High Lord, undercut by her illegitimacy. A ward and a bastard. A spymaster and a shadow. The Hawk and a worm. She knew enough without training that she could get by as an advisor, but the word of a Doctrina was valued more highly than that of an average advisor. And they were certainly more valued than a bastard.

Should she become a practicing Doctrina, she would be taken

seriously. At least in theory. The men of her father's court—what would be Asriel's court by the time she was put to that position—would likely still question her as they did now, leaving no space for her at their table. But then again, she would have a designated place.

The boat ride was long enough that she could hear the people around her shifting and finding different ways to occupy themselves. But Rhaella stayed where she was, her body leaned against the railing as she stared out at the ocean. She watched the way the sunlight moved across the sky as it reflected on the water. It was hypnotizing, and yet she continuously got swept into thought. Into memory. Into dreams.

In those daydreams, she was astride Egorion, traveling across the islands of Adristan and handling the business of her house. She was still the Hawk, fearless and useful and utterly faceless to the rest of the nation. She could drink at taverns and fuck who she pleased, so long as she was back in the house by a reasonable hour. Those days felt far away now, and Rhaella wondered if they'd ever be near to her again.

When they docked on the mainland, Stillgrove guards greeted them and helped them disembark. In their purple coat of arms, the Stillgrove men were gracious in unloading their bags and helping them down the rickety ramp. Not far from the docks stood Moldermouth—the castle that housed House Stillgrove. Their access to the fertile agriculture of the mainland made them formidable as keepers of taste. They contributed to Adristan by growing and supplying all of the food to everyone offshore.

Rhaella wondered if that offering was felt more deeply than the things House Veservus had to offer. Food was a tangible thing, and people were often wary of those who traded in information. And, having come of age in such a house, Rhaella wasn't sure she blamed them for feeling that way.

Around her, the rest of the Doctrinas muttered their thanks. The Superiors, however, remained ghostly silent. Rhaella chose to stay somewhere in the middle, nodding her thanks without speaking the words. Then she went on her way, dutifully falling into line with the rest of the Order.

The tower of the Dux Doctrina was further into the mainland, past Moldermouth and the lands surrounding it. Their path took them on foot through the dense woods that covered nearly a third of the mainland. The cleared walkway was windy, but the Order maintained a steadfast route. They wasted no time cutting straight through the trees and over uneven terrain.

Though there still remained a fair bit of their journey, the outline of the Silent Keep rose ominously in the distance. It was a formidable thing, standing taller and thinner than most castles. It was constructed of white stone with few windows, and it was rounded to perfection. The top was fashioned as a watchtower, and in the late-afternoon haze, Rhaella could make out guards watching them from above.

They were escorted inside where it was dark and cool. Some of the Doctrinas filed down the halls, disappearing into the dimly lit recesses of the tower. To herself, Rhaella decided that those must be the ordained Doctrinas. She and a few others remained in the receiving hall with the Superiors and the other trainees. She was glad to know that she wasn't the newcomer, at least.

A Mother Superior motioned for them to follow. "If you would follow us this way."

Rhaella and the rest of the trainees did as they were told, passing through a set of tall doors. But before she could take a surveying glance around the room to familiarize herself, she suddenly felt hands on her body, yanking her out of line. The same thing must have happened to the others, though, because shouts of protest sounded all around her.

A cloaked and masked Doctrina tugged at Rhaella's veil and jewelry, urging her to get them off faster than she could manage. With deft hands, she removed all of her jewelry and folded her veil across her arm. She stiffened, however, when those impatient hands tugged on her dress. She fought them for a moment, but when she turned to look at the others, they were also being stripped. Reluctantly, she followed suit, stepping out of her dress before falling back in line with her arms crossed firmly over her chest. She did her best to avoid staring at the others to protect their dignity, only hoping that they were doing the same.

Doctrinas came down the line, feeling their throats for lumps and their eyes and ears for imperfections. A few of the recruits were forced to turn in a circle. When the Mother Superior got to Rhaella, she lingered on her ears, snapping her fingers next to each one and testing for a reaction. Rhaella was careful to underplay her response, to keep hers as natural as possible. That should be enough to get them to pass her by without drawing attention to her natural-born abilities.

Only the Mother Superior pulled back to look over the rest of her, and when her eyes landed on Rhaella's hair, she saw the glint of dissatisfaction.

"Too long," the Mother Superior said without even a hint of feeling. "This won't do for a veil. Cut half its length."

"Wait, no," Rhaella said, looking around for someone who could advocate for her. Surely, one of these Doctrinas hailed from House Veservus. Surely, they would know how important hair was to her family. Surely, they wouldn't make her cut it. Would they?

Hands grabbed her from behind and she felt them tug on her braid. Then, without so much as a warning, shears began hacking at it, and tresses of hair fell to the floor in an ungraceful wave. A cry lodged itself in her throat, and she thought if she opened her mouth she might vomit.

Just like that, another connection to her family had been severed. She tried to remind herself that it was hair. It would grow back. But she'd kept her hair long for so many years that she'd forgotten how long it might take to grow back. She had to hope that it would be quick.

In what felt like the blink of an eye, the Doctrinas were done surveying the rest of the recruits. From there, they were led through another set of doors and into an even smaller room. This one was warm—almost uncomfortably so. The line of people ahead of her suddenly halted, tension rife throughout the gathered crowd. Rhaella peeked around the room—it wasn't difficult when she was already taller than most everyone else. Her eyes landed on a grand fireplace at the far end of the room, but it was the pokers that held her attention. They were topped with a welded image of the tower—the Order's sigil—and the tips of the pokers were already positioned in the flames as their lines were forced forward. Rhaella's stomach sank.

They were going to be branded.

Rhaella knew the Order was a lifetime commitment. She knew that once she entered these doors, she would never leave as a noble or a citizen again. She knew this required utter dedication and nothing less.

She could handle pain. She could handle fire-hot metal being pressed against her skin. *She could handle this,* she tried to convince herself. Silently, she recalled her youth, when a passing fortune teller spoke of fire in Rhaella's eyes. She considered that perhaps this was meant to happen after all. That entering the Order fulfilled some grand plan that had been laid out by the gods.

But as the screams of those before her dwindled out and the branded recruits were led away… as she drew closer to the front of the line… Rhaella's mind floated somewhere miles away from here. Somewhere she could stay young and play with her brother in an open field. Somewhere she held no responsibility and where the weight of expectation could no longer tear them apart.

When it was Rhaella's turn with the iron, she told herself she hardly felt the pain. That it was easy to grit her teeth and swallow her screams when the brand hit her left hip. That the pain was nothing.

This was a lie.

CHAPTER EIGHT

"And it was the noble House Midar who ultimately dealt the killing blow to the once-great King Edmund with the legendary sword, Veritas. The moment has since been commemorated by the sculptors within House Redspire."
—The Rise and Fall of the Kingdom of Adristan: An Anthology, *by the Collective Scholars of House Veservus*

3 Lightpel, in the Benevolent year 112 A.E.

One week. Asriel had only been without his sister for one week and he felt as though his life was coming apart at the seams. How Rhaella had juggled this many tasks from their father while keeping up with her training—let alone any semblance of a social life—astounded him. She must have only slept a handful of hours every night. And yet, Asriel couldn't recall a time when Rhaella had appeared anything other than put-together and presentable. She certainly never looked as though she felt anything like he did right now. The sheer exhaustion was killing him.

But at the very least, his father wasn't around to watch him struggle. The High Lord had returned to Isle Verdale, leaving seemingly endless miles of sea between them. He'd left Asriel with a list of instructions and a hard look that said failure was not an option. That, and the key. Though his father had not shared *where*, exactly, the key led to. Rather than point him in the right direction, Asriel's father expected him to search the Palace for the keyhole. Days continued to pass, and Asriel was afraid to even look. In reality, it was a reasonable expectation to have of the heir. And yet, his continuous shortcomings were not uncommon among his fellow heirs, either.

If there was one thing he had learned in his stay at the Palace so far, it was that none of them were ready to Ascend to power.

Nose deep in a historical text, Asriel counted off the heirs and their respective flaws in his head. They were fresh in his mind thanks to the meeting that had taken place about halfway through the week. It was strange to be in the same room as every other house's heir after so many years of distance. He wondered what sort of impression he made, but knew it couldn't be much worse than the impressions of anyone else.

House Lancor's heir was practically a child. House Oberon and House Aviatis's heirs showed little interest in politics. House Redspire's heir was a recluse. House Stillgrove's heir made no attempt to hide his opportunism. House Lightpike's heir was absent from duty, and his brother was insufferable. And House Midar's heir was one inconvenience away from attempting to abdicate… *again*. None of these things were secret. Asriel wanted to laugh at a future where each of them was in charge, but then he realized he'd be laughing at himself too.

The pile of work on his desk nearly threatened to topple over. Untouched missives and requests from residents on the island waited for him, and all Asriel could do was stare. Somehow, every time he scolded himself to get to work, the thought of moving felt more impossible.

Then, there were the ignored letters from Prince Virgil Midar.

They must have gone to Briarhall first. Kingsgrave was the reasonable location to send them once those went unanswered. The newest letter—the one atop the pile—was meant for Asriel.

Rhaella and their father had been right, as they often were, not to take the Prince for a fool. If Rhaella wouldn't answer him, then he'd get a response from the next reachable option. It was less of a question as to where Rhaella was and more of a demand. Asriel had half a mind to tell the heir that he had no right to know where his sister was, but diplomacy did not work that way. Not even for brutes like Virgil.

Rather than attempt to compose a reply—or work through the mountain of other tasks needing his attention—Asriel sat at a desk in one of the many empty studies with his feet up. Offensively bright light streamed through the tall windows, illuminating the freshly-dusted shelves along the wall. Asriel could count off all of the historical texts he'd been read as bedtime stories in childhood. Rather than hear of fairies and magical quests like normal children, however, Asriel had fallen asleep to the stories of the rise and fall of nations. Perhaps, he thought, that was why he felt suddenly drowsy as he stared into that corner.

He missed his room at the house. He missed his falcons, even the hateful ones that still nipped at his fingertips. The Palace felt so hollow when there was nothing happening. Sure, there were members of a few other houses staying in their own suites, but none went out of their way to make good faith with Asriel. He needed more than that; he needed there to be movement and noise and chaos to quell the loudness inside his head. If he was left to his own devices for too long—and one week was *decidedly* too long—it grinded him down into fine powder.

So he spent most of his days alone or with Barrett as his only companion. Even then, his guard was doing the work of several; only two others had been assigned to stay with them, and they were foot soldiers rather than guards. There simply were not enough men for a full rotation. If Barrett wasn't with him, he was doing things the other guards couldn't get done during their shifts. Which left Asriel relegated to the safety of the indoors. The grounds were too dangerous with the beasts roaming free in the untamed wild surrounding the castle.

The Palace of Many Rooms itself was secure, which was crucial considering it was the only neutral ground in Adristan. And, as such, no house was beholden to it by vows of servitude or contract. Each house had been given their own wing of the Palace, and each wing was full of novelties that showed off the best and brightest of their territories. If nothing else, it was a beautiful testament to why their power had been shared and divided the way it had been.

As for his own house, Asriel had practically grown up in the Veservus library. And then there were the archives that sat with the studies alongside the family suites. At a moment's notice, he could talk to the historians or the librarians or the archivists. And if he made nice with the other visiting nobles, he could talk to them, too.

Asriel had the entire Palace at his disposal, as long as none of the rooms were in use. But he didn't make any effort to take advantage of such resources. His was a very lonely existence. He hated this self-imposed isolation, and he wondered if it was the same sort of existence he had condemned Rhaella to.

Picking up the copy of the paper he'd found in his father's tent, Asriel glanced over the letters as he did every day, and he thought of his sister. If she had found this, she likely would have already decoded it by now. Beside their family's names was a *V* for vye. *No.* Most of the names were marked with a *K* for kwaw. *Maybe.* Alden had marked very few with *E* for ep—*yes*. The only ones were names Asriel did not recognize, though he knew them to be of various families and statuses.

Someone rapped at the door, and a scholar poked his head inside the study; he bowed at the waist before approaching the desk. The boy was young—likely not of age yet. House Veservus took scholars at any age, but it still surprised him. It was his father's opinion that one was never too young to learn how to learn, or something to that effect. As a child, Asriel had thought the ideal beautiful. But now, staring at such a fresh face, the thought just made him sad.

"My Lord," the boy said. "I've been tasked with confirming the dates of every High Lord's Ascension for a historical manuscript. There are a few texts with conflicting information regarding the line of succession in House Lancor. Do you have a definitive source, or shall I continue to cross-reference?"

Asriel refrained from rolling his eyes. "The Palace's library has the most up-to-date texts. I wouldn't bother with the archives unless something jumps out at you with its wrongness."

The boy shuffled on his feet for a moment. "But the archivists said—"

"The archivists are paid very much to do very little," Asriel said, cutting him off. "Refer to the library. Those texts are all hand-selected by the High Lord. Even the archivists must answer to them."

"Of course," the boy said, bowing again. "I'll see to it, my Lord."

The young scholar tried to shut the door on his way out but was stopped by a hand. When the door opened yet again, Barrett sauntered in, dressed in his soft gear. *His training gear.*

Asriel leaned his head back onto the seat and groaned loudly.

"Don't mope, you pansy," Barrett said, one hand going to the practice sword at his hip. "I'm only trying to help you."

"Help me lie to my father. Say that we did so much training that I can't possibly train any more."

Barrett snorted. "Perhaps if we can get you to hold your sword correctly, we'll be able to make that lie a convincing one. Get changed so we can make it to the Midar wing before lunch."

"I've had about enough of the Midar family," Asriel grumbled, rising to his feet.

"Why's that?"

Asriel followed his sworn sword out of the study and they made their way back toward the suite. He shoved his hands in his pockets and stared up at the high ceiling.

"Virgil wrote to me... *repeatedly*. He wants to know where Rhaella is."

"Alright," Barrett said slowly.

"I danced around it at the meeting," Asriel said. "But it seems I'm running out of room to do so. He's been quite persistent."

And every persistence spoke to a truth Asriel was not yet ready to face. He knew his father was a liar; that came with the trade. But this particular brand of urgency from Virgil had begun to scream at Asriel's instincts. And while he might not have been as quick-witted as his sister, he'd be brainless to ignore the glaring possibility. *That his father had never sent any sort of proposal.* That Virgil was, possibly, very willing to marry Rhaella, and that their father had not even given the man a chance.

In person, they had duty to hide behind. That, and a palace full of ears that had no business knowing any of this. Virgil didn't like him anyway, and Asriel didn't mind coming across as rude. All of this drove Asriel to pointedly ignore those instincts screaming at him to think deeper. To voice the question he kept running from.

Besides, there was months worth of information each of the heirs needed to catch up on. There was no time for Virgil to approach with questions about betrothal or deception or where Rhaella was. So, once everyone had left Kingsgrave for their home islands, there was a brief respite where Asriel thought that the Eighth Prince had finally given up. That was, until the letters started coming in.

Asriel hadn't the stomach to read them in full after merely skimming their contents. These were not letters meant for the heir, or even the pretend heir. These were letters meant for his sister's eyes and no one else.

The Eighth House's Prince spoke to her at first as though he knew her, offering inconsequential details about his life and asking about hers. There were references to jokes Asriel did not understand and callbacks to memories he did not have. Then, once those letters went unanswered, there was another inquiry about her well-being. He wanted to know if something had happened to her, and, worse yet, it seemed as though he *cared*. Virgil did not speak in code, the way many of the heirs did. His words were candid and direct in their meaning. There were no subjects he danced around.

"How do you intend to reply?"

Sighing, Asriel said, "I haven't decided yet. But if I don't reply soon, I have a feeling Virgil will sail all the way here just to beat the answers out of me."

Stifling a laugh, his guard said, "I wouldn't let that happen."

"Yes, because you can fend off a strongman on your own. The *strongest* strongman seen this generation, might I add."

"We have Egorion for the time being. I'm sure I can figure out how to command him to spit fire in the Prince's direction."

"He's not my dragon," Asriel said, unable to keep the note of longing out of his voice. "He's Rhaella's dragon, and he's a loyal beast at that."

After a weighted silence, Barrett said, "You still can try to claim one of the other dragons. They're all young and formidable. They're just as worthy as Egorion."

"Yes, but those dragons aren't from the patrilineal Veservus line, are they?" Asriel said bitterly. "They're the *other* dragons, bearing no relation to my father's beast. Those are no dragons for an heir, and so I shall have no dragon."

"You give yourself too little credit," Barrett said as they arrived at the suite. He opened the door and did a cursory sweep before motioning Asriel inside. Continuing, he said, "If you chose another dragon, the house would respect that decision."

"Now you give the *council* too much credit. They're all counting on my failure so they can option their children as the next most agreeable successor."

Asriel threw open his bedroom door and shucked off his nice clothes, pulling on a pair of loose pants that tied at the waist and a thin sleeveless shirt. He grabbed his practice sword from the corner he'd shoved it into, and he harnessed it at his hip before turning back to Barrett.

His guard stood in the open doorway, watching without making any effort to disguise it. And Barrett wasn't watching in the way that a guard watched over their charge, either. Barrett's eyes were too soft as he regarded Asriel, almost pitiful. In lieu of speaking, Barrett simply exhaled and shook his head.

"You can tell me I'm wrong. That my father would never allow such a thing," Asriel said. "But if I can't become what he needs me to be, he won't be able to fight it if the court rallies around a different potential heir."

"Your father's word trumps that of a few nobles," Barrett argued.

"And yet, we've set a precedent for killing powerful men who make inarguable decrees," Asriel pointed out, shouldering past Barrett as he made his way out the door.

"What is it that you want to hear, Asriel? That everything will work itself out? You have to *make* things work. I am no politician. I can do nothing to ease that part of your duty. But I can make you *stronger*, if you'll let me." He paused, and Asriel couldn't help but catch the small note of pleading that crept into his guard's voice when he spoke again. "Allow me to help you in that way."

"House Veservus's High Lord doesn't need to be strong," Asriel argued, navigating the halls toward the Midar wing. "I need to be smart, cunning, and decisive. In short, all of the things I am not. My strength will fail me in all of the tasks required of me. I don't see why I have to train."

"You're pouting like an inconvenienced child," Barrett said, finally sounding as frustrated as Asriel felt. He pushed open the doors to the training room with a huff. A few of the mats were already in use but no heads turned in their direction as they made their way toward an empty corner.

"Did you expect me to cheer with delight at the thought?" Asriel sneered.

"No, you soft sack," Barrett said, discarding his sheath on the ground. "Elbows up."

Asriel hated sweating. He hated feeling his muscles burn from the effort of training. Every time Barrett called for them to go again was another time too many. But there was no room to refuse. Asriel kept his arms up for as long as he could, drooping lower with every panting breath.

When Barrett knocked him on his ass for the tenth time, Asriel called for a break. He took calming breaths, pressing a hand to his abdomen.

Clutching his fingers to his shirt, he felt for the muscle beneath. There definitely were some there, but Asriel had never been carved from stone the way that their soldiers were. He had always done everything Barrett asked of him and he did all of the exercises—even through complaints—and yet it never yielded the desired results. His family's heritage bred willowy bodies. He and Rhaella were well over the height of most fully grown men, and yet they were nearly as thin as rails.

All of this work to be left mostly unseen. Upon first sight by an enemy, he'd be laughed off of the battlefield.

"You're looking stronger, stop worrying," Barrett said. "Can we go another round, or are you too tired?"

"You know I love it when you say that," Asriel said, sitting up. He stared at Barrett through the hair that had fallen in his face. His guard was pretty. Too pretty to have gone into the guard as a last resort. With his looks, he could have sat for portraits and the artists on Sandorne would have eaten him alive. Asriel was an artist of slightly-above-middling talent, but he thought he could attempt to do Barrett's beauty justice on a canvas.

His guard reached out a hand. "Here, up. We can stop for today."

"Thank the gods."

"You don't believe in the gods."

"Who else am I supposed to thank?"

Barrett smirked. "Me."

Asriel scoffed as he let Barrett help him to his feet. They stood like that for a moment, staring at one another and catching their breath. Barrett's endurance was better, that was without question. But he was tired. And all Asriel could do was stare back at him, apologetic and unable to put voice to such a feeling. What good were words when he couldn't change anything?

"I'm going to stretch," Asriel said, nodding toward a bench against the wall. "Why don't you stand guard from over there?"

It was a weak excuse, and it was one his guard saw right through. Even so, the half-attempted deceit wasn't one Barrett was willing to call out. He nodded his head with a soft, "As you say," before walking over and sitting on the bench. Immediately, his shoulders slumped and he rested his elbows on his knees. Asriel watched for a few seconds, making sure that Barrett intended to actually *rest* for a few minutes, before he began to stretch.

Using his good hand to stretch out his bad wrist, Asriel turned and was met with the sight of the most beautiful woman to have walked through the Palace doors. Dressed in a rich purple tunic and black pants that hugged every curve of her body—gold beads woven into the dozens of black braids of her hair and glittering gold rings adorning her fingers and her ears—she was unmistakably a Stillgrove.

Asriel jogged his memory, hunting for the few facts he knew about her, and most importantly her name. She was the third-born daughter, holding no real claim to her father's titles with two older brothers to take care of such a burden. The family made use of her all the same, though. Through her friendship with Rhaella, Asriel knew that she was beholden to no betrothals or vows, and thus he was free to saunter up to her with a smile on his face.

"Princess Stillgrove," he called out. "What good fortune has brought you to me?"

She slowed her pace with a guard at her side, a curious expression on her face as she dipped into a curtsy.

"Prince Veservus," she replied. "You honor me."

"The honor's mine," he said, dipping into a small bow and extending a hand. He was pleased when she took it. "I hear you know of my sister, Rhaella."

"We've been acquainted," the Princess said, one corner of her mouth lifting. She turned to her guard, saying, "Leave us."

Asriel waited for the guard to take up a post by the door before he turned back to the noblewoman. "Forgive me, Princess. As information is my trade, it seems I've done you a disservice by failing to remember your first name."

She chuckled. "Is that how your father prepares his heir to take over?"

Though it stung, Asriel forced himself to laugh in kind. What else could he do? He couldn't be rude to everyone who hurt his feelings. Were he to do so, he'd be no better than the Lightpikes, scorning and sneering at every turn.

"My father does his best to school me in lordship, but my skills are better put to use in the fields of wine and courting."

Her eyebrows raised in surprise as another laugh escaped her. "If this is how you speak to Ladies, I'm afraid to see how you'd command an entire court."

"I make commands in such a manner that compels people to listen," Asriel said deviously. "I can give you an example, if you'd like."

She straightened, folding her hands in front of her. "I'd love to see you try, vampire."

Blinking, Asriel was surprised he could control the laughter that wanted to bubble up. "Only part-vampire, I'm afraid. My family line has mingled with fae and elves and humans for centuries."

But he'd gotten to keep his fangs. And there was still a certain degree of compulsion he could conjure up, should he feel the need to do so. And it seemed this moment was one such case.

He took a step closer—not too close, though. He didn't want to frighten her. He folded his own hands behind his back, tilting his head to one side and letting his hair fall into his face. Asriel bided his time, letting the silence between them age like his other favorite vice. He let it simmer, settle, and then unsettle some.

When he'd had enough of it, he said, "You still haven't told me your name."

Unbothered, she tossed her braids over her shoulder. "Do you often use flattery to get what you want?"

"I'm not sure what it is you think I want," he said. "I'm simply making conversation."

"Everyone knows you hawks expect to leave conversations with your pockets full of information. If you'd like me to give you some, you'll have to give me some first."

Asriel cocked a brow. "Are you proposing a trade, Princess?"

"Perhaps I am, my Lord," she said. "Do you accept the terms?"

Hard-earned instinct kicked in, and Asriel stopped to consider the ramifications. Anything he could glean out of a Stillgrove would be of value. Her family would do just about anything to climb higher in status—not that they needed it. Seeing as they single-handedly oversaw one of the major exports of Adristan, they were easily one of the most powerful stronghold houses in the nation. They were a well-respected fae family. They were cordial enough when the time called for it, but they were equally as cutting when it came to their politics. If the heir, Gerard, could manage a higher degree of subtlety when entering sensitive discussions, Asriel thought they would have a real chance of becoming *the* most powerful house.

It wouldn't be worth telling her anything compromising. He would have to tell her something real, something that could arguably be used against him somehow, but nothing that would ever actually leave a mark.

"I have a bad wrist," he said at last. "A childhood accident with my sister rendered it feeble. I can hardly hold a sword properly, much to my guard's chagrin."

At Asriel's gesturing, she followed his eye to glance at Barrett.

"Why don't you use your other hand?"

He shrugged. "I can write with both hands. I can play more instruments than I can count on my fingers. I can even juggle." A humorless laugh. "But it feels wrong when I hold a sword in my left. Perhaps I'm inflexible, but I can't seem to grip the pommel correctly. I can with my right, but I tire quickly. It seems more feasible to attempt to rebuild its strength than retrain my left hand."

The Princess studied him for a moment, unabashedly letting her eyes rove over the planes of his face. He didn't fail to notice how those shining brown eyes lingered on his mouth. Then, she said sweetly, "My name is Galilea."

"Galilea," he echoed, tasting the shape of her name. "A name befitting its owner."

"You and your flattery," she said, but there was amusement written clearly across her face. She tilted her head toward the training mats behind them, urging Asriel to follow. He did. Galilea's clothes were fitted to move in, so she began stretching. She'd come to train, then. Why she was alone and not accompanied by either of her brothers piqued his curiosity, but he just assumed she'd come alone on her gryphon; the Stillgrove family was renowned for their riding skills.

He knelt on the ground beside her and went through all of the stretches Barrett said would help his wrist. "Does your father encourage swordplay for his daughter, Princess? Or only his sons?"

"Gerard is the heir. My younger brother Roman is his right hand, of sorts. It is of far more importance that they know how to fight than it is for me."

"And what do you do instead?"

She lifted her chin. "Whatever my father tells me to. Which rarely includes picking up a sword. My duties tend to focus on our main export. But these past months have taught me that it's a skill I shouldn't neglect."

Asriel's eyes lowered to her hands as she stretched, pressing against her knee as she lunged, and he wondered what kind of work those hands had seen. House Stillgrove was the house of grain and greenery, sure, but he wasn't sure what that entailed on a day to day basis for its children. Her nails were manicured and short—unlike the popular long, claw-like nails of others their age. There were no traces of dirt beneath them, and no chips or cracks that spoke to working with her hands.

"Might I see your rings?" Asriel asked, pointing to her hands.

She lifted a hand, gently placing it in his overturned palm. Asriel turned her wrist, slowly admiring the golden rings that glittered on each of her fingers, using the motion as cover while he examined what he felt there. He held on just long enough to feel the callouses that littered her fingers and her palms, and they told him exactly what kind of work it was that she did. And the longer she left her hand there, cool skin against his fever-hot, the more intensely he could feel the lingering hum of magic that clung there, clarifying his suspicions.

Galilea Stillgrove worked with poisons.

"Can I invite you for a drink after this, Princess? I've been told I'm very talented at making pleasing mixtures."

"And I have been told that I am an excellent judge of taste," she said. "I suppose we'll both find out if we live up to our reputations."

"Well, alright then," Asriel said, flashing her a smile. "What's your poison?"

Something flashed in her eyes, and Asriel knew he was correct. He resisted the urge to gloat or to make eyes at Barrett and ask him for his guard's praise. Instead, he fixed his eyes on Galilea and waited for her response. She shifted into a different stretch to avoid him, and that was when he knew he had her.

"It depends on the mood," Galilea said lightly. "Absinthe can be fun in the right company."

He hummed, pretending to consider that. "What about the Dux drinks?"

Galilea blanched, glancing at the people training on the other mats. "Why do you want to know about those?"

"We both know there's a market for them," Asriel shrugged.

"I don't deal in that," she said sharply. "And neither should you."

"Why not?"

She laughed in disbelief. "Your father has truly taught you nothing, hasn't he? Don't you know they're addictive?"

Asriel flinched. He did not know that, and the injury of such a thing stung. His idiocy was as familiar to him as an old friend, but he forced himself to maintain the mask of the charming heir. He continued to play the part of the lovable idiot rather than the frustratingly unfixable one.

He chuckled. "Forgive me. I shouldn't ask you to separate fact from fiction for me. That's my job, after all, not yours."

"I suggest you stick to your books instead of digging around in the black markets for a primary source."

"I'll remember that," he said, standing. "I had just finished my training when you arrived. The mat is yours. Good day, Princess."

"Asriel."

Pausing, he stared at her expectantly. There was a grave seriousness on her face that told him she wasn't simply humoring him when she spoke.

Steadily, she said, "I meant what I said."

Earnest words were few and far between among the nobility, and Asriel detected no falsity in her tone. But that simply meant he wasn't looking hard enough. He bowed to Galilea and crossed the room to the door without waiting for Barrett.

Barrett caught up a few paces later, jogging to keep up with him. "What was that about?"

"Did you know the Dux potions were addictive?"

Barrett stared at him for a few seconds before saying, "Yes."

"How did you know and I didn't?"

"I'm around more people who openly want to get high," Barrett said. "You have fancy tobacco and pipe weed. If you want the good stuff, you have to deal with the tariffs and the regulations. Potions are quick and cheap, if you know where to look." A moment later he added, "Not that I partake, but many in the guard do."

"How addictive would you say they are compared to other things?"

Barrett tossed up a hand. "I don't know, maybe more. When you dose them right, they can be hallucinogenic."

Asriel groaned, throwing a hand over his face. "Fuck."

"Rhaella is with trained professionals who know how to dose the potions correctly so that won't happen," Barrett said, daring to place a hand on his shoulder.

"Every day the fear that I've made a terrible mistake grows harder to ignore," Asriel said, shrugging off his guard's hand. "And there's nothing to do about it."

"Nothing to do but wait," Barrett confirmed.

In stewing silence, the two of them crossed through the Palace until they were back in the Veservus suite with the doors locked. Only then did Asriel allow himself the privilege of honesty. Of admitting the hard things—the things he didn't dare admit to anyone else—out loud to Barrett.

Collapsing onto the sofa, Asriel slouched forward and curled his fingers into fists.

"I want to know why my father hid these things from me. Why he pushed me into his decision without informing me wholly and dutifully. There is a motive there."

Barrett nodded. "As with everything your father does, there must be."

"He'll never tell me," Asriel said decisively. "We have to figure it out. I have to figure it out."

"Where do you want to start?"

Asriel raised his head. Exhaustion was all over his face, he knew that. But from the way Barrett was looking at him, that wasn't all there was. He suddenly felt a sheer force of will, a drive borne out of years' worth of falling just shy of expectations.

"I need to find the other library."

CHAPTER NINE

"Second trimester: The nausea persists. Aches in the lower back flare up after prolonged periods of sitting in the studio. I have recommended bed rest, though the princess refuses."
—*Notes from a Redspire midwife*

3 Lightpel, in the Benevolent year 112 A.E.

Travel did not agree with Aida's pregnancy. She avoided it when she could, but her aunts had ordered her to Kingsgrave to represent them at the trade meeting. It wasn't even a meeting with all of the houses, like the one they'd had a few days ago. She didn't understand why she needed to go. Or, at least, why one of her sisters couldn't go in her place.

Asa was being courted by various other houses and Alora was training with the guard like a common soldier. Adrianna was off on the mainland, learning new painting techniques. All things that were about as essential as discussing trade. But with her aunts keeping her secrets for her, she wasn't exactly in a position to refuse them anything.

She was too many weeks along to wear any of the dresses within her house's fashion, which left her wearing clothing much too conservative for her liking. But it covered her stomach, and that was what mattered.

More precarious than her appearance was the matter of her child's father. She hadn't heard from Hiram since before the royalists had surrendered. By now, House Lightpike had long since called back their troops. And yet it was Ramsey who responded to her letters, informing her of his brother's condition. He wasn't aware of *why* Aida had a right to know, but he answered all the same. That was a kindness she hadn't expected from the spare, who hardly knew her outside of the brief political meetings their houses had. Updates came sparsely, if at all. And, most frustrating of all, she knew neither of the Lightpike brothers would be at this meeting for her to ask, either.

Her mind ran over what she knew of the heirs that she would be meeting with. The Lancors were sending their heir and at least one or both of their spares. She liked the Lancor heir well enough, but it was the older spare, Freya, who she found most agreeable. All of the Stillgrove siblings were pleasant, if try-hard, and they typically went everywhere together. She had to admit, though, that her stomach sank when the missives said Asriel would be the only Veservus meeting her at the Palace.

She hadn't heard from Rhaella in *days*.

A few odd days here and there was nothing unusual. Rhaella did what she needed to when it was necessary, and though she was able to split her focus between duty and pleasure, sometimes things took priority over sending her friend a letter. But as long as it was feasible, they were in correspondence nearly every day. Neither of them were ever far from a brazier. Even when times were desperate, they could resort to the old magics and toss letters in a common fire.

But Aida couldn't shake the image of Rhaella crawling through her window, soaking wet and desperate. The High Lord of House Veservus was not a desperate man—her aunts had made that clear—and her conversations with Rhaella had only affirmed that fact. High Lord Alden Veservus was logical and calculating. For him to leave such sensitive documents where his hawk-like daughter could find them felt... wrong. It felt logical and calculated, just like everything else he did. True, Aida did not have the face to face experience with him to say for certain, but she knew Rhaella well enough. She *trusted* Rhaella well enough.

Aida's worry occupied her time long enough for the ship to have docked by the time she came back to attention. Ships bearing other house banners were in the port as well, unloading their Princes' and Princesses' things onto the lined pathway that led up to the Palace doors. At first, Aida was surprised to see the lack of a Veservus ship. But then she thought on it for a moment, and things made sense. The Third High Lord had no doubt sent his son ahead of the rest. She scoffed at the thought of poor Asriel waiting in the Palace for the rest of them. He had probably passed the time by twirling his fingers and making eyes at his guards.

Sure enough, moments later, Prince Asriel strolled out of the Palace of Many Rooms as though he owned it. His hands were in the pockets of his well-tailored slacks and he met her eyes with an easy smile. Once their eyes locked, however, his skin visibly blanched.

That was all the confirmation Aida needed, but she was not about to let him off easy. She stalked over to the Third Prince and crossed her arms.

"Where's Rhaella?"

The tightness that took over him, the way he cowered, said what words couldn't.

"Please don't say anything," was all he said.

And so as they entered the Palace, Aida's blithe expression never faltered, greeting the other heirs as though nothing was wrong. But every time Asriel's eyes lingered too long on the flowing panels of fabric covering her stomach, she sharpened her stare at him. Minutely, she shook her head. He had no right to eye her belly with suspicion, even if his intuition was correct. Asriel needed to remember that she now knew one of *his* secrets, and that she was not above spilling it if pushed.

CHAPTER TEN

"[The Palace of Many Rooms] is structured as something of a museum of each house. There is a wing dedicated to displaying the main responsibility and pride of each one. Congresses, parties, and general meetings are often held in the Palace, but the nobles can visit whenever they like and stay as long as they wish."
—The Commoner's Guide to the Islands of Adristan, *by Scholar Eculid*

3 Lightpel, in the Benevolent year 112 A.E.

The room the Mediators led them into was too cold. Each room in the Palace was temperature-controlled thanks to some spell or other performed by the Aviatis priestesses, but the conference rooms were kept at a chill that was beyond comfortable. If Asriel had been a smarter man, he would have worn the layers of traditional clothing that his father usually donned—a doublet on top of his thin shirt, a patterned vest, or even a coat. He thought the poet's shirt and house amulet hanging around his neck would be enough to represent himself.

A different Mediator than the one who had led them to the room was handing out a pile of documents related to what they'd be discussing as they briefed the seated heirs. Asriel was seated beneath one of the tall windows near the center of the table. To his right sat Ezra Lancor, eyes fixed solidly on the surface of the table. Across from him sat Gerard Stillgrove and his brother; they had their heads bowed together, fixed in quiet conversation. Aida Redspire sat quietly to Asriel's left, making no effort to mask the hard stare on her face. Scattered between them were the masters of trade from each house, except for House Veservus. Asriel would be representing his house alone.

"The remaining heirs sent word with excuses for their absence," the Mediator continued. "I'm not sure if you'd like me to list them off."

"That won't be necessary, thank you," Aida said, smiling at the Mediator. "We'd like to get started, if you please."

Understanding that they were being dismissed, the Mediator bowed slightly. "You need only ring the bell should you require assistance."

Once the Mediator shut the door behind themself, the air seemed to thicken in the room. Asriel was hardly ever alone with other heirs, and even now they weren't *truly* alone thanks to the presence of the guards and the trademasters.

The trademasters were seated councilmen—an essential piece of the Concilium threshold. Every house had masters of trade, coin, strategy, battle, and more. Their titles varied based on each house's traditions, but ultimately they always distilled down to the same core focuses. Asriel held no love for the Veservus council. His father's friends and distant relatives were condescending at best, and downright disrespectful at worst, and so he expected no better of the other houses. Which was why, although it raised his nerves to be the sole representative of his house, Asriel was thankful he didn't have to pretend to respect them for the day.

Even so, he still wanted them to think highly of him.

"So," Asriel said. "Shall we get started?"

"What's the rush?" Gerard said. "We've got all day for formalities. How is everyone?"

"No offense, Gerard," Aida said, "but I didn't come here to talk about my life. We're here to discuss issues with the trade routes."

"What is there to discuss?" Gerard asked, tossing the documents back onto the table. "They've had problems before and were fixed with little trouble. This meeting is merely a formality."

"That's not true," Ezra said quietly from the other end of the table.

Every head turned toward the First House heir. He was already crimson with embarrassment, but there was determination in the set of his jaw.

"House Lancor has had a hard time getting into the ports of three other houses. At first, we thought it was that the seas have been eroding at the land, making the rocks more jagged. We've lost one ship already, and had delays on two of our major exports. A pattern is beginning to form."

The other heirs sat in stunned silence for a few beats while Asriel merely nodded his head, writing down what Ezra had said.

"That makes sense," Roman Stillgrove said. "We've heard of our spice shipments taking a few extra days to import. I thought it might be the island weather, but now I see that must not be the case."

As the others continued asking Ezra questions, Asriel did his best to listen and transcribe everything. He went from complete sentences, to shorthand, to shorthand of his shorthand. Cursing himself for his inability to write quicker, he kept his head down and tried to write as neatly as possible without missing anything.

"Asriel," Gerard said sharply. Not in an unfriendly way, but with a tone that demanded attention.

His head snapped up, and he stared at the Stillgrove heir with what he hoped was a passive expression.

Gerard gestured with a heavily-ringed hand. "How are the markets on your island? Isle Verdale isn't very crowded these days, I hear."

He and his brother snickered at that and Aida glared at them in warning. Asriel felt his stomach drop as he wracked his mind for the most diplomatic way to respond to the snide comment. How his father would expect him to respond.

Asriel cleared his throat. "I wouldn't know, actually. I haven't been home since the war. Instead, I've been here, doing my studies and training in the most abundant cultural center in the nation."

"I don't need the whole speech," Gerard said dismissively.

The Stillgrove master of trade said, "Surely someone at home is keeping you in the know. How do the markets compare to how they were before?"

Asriel hardly visited the markets. At least, not the ones they were asking about. His father wasn't in favor of his intermingling with the common people, and so Asriel went out when his father was otherwise occupied. The times Asriel was able to make it to the markets during the day were few and far between, and from what he could tell, they were reasonably thriving. The night markets flourished without issue, but that wasn't what Gerard had asked of him.

"I haven't been informed of a substantial difference from before," Asriel said surely.

"That's... not what my sister and I discussed," Aida said slowly. She shot Asriel a look that might have been apologetic before addressing the rest of the table. "Princess Asa is on a tour of the islands, meeting potential suitors. Last we spoke, she complained that the markets were out of her favorite berries that you can only find on the mainland."

"So it's a little bit of everything, then," Gerard said, rubbing his temples. "This is a bigger mess than I anticipated. I hope we're all comfortable, I think we're going to be here for a while."

Asriel resisted the urge to groan. "I like to have tea while I think. Would anyone else care for some?"

To his chagrin, all of the present parties enthusiastically agreed. Asriel rose to his feet, excusing himself to get the tea as promised. Normally, he'd send for someone to bring it directly to him, and he was sure the others would do the same. But the air in that room grew heavier with each passing second,r and Asriel thought he might suffocate if he didn't escape for a bit.

Barrett followed him out, hastily trying to keep up. His armor clattered against the sword holstered at his hip, and the sound was grating.

"Do you *have* to wear that?" Asriel snapped without turning around. "Do you think the Lancor heir is going to stab me? You could've worn your soft armor."

A sharp intake of breath. Then, "Asriel, this is my uniform."

"Yes, well, we all shrink beneath the weight of duty, don't we?" He could hear the bitterness in his voice, and he hated it. But he also couldn't bring himself to stop. "You have your noisy armor, and I have to sit through a meeting where I am ill-prepared to answer such simple questions."

"Is this about what Aida said? It's not an affront against you to not know everything going on at home."

"No, but it is humiliating all the same," Asriel said. "And what does Aida know? Her sister spends a few days on the island, and she thinks she knows everything about our house? Ridiculous."

"She's not claiming as much and you know that. Be reasonable."

"Reasonable," Asriel scoffed. "My finest trait."

"You're being childish," Barrett said, his temper wearing thin. "Get the damned tea and return to the meeting with your wits about you. They don't know everything about their houses, so why should you?"

"They all have their masters to assist them. I am alone. I know almost nothing."

"You know enough to walk back in there with your head held high," Barrett insisted. "Accept what you don't know. *Learn* from these people."

Before Asriel could reply, another voice chimed in, "Am I interrupting something?"

Both of their heads snapped toward the sound. Barrett took a defensive step in front of Asriel, one hand on the pommel of his sword. A redheaded beauty stepped into the light, a relaxed smile on her face despite the raised hackles of Asriel's guard. She herself was unguarded.

Asriel studied her. Something about her was so familiar. The burnt orange hair, the splattering of freckles across her nose and cheeks, and the brilliant emerald green of her eyes came together to paint a clear picture. Not to mention her height and the strong build of her arms and shoulders. She wasn't as tall as her brothers, but she nearly matched Asriel in stature.

"Freya," he breathed. The woman he'd been promised to since birth. Quickly, he schooled his expression so as not to look too eager. Clearing his throat, he said, "I haven't had the pleasure."

He bowed deeply at the waist, accepting the hand that she proffered.

There was a smirk on her face as she asked, "How did you know me?"

"I've always known you," he said smoothly. "We're fated."

He ignored Barrett's scoff behind him. The same way he ignored the fact that he and Freya had briefly interacted at various events over the years. Same as the fact that it shouldn't have taken him so much as a moment to recognize her.

She hid her giggle behind an ungloved hand. Asriel had thought that the fashion was more conservative over on Segsiege, but it delighted him to think that such things didn't quite matter to her.

"Really, though. How did you know?"

"Your hair," he admitted, daring to reach out and twirl a lock around his finger. "It's rather unique on the islands."

"I could've been a mainland girl," she said, smiling.

He smiled back. "But you're not."

Barrett cleared his throat. "If I may, Asriel. The tea."

"Right, yes," he said. "Freya, if you'd care to join me, I'm in the middle of bringing tea to the rest of my company in the conference room."

"How very noble of you," she replied, looping her arm through his. She led him toward the kitchens. "Are you a lover of tea, my Lord?"

He snorted. "We're past that. Call me Asriel."

"Just like your guard does?" She turned over her shoulder to glance at Barrett. "Very well, Asriel. Are you a lover of tea?"

"More like a hater of meetings," he said. "I find them heinous to sit through."

Asriel halfway listened to her response, but as they walked, it was his father's voice he heard in his mind—even in his absence, the High Lord's words hung in the air. Asking her to accompany him as he brought the tea meant little aside from fostering an opportunity for conversation. But as long as they were in the kitchen, he could make his father proud.

Courtships were revered in Adristan. It was never as simple as moving from interest in one another to marriage. If he wanted to marry Freya, Asriel was going to have to pass several rites of tradition. Though he couldn't recall all of them off the top of his head.

One of the easiest to pass, however, was the simple act of preparing a meal together. What went better with tea than a platter of offerings?

As they passed into the kitchens, Asriel signaled for a jug of hot water. He sorted through the cabinets, pulling out a platter and setting the tea cups atop it. Freya followed him into the pantry, detailing the journey from Segsiege to Kingsgrave as they went. Asriel listened, making small comments as he pulled various fruits and cheeses down from the shelves. Freya took whatever was handed to her without question, which sent a thrill through him.

"What flavor of tea are we preparing?"

Asriel liked that she said *we*. "Black tea should be suitable for everyone as long as there's enough cream and sugar. For myself, I prefer hardly any. Can you help me with this platter?"

They set about attractively arranging the fruits and cheeses and crackers on the platter. Freya pulled scones from the counter top, where a row of other freshly-baked pastries laid in wait. She expertly placed them among the rest. Tea cups were nestled between bundles of grapes. And when the jug of hot water was brought to them, Asriel set it in the center. Propping open the lid, he dropped the tea leaves inside and hoisted the platter into his hands.

This was sure to be a suitable meal for their waiting peers. And having prepared it with Freya, Asriel could count them as having passed the first rite of passage. He wondered if she knew it, too. Whether that was the reason for the easy smile on her face.

The walk back to their meeting room was short, though Asriel found himself wishing it had stretched out even a bit. Too soon, they were back, being greeted by the sound of chittering over trade.

"Took you long enough," Gerard quipped as they entered.

"And you brought a friend," Roman noted.

"Prince Gerard, Prince Roman," Freya said curtsying, inclining her head toward each of the heirs and spares. "Princess Aida."

"Where were we?" Asriel asked, arranging the tea set on the table.

"I believe we're due for a break. Please, sit," Gerard said. "I'm sure you're not so eager to get back to business now that your betrothed is here."

Freya took the seat between her brother and Asriel. Fitting, he supposed. She looked between everyone, sitting tall in her seat as though she was used to having all of the attention on her. With hands folded in front of her on the table, she fixed her gaze on Gerard.

"It's actually the first time we've met," she said. "Informally, at least. Our fathers haven't arranged time for Asriel to court me yet."

"Been busy, I suppose," Asriel muttered. "You know how that goes."

"I can't say I do," Gerard said. "Fifth House doesn't typically secure betrothals that far in advance. My siblings and I remain free agents."

"Speaking of siblings, we heard you met with our sister Galilea yesterday," Roman said. His tone was measured, but there was a suggestive glint in his eye. "She's lurking around here somewhere."

"I did," he replied plainly. "We got to talking."

Asriel swallowed. The Princess had found him in the library as he searched the room for any signs of indiscretion. She wordlessly handed him a book on poisons before attempting to walk away. Asriel didn't let her slip away so easily, though. From there, they *did* get to talking, and he found that she was a pleasant person to talk to when she wasn't scolding him for all the things he was ignorant of. And then, he and Galilea had done more than just *talk*, but he wasn't about to admit that in front of her siblings, let alone his future *wife*. He hoped Galilea hadn't let anything slip to her brothers, either.

Asriel found that there were far too many eyes on him for his comfort. His eyes darted around the table in search of a distraction, landing on Aida and her suspiciously swollen belly. The Redspire sisters were all notably petite, and the fashion of their house typically wasn't so modest. In the few brief interactions he'd had with the Fourth Princess, she'd never been so… covered.

"Aida," he drawled. "You're betrothed to the son of a nobleman within your house, aren't you? How is that going?"

She shot him a glare. They all knew that her betrothal had mysteriously fizzled out only a few short weeks ago. "The son of one of our allies in a minor house, actually. He attended school on your island. I thought you might've done your studies at the same time as him."

"I wanted to go to school on your island," Roman said to Asriel, an obvious attempt at a diversion. "But my father insisted I be trained at home. Do you ever get to visit the school, now that you're finished with your education?"

Asriel was most definitely *not* finished with his education; at least, by his father's standards. He had also never stepped foot in the classrooms at the Academy beyond making appearances. Foolishly, he was under the impression that the rest of the heirs had received their education at home with tutors, scattered and inconsistent and he had been.

"Here and there," Asriel said, the lie coming effortlessly.

"I want to hear more about the Veservus schools," Aida said, her face hardening. "I'm sure your future bride would love to know as well."

Clearing his throat, Asriel said, "We all know that my house facilitates education on every island. It isn't just the schools on Isle Verdale. Private or public, paid for or free. If you've attended an academy through any major house, you've attended a Veservus school."

"And what about the lesser houses?" Ezra asked.

"There are so many on each of the islands that we end up sharing space with them more often than you'd think," Asriel said. "They're welcome to attend under their own banners."

"You shouldn't call them lesser houses," Freya scolded her brother. "They're the minor houses."

"Does the verbiage matter?" Roman prompted. "They have less political power. Thus, they are the lesser houses."

"They are represented at this very meeting!" Freya said. "Our own master of trade is a common, working man."

Every head turned toward the orange-cloaked man at the corner of the table. He bowed his head modestly, chafing beneath the sudden influx of attention. He raised a hand, and it was clear that they were the hands of a worker. Vicious callouses covered the pads of his fingers, and there were several cuts littered across his skin.

Asriel knew that the Lancor's often employed commoners among their staff, but it still seemed like a strange custom to him. He hadn't seen any other house exhibit such an attention to the common folk before, and it was almost refreshing. Though the common people of House Veservus could rise through the ranks of status through their level of education, Asriel's father had never employed someone who hadn't already completed that education in its entirety. And as for the rest of the house councils, many of the other High Lords often opted to appoint their kin or other nobles who carried the same magic as them.

"My Lords, my Ladies," a Mediator said, peeking their head through the door. "Apologies for the interruption. The Third Prince is required to attend his duties in the archives."

The archives were likely the only thing that would be more tedious than this meeting. He sucked in a breath and avoided rolling his eyes. "Can it wait? We're in the middle of something."

"Don't shirk duty on our account," Gerard said, waving a hand. "I'm sure we can pull enough information all the same."

That stung, hitting the never-healed wound in Asriel's chest. He wasn't needed for what seemed to be a serious meeting. Taking the dismissal for what it was, he rose to his feet and headed for the door. He was prepared to follow the Mediator out with little more than Barrett and his dignity, but the sweetest sound carried over the room.

"I'll come with you," Freya said, hurrying around the table.

The Mediator eyed Asriel, seemingly for his consent to include her in his duties. He gave a curt dip of his chin, welcoming her. Barrett, noble as always, dipped low at the waist.

"My Lady," he said.

"Soon enough," she said brightly, taking Asriel's arm.

That warmed Asriel, somewhat. Not only the affection she showed him immediately, but also the familiarity she showed Barrett. He didn't think any marriage would work for him if his spouse couldn't show kindness to Barrett. He didn't give any more thought to the particular *brand* of kindness Asriel showed him, though. Or how a spouse might react to such a thing.

The archives awaited them.

"Have you been down this way before?" Asriel asked.

Freya shook her head. "I haven't explored much of what the Palace has to offer, in fact. I've only really been to the Lancor wing, and our shop there."

"And a fine shop it is," Asriel said, though he'd never been there before.

The walk took them into the Veservus wing, passing the ornate library doors to stand in front of an unremarkable rounded door, much shorter than Asriel. The top of it only came to his chest. It was uncomfortable to duck through the threshold once the Mediator unlocked the door.

"I can go no further," the Mediator said, remaining outside. "Only archivists—and you, my Lord—are allowed in the archives. And any guests you bring."

"Not so fast," a deep voice said from within.

Heads turned to see an elderly archivist standing with a pile of scrolls in hand. He looked both Barrett and Freya over with displeasure.

"Master Euclid," Asriel said. "These people are my friends. They may accompany me into your archives."

"There's no need for swordsmen down here," the old man continued. "If he wants to come in, he must disarm."

Asriel and Barrett looked at each other for a moment, holding a silent conversation before Asriel nodded for him to go ahead. With care,

Barrett removed his weapons and handed them to the Mediator on the other side of the doorway.

"And who is this?" Master Euclid asked, gesturing toward Freya.

"She is my betrothed," Asriel said, putting an arm around her waist. "She will not be parted from me."

After a pause, the man said, "Very well. Close the door."

Barrett obeyed before rounding out their little party. When the archivist departed into the room without a word, they knew to follow.

Asriel hated coming to the archives. They were dank and had an air of foreboding to them. There were so many archivists within it who he saw once and never again that he had to wonder if these shelves went so deep they never found their way out.

The front room was full of cursory information—the most recent histories that were still too old for the scholars to keep as current. After only a dozen or so rows of dimly-lit shelves, however, the room sloped downward into darkness. A carved stone staircase marked the only way forward. The stairwell was dark, and Asriel wasn't ashamed to take Freya's hand for his own comfort, though for the sake of appearances, it would seem as though he was the one comforting her.

"Bit dark," she muttered.

"I can see," Asriel said, his eyes adjusting preternaturally. He couldn't see as crisp as he could in daylight, but he could still make out shapes more definitively than a human's eyes could. He could see enough to manage as he and Freya descended lower and lower beneath the ground floor of the Palace. Asriel had no idea how many stairs there were in total, but he decided that there were far too many for any person to descend—let alone make the ascent back up.

At last, the floor leveled out as they reached the end of the staircase. There were lanterns every few steps, lighting the spaces between the shelves. And there were hundreds upon thousands of scrolls, books, and boxes stretched out as far as the eye could see.

"It's good that you came," Master Euclid said. "We spoke with one of the young scholars regarding a discrepancy in the texts. He said you referred him back to his masters, but they are the ones who sent him to us in the first place. We were hoping you could sort through the data and let us know what is correct."

"O-okay," Asriel stuttered. "I wouldn't presume to think I know better than you, though, Master Euclid."

"You are the authority on such matters," the old man said. "If the scholars disagree with us, we must defer to you."

A chill went through Asriel. "Of course," he said briskly, trying to keep his tone level. He did not enjoy having his gaps in knowledge so swiftly corrected. "Show me the texts."

Master Euclid walked further into the shelves. Asriel turned back to Barrett, who took up a post beneath the archway that led to the stairwell. Swallowing thickly, Asriel followed the archivist with Freya on his heels. She seemed wholly at home, which he supposed was nice. Perhaps in their future together, he could trust that he'd be able to bring her along on such tedious tasks. He almost enjoyed the idea of such a thing.

"Here," the archivist said at last. "This collection of dates should lead you to the correct information, which will be upstairs with the scholars."

"Fine, thanks," Asriel said gruffly. They'd come all this way for one measly book. Wonderful.

He took the tome—which was more like a stack of sheets bound together—in hand and started making his way toward the staircase. He hadn't made it very far, though, when Master Euclid cleared his throat, stopping Asriel in his tracks.

"The tomes must be studied in front of their home on the shelf," he said. "Lest we lose track of any."

Asriel nodded and returned the book to its post, laying it flat on the small section of shelf left empty. He knew that rule, of course. It was his duty to know such things. He didn't require constant reminders on the functions of his house. Not from the archivists, not from his sister, not from *anyone*.

His eyes ghosted over the fading text, noting the dates and names of the Lancor lineage. Tracing his fingers over Freya's ancestors' names, he committed the facts to memory. He felt Freya reading over his shoulder, examining her own history as though it were new to her.

After scouring several pages, Asriel shut the book and set it back in its place. "I have what I need. Let's head to the scholars."

As he and Freya made their way back up the stairs, Asriel miserably wondered why the archivists and scholars couldn't just compare notes themselves. Why did he have to be involved? The scholars were only one door down from the entrance to the archives. Their room, however, was full of tall windows that let in plenty of sunlight. Asriel was thankful for that, as well as for the noise. The scholars worked in more organized chaos, with the quiet buzz of constant conversation hanging over the room. As they crossed the carpeted floors, the young scholar who had first approached Asriel walked by with his arms full of scrolls.

"You, young scholar," Asriel said, whistling sharply.

"My Lord," the boy said, bowing deeply and dropping some scrolls in the process. He fumbled for them, which caused him to only drop more.

"Here," Freya said breezily, crouching down. "Let me help."

The boy turned pink all the way to his ears. "Thank you, Lady."

"She's to be the Lady of your house someday," Asriel said proudly. "Now, go tell your masters that I've consulted the archives. Have them collect what each of their texts say and bring me their findings. I'll be in the conference room."

"Yes, my Lord," the boy said, bowing once again.

Once the boy walked away, Freya said, "You're not collecting the data yourself?"

Asriel shook his head. "I'll compare it all once they bring it to me. The scholars don't like me much, so I avoid dealing with them when I can."

Even as she took his arm, her brow furrowed. "For someone who hates meetings, you're very eager to get back."

"I survive the dredges of duty by coasting on my mediocrity," he said lightly, playing it off as a joke instead of the sad truth it was.

To his relief, she giggled. That was enough to set Asriel back on track to take the reins of their exchange. He led her back to the cold conference room with a series of lighthearted comments and carefully picked-apart bits of information about himself. The more he gave, the more Freya gave in return.

He was used to these sorts of conversations. Often, they were more like verbal exchanges in search of a greater depth of understanding. He had

138

grown up watching his father speak to people this way. Although his status as the High Lord typically prompted people to acquiesce more frequently than they would if he were a regular man. Still, his father commanded respect, and people addressed him in kind. Someday, people would speak to Asriel that way.

For now, though, they would continue to look at him with contempt—scoffing when he entered the room just as Gerard and Roman did. They also tended to roll their eyes, the way Aida did… Or they would avoid looking at him altogether, the way Ezra did.

Asriel tried not to pay them any mind as he took his seat and waited for the others to settle down. They were never going to give him the respect he was owed, not while the wound of treachery was still so fresh. If he wanted respect, he was going to have to take it for himself. And the way to do that was by proving his usefulness—which he still had yet to prove to himself or his father. But there were ways of getting around that. Ways his father had taught him that he knew just as well as strategy.

Asriel knew how to pick apart stranger's secrets like carrion. How to turn the bits of flesh into a feast.

"So," he said. "I hear the Aviatis heir still hasn't declared herself. Isn't that strange? She's already twenty-four."

"Word is she's busy," Roman said. "Fulfilling her duties as the High Priestess."

The Sixth House was one of the oldest in Adristan, dating back to the early days of the old world when kings still ruled. The namesake family were almost exclusively high-ranking figures in the Lucerian priesthood aside from those who had Ascended to lordship. Their current High Lord, Zerin Aviatis, had never been a priestess. She had lived her early years enjoying every luxury afforded to a Princess and heir before Ascending.

Her chosen heir, Raven Aviatis, had not followed suit.

Freya frowned. "How can Princess Raven be the High Priestess *and* the heir to the High Lord?"

"You can't, technically," Asriel said. "There's that saying from the old school religions. 'You can't serve two masters.' Raven will have to give up her position in the priesthood in order to Ascend someday. But her aunt is young, and isn't likely to give up lordship any time soon."

"I didn't declare until I was twenty-five," Gerard said. "It's a pointless ceremony. You can do it at any point in time."

Asriel turned toward Ezra. "You were *just* named heir, weren't you?"

"Formally, yes," Ezra answered.

Freya leaned forward on her elbows. "When did *you* declare, Asriel?"

He widened his eyes in surprise. "At twenty, when I was named. I'm surprised anyone would wait."

"You typically know you're going to be named heir years before it actually happens," Gerard said. "There's no rush to get it on paper."

Asriel hummed. "I have to disagree."

Roman grinned smugly. "That's because you have to."

Defeated, Asriel sat back in his chair. These were the trials every heir had to live through, he told himself. He was determined to come out stronger and more fortified on the other side of it. He needed to be strong enough to carry the weighted burdens that came with Ascending. There was no alternative for his future.

Asriel had been keenly aware of what would happen should he fail for longer than he cared to think about. If he were to misstep along the way, his family wouldn't be able to look at him the same. And he wasn't sure he could face *them* ever again. But there, in the back of his mind, a small voice dared to disagree.

Somewhere, deep inside of himself, Asriel couldn't quell the hope that even if he failed, he might still be able to face *himself* in the mirror.

CHAPTER ELEVEN

"Betrothals are not unheard of in Adristan. They are often utilized for political reasons, but not every house sees them as such. Regardless, wedding and marriage ceremonies follow certain procedures. In order to pass from courtship to marriage, the couple must engage in several different ceremonies to cement their commitment to one other."

—Wedding Traditions, *revised by High Lord Alden Veservus and High Lord Zerin Aviatis*

4 Lightpel, in the Benevolent year 112 A.E.

Virgil's skin was irritated, but he resisted the urge to scratch behind his ear thanks to the dozens of threats Bianca had sent his way already. Instead, he rolled his shoulders and neck, trying to chase away the sensation. From behind, his cousin slapped his shoulder.

"I have a needle precariously close to your *skull*. You'd do well to keep still," Bianca snapped.

Virgil sat cross-legged on the floor of his bedroom while Bianca sat on his bed, using a buzzing needle to etch a tiny design into his skin. He had asked for claw marks for his first tattoo, hesitant but curious when he saw the device Bianca had brought. At first sight, he had mistaken it for some sort of quill. But when Bianca wound up the feathered tail, it began vibrating thanks to a series of gears inside of it. Once the tip was dipped in ink, it created friction that pressed the ink into the skin and sent chills throughout Virgil's body.

Meanwhile, Mila lounged in a chair she had dragged from the sitting room, leaning back with her feet propped on the windowsill. She watched them with half-shut eyes, laughing quietly to herself every time her eyes ghosted over the papers in Virgil's hands.

"Find anything interesting yet?" Mila quipped.

"Plenty," Virgil said with a grumble.

With a cheery voice, Bianca read over his shoulder. *"House Veservus*

141

are known for their strategic political marriages. They set betrothals far in advance—"

"Stop that," Virgil said, shoving the papers out of sight.

"Oh, he's blushing, Bianca," Mila crooned. "We shouldn't tease him."

"Why shouldn't we?" Bianca argued. "It's good for his character."

"Leïch aiyy," Virgil said. *Fuck off.* "*You* are the one who encouraged me to look into pursuing her. Should I do this in secret beneath the covers with a single candle at my bedside?"

"You'd be concerned if we weren't making fun," Bianca said, fluffing up his hair. "You'd wonder why we were all doom and gloom instead of letting you dampen the mood."

"We'd make you look downright *cheery*," added Mila.

"It would make me nervous," he muttered. "If the day comes where I ever see you two without smiles, then I'll know hope is lost."

Bianca clucked her tongue and set the needle aside before leaning down and hugging Virgil around his neck. She rested her cheek atop his head as she said, "Now I feel bad!"

"Don't," Virgil said. Tossing the stack of papers onto the bed, he said, "I don't know if her father will agree to a courtship. He still hasn't answered me."

"He'd be a fool not to," Bianca said, setting the papers aside. "It would be an advantageous match for his daughter *and* for his house. They need it more than they're willing to admit."

"Watch it," Virgil warned. "The Veservus family are good people. What their subjects chose to do isn't their fault."

"Did the heir ever write you back?" Mila asked.

Gods, had he. After his proposal had gone ignored, Virgil had tried writing to Rhaella. And when *she* ignored him, he knew something was off. So he'd taken to contacting the Prince directly. In an aggressively timely manner, Asriel responded with a letter full of diplomatic bullshit. Excuses and non-answers as to where his sister was. Busy studying, busy furthering her education to the betterment of her house. What did any of those words mean in context?

It meant they were hiding something.

Virgil had held up his end of the bargain, defending them to any noble who questioned their reputation. But the Third High Lord and his heir were practiced liars... And not well-practiced ones, at that. Virgil caught onto every piss-poor attempt they made with little effort. Maybe it worked on the rest of the nobles who enjoyed the wordplay they all partook in, but it didn't work on him. He couldn't stand pretty words used to dress up uglier meanings.

"He didn't say anything of note," Virgil answered after a pause. "None of my questions received an answer. I still don't know why I haven't heard from her."

"You could just travel to Isle Verdale," Mila suggested. "Show up and present the High Lord with an offer he can't refuse. Perhaps he appreciates action over words."

Virgil rolled his eyes. "He's the Lord of House Veservus, for the gods sakes. All he cares about are information and words." Virgil paused, seeming to think things over. "But it might be worth paying him a visit."

"It couldn't hurt," Mila said. "It'll look better if you go with your father's blessing, though."

"I already have it," Virgil said. "He's insistent I marry as soon as possible. The fact that I'm presenting him with even so much as a name is going to count as a victory in his mind."

"Then you have nothing to worry about," Bianca said. "Now sit still so I can finish this."

It was a small design—only four lines about the length of a finger—which she finished within minutes. Bianca set the quill and ink aside and began cleaning his tattoo with a liquid that smelled clinical. Virgil's skin was *sensitive* and he was very aware of the skin there, but there was no pain. Not that bad for a first tattoo, all things considered.

"You're going to want to put an ointment on this a few times a day. Whenever it feels dry, or whenever you remember."

"How's it look?" He reached a hand up reflexively, and was once again shot down.

"You gave me an easy design. It's some of my finest work." She rose, lightly smacking his shoulder.

As his cousins continued chatting, Virgil strolled over to the mirror atop his dresser and surveyed Bianca's work. Pushing a few strands of his hair aside, he admired the claw marks that were crisper and even more refined than what he'd had in mind.

Mila said, "I think I would like to get married someday, after all."

"Get married or be married?" Bianca asked drily.

"Get married," her sister replied with a dreamy look on her face. "The notion is so romantic, isn't it? Binding yourself to another in the presence of all the houses. I'll get to wear a few dresses and dance and be the center of attention for several days."

Virgil scrunched his nose. "I think you've actually just changed my mind."

They all laughed, and it was a joyous sound until pounding at the door startled them into silence. Virgil went to answer but Uncle Nicholas burst into the room before he could open the door. He wasn't wearing his Doctrina robes, which was an unsettling sight. Whatever urged him into the room had done so without giving him the chance to dress in full regalia. Virgil's stomach sank.

"What are you doing here?" Uncle Nicholas demanded, clutching Virgil's shirt in a fist. Ignoring the girls barking out in protest in the back, he said, "You're supposed to be on Kingsgrave at the trade meeting. Why are you *home?*"

"Relax," Virgil said, taking breaths to steady himself as his nerves set his body alight at the sudden intrusion. "I sent word notifying them of my absence. And someone there owes me a favor. I'll get the rundown from them."

He hadn't included that tidbit of his letter to Prince Asriel when recounting it to Bianca, but it didn't matter. If Asriel wouldn't own up to what was going on with Rhaella, he'd have to pay up with information about trade.

"Idiot," Uncle Nicholas sneered, shoving away from him. "Your father is fuming."

The words momentarily floored Virgil. If only for a few seconds, he was a teenage boy again, shirking duty without fear of consequence. Since then, he had become intimately familiar with consequence. It was his lover. His most constant friend. It was all he knew and all he had.

The High Lord was supposed to be tied up in meetings with the minor houses of Greenisle, keeping him out of Castle Silverfort for at least two days. Long enough that Virgil's absence at the trade meeting could go unnoticed and unremarked upon.

Virgil shook himself out of his stupor. "I'll speak with him."

"Yes," Uncle Nicholas said. "You will."

They both stormed out of the room, silently fighting to get ahead of the other, before Uncle Nicholas stopped in the doorway and turned to look at the girls with derision.

"The High Lord is going to want to speak with both of you once he's through with his son. Be ready. And *don't* make me come get you."

"Don't talk to them like that," Virgil said calmly. The threat beneath his words was clear; he didn't need to take on a tone for it to have the right effect. As intended, his uncle's eyes briefly widened before narrowing again. Without another word, Virgil shouldered past him and walked down the hall.

As he walked, paws patted against the marble floors and caught pace with him. His pet wolf, Stollas, nuzzled his snout against Virgil's knee. He leaned down and petted the wolf on the head.

"We're in trouble, boy," he murmured. "You won't want to hear this."

Still, the wolf followed him dutifully into the great hall. It was crowded with people today—nobles who were insistent on meeting with the High Lord upon his return. A posse of advisors second to the Dux Doctrina—as well as children and relatives of those who worked in House Midar—were eager to snag themselves a match that would uplift their family's status.

Virgil strode past all of them, straight to the ornate chair his father sat on. The High Lord wasn't proud; he'd had the dais whittled down after the house's construction, saying it made the hall look too much like a throne room. None of that stopped his seat from appearing as one all the same, however. It had been carved from black wood and fashioned with swirling patterns. Miniature columns held up the arms, and they were fronted with the heads of snarling wolves. It was a masterful piece of furniture. The Lancors, however many generations back, had done a masterful job with it.

Taking no notice of the man prattling on to his father, Virgil cleared his throat theatrically. The gathered nobles scattered around the room, startled by either him or the wolf, but they left the space in front of the throne clear for both of them nonetheless.

"You're supposed to be on Kingsgrave," his father said, not commenting on the intrusion.

"I had other matters to handle here," Virgil said.

"Did you?" The High Lord scoffed, a chilling sound. "So there's business going on in my own house that even I'm not aware of?"

Virgil bit the inside of his cheek. "If we could speak in private—"

"What for? So you can make excuses for yourself? I won't have it," his father said. "What was so important that you had to miss the trade meeting?"

"I'm handling what you asked of me," Virgil growled. "What you tasked me with that day in the war tent."

Confusion flitted across the High Lord's face before realization cleared it. What replaced it might have been described as satisfaction. Slowly, he began nodding his head.

"That's comforting to hear," he said. "Yet you're neglecting your other duties to do so. That cannot stand."

Virgil said, "I have a contact who owes me information."

His father arched a brow. "Very resourceful. Even so, I cannot let your wills slide. You sacrificed one meeting, so now you'll attend another. You were supposed to travel to the Silent Keep once you came of age, and you were to declare yourself to the Mothers and Fathers Superior there. You still haven't. I didn't push the issue back then because you had just returned from another one of your abdication stints. That, and your uncle being our Doctrina bought us time, but that time has since run out."

"So I have to do that," Virgil sighed. "Have all of the other heirs declared themselves?"

"Of the seven other stronghold houses, six have declared. Only you and the heir to House Aviatis have yet to do so," his father said. "Of the dozens of minor houses, only a few have declared. But the eight stronghold houses are the Order's priority."

"Well," Virgil said. "At least we won't be last."

"Your attempts at humor are appreciated," his father said drily, "but unnecessary. You'll set sail first thing tomorrow morning." Somewhere in the back of the room, Virgil heard a commotion as the door opened. "Here come your cousins. You can ask them to come with you, if it pleases you. Just get it done."

Virgil glanced over his shoulder. Indeed, Bianca and Mila had made their way into the great hall. They each had their hands folded, standing as picturesque as they could. Something was cowed in Mila's posture, and Virgil didn't like it.

"Good, you're here," the High Lord said to them. "Virgil, you might as well hear this."

Frost seemed to settle over the hall, even though it was the dead of summer. Virgil had received plenty of punishing tasks in this room over the years, as had his cousins. But there was something hardened in his father's expression. Something unrelenting. Those weren't the eyes of a stern parent and an uncle who had to deal with rebellious children. His somber face was that of a ruler who could not bend, even for his kin.

Dissatisfied with the nearness of the nobles gathered at court, Virgil's father snapped his fingers. At once, the lower ranking advisors moved into action. They swept around the room, making conversation with the gaggles of people so that they would remain occupied for what was, evidently, a private conversation.

"Both of you broke your word," the High Lord started. "After concluding your service in the North, you were supposed to tour the mainland and assist the nurses with their duties, yet you defied me. In coming to stay with our main camp and attending dinners you were not invited to, you have made my word look *weak*. You have disobeyed direct orders. How am I to command respect if I cannot command even my own blood?"

"There was never any ill intent, Uncle," Bianca said.

"I know that, and yet it doesn't change anything. You still disobeyed a direct order. That cannot be without consequence. You want to be by Virgil's side, regardless of what I say? Fine. Bianca, you'll become Lord Commander once Virgil Ascends. And until that time comes, you'll go back into the academy in preparation."

"Father—" Virgil started.

"It's fine," Bianca muttered to him. "I want to be commander. It'll be an honor."

"Yes, it will be," Virgil's father said. "As for you, Mila—"

147

"If I may, Uncle," Mila said, lifting her chin. "For many years, I have refused to participate in finding a match that will benefit our house. You and my mother argued with me plenty over that. But I've changed my mind. If you find me a suitable match, I'll go through with it."

The High Lord lifted a brow. "Now *that* is a surprise as well. Did the three of you come back from the battlefield with your minds righted?" Virgil flinched. His father continued, "This does change things. You're aware that I have final say in who the match is?"

Mila nodded. "I accept that."

Virgil's father waved a hand. "That's all, then. The rest of the day is yours."

Effectively, they were dismissed. Virgil, with his latest inane task; Bianca, with her future now mapped out for her; and Mila, with the world open to her as long as her uncle approved it. All the bearings of nobility beat against them as the current beat at the shoreline. The formality of it all set Virgil on a high cliff, looking down at the subjects around him as he attempted to keep his balance. One misstep, and he was sure to go tumbling toward the rocky surface below.

As they made to exit the great hall, the Dux Doctrina entered, now in his robes. He also wore a mask of reworked black metal, with chains that swept across the planes of his face. Dark eyes blinked from behind the metal, seemingly unaffected by its weight.

Bianca and Mila shouldered past him without a word. When Virgil tried to pass, however, his uncle caught him by the arm.

"Your cousin is doing her house a great favor. In turn, she does her nation a great favor. That must please you, to know that your closest friend wants to do what is good and right."

"As we all do," Virgil said, yanking his arm free. "You don't have to gloat."

"Gloat?" His uncle reared back slightly. "I never gloat, Virgil. What I do is remind you that there are players in this game aside from yourself. You would be wise to remember that your actions don't affect just you."

"I am *violently* aware of that, thank you," Virgil growled.

"Then you need to act like it," his uncle said. "*Act* like the future High Lord, not like the drunken, irresponsible loaf you've proven yourself to be up until now."

Taking a step closer, Virgil looked down his nose at his uncle. They were both well aware that Virgil was bigger, stronger, and angrier than him. It wouldn't take much for Virgil to overtake him.

"I won your war for you," he said with deathly calm. "You can speak down on me all you like, but you do not get to call me loafish."

Uncle Nicholas gave him a long look up and down. "Then why are you spending your days lounging about, getting drunk, while you neglect your responsibilities?"

"You think my father was a saint before his Ascension? I'm not hurting anyone. I've already agreed to take up my fate. Let me have my fun while I still can."

"Do what you like," his uncle said, circling to step around him. "Just remember that there are eyes on you as you do."

Doctrina Nicholas strolled back to his circle of peers and they began whispering amongst themselves. Their eyes occasionally flitted toward Virgil, and he found himself feeling uncomfortably exposed. But that feeling could be numbed. He slipped out of the hall and caught up with his cousins, Stollas at his heels.

"I have to travel to the mainland tomorrow morning," he said. "Do either of you want to accompany me?"

"Depends," Bianca said. "What for?"

"I have to visit the Dux and declare myself as heir."

Bianca made a face. "You have to travel all that way just for that?"

"It's symbolic," he said. "I was supposed to go when I turned twenty, but we all know where I was then."

That sobered them all. None of them liked to reflect on Virgil's younger days. The fighting pits were his home back then, and bloodied knuckles and bruised cheekbones were his constants. It wasn't fair of his uncle to act like he was still there, fighting other desperate bodies because he couldn't fight himself.

Too soon, the three of them arrived back at his rooms, where Declan and Eric were standing watch. That annoyed Virgil, too, but he knew they *had* to act like watchdogs, even if he couldn't truly accept them as his guards.

"I want to go for a walk," he said.

Wordlessly, Virgil pushed open his door and led both his guards and his cousins to the tapestry hanging in the furthest corner of the sitting room. Eric held it aside so Virgil could take the jar of half-melted clay from his dresser and dip his fingers into it before drawing a symbol on the empty wall beneath. The wall seemed to shudder for a moment before a section carved itself out and pushed deeper in, revealing the door that was now opening.

The cavernous space it led to was dark, but Virgil had been through here before. Declan went first, having produced a lantern from somewhere hidden when Virgil wasn't looking. Patting his leg so Stollas would follow, Virgil ducked inside. His cousins followed next, shoving each other to see who would go first. Eric rounded out the back, pulling the tapestry over the now-open space and sealing them into the murky gray darkness.

The tunnel took them downwards before snaking right and then left again. Virgil kept one hand against the cobblestone wall to steady himself against the debris littered across the floor. His boots kept kicking loose rocks and slipping over piles of dirt. Since he was the only one who used this tunnel—and he used it rarely at that—it had seen better days.

A final swerve to the left led them to another wall. Virgil produced the jar of clay again and drew the same symbol, opening yet another door. The threshold left in the wake of it led to the green outdoors and a sectioned-off part of land that belonged to the family. Stollas took off running toward a tall iron fence a few yards ahead that effectively gated them in and kept anything else out. The five of them crossed the short expanse of land quickly, and they made light work of heaving themselves through a section of missing bars.

It was easy for Virgil and his cousins in their comfortable clothes, but the guards made a noisy, awkward effort with their armor. Once on the other side of the fence, Virgil put his hands in his pockets and began walking. Eric kept pace with him while Declan hung back a few steps. The girls sped ahead, basking in the mid-afternoon sun. Stollas, as expected, ran off on his own.

"Where do you want to go?" Mila asked.

"I just want to clear my head," Virgil replied. "There shouldn't be any beasts this way."

"Shouldn't," Eric muttered. "Doesn't mean *aren't*."

"We're fine," Virgil insisted, patting Airslinger at his hip.

For a while, they walked in silence, passing through trees and stepping over roots and fallen branches. A river babbled in the distance and there were birds chirping from above. The whole thing had an almost musical effect on the forest.

The babbling got louder even though they weren't any closer to the river, and it wasn't until they were nearly upon the fountain that Virgil realized that's where the sound was coming from. It was taller than he was. Gray stone had been molded into the image of a giant elk with magnificent horns protruding from its head, and between its front hooves was a giant bowl where the water that poured from its mouth and eyes dripped into. It was only a light stream; the bowl wasn't even halfway full.

"Gods," Bianca hissed. "What is this thing?"

"It's from the Lucerians," Virgil said, approaching calmly. "Back when Adristan was reforming itself from the ashes of the old world, the priestesses went around the islands and constructed monuments for their religion. We stopped paying attention to them long ago, so most of them are in disarray now."

"It looks like a deer," Eric said.

"It's a giant elk," Bianca said, peering closer. "We don't have them here."

"There's a few," Virgil said. "They aren't wild, though. They're mostly domesticated."

Declan ran his hand over the carved rock; its surface was crawling with moss and ivy and there were substantial cracks to be seen. "What is a lone fountain doing out in the forest?"

"If I'm right," Virgil said, "I think it's an altar for a bride and groom to leave offerings before a potential marriage."

Eric burst out laughing. "Is that why we're here?"

Virgil glared at his guard. "No. The priestesses had them built close to the houses for convenience. I wanted to go for a walk, and it's in the vicinity."

"So it's a coincidence," Declan said, half question and half-suggestion.

Letting his fingertips swim on the surface of the collected water,

151

Virgil considered for a moment. "Not that, either. The topic just keeps coming up."

Talking about it made Virgil uncomfortable. Perhaps because the more people knew, the more real it felt. And maybe because part of him was afraid to pursue Rhaella. Marriage had seemed like such a faraway thing for so long. It felt wrong not to be pushing it off any longer, even after that conversation between him and his father in the war tent.

He hadn't even *tried* to find marriageable qualities in the Hawk. But when he put together their months of communication with the ease he found talking to her in person, he could envision a version of his future where he didn't cringe to picture someone beside him.

On an exhale, he said, "Or maybe that *is* why we're here. I want High Lord Veservus to give me an answer."

"This is the most eager I've ever seen you about the prospect," Declan said.

"Any amount of eagerness would be the most you'd get out of him," Bianca said. "He was outright opposed until he met her."

"I still am, mostly," Virgil said, brushing moss and dirt from his hands. "There's aspects of it I'm not particularly enthused about, but my father's going to pair me with some nobleman's daughters if I don't choose myself. This way, I can at least ensure it's someone I *like*." He paused, taking a deep breath before admitting the rest out loud. "And I like her."

The confession held more finality than he cared to think about.

"What don't you like about it?" Declan asked, removing an apple from his pocket. He took out a dagger and began carving off the skin. "Marriage, I mean. Not Rhaella."

"Well, look at my parents," Virgil said, blowing air out of pursed lips. "They aren't in love anymore. At least, my mother isn't. But he has to travel to the mainland every so often to see her because when you're a High Lord and you're married, there's certain things you *have* to do with your spouse. The marriage bonds make it that way. Obligation makes a mockery out of love."

"We wouldn't know anything about obligation, would we?" Eric asked, eating the apple skin as Declan handed it to him. Moving on, he asked, "What're the marriage bonds like?"

Circling the fountain, Mila said, "Other cultures have called them soulmates, or just mates. It's a very intense thing. You become very possessive over one another, and your life in general feels incomplete without them. In those other cultures, you can find that person without getting married. Some even think it's predetermined. Here, though, whatever magic they do during the wedding ceremony essentially mates you. That doesn't go away if you fall out of love or physically separate yourselves. You're still attached, even if you're not in love."

"And you want that?" Bianca asked, scrunching her nose.

"I'm willing to take the risk," Mila said. She knelt and picked up a stone off the ground, clutching it to her chest before placing it in the fountain's bowl.

"So, you find someone and they become your mate," Declan said. "And in other cultures, you find your mate and then you may or may not marry them."

"Essentially."

To Virgil, Declan said, "So you don't want a mate."

Virgil shrugged. "My parents are mated, and look at them. He only sees her because the magic makes him incapable of completing his High Lord duties without doing so. It's all very political. I'm sure it wouldn't be so bad with a love match, but those are hard to come by."

"You and Rhaella seem well-matched," Eric said, surprisingly earnest. "At least from what little we witnessed."

"I think I agree," Virgil said, sighing heavily. "I just hope she does too."

"It'll work out," Bianca said. "I have a feeling you wouldn't have entertained the idea if she wasn't worth the risk."

Virgil sat before the fountain, contemplating its purpose and everything that had been put into constructing it. People had to believe in its powers firmly in order to make such efforts to place them all over the islands. Maybe that should have assured him of its truth, but he couldn't wrap his mind around such a thing the same way Mila did. She came to sit beside him, resting her head on his shoulder.

"If her father agrees, and I marry her, she'll become the Lady of our house. Because someday, I'm going to be High Lord."

Virgil choked up slightly, swallowing past the lump in his throat. He stared up at Bianca, tall and proud. She was beloved by everyone who met her, and she was capable of leading the army just as well as he was. Her mother was up for consideration as the heir in her youth, but it was ultimately Virgil's father who had taken the title. Somehow, he still felt that he had robbed Bianca of her birthright. And even now, she was being ordered to serve under him. Commands were quick blades dashed across their desires.

"It should've been you," Virgil said into the quiet.

"Don't say that," Bianca said firmly. "I'm not a leader. You are."

"I don't want to be."

"That doesn't mean you aren't," she said. "I see the way your men look at you. They revere you, but not like you're some kind of god. It's like they see you as one of their own."

"Good," Virgil said. "I don't want to be anywhere above them. What I do and say isn't any more important than the things they do."

"It holds more weight, though" Bianca said. "Uncle Vincent wouldn't be so uptight if it didn't."

"My men like you just as much," it was an obvious deflection, but she let it slide. Waiting to see where the thought would take him. "They know you. And you're better with people, anyway. I don't like pretending with people just so they don't think I'm being rude."

Declan said, "Then don't pretend. You never do with us, and we respect you for it."

"I have to," he moaned.

"You don't have to just because your father does," Mila said. "If we all did what your father wanted, we'd be a much more rigid house."

That wasn't untrue, but it didn't make things any easier. Virgil still had the weight of expectation wearing him down. He was strong, he could carry the weight no doubt. He just wondered how long he'd have to.

For now, all he wanted to do was complain as the sun began to set on them. In the quiet, surrounded by the few people he could trust, the sound of the fountain's babbling carried them into the dark of night.

CHAPTER TWELVE

"Though you have every right to deny me, I would still beg of you for nothing more than a reason."
—Letter from Rhaella of House Veservus to Virgil Midar

4 Lightpel, in the Benevolent year 112 A.E.

The clanging of bells woke the Progenies in their dorms every morning at precisely sunrise. Rhaella didn't have a roommate, which offered her the slightest bit of privacy between meals and training. And it was spacious enough that she could get up and stretch if she felt like it. In the corner, a bookshelf sat with heavy tomes on any subject she could want to study. And though the room itself felt dark, her window was large and had an enviable view.

She was so tired of being here.

Only a week and some change had passed, but it felt like it'd been longer. Thus far, she hadn't been allowed to send out or receive letters, and she wondered if her family had even written. Or if any of her friends had, for that matter. On her desk, Rhaella had a pile of letters that remained unsent. The Superiors had promised access to mail at some undetermined point, and Rhaella would be ready for that day.

The bells rang again, this time a warning to get to morning inspection. Quickly, she dressed in her regulation clothes—loose-fitted gray pants and a sleeveless shirt. Her gray robes were only mandatory during seated classes and on-sight training, as well as during public appearances. After plaiting what was left of her hair, she pulled on her black boots, laced them up, and made her way downstairs.

Superiors waited in the foyer where all of the staircases emptied to line the Progenies up and give them their first checkup of the day. Rhaella

155

made her way to the shortest line and waited her turn. She kept her eyes down, but cast her focus throughout the room. There weren't many Progenies in her class. Last she had counted, there were only a few dozen—somewhere around fifty of them at most. Her class was comprised of young men, women, and genderless folk. Though more women were present than anyone else. By her own estimation, Rhaella was one of the oldest there, though the rest weren't significantly younger.

Once it was her turn, she held her hands behind her back and stepped onto the scale. She turned her eyes toward the ceiling, not eager to fixate on how much she currently weighed.

The Mother Superior *tsked*. "You've lost weight. I'm ordering the mess hall to give you extra protein at breakfast. Now, open."

Stepping off of the scale, Rhaella opened her mouth and let the Mother Superior inspect her tongue with a depressor. Then, she pressed light fingertips against Rhaella's throat. Satisfied, she nodded and took note of everything. Finally, she loaded a small tray with tiny cups filled with different colored liquids and handed them to Rhaella.

She took a drink from each cup, one after another, swallowing hard against the harsh bitterness. Some of them were sweet, but only slightly. The Mother Superior checked Rhaella's throat once more after she had finished with each cup before sending her on her way for morning class.

The Superiors still hadn't noticed that their potions had virtually no effect on Rhaella.

She still wasn't sure why, but when she drank them, she never felt the urge to cough or groan or fully collapse like some of the other Progenies. Drinking the potions had the same effect as poorly-flavored water; it didn't taste good, but did not harm or benefit her either. Some of her peers had been sick ever since they'd arrived. And when asked about it, the Superiors simply explained that some students would need more time than others to adjust to whatever mix of herbs they were being given each day.

During class, Rhaella and her fellow Progenies studied all of the herbs the Dux utilized, and there were plenty of books on the topic of potion-making, but she hadn't found anything useful thus far.

The gym was sparsely filled with people sparring, either with practice swords or their fists. Most mornings, unless otherwise stated, Rhaella started her days here. This was inarguably her favorite part of the day. Mainly because they let her use a bow and arrow. She'd spent most of her first night worrying that she was going to lose her skill over the course of her time in the Silent Keep, so when her and the other Progenies were brought into the training ring and she saw the quivers full of arrows along the sides of the room, she couldn't squash the burst of relief that opened up in her heart.

She stretched by herself in a back corner, taking extra care of her shoulders and upper back, before pulling a hefty bow and a sheath of arrows from the rack. There were only three free targets, but she made good use of them, firing arrow after arrow and hitting the bullseye more often than not. And when she ran out of arrows, she went to the targets and yanked them out one by one, refilling her sheath before continuing to fire. There was something calming in the repetition of the motion.

With each fire of her bow, Rhaella recalled each of the many times her father had sent her away for the purpose of teaching her a lesson. She had once complained about attending mass at the tender age of seven, and so she was sent to stay with the Lightpikes as their ward for an entire fall season. *Thwack*. Rhaella had gotten caught sneaking out on Egorion once when she was sixteen and naive, and so her father sent her to the Palace of Many Rooms for the entirety of winter. *Thwack*. Rhaella had purposefully spilled her glass during a dinner with emissaries at eleven, so she was sent to the Dux to learn manners for an entire summer. *Thwack-thwack-thwack*.

This was far from her first time stepping through the gates of the Silent Keep. Her early adolescence had been marked by her attendance in their etiquette program, which taught her all manners of how to behave like a noble Lady. The other attendants were fellow spares and siblings to the heirs apparent. They were children who were not worth the effort of being taught by their High Lords.

If there was any lesson Rhaella had learned quickly, it was that she was disposable to her father.

At first, the realization made her cry. Then, it morphed into a desperate need to prove her usefulness. To make herself indisposable.

That had been easy enough. Simply put, Rhaella *was* useful. Even her father could see that within her. That was why his punishments were so severe. She could respect his methods. Only now, she wondered if she had done *too* good a job of proving herself.

Only once her back began to protest did she give up for the day, finishing off with more stretching. The bells rang at the top of the hour, freeing them to freshen up before grabbing breakfast.

The washrooms were, unfortunately, communal. Rhaella did her business, washing her body and hair before hurrying back to her room. Before donning her robes, she applied a cream to the brand marring her hip. It was ugly and swollen this morning, looking about as angry as she felt. The gray robes didn't help either, since they were itchier than she expected the black ones were. These ones were thicker, after all. And perhaps this, too, was a punishment meant to break down their spirits.

She braided her hair back in an elaborate pattern at the top of her head before it devolved into a simple plait, which now barely grazed the back of her neck. She found it hard to look at her reflection these days. Not only because of the hair, but because of the dark circles beneath her eyes. She used to bear a lack of sleep better, as well as unwanted responsibilities, but she supposed she might be reaching her limit.

As promised, the Mother Superior who had inspected her that morning had ordered the mess hall to give her extra protein. Instead of one serving of roasted pork, she received two alongside shredded potatoes and mixed charred vegetables. At the table aside from the serving line, she added a sprinkle of cheese to her potatoes and poured a light helping of syrup over her vegetables. Finding an empty seat at one of the long tables, she sat and kept to herself as she ate.

Though the potions had no effect on her functioning, they did leave an awful taste in her mouth. The potion that was meant to heighten their senses tasted of orange and wormwood. The one that harnessed their energy to create a protective force field around them tasted of blackberries, ginger, and dill. And the nastiest one, in Rhaella's opinion, was the black coffee and vinegar that bound them to the Order for life. Shuddering, she chugged down half a glass of water to try and chase the lingering flavor away.

She glanced around the room as though she were merely taking in the scenery, but her eyes found a group of Superiors huddled near the door, watching the Progenies as they ate. They were muttering to one another and making observations. Rhaella feared the things they were saying about her.

She wondered if they would make note of her sitting alone during meals, as well as during classes, and mark her as a recluse. That was sure to harm her standing.

Ghosting her eyes over the room again, Rhaella spotted her peers at the other end of the table. Some of their skin had turned pallid, their hair limp. Despite the side effects, though, excitement still sparkled in their eyes. Like this truly was an honor they were happy to have been tasked with.

Rhaella scooted closer to them, pushing her half-eaten tray with her. She offered a smile to the group of Progenies, and though she had been trying for warmth, it felt more practiced. Diplomatic, even.

"Hello," she said sweetly. "I'm Rhaella. And your names are…?"

"Hi Rhaella," a pretty brunette said. "My name's Edina of House Lightpike. This is Asher of Segsiege, Wilcox of Scalesound, Fawn of Greenisle, and Darius of the mainland. *My* family works in House Lightpike. The rest of theirs just live on the islands."

Though she bristled at that, Rhaella let out a friendly chuckle. She decided immediately that she did not like Edina.

"I've never met anyone that wasn't from Isle Verdale," Rhaella said. "What's it like out there?"

Each of them looked to be likely candidates, except for Darius. He was broad shouldered and muscular, and he looked as though he could have descended from a family of strongmen. Though maybe his muscles had been earned through years of manual labor. Because he hailed from the mainland, he had likely worked in the Stillgrove farms before coming here. Agriculture was a well-paying job.

Absently, Rhaella wondered what might have convinced him to abandon such steady work for the Order. She kept her eyes fixed on him, blinking prettily so that he'd feel compelled to respond.

Thankfully, he did. "The mainland is convenient in that we have access to the borders of the other nations. I've been able to travel quite a bit in my short life."

"And you prefer the stability here to traveling?"

Darius shrugged. "The Order offered to pay for my sister's schooling if a family member volunteered."

Rhaella frowned. There were schools that took students free of charge. For his sister to require a paid education meant that she was aiming for a higher position, likely one within the houses themselves. And, it likely meant that she didn't have any family connections to get her there.

"Which school is your sister attending?" Rhaella propped her chin in her hand to feign casualty.

"The school for archivists on Isle Verdale."

The words pierced her heart. *One of her father's schools.* She knew they could be expensive, and she knew that not everyone could afford the tuition. But, for once, she was completely blindsided by the information presented to her. The Order paying for students to attend as long as they received a body in return was not forbidden, per se. But she doubted it was the sort of trade her father would encourage.

"What brings you into the Order, Rhaella?" Fawn asked her.

She was the one from Greenisle—the island Virgil lived on. A pang of jealousy hit her out of nowhere. They looked to be roughly the same age, and Fawn was pretty and held eye contact as she spoke. A treacherous corner of Rhaella's mind wondered if Fawn had been the sort of girl Virgil would have preferred to spend his nights with.

Remembering she needed to answer, Rhaella coughed. "My brother thought I would like it."

It wasn't a lie, but it wasn't the truth, either.

Darius barked out a laugh. "And that was enough to convince you?"

"What can I say?" Rhaella shrugged.

"Can't blame you," Asher—the boy from the Lancors' island—said. "Frankly, I think we've got the best gig in Adristan."

The others whooped and smiled and nodded in agreement. Rhaella just blinked. These people truly wanted to be here. It made her feel like a *fraud.* Even with their wan faces and drained eyes—even with the nasty side effects of the potions and the exhausting schedule—they *wanted* to become members of the Dux Doctrina. They had had a *choice* in the matter.

Among these young Progenies somewhere was a future Dogan. Perhaps *several* future Dogans. If her father hadn't predetermined that she'd serve Asriel, who among these Progenies would her brother be willing to choose for himself? She couldn't picture any of them spending a lifetime with her brother.

She wished she could be like them, accepting the path they had all chosen. And in another life, this very well may have been the path she had decided on. But this was a different path entirely. Robbed of her choice in the matter, Rhaella couldn't help but wish for a way out.

Too soon, those damned bells rang again for their next class. Rhaella gathered herself and her things and made her way toward the classrooms on the third floor. After breakfast, she had history, followed by potions. Then, a quick lunch break before the most important class, at least according to the Order. *Advisory.*

In Advisory, each Progeny studied how Doctrinas both past and present could best advise their future High Lords. It was the official position of the Dux that no Doctrina could serve their High Lord effectively without this rigorous attention to how history impacted the future. To how Doctrinas had guided the hands of the High Lords for as long as their nation had existed. *Longer.*

Rhaella, for her part, did not pay much attention in this class. She knew her brother up and down, and she knew the functions of House Veservus just as well. She was all too familiar with the politics they would face every day. She knew how her brother was likely to react, and she knew what course of action would be best to take in any given scenario. The first twenty five years of her life had been dedicated to learning such things. If she didn't know them by now, she was as disposable as her father believed her to be.

The door to the classroom opened in the middle of the Father Superior's lecture. It might have been a momentary relief, except it was the Reverend Mother who walked in. Rhaella's eyes ducked as Reverend Mother Locasta's gaze swept across the room. She felt it wash over her like sticky, unforgiving syrup, coating her entire being. It took considerable effort to fight off a shudder.

"Reverend Mother," the Father Superior said, bowing low at the waist.

"Continue your class," she said callously. "I am here to watch."

"Of course," the Father Superior said, bowing again. He continued on with his lecture, putting on a bit of a show for the Reverend Mother.

The hour went by slowly as the Reverend Mother watched, and it took every ounce of self-control Rhaella possessed not to sprint down the hall once the bells rang again, signaling that class was over.

Later, they would have lessons on how to expand their senses with the help of the potions. But first, there was a free hour for Progenies to study, practice, train, or do whatever they pleased on their own. In these quiet moments, Rhaella went to the library. There was something familiar and comforting about cozying up between the shelves with a book.

She made herself comfortable at a table near the door, where there were a few shelves within walking distance, but she remained in sight of the exit. The herbology book she had picked up was supposed to help her understand why the potions weren't taking effect on her yet, but nothing she had seen so far was helping. She tracked her place on each page with a finger, memorizing entire passages at a time, but it wasn't enough. Not yet. She needed to understand what other elements were at play here.

Rhaella studied until she had committed the information to such perfect memory that she could have recited the contents of each page with her eyes closed.

Perhaps it was the amount of focus this task took that distracted her from hearing the heavy boots coming her way, but they startled her on arrival nonetheless. When a figure stopped in front of her table, she tensed in anticipation and looked up.

Virgil Midar stood stock-still in front of her, looking like he'd just seen a ghost.

After a painful silence, he said, "What are you doing here?"

Swallowing past the dryness, she croaked out, "What are *you* doing here?"

For a beat, she thought he looked crestfallen. Quickly, he pulled himself to stand up straighter, carrying himself the way any heir would around any Doctrina.

"I didn't know you joined the Order," he said. A trace of bitterness lingered in his voice despite his clear efforts to mask it.

Biting her lip, she debated how much truth to give him. She recalled the gentleness with which Virgil had bandaged her hands back at camp. How he'd done so because of the honesty that had always existed between the two of them. How the sweetness of that memory was now diluted by his rejection of her. How that still stung. Despite that hurt, however, she couldn't bring herself to come up with a believable excuse.

Quietly—blasphemously—she whispered, "My father made me."

He nodded, a hushed violence clouding his eyes. "Of course," he said, like it made all the sense in the world. "We all have our duties."

She knew that he was choked by duty the same way she was. And if she was able to, she would tell him as much. But she was prideful.

If Virgil didn't want her, she had no obligation to comfort him. Though, why he would require comforting was still unclear to her. Rhaella didn't know how many listening ears there were in the library—ears that could hide beyond her preternatural hearing—but she didn't dare risk it. Despite that fear, however, she spoke. Because silence and wondering would kill her quicker than any potion could.

"If you had ever bothered to answer my letter," she began, "you would know that I was on the ship before I could read yours."

He frowned. "What letter?"

"The one I sent not even a fortnight ago," she said sharply. "I wanted to know why."

Head tilted, he said, "Why *what?*"

Was he being cruel? "I wanted to know why you and your house rejected my father's offer. I thought you owed me at least that much."

"Rhaella, I need you to explain what offer it is that you're talking about."

She rubbed a hand across her forehead. He had to think her a fool if he was continuing on this way. "If you're going to make me say it aloud, then fine. I wanted to know why my father's proposal was unacceptable to you. Maybe I misread the situation, but I didn't think you would ignore me over that. I thought you better than that."

"Proposal...?" Virgil trailed off as he narrowed his eyes. "*Your* father never responded to *my* proposal. I never received anything from him, before or after."

Rhaella didn't know Virgil's tells well enough yet to know whether or not he was lying. There was no way to know for sure. But she thought he might be telling the truth in that moment. If she could trust the look in his eyes and the tension in his face, then she could at least guess at his intentions. Still, the uncertainty brought up feelings she didn't dare acknowledge.

"Swear it," she whispered. She knew him well enough by now to know that he was likely armed.

His hand went to the dagger at his hip and his eyes ghosted around the room. There were few people scattered around, but the room wasn't empty either. Finally, he asked, "Is there anywhere else we can talk?"

Rhaella glanced toward the shelves, raising a brow. Virgil nodded, motioning for her to walk ahead of him. She rose to her feet, and when she turned and walked deeper into the shelves, she felt Virgil's footsteps behind her more than she heard them. She traced her hands along the spines as they passed, grasping for even an ounce of comfort among the tomes. And when she glanced back, she saw Virgil running his fingers over the same ones she'd touched only moments previously.

Turning back to face forward, Rhaella asked, "What did your father send you all the way to the Silent Keep for?"

There was a drawn-out silence on his end, and, for a moment, she was convinced that Virgil wasn't going to answer her. It was a rare insecurity for her, and she wished desperately that it would go away, but even she couldn't strong-arm her own feelings into submission. And it was that very introspection that cost her enough awareness for Virgil to surprise her… *again*. He kept doing that, she thought to herself. But even still, she found it not altogether unpleasant when she felt his fingertips grasp the end of her now-shortened braid, and tug just the slightest bit.

He removed his hand almost immediately—almost as though he hadn't meant to do such a thing—and she felt colder at the loss of contact.

"I didn't expect you to cut your hair." His voice was full of gravel as he spoke.

A chill traveled all the way down her spine. "That wasn't my choice, either."

"You seem to have few of those lately." His tone was much darker this time.

"You'd be surprised," she said, tossing a sad smile over her shoulder.

He shook his head. "I had to present myself as the heir to the Order.

I would've continued putting it off, but I pissed off my father, and so he sent me here as punishment."

Rhaella huffed a laugh. By now, they had made it to the furthest row of shelves, well away from the other Progenies and Superiors milling about the library. There wasn't even a window down this way, and they were encased in shadow.

Rhaella turned to face Virgil, struck by how close he was. How it would only take a step or two forward to press their bodies flush. Slowly, he unsheathed his dagger and held it above the skin of his palm.

Meeting her eyes, he asked, "What do you want me to swear?"

She lifted her chin, forcing herself to stay strong. "That you never received word from my father offering my hand in marriage, and you never sent a rejection."

"I'll cut off a pound of flesh if that'll make you believe me," he said, digging the blade into his skin.

"You don't have to go that far," she said. "I believe you."

He handed her the blade. "Your turn. Swear that, to your knowledge, you never received my request for the opportunity to court you."

Without hesitation, Rhaella sliced open her palm. When she reached out her bloodied hand for his, he shook it firmly. Which left them staring at each other, hands slick with one another's blood. All that was left was the horrible truth that hung in the air between them.

"Well, that's out then. What do we do now?"

"I only just got here," she said helplessly. "I can't just leave."

"Doesn't it bother you that one or both of our fathers lied to us?"

"It does," she said, leaning her head against a shelf. "I usually catch my father when he lies, but I was so hurt by the idea that you would…"

"Reject you?" He finished. "Not a chance."

"I'm sorry," she whispered.

"I'm not blaming you," he said, and the gentleness in his tone nearly broke her. Then, after some consideration, he added, "You look tired."

"I *am* tired," she replied, helpless to quell the urge to tell him too much.

Virgil spoke what sounded like a curse, only the words were

something Rhaella could not understand. She frowned, tilting her head. She was passable in several languages, but only fluent in Vessial and the common tongue. Whatever Virgil had said was from some language she hadn't come across before.

He must have seen the confusion on her face, though, and realized that she couldn't understand him. He shook his head as he loosed a disbelieving laugh.

"I thought you'd have known that, too," he muttered, practically to himself. "But then I suppose the Hawk can't see everything at once."

She tried to ask what he meant, but a yawn forced its way out instead. Covering her mouth with her arm, she let it out, feeling the weight of this day and these weeks weighing her down. When she composed herself again, she found Virgil studying her intently.

Deflated, he asked, "Where did your wings go, little bird?"

Heat threatened to crawl up her throat and force its way out in the form of violent tears, and even the thought mortified her. Instead, she made a point to remain silent.

"These are not the circumstances under which I wanted to see you again," Virgil said.

"What would your preferred circumstances have been?" Rhaella tilted her face up to stare into his eyes. It wouldn't take much to close the distance at this rate.

His eyes searched her face, and she took no small pleasure in the way they lingered on her mouth. She parted her lips slightly, asking him. Begging him.

When he took a step back and blinked back the warmth in his eyes, she told herself he was simply doing the noble thing. "Nothing I can tell you now."

She nodded her head. She understood. *Of course* she understood.

"I said I'd bring back a book on gold for my uncle," he said, half-apologetic.

"Gold," she muttered, calling the layout of the library to mind. "There's a few down this way."

Virgil followed her through another set of shelves until they reached the section they were looking for. There were only four or five tomes on gold, and he read the first few pages of each before deciding which to take. Rhaella waited patiently beside him, reading what she could see over his arm.

"I'd better be going now," he murmured.

"I'll write when I can," she said, half a question. There was only room for halves between them now.

Through half-shut eyes that drank her face in greedily, he said, "Please do."

Virgil sped out of the library with no more than a parting bow, but Rhaella didn't miss the measured breaths he took before leaving. The discomfort he seemed to be in. If it was anything like the discomfort she felt now, she empathized.

She considered returning to her room and easing the discomfort with her hand and a little imagination, but those cursed bells rang again and her time was no longer her own. It was time for her next class.

Before she could even enter the potions classroom, Rhaella heard coughing and retching from inside. Cautiously, she poked her head inside and saw groups of students clustered around tiny cauldrons that emitted varying shades of smoke.

The Mother Superior turned her head. Sharply, she said, "You're late."

Rhaella bowed slightly. "Apologies, Mother Superior."

She pointed toward one of the long tables. "Join that group."

Her allotted group had already begun mixing ingredients. Rhaella sidled up to the table and began handing herbs to the person holding a ladle in the cauldron as they called out for them. He was adding too much cardamom, but no one was correcting him, and so Rhaella didn't either. It stank from the mix of herbs that did not blend together, and the smoke was turning an unfortunate shade of greenish-gray. When the Progeny held out a spoonful for someone to taste, no one volunteered.

Reluctantly, Rhaella held her hand out to take the ladle from the boy. Bringing it to her lips, she took a deep breath in. The liquid rushed into her mouth, and the touch of it sent a fiery tingle across her skin. Immediately, she began to feel dizzy from the rush of aroma.

She put the ladle back in the cauldron, assuring her classmate that it tasted right, but there was too high a percentage of each ingredient. Unwittingly, he had created a batch that was doubly effective to what they were given every morning. That wasn't what concerned Rhaella, though.

The fact that it took this high of a dosage to feel the effects could only mean one thing.

Her tolerance was higher than the Doctrinas had anticipated.

Rhaella didn't think she had a high tolerance for just about any substance. A few goblets of wine gave her a splitting headache the next morning. One too many hits of pipe weed rendered her sluggish. She didn't dare bother with the more experimental drugs sometimes offered to her at taverns and dance halls because she knew that to do so would be to invite trouble into her life. So for her to be nearly immune to a few specific mixes of spices and herbs was nonsensical.

And yet.

The following morning, when she received her morning inspection, she took a few sips from the first of several potions—enough that it should've had an effect—before spilling the rest on herself. When the irritated Mother Superior gave her another dose, Rhaella downed it without hesitation.

The extra potion settled in her stomach and set a fire in her body. Just as she expected, her senses pulsated with renewed vigor. Her ears popped and the sounds of the room suddenly became crisper. She saw the Mother Superior before her with a fiercer sharpness than she had previously, and her hands shook—overwhelmed by the texture of the fabric touching her body.

She downed the rest of the potions as directed, feeling nothing from the rest of them. She had learned enough for one day.

Instinct pushed Rhaella to confront the Superiors about this revelation, but quieter suspicion pushed her to keep the information to herself. On one hand, if Rhaella informed the Order that she had built a tolerance to their potions, they'd be able to assist her in finding the correct dosage. On the other hand, however, correct dosages would mean that her skin would turn wan, and she would be just as sick as her peers had been this whole time. Not to mention the fact that they would alter the functioning of her brain irrevocably.

The correct dosages of these potions would change her in a way that could never be undone. And Rhaella was not too proud to admit that the notion of such a thing stuck a cord of fear in her heart.

No, she told herself. *She would continue to go without.*

Rhaella started showing up late to potions class regularly after that. Not so late that she'd be reprimanded in any serious way, like being put on an extra chore rotation, but late enough that she missed the context given at the beginning of class. She started asking foolish questions on purpose. She mismatched herbs in her pairings and misidentified them when quizzed.

She maintained this act for about a week or so, just long enough to catch the attention of the Mother Superior. So when Rhaella came to her, near tears, asking for any spare herbs so she might practice on her own and catch up on the work she'd fallen behind on, the Mother Superior was sympathetic and handed her a bundle of herbs without a question.

It took a few tries to pinpoint exactly what her tolerance was to the potions, but once she had figured that part out, she could begin the real work. Making herself immune to these particular brews was going to take time, of which she had plenty. She only hoped her stomach was willing to put up with the task. Mithridatism was such a delicate practice, after all.

The first few days, she vomited endlessly. The aftertaste had her skipping meals and holing up in her bed any time she wasn't in class. It didn't look suspicious to the Superiors, though, if everyone else was doing the same. The following days were easier, but not by much. She only felt like vomiting immediately after taking her allotted dosage.

After a full week of slowly increasing her tolerance, Rhaella allowed herself a real meal—her first since she'd started this process. She got the food down easily enough, and was able to make conversation with the peers she'd struck up a friendship with. And though they certainly thought themselves friends, Rhaella couldn't bring herself to care about any of them in any real capacity. Cruel as that might sound, she knew it was better to appear friendly and approachable to her Superiors.

It was only after she dragged herself out of bed and to the washroom hours after dinner had passed that the sickness returned. There, hunched over the edge of the chamberpot and sticky with sweat, Rhaella allowed herself to start crying for the first time. If she were home, she wouldn't have to do any of this. She didn't want to anymore. She was so very tired.

Spitting out the nauseating phlegm, she took a few steadying breaths.

Rising to her feet, she went to wash her hands and face. A mirror was above the washbowl, showing her just how ghastly she looked. And beneath the sadness and exhaustion, there was the feeling she never allowed to the surface.

Rage.

Hunched over the washbowl, she continued breathing herself back into some semblance of calm. It didn't work. That humiliating vulnerability was still written all over her face, and she couldn't stand the look of it. A few rogue tears slipped down her cheeks, mocking her.

"Ŭ afnaw swa zyisha," she said to her reflection. "You are a *hawk.*"

Her reflection stared back at her, full of tears and mucus and disgustingly raw emotion. Breathing and encouragement did nothing to dwindle the amount of things that had come brimming to the surface that night—nausea or otherwise. But she had reached her maximum capacity for processing things that day.

She went back to bed.

CHAPTER THIRTEEN

"May the dead lie where the future leads."
—*Lucerian Proverb*

22 Lightpel, in the Benevolent year 112 A.E.

From the moment he saw the lackluster spread at breakfast, Asriel should have known to stay in bed that morning. The lemon tarts were too sour and his coffee was too milky and nothing was quite right. If things could go his way, he'd want everyone else to leave the Palace so he could have some goddamn peace. Another voice whispered that that would be more than he deserved, but he was happy to ignore it. He was content to pace the halls, ducking into random doorways whenever someone threatened to pass by. Barrett was several paces behind, not close enough to talk to. Just as well, he thought. He didn't feel like talking anyway.

On his first sweep through the Palace, Asriel passed the entrances to each wing, debating where to stop first. On his second lap, and after a lot of consideration, he settled on spending the early hours of the day in the Redspire wing. It was an easy way to pass time, considering the main attraction was a museum, and he didn't feel up to much more than standing and staring at things.

On the walls, far above where he could crane his neck to see, paintings were hung frame to frame. There were all sorts of styles and techniques, and he challenged himself to identify each of them. A quick look into the brochure he kept in-hand informed him whether he was correct or not, and Asriel was pleased to find that he got most of them right. Art, at least, was easy for him to memorize.

There was a labyrinth of statues around the floor. In every direction,

171

there were life-size figures of the historical greats of Adristan, some of them Asriel's own ancestors. He searched for his own features among the stone, some hint of detail that would show him where his face deviated from his father's and changed into his mother's.

Asriel's mother had light brown hair and soft features. A complete departure from the white-blonde and sharp angles of the Veservus line. Any further details, and Asriel's father shut off faster than was reasonable. He didn't get *choked up* talking about his late wife, per se, but there was a sadness that overtook him when he brought the subject up that never existed there otherwise. When it came to Lady Adria of House Erestine, he was rendered helpless.

Asriel wanted to find pieces of her where he could. Was she assertive and resilient, making her an excellent match for his father? Or was she more like her son; laid-back and unconcerned with things like deadlines and scoldings?

The sculptures didn't reveal his family's secrets to him, and neither did the paintings.

Asriel left the museum, and he couldn't help but notice that the halls were unusually crowded for this time of day. He noticed colors and faces from each of the houses in the mob, but there was a notable excess of Midar soldiers milling about as well. Asriel hadn't heard whether or not the Prince had arrived at the Palace, but the further he walked, the more certain he was that there was at least *some* manner of Midar noble in their midst—even if it wasn't Prince Virgil himself.

He was about to turn a corner when his ears tingled and he *froze*. Their father had spent an excessive amount of time dedicated to training that instinct in both of his children. It was the very same instinct that told them there was an important conversation happening nearby. One that he would probably be interested in making himself privy to.

Sparing a cautious glance around the corner, Asriel found two more Midar soldiers talking and laughing, but their words were still too muddled for him to make them out. So he closed his eyes and loosed a breath, attempting to clear his thoughts. And when he opened his eyes, the voices of the soldiers sounded clearer. Magnified, almost. As if they were projecting.

"...and after we leave here, Princess Mila wants to stop on Sandorne to take in the art."

"There's good wine on Sandorne. At the very least, we'll have a good time."

"We certainly will. And there will be plenty for the Princess to do. I'm just relieved that Virgil didn't decide to join us."

"I feel sorry for him. He seems downright *heartbroken*."

"Wouldn't you be? If you found the woman you'd chosen to be your future bride had taken a vow of chastity, I think you'd also be upset." The soldier huffed a humorless laugh. "And get this. According to him, she looked *miserable*. It'd be one thing if she was happy with it, but who'd be happy joining the Dux?"

Asriel stiffened. They couldn't be talking about...

He considered the ramifications of his sister's unhappiness with the Dux. She couldn't be expected to get through her training with a smile on her face, but surely she shouldn't be miserable either. None of the Doctrinas he'd encountered ever looked particularly *happy*. Though they never seemed to show any discernible emotion either. They had always possessed a serene neutrality, as was required in their code of conduct. An overly excited Doctrina was good to no one.

But then again, a depressed one was a nonstarter.

With a fierce curdling in his gut, Asriel turned in search of another route to the kitchens. He'd heard enough gossip from foot soldiers for one day. They knew nothing of the intricacies of politics, and were likely parroting misquotes from their own superiors. Virgil knew nothing of Rhaella, Asriel decided. Nothing that mattered, anyway.

"What did you hear?" Barrett asked, matching his pace.

"Nothing of note," Asriel snapped.

He told himself that he'd done them both a favor, actually. Rhaella got to expand her powers, and he got an edge on the rest of the future Lordlings. Asriel had always taken care of Rhaella when he could. He had always tried to bring her into meetings she had no access to, he tried to defend her to the nobles and sneering Lords, and he had always worked to give her brilliant opinions a place in his proceedings. Rhaella *knew* this. Just like she *had* to know that he would continue to do as much once he was High Lord and she was his Doctrina.

Perhaps reassurance was what she required. He could write her, but he didn't want to overplay his hand. His sister did poorly when spoiled with compliments; she writhed beneath them as if they were a damp blanket she couldn't wait to be rid of. Praise did not become her when she had full confidence in her own abilities.

Storming all the way to the library, Asriel stalked through the shelves with a vengeance. Determination set his jaw. Failure would not be his today. Barrett kept pace beside him, tracing his hand along the shelves. Asriel's fingers tapped along the spine of each book, listening for a hollow-sounding resonance. They combed through each shelf, tapping and tapping.

At last, the tap of his finger echoed, sounding hollow and almost dull.

As he pulled the book from the shelf, Asriel reached around and felt around for the lock he knew was there. At last, he felt the texture he had been searching for. The metal had been fashioned into a unique shape, and he now knew it by touch alone. Fumbling for the key, Asriel glanced around only once before shoving it into the lock. With a soft *click*, the lock gave way, and he smiled.

A piece of the shelf gave way first, swinging toward them. Asriel slipped through the small doorway that opened before him. Barrett followed, quickly shutting it behind them. And the hidden room was so dark that even his preternatural sight couldn't quite make out the shapes of things.

"Barrett," Asriel said in a hushed voice. "Light some candles, would you?"

A few moments—and a couple of match-strikes later—there was light in the tiny library. It was more of a grand office than a true library, but the deep-set shelves lined three of the four walls, giving it the feel of a library nonetheless. In between two of the walls, in the deepest corner of the room, there was an empty section of stone that looked more weathered than the rest. There were a few taller scrolls leaned against it, tied with string to keep them closed.

A desk sat littered with papers. There were half-melted candles, gold watches, and ceramic bowls littering its surface in an almost-frenzied fashion. There was a creaky chair sitting behind the desk that looked like it hadn't been sat in in a long while. Asriel whistled as he took a seat and began sorting through the mess atop the desk.

His father had left the place in utter disarray.

He pointed to a sconce. "Bring that lantern here, please."

Barrett obeyed, bringing it closer to shine more light on the desk. Asriel stacked the bowls on top of each other before placing the candles inside, and piled all of the papers together neatly. Then, once he had an orderly stack, his eyes glossed over the words on every page. He wasn't really reading, so much as he was sensing what each one said. As he worked his way through the pile, discarding page after page, he realized that there was absolutely no structure to this mess. It was entirely unorganized and familiarly chaotic.

As he continued to read, Asriel ran his hands over the surface of the desk. It was shabbily crafted and entirely unlike any of the furniture he had seen both here and in his rooms back at Briarhall. When he pulled open one of the drawers, the bottom of it rattled, as did everything inside. Asriel lifted the pile of papers out, expecting to find that a key or trinket was the culprit, but there was nothing he could see that would have made the noise. And yet, when he slammed the drawer shut with his boot, that rattle mocked him yet again.

His ears tingled again.

Slowly, Asriel reopened the drawer and pressed his hand against the bottom. And when he found that it wobbled beneath his touch, he almost couldn't contain his pleasure. For once, he had solved something on his *own*. Without the help of his father or his sister. A false bottom was exciting. It meant that there was something worth hiding in there.

"Help me with this," he said, glancing up at Barrett.

Barrett set the lantern down on the desk, minding the piles of old paper that were sure to catch fire if brought too close to the flame. Asriel and Barrett each stuck one hand in the drawer, tugging upwards, until they lifted the heavy sheet of wood out of the way. It landed on the floor with a clatter.

Beneath that false bottom of the creaky drawer, another pile of haphazardly organized papers blinked up at him.

Despite the victory, Asriel's happiness dimmed. He felt as though he'd gone searching in quest of some foreign treasure. Instead, reality greeted him with a *chore*. Now, rather than magically solving all of his problems, these papers faced Asriel with more to sort through than he had bargained for.

"What fun," Asriel said, hoisting them into his hands. "With any luck, these are my father's health records. Or, perhaps it's his diary! One can only *hope* for such entertainment in such a dull study."

But when he held the page up to the light, he saw that it was a certificate decorated with the sigil of the Dux Doctrina. The edges of it had curdled and turned brown as if it had been in proximity to extreme heat. The ink had faded some, but not so much that Asriel couldn't make it out.

"What is it?" Barrett asked, picking up the lantern once more.

"It's a record of my father receiving his Doctrina," Asriel said, looking up in disbelief. "And it's not Dogan."

Barrett shrugged. "So?"

"He never mentioned having a Doctrina aside from Dogan. He's always said that Dogan has served him for over two decades. As long as he's been High Lord. If Dogan isn't the only Doctrina to have served House Veservus in his lifetime, my father completely omitted that fact."

"Well, *also* according to your father," Barrett pointed out, "High Lords often start off by inheriting the Doctrinas from their predecessors before choosing their own. It was probably the Doctrina assigned to your grandsire."

"It's not," Asriel said, shaking his head. "Grandfather's Doctrina was an old man like him. This person was young, if I'm counting the years off correctly."

"Is it anything to worry about? Does it really matter?"

"It probably doesn't mean anything, but…" Asriel shook his head. "I don't know why he'd make it sound like Dogan's been his one and only Doctrina. If nothing else, it's another lie from him. Another misdirection." Asriel paused, taking a moment to decide whether or not he wanted to reveal this specific truth to Barrett. This *vulnerability*. "Why does he continually refuse to tell me things?"

"He's going to tell you eventually," Barrett reassured him. "Once he sees how well you're doing here, he's going to bring you in on his plans, but you'd do well to remember that the High Lord of the house of secrets has never offered information freely. And, someday, you'll likely have to hold the same number of secrets, no matter how much you may wish to let someone in on them."

Asriel considered the map of family trees he'd found in the tent. The markings that could have meant anything. He opened his mouth to respond, but there was a *thump* that drew both his and Barrett's attention. They froze, waiting for it to happen again, hoping to discern where the sound was coming from. When there was another *thump*—one that sent a flurry of dust raining down from the ceiling—Barrett moved into action. He drew his sword and ran for the door.

"Don't open that," Asriel said. "It's not coming from there."

"Where else would it be coming from—"

Thump.

Following his ears, which were practically singing, Asriel stared with wide eyes at the corner of the room. The scrolls that were standing against it had fallen over, and a few of them even rolled slightly away. Asriel dared a step forward, only to be stopped by Barrett, who put an arm in front of his chest.

"Let me," his guard said, eyes on the wall.

The two of them continued forward, Barrett leading, until they were within striking distance of the wall. Barrett turned his sword so that the pommel knocked against the stone. It was hollow-sounding. Different, somehow, than the average wall. It sounded a lot like the false door in the library they had passed through before this one.

Barrett said, "This must lead somewhere. I think it's a door that was sealed up."

"Or maybe it blends in," Asriel said, already springing into motion. "We need clay. Search the drawers, the shelves, wherever."

A hectic search followed, and the two of them made a larger mess than the one they'd walked into. But sure enough, they found a jar of clay in one of the desk drawers. Asriel muttered to himself, scanning the shelves until he found a book with the information he'd need.

"I don't have the damned symbols memorized," he muttered, handing the book to Barrett. "Hold it open."

Copying the image he saw in the text, Asriel scooped clay with his fingers and drew on the wall. As he'd suspected, the wall seemed to shudder once before caving in on itself in the shape of a rounded door. It slid behind the wall, leaving the gaping mouth of a doorway open to them.

Asriel looked at Barrett, who was already looking at him.

"Should we go inside?"

Barrett shut the book and set it on the floor. He held his sword aloft, soft determination on his face. He shrugged blithely. "I have to follow you if you go."

"You're honorable," Asriel said drily. "Let's go."

The doorway swallowed them whole, and they went into impossible darkness. It was damp inside. The cavernous space didn't take the shape of a stairwell until Barrett nearly tripped down the steps, and it was only when Asriel knotted a fist into the back of his shirt that he stopped falling.

"How far down do you wager this goes?" Barrett asked, carefully holding up the lantern.

"Well," Asriel said. "The Palace is the only part of the island still in use. We're so high on the land that it could go all the way down until sea level. Lower, even."

"I don't want to go underwater," Barrett said, fear trickling into the edges of his voice.

"If I think we get that deep, we'll turn around," Asriel said, turning to look at his guard. "I promise."

The stairs got wider the lower they went, and eventually Asriel and Barrett were able to walk side by side without brushing against each other. Asriel kept his shoulder pressed against Barrett's because Barrett had the light. As advanced as Asriel's eyesight was, he still needed a moment to adjust to the pitch-blackness.

Finally, they reached a landing with openings in every direction that appeared to lead somewhere deeper inside the island. Some of the archways were round, with words and symbols carved at their apex. Some of them were square, and their corners were ornate in a rugged sort of way. Even in the dark, Asriel could see that some of the openings led to hallways, and some to more stairwells that went even further down.

As he looked around, he noticed that the walls were mainly tightly-packed earth. And it wasn't just the doorways that had writing above them.

On every bit of empty space, there were carvings along the wall. Peering closer, they were names, titles, family lines…

"I know where we are," Asriel breathed. "These are the catacombs."

"I gathered that much," Barrett said, walking the lantern to each opening. "What I want to know is why your father's guarded library has a secret entrance to them. I thought every house had access from the Palace."

"We do," Asriel said. "There's a door in our suite, and there's one in the regular library, and they both lead to our family tombs. We also have access to the servant tunnels that are sealed to the rest of the houses, but I haven't ventured that far yet. As far as I know, we're the only ones who have access to them," he paused, pacing as he explained the setup to Barrett. "The study is in the middle, with easy access to both of them, but those tunnels don't lead to the catacombs. I don't know where the other entrances are, or where they may lead, but I have never found access to them through those doors."

"From what I can see," Barrett said, "most of these are long hallways that lead elsewhere. But this one here is just a room. There's a wall just over there, see?"

He pointed to the doorway to the immediate right of the landing which led to a shallow room, which was only about the size of a very large closet. Asriel stuck his head inside, finding it bare of any furniture. Relieved that he hadn't stumbled upon a casket, Asriel stepped confidently inside. As he ran his hands along the walls, he found more dense earth mixed in with some concrete bricks.

"Maybe they closed off the rest of this tunnel," he mused. "Or maybe it's my father's future tomb."

Suddenly, he hissed, drawing his hand away from the wall.

"What happened?" Barrett asked.

"Something cut my finger," Asriel said, holding it up. It was bleeding.

"Gods," Barrett said, setting the lantern down. He approached with a handkerchief. "You need to be swaddled like an infant. What on earth could have cut you?"

Asriel glanced at the wall, expecting to see jagged rocks or roots of long-dead trees sticking out. But now that his vampiric eyes had adjusted to the dark, he could make out flashes of white and cream among the earthy brown. Reaching between the bricks, his fingers grasped onto a piece of white and tugged. It came away freely, revealing itself to be a scrap of parchment.

Asriel dusted off the worst of the dirt and read, finding only uninteresting collections of expenses related to the house. Whatever his father was hiding, he would have to dig deeper to uncover it. His arm was deep in the wall now, and dirt was caked into the sleeve of his blouse all the way up to the bicep. Every time he pulled out an unimportant, dirt-covered document, he thrust it at Barrett for safe-keeping.

Finally, once he was dug in up to his shoulder, Asriel's fingers graced the corner of a page. This one felt different, somehow. It was crinkled and soggy. He yanked it out of the wall with enough force to send him stumbling back a few steps, and he began to read it. Asriel looked over the paper with ghostly wonder.

At some point in the past, it had been rolled into a tube, and the edges now forever-curled in toward each other. Asriel struggled to keep it flat enough to read for a moment, but soon enough Barrett was at his side, offering a hand. When the roll was fully unfurled, it was nearly as long as Asriel's torso.

The parchment before him now was similar to the one from the tent, except for a few key differences. Instead of a list, it was a giant map of names with lines drawn to connect each of them. The various colors on the page were easily discernible, even in the dull light, and Asriel was enraptured. The light red lines drawn between spouses must have represented marriages. Blue most likely represented parent and child. Yellow likely stood for siblings, possibly cousins. And the pen markings above each name were written in that same Vessial shorthand for *Y, N*, and *M*.

"I need to trace this," he said.

Barrett raised one brow. "You brought supplies?"

Asriel patted his pocket, where a hunk of charcoal and thin sheets of paper waited. They crinkled against the pressure from his hand.

"Look at you, being prepared," Barrett teased. "Maybe our time at the Palace has done you some good after all."

"Make your jokes," he said. "But when I piece together what all this secrecy is for, you won't be laughing. Now, quickly," Asriel said, setting the page on the floor. He gathered stones from where they were strewn around the floor, and he set them atop the corners to keep the parchment flat. "If we hold a few pages together, I can copy an approximation of this."

It took nearly half of his charcoal stick—and several passes between his left and right hands—but soon enough Asriel had a copy of the map on six separate pages. Once he was finished, he rose to his feet and dusted off his hands as he surveyed his work.

"Let's see if there's anything else worth copying while I still have some charcoal."

"You're not usually like this," Barrett noted. "You're so... *motivated*."

"My father has so many layers of hidden documents," Asriel said, digging into the wall again. "Why do you think that is?"

"If I had to guess," Barrett said, "it would be because he's in charge of all of the sensitive information in the nation. That requires security."

"Yes, but why hide things from his son and heir? He gave me the key to that room, sure. But he didn't tell me about the door that leads down here or the room we're in now."

"And yet you found them. Perhaps he trusts you to figure out his secrets on your own."

"This means something, Barrett," Asriel insisted. "What if he *did* expect me to find all of these hidden rooms, but he planted unimportant documents at the forefront? If our positions were reversed, I would expect myself to give up after finding those."

Barrett paused, thinking. In the meantime, Asriel's fingers grasped onto yet another aged sheet of parchment. He yanked it out of the wall and it was covered in gunk, but mostly in one piece. This one, too, was a map. Only, this one was of the Palace.

Markings had been placed around the entirety of the building, and there were at least several dozen of them. There was a star over the Veservus suite, as well as the section of the library where Asriel knew there was a hidden door. And on the reverse side of the parchment, web-like lines criss-crossed over one another, pooling at certain points.

Grinning wickedly, Asriel looked at Barrett. "These are the rest of the hidden doors. It's a map to each of them. And, if I'm reading right, where they lead into the catacombs."

Barrett started to return the smile, but before he could respond, another *thump* sounded. It was the first since they'd descended the stairs. They watched each other for a moment, considering their options. Quickly, Asriel set the map on the ground and covered it with the few papers he had left. His wrist ached as he started copying, but he was moving quicker than he had before.

"I don't like this, Asriel."

"I just need a little more," he said. "It's not like we can even enter the catacombs through these other doors. We don't have access to them that easily. If that were the case, someone would have gotten into our suite by now. Even *we* needed clay to get in here. We're warded against each other. I just want to have this one thing. I want to have something none of the other heirs have."

"You have no way of knowing what they know or do not know," Barrett reasoned.

"If this was something the others knew about," Asriel said, "my father wouldn't have hidden it all the way down here."

"Fair enough," Barrett acquiesced. "So what about someone who knows all of the clay symbols? Wouldn't they have master access?"

Asriel sighed. "My father explained this to me before. Something about the priestesses setting protection spells across the whole Palace to avoid things like that. I don't really understand how their magic works."

"It's not all that complicated," Barrett said. "And it's not the priestesses that have magic. It's the race of elves the Aviatis family descend from. A lot of them just happen to be priestesses."

"I knew that," Asriel lied. "Why do you know so much about Aviatis priestesses, anyway?"

"A lot of their men join the guard," Barrett answered. "A lot of their genderless folk, too. If they don't want to serve their house by becoming monks, that is."

"Not many women leave the Sixth House?"

"From my understanding, they consider it a great honor to join the priesthood. Not many forsake the opportunity."

"So you met them while studying on Greenisle," Asriel said.

"While *training* on Greenisle, yes," he corrected. "We spent a lot of time in classrooms, but most of it was field training."

Asriel paused. "You don't talk about Greenisle much."

Barrett shot him a look. "You don't ask much."

And there it was. The crux of Asriel's problems. The answer had been there all along; he simply didn't have the foresight to ask the question. Barrett had already offered him a grand amount of vulnerability—if sharing their bodies could be considered as much—and yet Asriel knew so little about his experience being schooled across two different islands.

"I'm sorry," he said quietly. "That's thoughtless of me."

"You don't have to be sorry," Barrett said, and it sounded genuine. "You've got a lot of other, more important things to remember."

"Don't say that—" Asriel started, but he stopped short, holding up a hand. "Do you feel that?"

There, in the dirt room, the air around them was almost silent. But in the stillness, Asriel could hear the slightest sound running beneath their feet. It was almost tinny. The longer he thought about it, it was a vibration whose frequency was so high that Barrett likely couldn't even hear it. But it could certainly be *felt*. Already, the disruption had him feeling slightly dizzy.

Holding up the lantern, Barrett said, "Catacombs are tombs, aren't they?"

"Among other things, yes," Asriel said.

In a very small voice, his guard said, "What else is down here?"

That vibration sounded again. Asriel felt it before he heard it, and before Barrett noticed at all. Once it grew louder—and closer—neither of them could ignore it. They shared a frightened look that spoke to their agreement; it was time to leave.

Asriel shoved the map back in place, and Barrett placed all of the useless documents back where they were, or at least his closest approximation of it. After a brief moment, the vibrations turned into more of a rumbling, and Asriel found himself spotting the stairs. Readying himself to bolt up them, should the need arise. Before he could get very far, though, Barrett had grabbed Asriel's wrist and pulled him back inside, shoving him against the wall as he shielded Asriel's body with his own.

"What are you—"

Barrett shushed him fiercely, leaving no room for arguments. Asriel could see nothing aside from Barrett's armored arm blocking his view. His guard's body pressed him into the wall, and the packed-earth gave a little bit where his body dug in. Dirt now dusted his shoulders, leaving Asriel in desperate need of a clean shirt.

And then he heard it. The slithering. The sound of an underbelly dragging itself across the floor. Scales, clinking against the scattered stones on the ground. When he inhaled next, his breath was shaky. Barrett put his palm over Asriel's mouth to quiet him. Looking Asriel directly in the eyes, his guard silently beseeched him to hold his breath.

At last, the sound got closer before fading away as the thing picked a different tunnel to travel down. Barrett lowered his hand from Asriel's mouth but did not step back.

"Are you alright?"

Stiffly, Asriel nodded. "I want to go back upstairs."

"Hurry," Barrett urged. "This way."

They made it back to the landing at the bottom of the stairs before they heard the most horrible sound. It was a screeching so loud, so close by, that it echoed through the catacombs and shook the walls so hard that more dust rained down on them. Beneath their feet, rats scurried away from the sound.

"Up the stairs," Asriel said, hauling Barrett behind him. "Hold the wall. Let's go!"

Thank the gods they had left the library door open. Once they had thrown themselves inside, Asriel scrambled for the clay and drew the symbol that would shut and lock the door. Then, mindlessly, he picked up the fallen scrolls and set them against the wall just as they had been before.

As if in a daze, Asriel kept his eyes on the wall where the door was now hidden. "My father used to read us textbooks when we were little. In them, there was information about all the kinds of dragons that roam Adristan. There are the winged, four-legged ones, like Egorion. Those can be found all over. Then there are the two-legged winged ones called wyverns who live on Sandorne. Then, there are the beasts of Kingsgrave. The drakes, four-legged and wingless, who roam the island as their domain.

And then there are the wyrms, wingless and legless, who slither on their bellies wandering for food."

"And where do those live?" Barrett asked quietly.

Asriel swallowed dryly. "Beneath the Palace."

"Right," Barrett nodded. Then, "Can we get away from that door, please?"

"Gladly," Asriel said, lunging for the exit.

They emerged back into the library proper and Asriel locked the secret shelf-door behind him. There was no one else in the library; he'd started to notice that as a theme. There were rarely patrons in any of the Palace rooms that were open to the public. But then again, with such few guests at the moment, he supposed that everyone preferred to keep to themselves.

"I don't want to look at books for the rest of the evening," Asriel said, rubbing his eyes.

"Agreed," Barrett replied quickly.

Adrenaline coursed through his veins, refusing to allow his pulse to settle. Even with the war having passed, Asriel had never come so close to real danger. Men with blades were one thing, but a wyrm was an entirely different beast.

He'd found his father's secret library and *then some*, which should have made him proud. But at the moment, Asriel only felt fear. Maybe the rest would come later.

There was one advantage he had now, though. In Adristan, swords and brute force did not equate to power. Truthfully, in Adristan, knowledge was the real power. And Asriel now had knowledge that no other heir could make a claim to. Smiling to himself, Asriel let out a breathless chuckle. Who else knew the Palace as well as he did? Where the Many Rooms were shut to the rest of them, he now had a master key. And as Asriel searched inside himself, he determined that such information could be bought for the price of his pride. If the other heirs had equally-weighted secrets of their own to share, Asriel would be willing to part with this one. As long as it meant he would finally be taken seriously.

CHAPTER FOURTEEN

"Let no man, no war, and no kings stop us from dancing."
—*Proverb among the common people of Adristan*

23 Lightpel, in the Benevolent year 112 A.E.

The skies were stormy on the way back to Greenisle, and by the time the ship docked, Virgil was soaked to the bone. His clothes were a sopping mess. His hair was stuck to his face. By now, he should have been trembling with cold. Sickness should've been threatening him. But all he felt was a familiar, welcoming numbness.

He disembarked, but not before helping the crew haul their supplies into the covered safety of the port. Grunting, he refused offers of thanks and made his way up to the house. Stollas greeted him at the door, whining softly as he nuzzled Virgil's legs.

"I'm fine, boy," he said softly. "Just a little damp."

That was the understatement of the century, but Virgil held the truth within him as he discarded his wet boots in the entryway and stalked down the halls to find his father. As usual, court was in full swing. Nobles—both local and visiting—filled the hall with drinks in hand. There was a loud buzz of conversation hovering above the air, though it seemed to dull itself when Virgil entered the room. Heads turned in his direction to watch the heir charge through the hall, sopping wet with a wolf on his heels. But he paid them no mind, eyes narrowing in where his uncle stood at his father's side.

"A librarian is drying off the book you asked for," Virgil said flatly. "It got wet during the storm."

His uncle, in full Doctrina regalia, bowed his head in thanks. "I'll look for it in the library myself. Thank you, nephew."

Turning to his father, Virgil said, "We need to talk."

"Yes, we do," his father agreed. "But you've only just arrived after your vacation. Have a drink. Your cousins are around here somewhere."

"I was gone for two and a half weeks," Virgil insisted. "They can wait."

"Fine," his father said, rising to his feet. "We'll talk, and then you can come back and have a drink."

"You're in good spirits," Virgil noted, keeping pace with his father out of the hall. He ignored his uncle quietly trailing behind them. Stollas, however, did not; he bumped his head against Uncle Nicholas's leg, attempting to trip him.

His father huffed a laugh. "I always enjoy being at court."

Virgil whistled at Stollas, pointing down the hall toward the kennels. The wolf was smart enough to find his way back on his own, but with any luck the kennel master would be waiting for him anyway.

Once they were shut into a conference room, Virgil deflated against the wall. Sighing, he said, "My proposal isn't going to work out."

"Why's that?"

He dragged a palm down his face. "Because they sent her to the Dux Doctrina."

His uncle seemed to perk up at that. "Who?"

Virgil glared before saying, "Rhaella of House Veservus."

"Oh," his father said, waving a hand dismissively. "Had I known that's who you were proposing, I would have discouraged it from the start."

"You told me I could choose a bride," Virgil said darkly. "I chose her."

"And now you can't have her," his father finished, taking a seat at one of the mismatched chairs along the table. "What do you want me to do about it?"

"Is there any way to stop it?" Virgil faced his uncle then, desperate enough to seek out his advice. "She hasn't been there long. Can she leave before she takes her vows?"

"Progenies take their vows upon arrival," his uncle said solemnly. "She belongs to the Order now."

Virgil raked a hand through his hair. "What if she didn't choose to enter the Order? Isn't there some article in the laws preventing forced submission?"

"The Order takes great care with who they accept into their ranks," his uncle argued. "They would not have done so lightly. It would be a great offense to suggest she was forced, and we are in no state to initiate more conflict."

"She looks sick, and *miserable*, and—"

"The transition period is hard on Progenies," his uncle cut him off. "Even I was like that once. I was sick nearly every day for a full month. The body needs time to adjust to the Order's processes."

Virgil hung his head. "So it's over, then? There's nothing I can do?"

"That's actually what I wanted to bring to your attention," his father said. "I wanted to offer you something to sweeten our deal."

"How so?" Virgil didn't imagine anything could undo how his mood had soured.

"Once you choose a bride, I'll protect you from the priestesses and insist that the affair be taken care of quietly and without fuss," his father said. "You won't have to worry about them insisting on ceremony and tradition. All you have to do is find a bride, and the rest can be handled away from prying eyes."

It was a touching offer, and it was one Virgil would have jumped at if he had been granted permission to marry Rhaella. It was also more kindness than his father had extended to him in years. Some time ago, before Virgil had given in to his wildness and attempted to abdicate, his father was like this more frequently. Ferocity aside, there had always been a softness between the two of them. An acknowledgement that it was not easy to be a Midar, and a will to ease that difficulty. He'd irrevocably marred that good will with his insolence, so it warmed him to receive even an echo of that same kindness again. He had missed it more than he was willing to admit.

Regardless, knowing full well he was going to do everything he could to avoid such a marriage, Virgil stalled for time. "Thank you, Father."

Nodding, his father stood. "Let's return to the festivities."

"I need to dry off first," Virgil insisted, heading in the direction of his room.

"Do that," his father said, walking away. "I'll see you in the great hall."

Virgil's uncle hung back, staring at him with a knowing smile. When he quirked a brow in question, his uncle said, "I can keep you updated on how the Veservus girl fares."

"That won't be necessary," Virgil glowered, shouldering past his uncle.

The walk back to his room was, for once, unaccompanied by guards. He needed the silence, because if there was any sound at all, he thought he might've screamed just to be louder. Just to exert control over one small aspect of his uncomfortably large life.

If there was anything he hated, it was feeling small. Powerless. At every perceived avenue of control, there was a blockage that sent him stumbling. Could he take several more decades of this? Could he handle the pressure of not just his father, but an entire nation depending on him to make the right decisions? No matter how many times Virgil calculated the mental math, his father didn't quite seem to understand that the outcome was always a resounding no.

In the sanctity of his bedroom, he stripped down to his skin and pulled on dry clothes. These were much fancier clothes—far more suitable to be seen in. If he was good just long enough to have a few drinks, then he could unwind some. Perhaps pipe weed would be faster. Maybe he'd see if Bianca had any.

When he returned to the great hall, his cousins were waiting for him near the door with a fresh glass in hand. He accepted it with thanks before downing it in one gulp.

"Declan told us," Mila said, squeezing his arm. "We're so sorry, cousin."

"Don't pity me," he said, handing the empty glass off to a passing server. "It was bound to happen. I waited too long."

"You could still bed her," Bianca said, sipping her drink. "Should the opportunity present itself, I mean."

"Don't be crude," Virgil snapped, feeling himself turn red.

"What?" She shrugged. "You think *all* Doctrinas adhere to their vow of chastity? I highly doubt it."

"I can't ask her to break a sacred vow," he said. "According to my

189

uncle, that's the sort of thing that would get her punished."

"And what does our goody goody uncle know?" Bianca laughed. "Neither him nor your father were the troublemakers of the family."

"No, that's *your mother*," Virgil pointed out.

"Precisely," Bianca said with a wink. "Uncle Nicholas is just trying to save face for his precious Order. I wouldn't take anything he says too seriously."

Virgil grunted, crossing his arms as they surveyed the masses at court. There were a handful of Doctrinas present aside from Uncle Nicholas. They were visitors who tended to his uncle's needs so he wouldn't have to travel to the Silent Keep as often. They were all dressed in black, signifying their presence as practicing Doctrinas, though they weren't assigned to a High Lord and they saw out the will of their Superiors. Each of the visitors also sported different styling, showcasing the full range of what a Doctrina's dress might look like. Some of them had heavy headdresses covering their faces, while some of them stuck to the simplistic veils and fitted masks.

If anything, the wide range of their appearances made them more unsettling to look at as a group. If they held this much power without some sort of uniform like the major houses had adopted, Virgil couldn't imagine what it might take to maintain a united front.

The Doctrinas were drinking and mingling and laughing, appearing entirely normal apart from their dress. Once Rhaella was a practicing Doctrina, he might see her at court just like this and be able to talk and laugh and drink with her, too. They could write each other letters and maintain the friendship they'd only just started to build. It would take some relearning of where the boundaries in their relationship lie, but for her, Virgil could imagine the work might prove to be a worthy investment.

He would have to become content with the fact that they both knew they desired more than friendship, but it would be worth it just to keep each other in their respective lives. He hadn't been raised religious, or even spiritual, but he could at least accept that there was a larger plan for things that he was not privy to.

"Do you have any pipe weed?" The question came out blunt and clumsy on the tail of so many revelations at once, but Virgil didn't have the energy to mask his attitude as anything else.

Mila patted the boning of her corset, nodding jovially. "From the mainland."

He raised a brow. "Shall we take a walk around the grounds?"

"Please," the sisters said in unison, following Virgil out.

Both Declan and Eric followed them out as well, keeping a respectable distance while in view of the court, but catching up to them once they were outside.

The storm had tapered off, leaving only a humid chill in the air. Virgil took Mila's weed and pulled his pipe from his pocket. Receiving a match from Declan, he lit the pipe and inhaled deeply. The pipe was passed between the five of them, and after a few hits, Virgil let out a light chuckle.

"I love good pipe weed," he said dreamily.

"Gods, it's so hard to come by on this forsaken island," Eric moaned.

"It's the tariffs," Mila said. "Uncle Vincent won't lower them."

"I'll do it," Virgil said, blowing smoke toward the cloudy sky. "Just give me a few years."

"Now you're *excited* about Ascending," Bianca teased.

Eric clapped him on the back. "If lower tariffs on pipe weed is to be your first order of business, then you're already the best High Lord we've had in a generation."

"And how many High Lords have you lived through?" Declan said.

Frowning, Eric began counting off on his fingers before throwing Declan a crude gesture. They all laughed as they continued to pass the pipe back and forth. But somewhere in the distance, they heard yelling. Some paces away, toward the gates, a guard was sprinting toward them full-force, a frantic look on his face.

"Virgil!" His voice carried over the wind. "Virgil!"

Declan and Eric stepped to the front of their group, awaiting what their comrade had to say. The guard skidded to a stop in front of them, doubling over as he panted to catch his breath. "You've got to come to town. *Now.*"

"What's wrong?" Virgil stepped past his cousins and around his guards. "Tell me."

The guard gulped. "It's the fighting pits. They're out of control. A few people are hurt, beaten to bloody pulps. It's getting ugly."

"Take me there," he commanded. Turning to his cousins, he said, "Go back inside and keep my father busy."

"You're thoughtless if you think we're staying here," Bianca said, storming straight ahead.

Mila, however, hung back. "I'll stay. Don't worry, Virgil."

Eric took her arm. "I'll escort her. The rest of you, go."

Once Mila and Eric's silhouettes faded toward the house, the rest of the party took off running to the edge of the grounds. The land surrounding Castle Silverfort was nothing but an expanse of rocks and grass, not fertile enough to grow anything but not level enough for festivities either. Every step of the way, Virgil had to be mindful not to trip over any of the jagged rocks that threatened to topple him.

No gates or high walls bordered the Midar lands, and at the edge of the grounds, there was a watchtower to keep track of anyone who came or went from the house. High in the lookout, several guards milled about, tending to the firepit. At the base there were two guards who stood at full attention, their armor glinting in the moonlight. Virgil slowed his pace, and his guards and Bianca followed instinctually. He knew that the risk of these watchmen reporting back to their superiors was high, and he also knew that whatever they reported would eventually make its way to the ears of the Doctrina. He would need to tread carefully.

Coolly, Virgil acknowledged them with a brisk, "Evening."

"Evening," the watchmen replied. They bowed their heads respectfully to him and Bianca, and regarded their brothers-in-arms with nothing more than a quick nod.

Beyond the watchtower, there was even more untended land. The trodden path curved away from the house, leading down hill toward the main roads, and the watchtower fell out of view the further they walked. Now, confident that he and his party wouldn't be seen, they all began to run. Bianca's gown didn't slow her one bit, and she could outrun him even on her worst days. He felt an odd mix of pride at his cousin's abilities, and anxiety at the fear that this could go wrong at any second.

Past the barren lands behind Castle Silverfort, there was a neighborhood called Id Rawkshe. It housed many of the nobility who resided on Greenisle, and it had managed to maintain its regal appearance throughout the war, despite the hit that so many other neighborhoods had taken during the struggle. The roads in Id Rawkshe were neatly paved before them, which made it easier to sprint through the streets. House Salgrat—the minor house where his mother hailed from—oversaw the happenings of the neighborhood and the cities beyond.

On a normal night, nobody and nothing passed through the streets that went unseen. Everyone of importance was at court tonight, though, which meant that there were no lanterns to light their way and there was no foot traffic to slow them down. It was equal parts nuisance and aid in their mission.

As they turned through alleys, lights began to sparkle in the distance. And as they crested the top of the hill, the heart of Zcïpïl—the capital city—unfurled before them, and they were all silent as they took it in. The city was full and glittering and *alive* with the thrum of happy people, and the sight of such liveliness even after the war made that same flicker of pride burn bright in his chest. On any other night, Virgil likely would've bartered with the street vendors offering smoked meats or fallen into bed with any number of the courtesans currently batting their lashes at him. Instead, he was full of buzzing nerves—and the pipeweed in his system wasn't helping matters either.

This was far from the first time he'd heard of the fighting pits getting rowdy, but it was most definitely the first time they'd called for his help to settle them.

"Pull up your hoods," Virgil said. "This is not a night we want to get recognized."

Sensation hit them from every side as they passed into the city proper. Buskers were gathered on street corners, playing music from weathered instruments. Young girls held hands, twirling each other around and squealing with laughter as their bare feet kicked up clouds of dirt. And people of all ages stared up at the stars—taking in the beauty of such a clear night sky on the heels of such unrest.

The roads still weren't paved in this part of the city, although Virgil had been campaigning to change that for years. But no matter how hard he campaigned for it, his father had yet to make it a priority. With the war looming, it had been set aside as a goal for a distant future. Even now that they were past the worst of the fighting, his father still hadn't allocated resources for the repairs because of the uprisings that threatened to draw them back into battle. But these people didn't seem to mind the dirt roads. They danced and strolled along the uneven, rocky ground the same way they would march down a finely cobblestoned path.

The deeper they went, the people grew sparse and the lanterns were few and far between. The quiet darkness of the city's underbelly welcomed them into its cool embrace. None of this was new territory for Virgil. His fists clenched as they turned into the alley that would take them to the tavern he used to frequent; it was crowded with folk looking for trouble. Luckily, they had the password for just that.

Yves, the soldier who had accompanied them, stepped up to an unsuspecting doorway and knocked three times. A slit near the top opened, and a pair of narrowed eyes blinked back at the four of them.

"I want to get my boots shined by Jameson," the soldier said.

The slit in the door slammed shut, and a series of locks clicking into place followed the sound. No longer just a pair of blinking eyes, the man behind the door was an equally displeased fellow. But he stepped aside to let them pass without argument. Virgil pulled his hood low when the man's eyes lingered on him for too long.

It was loud. There was jeering and shouts of fury and praise—the two sounds were nearly indistinguishable amidst the chaos. There were tables pushed against the edges of the room with rickety wooden chairs around them. A few patrons sat drinking ale and wine, and some even braved the food. The majority of the space, however, had been hollowed out to make room for the main attraction. The bowl-shaped fighting pit was full of dirt and dried blood, and there were three men facing off in the middle of it.

As they got closer, Virgil realized one of them was holding another's arms back while his partner beat the living piss out of him. The crowd hollered, tossing silver and bronze coins into the pit at their feet. It wasn't a fair fight, and that was exactly what these people craved, apparently.

"They're going to kill him," Bianca said. She took a step forward, but Virgil grabbed her shoulder, keeping her at his side. "We can't just watch!"

"We're not going to watch," Virgil said, voice low and dangerous.

He pointed to a door on the other side of the room. "Go find any fighters waiting back there and kick them out. Use any means necessary. Declan, Yves, watch the crowd."

"Gladly," Bianca said, cracking her knuckles.

Virgil removed his doublet, tossing the royal blue thing onto the ground. His shirt followed quickly after. He only wished he'd had the foresight to bandage his hands before running here. Patching up the cuts after was so tedious. Spitting on the floor, he scuffed his shoes to give them grip. Then, he stepped out of the shadows.

The crowd quieted as he hopped down into the pit. The fighters hadn't noticed him yet, but they had noticed the sudden hush that *had* fallen across the room. To the people among the fringes of the crowd, he likely appeared to be nobody. An oddly large man, maybe. Some poor soul looking to prove his worth. But they would realize their error soon enough.

One by one, each of the three fighters stopped and turned in his direction. The first one—in the middle of being beaten by the other two—paled at the prospect of a third person joining in his misery. Virgil shook his head slightly.

To the two, he said, "It looks like my friend is short a partner."

As he realized that Virgil was there as an ally, the beaten man went slack with relief. The men holding him widened their eyes, but they kept their grips on the poor man.

"Prince Virgil," one stammered out. "M-my Lord."

"Don't bother bowing," Virgil said. "I'm not fond of it."

The one who had been punching the victim asked, "What are you doing here?"

"What's it look like I'm doing?" Virgil opened his arms wide. "These are the fighting pits."

"I… I don't understand."

Virgil pointed at the man they were beating. "My friend here doesn't seem to be putting up much of a fight. You should let him go and fight someone more worthy of your combined talents."

Immediately, they let go of the man and shoved him away. He scrambled out of the fighting pits like it was his only chance, but not before bowing at the waist and stuttering out, "Thank you, my Lord. Thank you."

The room was utterly still after that. Virgil merely continued staring at the two men, who were now pale and shaking. Good. He had never been a fan of cocky men.

"So?" He gestured around the pit. "Shall we begin?"

Someone in the crowd began cheering, and it wasn't long before the others joined in. There was shouting—some of it unintelligible—and a rhythmic chant broke out before Virgil could make out what they were saying.

"Fight the heir! Fight the heir!"

One of the men shoved the other before pointing toward Virgil, clearly egging his friend on. They looked around the room, taking in all of the cheers from the crowd. Still, they seemed hesitant.

"You'll fight a man who can't even hit you back but I'm too strong a challenger?" Virgil sneered. "How *brave*."

One gulped. "We mean no disrespect—"

"It's quite disrespectful to deny the heir to your house the opportunity," Declan spoke up from where he sat on the upper rim of the pit—one leg casually dangling off the edge.

Whistles and hollering abounded. Virgil made a slow circle around the ring, looking up at the waiting audience around the edges of the room. Maybe some of the people here tonight had also been here five years ago, when *he* had been the main attraction. He wondered if they recalled witnessing his superior strength in action. If the fighters that had come along since were boring to them. They were entertained by filth and unfairness, and it disgusted him.

Drunk, incoherent yelling sounded from the opposite end of the pit. Several people were attempting to hold back a very persistent man who was now attempting to make his way into the pit. No matter how the crowd tried to slow him, it didn't work; he lowered himself in and shoved past the first two fighters.

"I'll fight the noble heir," he slurred. He spit at Virgil's feet, jeering. "If you can be called that."

Warning tickled at the back of Virgil's mind as he sized up the new competitor. Despite his slurred speech, he stood firmly on his feet. He was large—not quite as tall as Virgil, but still taller than the average man. And he was built. From the looks of things, he could've worked in the steel mines or the forges. Virgil visited those regularly, though. And he didn't recognize this man.

So he felt no remorse deflecting the first punch the man threw and hitting him square in the jaw.

Virgil kept a tight leash on his strength; he'd learned that lesson the hard way. Usually, he made it a point to channel his energy to every part of his body to siphon it somewhat. But now, he let go of a modicum of that control and let the energy flow straight into his fists. He made sure to keep a handle on how *much* power he let loose, however, lest he kill the man But he was not above teaching the man—and the rest of his jeering friends—a lesson.

The man fell back with a cry, blood spilling from his mouth. He stumbled without falling, catching himself in his drunken stupor. Virgil didn't let up though. He dealt out hit after hit, landing punches on the man's jaw, his shoulder, his gut.

When it became clear that the man was no match for Virgil, his friends started to jump in the pit. At first, there were only two of them. Then, two more joined, until Virgil was faced with five drunk, angry men. They tried to strike in a formation that was sloppy at best. It was a valiant effort, though, and Virgil held back for a moment to let them relish in the glory of their idiocy. They surrounded him on all sides, throwing out poorly-formed punches and kicks.

At last, Virgil grew annoyed. He let a little more of his power loose, and then he began taking the men down. Giving in to his darker desires. The ones he had kept buried since the last time he was in these pits. He let out a growl and reared back his arms. One by one, he dealt out stunning blows that sent the men to their knees until he was the only one left standing.

His knuckles were bleeding, and he was breathing a little heavier than before, but all he could think was how tedious that had been.

Looking up, the room had gone quiet once more. Stunned into silence at the sight of their heir as he knocked a horde of men unconscious. It should have been impossible. And for a normal man, it might have been.

Another burst of noise, and then Bianca was dragging three men out by their shirt collars as though they weighed nothing. They protested loudly, but she continued dragging them across the room until she reached the door that Declan held open. And once the fighters were thrown outside, she dusted off her hands and turned to her cousin.

Virgil made another circle around the ring, this one wider. The deep timbre of his voice echoed off the walls as he called out, "House Midar allows you to keep this fetid place open so long as you don't give us a headache. This," he said, holding up his bloodied knuckles, "is a headache. Don't let it happen again."

With that, he met Bianca, Declan, and Yves at the door and stormed out into the night. He realized far too late that he'd left his shirt and doublet inside, but it was of no consequence to him. They'd find another shirt from a vendor on the way home. All he wanted to do right now was bandage his hands.

"We need to start sending a few of our men there every night," Virgil said. "Keep a rotation of spies and soldiers in there and do *not* allow them to make themselves known. At the first sign of royalist sympathies, we swarm in and shut that shit down."

"Of course," Declan said.

"Are you okay?" Bianca asked, her voice a ghostly whisper.

Gruffly, Virgil replied, "Don't ask me that."

He was too exposed to go unnoticed as they made their way back through town. People began calling out to him, thanking him for his service and offering free meals and wares. All of it went ignored. There was only a loud ringing in Virgil's ears that he couldn't think past. A generous vendor offered him a shirt, and when he tried to refuse payment, Declan shoved triple the cost into the man's hands.

It wasn't until they were halfway up the road that Virgil's hands started shaking. Memories of his younger years—the damage he had caused in those very fighting pits—came to him in flashes. He rubbed an arm across his face, trying to dull the visions that flashed behind his eyelids. Part of him had hoped that fighting would quell the raging unease in his stomach, but it hadn't. Now, all he felt was disgust. Some of it for the onlookers who had let a defenseless man be beaten. The rest reserved for himself for resorting to violence to solve his problems.

Virgil scoffed. He really was a Midar at his core. They dealt in violence. When he was a small, sensitive boy, it was still acceptable for him to abhor it. It only became unacceptable once he had aged into his role as the heir and was old enough to let his bloodline down.

Declan led the pack as they approached the border of the house. The guards at their post tried to peek around him to see why Virgil was bloodied and cranky, but Declan blocked their view.

"Leave him be," Declan said. "Let us pass."

"Of course," they said, bowing as they went.

If Virgil made a spectacle of himself, he didn't quite care. He'd given the fighting pits a warning. If they didn't heed it, he had an excuse to return and make another example of another drunken, proud man. And, in turn, that would justify the inadequacy he felt toward himself. Maybe then, his father would take notice and name another heir. It was all he could hope for.

But even as he thought it, it felt like a futile hope. Not unlike the vast majority of his hopes nowadays.

CHAPTER FIFTEEN

"Thanks to the advanced hearing and sight in those with vampiric heritage, the founding Veservus family established themselves as a formidable beacon of knowledge. However, they commonly used these gifts for spying, as well."
—The High Lords of Adristan: A History, *by Gawain Redspire*

13 Midanae, in the Benevolent year 112 A.E.

Breakfast was always the most difficult meal of the day.

Rhaella's days were defined by stoic routine. She awoke, took her first dose of various poisons, received her examination, and drank down her next dose of potions. An hour of physical training followed. Sometimes before she ate, but most often after, she had a bath. She dressed herself and braided her choppy haircut into something passable. If she hadn't already, then she could eat her first meal of the day. Mixing with her mithridatism dose and her Dux potions made the food taste disgusting. It had taken days for her to be able to keep food down with a straight face. Those days were spent eating alone in her bedroom, with food she had smuggled out of the mess hall. The Superiors were still not satisfied with her weight.

But her efforts were paying off.

She'd taken notice immediately once the Superiors increased the dosage in the morning potions. The aroma of the potions themselves had given it away. But it was the effects they had on her peers that solidified her guess. The Progenies were changing; slowly, not all at once. As far as the ones she occasionally shared meals with, she could see that their eyes were changing color. The lower their tolerance, the more drastic the change. Edina, for example, only had to blink before her eyes shifted into a stark gray whenever they discussed advising; it was a chilling difference from her usual green. Rhaella wasn't too proud to admit that she mistakenly thought Dogan's eyes were a murky mix of blue and gray, and that was why she had never noticed the subtle change.

A few of her classmates had a different energy about them when they walked the halls. There was a smoothness that wasn't there before. An anticipatory speed with which they turned corners without running into anyone on the other side. They could sense one another better and from there, could adjust the way they moved around each other based on that. Ordinary, unremarkable people with little to no magical gifts were suddenly moving about the world with advanced senses and a broader lens. Things Rhaella could do naturally, and therefore hadn't been caught yet.

Yet.

Eventually, though, the Superiors were going to take notice that Rhaella's eyes remained icy blue whether or not she was accessing the logical side of her brain where the Dux resided. It was a smug sort of satisfaction to know that she had enough skill to make it this far without taking the potions to any effect. But she was unsure how much further natural talent would carry her. If she could just get the dosage right, perhaps the mithridatism could expose her to the right herbal mixture that would change her eye color without altering her brain.

Her mind was running through numbers, and she felt it as her eyes slightly glazed over while her body moved through the motions of eating breakfast. Distantly, she heard herself responding to the conversation the table was having. Her fingers itched to trace along the surface of the wooden table, drawing out figures as she saw them in her mind, but she kept still. The clarity of the images she could see in her mind, paired with her habit of drawing invisible words on surfaces, would invite conversations she did not have the energy for.

Rhaella's mind nagged at her to tune back in. To pay attention. She looked up to find Edina and Darius staring at her expectantly.

She let out a breathy laugh, tucking a strand of loose hair behind her ear. "I'm sorry, what was that?"

"I asked if you're ready for the trials to start," Darius said. "I know I'm not."

"Oh, those," Rhaella sighed. "As ready as I will be, I suppose."

The trials were expected to begin any day now. The Superiors wouldn't say exactly when. In fact, they offered the Progenies almost no information that could help them prepare. The history books were no help, either. Any listed text in the directory that might have been useful was locked away in the restricted section. When she was a curious child, Dogan had always remained tight-lipped about it when she asked. Though he *did* admit that the trials would be both physical and mental. Which was incredibly unhelpful in this moment.

"My father told me that we're going to have to make potions in front of all of the Superiors," Edina said. "Which I feel very ready to do."

"That doesn't sound too bad," Rhaella agreed. In fact, it sounded too *easy* compared to all they had endured so far in the name of training.

"How are your classes?" Darius continued.

"I heard from Asher that you've been slacking in potions class," Edina said, a tad too cheerful.

"I get caught up studying in the library," Rhaella answered flatly. "Bad habit."

Edina shook her head, pursed lips curving up into a cat-like smirk. "That could reflect poorly on your performance evaluation."

As if Rhaella was concerned about a thing like that. Matching Edina's energy, though, she tossed her braid over her shoulder and sat up a bit straighter, raising one quizzical brow.

"I've stayed after class to make up for the time I've missed. Mother Superior complimented my initiative, and she even let it slip that my performance evaluation was already being put together. She might have even hinted that she had only good things to say." Rhaella paused to let her words sink in. "She didn't tell you that when you spoke with her?"

Rhaella had had no such conversation with Mother Superior, but Edina didn't need to know that. What she needed to do was go after their instructor and hound her for details, ultimately making herself look a fool.

Edina frowned. "I haven't spoken with Mother Superior one on one. I didn't know that *any* of the Superiors were around for extra help."

"Have you tried asking?" Rhaella kept her expression carefully blank, just barely bordering on condescension.

Darius nodded in agreement. "I've spoken with a few of the Fathers Superior for help with my physical training. They're very helpful once you get to know them."

Edina looked horrified to discover that there were resources available to everyone that hadn't been handed directly to her. Haughtily, Rhaella thought Edina might be jealous that *Rhaella* had supposedly taken advantage of resources before she had.

"*Progenies*," a voice rang throughout the room.

The speaker wasn't present; that was clear from the tinny echo that followed the word. It was another trick of the magic derived from the potions. Vocal projection was an advanced skill, accomplished after years and years of drinking poison.

"*Gather in the auditorium. There will be an assembly beginning promptly in fifteen minutes. Full dress is required. No books, no supplies. Sit according to your room assignments. That is all.*"

Rhaella rolled her eyes, muttering, "As you say."

She gathered up her things and left her peers to change into her robes. There would be no time for a bath, but she hadn't pushed herself in the gym, so it was fine. Rushing back to her bedroom, she found a clean gray robe. Her hair was a mess but seven minutes had already passed and it would take another four to reach the auditorium. She hated looking at her hair. It was short and uneven and carelessly done. Nearly two months in the Order and it had grown half the length of her pointer finger. It wasn't enough.

The auditorium was shaped like a massive cone. It had a draft thanks to all of the high windows near the balcony seats, and the wood was rotting after years of use and no upkeep. Having no roommate and a corner bedroom, she went to sit in one of the furthest back rows, high above the rest where the draft was coming in. Other Progenies were still filling in the rows in front of her, and a table was set on the dais in the center where the room bottlenecked.

The air in the room shifted once the Reverend Mother entered. Their fifteen minute window had closed; anyone late would be reprimanded privately after this. Doors were shut and curtains were drawn over window panes, sending the room into murky darkness. One of the Fathers Superior conjured a ball of light between his hands and set it on the table, illuminating the faces seated there.

"Your trials begin now," Reverend Mother Locasta said, her voice slightly amplified by magic.

Gasps rang through the room. They knew it would be soon, but they had no idea it would be instantaneous. Rhaella sucked in a sharp breath, settling her nerves. It would be fine. She would be fine.

"The Progeny class will be split up into groups. These groups matter for our records only. We trust that you will hold onto your group number once assigned. If your group number is anything other than one, you will continue with your regular studies until you are told otherwise. For all the members of group one, report to the atrium."

They were called up to the dais in order of family names after that. Rhaella sank into her chair, getting comfortable for the long wait ahead. Every time a body approached the table of Superiors, they received a number and went out either door. She watched as her classmates went out the left door, sagging with relief, or the right door, tense with anticipation.

"Progeny Rhaella," they called.

Rhaella made her way down the stairs, restless and eager to go on with her day. There was a book she wanted to check out from the library and she had a pile of history homework to complete. If there was time after that, she wanted to hit something with her arrows. Hard.

She approached the dais, her shoes scraping softly against the steps. Reverend Mother Locasta gave her a once-over but said nothing. To her right, a Father Superior cleared his throat.

Quietly, he asked, "Family name?"

"Veservus," she supplied. She kept her voice low, lest any of her peers find out a noble was among them. An attentive classmate might have noticed, and yet she hadn't encountered one who was.

The Father Superior nodded. "Group one."

The floor dropped out from beneath her. On shaky legs, she started to step down from the dais, only remembering to nod and bow to the Superiors once she was three steps down. She exited to the right, following the rest of her peers toward the atrium.

The request that they all don full dress should have alerted her. Ritual and tradition were everyday occurrences, but the explicit reminder for what seemed like a routine assembly should have set off alarm bells in her head. She had either been careless or too hopeful, even after all this time. Neither made her feel better about herself.

Chiding herself, she redid her braid as she walked.

The right hand door opened onto a grassy field that stretched toward the edges of the Order's lands. A gate caged them in just before the tree line began again, and the forest felt dense and mysterious. There were no citizens from either Adristan or Steephelm that lived here. With a shiver, Rhaella thought the gates were meant to keep them in just as much as they were meant to keep whatever lay within out.

On the other side of the trees there was a cluster of small villages. They weren't under Adristan's jurisdiction, but the people there had been affected by the conflict all the same. Over the course of the past months, Rhaella had visited with groups of soldiers to gather supplies for the war effort, and as she thought about them now she wondered how they were faring. She wanted to know if their efforts at conservation had proven to be of any use at all. She also couldn't help but think that her brother should have at *least* participated in those efforts. But his lack of involvement wasn't out of the ordinary. If he was trapped in the Palace as their father had said, then it was likely he *couldn't* have had anything to do with them.

She pushed open the door to the atrium and felt a wave of memory wash over her. During the summer she'd spent with the Order, they had housed her here. The building stood four stories tall, and there were windows commanding every bit of space that wasn't a doorway or a completely-full library shelf. Some of the doors opened onto studies. Others to guest rooms. But so many more of them were filled to the brim with confidential documents.

Every single one of them was locked.

Balconies lined the edge of every floor, allowing anyone to peer at the whole of the place from every angle, and as she joined the crowd of Progenies lingering in the center of the first floor, Rhaella felt unsettled to know that her Superiors could be anywhere. All around her, they silently watched everything that happened, backlit by the blinding sun that streamed in through all the glass.

As if they had heard her thoughts, covers slammed over windows, similarly to how they had in the auditorium. Every door in front of them slammed shut except for one near the end of the long hall on the other side of the room. Through the dim light, the Progenies stared at each other. And as though they could all sense there was nowhere else to go but forward, they walked together.

When they were more than halfway down the hall, a Superior materialized out of nowhere. Realistically, they probably slipped out of one of the many doors that lined either side of the hall, but it was so sudden that several of the Progenies flinched. Small gasps sounded all around her. The Superior seemed to notice, and Rhaella watched the corner of her mouth twitch as she forced down a smile. She appeared not to be much older than the rest of them, which meant she hadn't been picked up by a High Lord yet.

"This way please," she said, turning. She pointed to various rooms as they passed. "You'll be sorted here."

The hall had become noticeably cramped, with all of them standing shoulder to shoulder, wall to wall. The crowd had to be larger than just her incoming class. Some might have been Brothers and Sisters Superior, retaking their trials to ascertain if they were still fit to be selected by a High Lord. But Doctrinas were needed for more than just service within the major houses; lesser houses received guidance from the Dux as well. Then, there were the needs of the Silent Keep. Their own system of checks and balances required untethered Doctrinas. Beyond that, the Keep needed cooks, accountants, record keepers, and so much more... And with their forces depleted by the war, the Doctrinas' numbers were well-below what they should have been.

As the Superior pointed, she called out names, sending Progenies into rooms. Rhaella followed the orders she had been given, finding a small room that was empty except for a bench against the far wall. She turned to look out of the door and found it already shut. The walls were so thick that even her ears couldn't pick up any sound from the other side.

Rhaella blew out a heavy breath. "Alright," she muttered to herself.

Crossing the room, she sat and folded her arms across her chest. Years ago, when she had spent her summers in their etiquette course, the Dux had housed them within the atrium. It hadn't been updated to match the changing fashions then either. It was still sparsely decorated and bare of any personality. But she hadn't been there to admire the scenery then, and she certainly wouldn't be doing so now. Once they called her out, which shouldn't be long from now, she would be free of this room.

She repeated that thought to herself for the entirety of the first hour.

By the second hour, she was restless and had taken to pacing the length. She studied every inch of the walls and learned their imperfections. She ran her hands along their surfaces, searching for hidden compartments or loose paneling. Hidden doors always made themselves known one way or another. She found none, likely thanks to the magic concealing them. Maybe if the potions had worked on her, she would be able to unlock such secrets.

That sent another wave of nerves through her. She had confidence in herself and her skillset. This, however, would be an opening for her superiors to notice that she hadn't been affected by the potions in the same way everyone else had. Even if they forced her to take a higher dose, she should be able to withstand quite a high solution. Certainly they would take notice of such a thing then.

By the third hour, she was reciting house histories aloud to keep her mind sharp. She started with the origin of the islands before moving to the killing of the tyrant king, then to the alliance of the eight stronghold houses and the forming of Adristan. She walked up and down the room, spouting facts to no one, trying desperately to calm her nerves.

Another half-hour passed and Rhaella pressed her ear against the door, listening for any hint that her turn was coming up soon. She let her eyes glaze over, sending all of her focus into her hearing. Faintly, she heard the slight rustling sound as bodies passed through the hallway. If she focused enough, she could almost sketch out the vision in her mind: A Superior roaming the halls, searching for the next Progeny to test.

Desperately, Rhaella hoped it would be her, and she stepped away from the door in anticipation. She hoped she looked occupied with her study of the tiling on the wall, lest one of the Superiors catch her in a moment of unreadiness.

Still, none came for her.

She'd resigned herself to the bench, nearly half-asleep from a combination of boredom and genuine exhaustion, when the door suddenly opened. A Superior stood on the other side of the threshold, expectant and eerily patient. Rhaella jumped to her feet, smoothing out her robes as she made her way toward the door. She followed the silent Superior out into the hall, and they passed a few doors before reaching the end of the hall. The door to Rhaella's right opened of its own volition, and she was ushered inside.

The Reverend Mother sat at a table in the center of the room alongside a few Superiors. Rhaella started to bow before righting herself into a curtsy.

"Sit here, girl," Reverend Mother Locasta said, gesturing towards the only empty chair.

Rhaella did as she was bid, sitting ramrod straight and folding her hands in her lap. The panel of her betters stared at her without offering instruction. She knew better than to question them; to speak before being spoken to. The staring continued wordlessly for what felt like many minutes. Rhaella kept her composure, fighting hard not to fidget or avoid their eyes.

Time passed, and then one of the Mothers Superior cleared her throat.

"Speak."

Unsure of what to say, Rhaella tilted her head. She searched for the right words, knowing there were certainly right and wrong answers. What would be the most logical thing to say when prompted? Everything that came to her seemed too obvious or too nonsensical for a trial. They wouldn't command her to speak without a concrete notion of what they wanted to hear from her.

She decided she was thinking too hard and said something that felt obvious, but was also plainly clear as something she needed to know and to say.

The Order's motto left her mouth in a steady flow. "We hold steady the hand that wields the reins."

There was no acknowledgement of correctness, no assurance that she had given them what they wanted. The Mother Superior merely continued on, her words brisk and her tone immovable.

"Feel."

Rhaella stared at the hands of the Superiors, noticing how each of their palms were pressed against the table. She mirrored the pose, her fingertips scratching against the rough wooden surface. Running her palms along the length of it, its texture and craftsmanship spoke to her.

"Speak."

Hesitantly, she said, "It's poplar, not from the forests of Segsiege. House Lancor did not build this."

"And who did?"

Rhaella continued running her hands along the table, feeling for clues. There wasn't a coat of varnish atop the wood. It also hadn't been sanded down correctly. "A hobbyist builder from the mainland."

By now, she noticed the Superior at the end of the table taking furious notes at every command. She wanted to stare, willing her eyes to latch onto what was being written, but the Mother Superior across the table continued to throw commands at her.

"Smell."

She sniffed the air, catching notes of rotting berries and cinnamon. Her lip curled, put off by the combination.

"Speak."

"Aged blackberry, maybe a few blueberries mixed in. Just past the safe period for consumption. Cinnamon, not fresh. Not aged, either."

"Look."

Now, she let her eyes wander the room. It was dark; only a few candles were lit around the perimeter of the room. A human would not be able to make out shapes in this murkiness unless they were drunk on the Dux potions. But Rhaella was not human. Not in any way that mattered. Her eyes adjusted, and she could make out the shimmering light glowing just above the heads of the Superiors. It wasn't the sort of light that cast out a glow or illuminated the space around it. No, it looked more like threads of captured sunlight.

"Speak."

"Frozen lightning." She swallowed past the dryness in her mouth and throat. "A weapon captured and forged on Greenisle. It hasn't been in fashion in battle for many years. There's a shroud of darkness around it, making it harder to see."

"Listen."

For this, she lowered her eyes so that her superiors wouldn't notice how they glazed over as she listened for whatever nearly silent sound they wanted her to locate. At first, there was nothing. The potions allowed Doctrinas to master themselves down to their breath and pulse. She could hear those of the people in front of her. But there, muffled by the robes of the Father Superior to the right, was a slight ticking.

"Speak."

She turned to the Father Superior. "You have a pocket watch hidden in your robes."

"Taste."

Opening her mouth, she expected to taste that strange mix of berry and cinnamon. But the air was sweet, almost sickly so. She wanted to drink it in; it reminded her of youth and lack of responsibility. It made her heart ache with missing Asriel. She thought of splitting pastries with him, eating beneath tables at banquets as they hid from their father.

"Speak."

"Cake," she said, biting back a smile. "Honey cake with thick frosting."

The Superiors looked to the Reverend Mother, who showed no emotion. When she stood, the rest of the table did too. Rhaella hastily followed.

"Very good, Progeny Rhaella," Reverend Mother Locasta said. "You've been excelling in your studies, and that has not gone unnoticed. The Order commends you. If you keep this up, you'll make a valuable Doctrina to your High Lord."

She opened her mouth to say thank you, and then closed it. She still had not been prompted to speak.

"There is only the matter of your emotions," Reverend Mother Locasta continued. "You show too much on your face when recalling things. You must work on schooling your face, and keeping the rest of your studies up."

"As a reward for passing your trial," a Mother Superior said, "you will be granted access to the mailroom tomorrow morning. You may send out or read any letters you've received before breakfast."

Effectively dismissed, Rhaella bowed too low to correct into a curtsy. She turned on her heel and headed straight for the door that was already open where the young Superior waited on the other side.

"You're free to return to your room," the Superior said. "Get some rest for tomorrow."

It was uncharacteristically kind of someone of her status, and Rhaella almost didn't trust it as sincere. But she was allowed to leave the atrium, and when she walked outside she was startled to find that it was barely sunset. They were probably still serving dinner in the tower. She could have a good meal if she wanted to. But her body suddenly ached as if every muscle and joint had taken a giant exhale. All she wanted to do now was to sleep, but she was determined to ready her letters before anything else..

The pile of letters she had been composing since her arrival was hidden in a drawer. Digging them out, she quickly scanned their contents. Some of them were horribly out of touch with how she was feeling now. Impulsive thoughts put to page when she needed to distract herself from this new reality. Discarding those impulsive missives, she settled in with a fresh pile of parchment and a pot of ink. Her pen hovered over the page, her mind suddenly empty of the words that had been jumbled around in there for weeks. She hadn't even decided who to write to first. She missed Asriel, but she found she had nothing to say to him. And yet somehow she also had *everything* to say to him. And that was too much for her to untangle right now.

Gods, she didn't want to write to her father either.

Aida's face came to mind and the words came effortlessly. Rhaella kept her composure as she wrote to her friend, letting her know that she was okay and safely tucked away in the Silent Keep. She told Aida not to worry, and she kept control of herself while she did it. A few tears bubbled up to the surface, though, when she asked how her and the baby were faring. Then, conscious of the fact that someone may read the letter before Aida could, Rhaella scribbled out her initial wording, and instead asked how her friend's *condition* had been as of late.

After she had signed and dated the first letter, Rhaella reached for a fresh page and considered who to write to next. Much of her correspondence was political, and her house did not need her to keep that up while in training with the Dux. And she wanted to reserve this gift from her superiors for friends and family.

How many of those did she have when she wasn't the Hawk?

She could think of at least one besides Aida.

Dipping her pen in the ink pot again, she hesitated only once before beginning to write.

Virgil…

It was difficult to say what she felt while keeping in mind that someone else may read it. She thought of his odious uncle, the Doctrina. The way he'd glared at her as though she were a boil and not a diplomat.

And it was even more difficult to carefully manage her words after recalling the intensity of Virgil's gaze on her in the library. She felt the heat of his breath prickling her skin, a sensation she'd imagined countless times before.

In another world, she'd acted on her feelings with the same boldness she'd shown him in every other regard. She'd never hesitated to tell Virgil exactly what she thought—which might have been a miscalculation, but she couldn't help herself around him. Something about him felt so *safe*.

And while she was not vain, she also was not an idiot. It didn't surprise her that Virgil's thoughts had drifted to marriage the same way hers had. What shocked her was that somehow the mere option was taken away from them before they could decide for themselves. If she dwelt on such a thing for too long, it made her sick to her stomach. Not in the same way the potions did, but with the gutting knowledge that there was another option for her life that had been ripped away before she knew it was within her reach.

There had been no time for him to propose sooner; even a few days sooner would have felt so fast. If she was honest with herself, it had felt fast as it were. They had only been acquainted for a few months through letters, and in person for even less time. Had he proposed while she was at camp, she might've been taken aback. Frightened by the idea of such a real future. And it wasn't as though she didn't want that future either. Rather, she had never been *allowed* to want.

If she had been given just a little bit of time to think about things, Rhaella likely would've said yes.

But they were too late and now she was beholden to her vows.

Perhaps she was a fool for other reasons. For hesitating. For keeping to herself, as she had always been taught to. Begrudgingly, she thought of every other awful habit she'd adopted for her family's sake. She'd already been chastised for one of them—for not keeping her face schooled regardless of the circumstances. Her father had mastered that one—although Asriel still had yet to do the same. But for Rhaella, hiding her true feelings was a task. And it was even more difficult when she was sleep-deprived and lonely and thinking of childhood memories.

Rhaella blinked back to the present. Back to the several pages she had written to Virgil without really meaning to. She read the entire thing back and found nothing compromising. It *was* vulnerable, but she refused to shy away from that. It felt silly at this point.

Folding all of her letters up, she stamped them closed with the Dux's sigil and set them aside on her desk. Then, she shucked off her robes and collapsed into bed, letting the day fall away with no more thoughts.

Before the sun was fully risen, Rhaella awoke, dressed for physical training, and then made her way to the mailroom. There were a few other early-risen Progenies in there as well. Others who had successfully handled their first trial. Rhaella kept to herself and placed her letters in an unoccupied brazier before checking her mailbox. At first, she thought she'd opened the wrong box because this one was empty. Then, with a sinking feeling, she accepted that her family simply hadn't written her yet. Slamming the box shut, she left the mailroom.

The same young Superior from yesterday was waiting outside, so close to the door that Rhaella nearly ran into her. Apologizing profusely, she stepped back into a bow-curtsy and tried to pass by.

The Superior smiled slightly in that same knowing way. "Progeny Rhaella. The Superiors sent me to speak with you."

"Sister Superior," she replied dutifully. "What is it?"

She chuckled. "They sent me to tell you that you'll be making your rounds beginning next week. Be sure to make arrangements to miss a few weeks of class. It's time to see the islands, Progeny."

Rhaella bit back a retort that she'd already seen the islands along with most of the houses. She bowed again before hurrying to the gym. Making the rounds meant she would get to meet with each of the stronghold houses and shadow a practicing Doctrina. It meant *freedom*.

It meant seeing her family and friends again, not even three months

213

into her training.

For the rest of the day, she failed at the simple task Reverend Mother Locasta had given her. She couldn't help but smile.

CHAPTER SIXTEEN

"I have found that the races aside from elves, fae, and the like take to the potions more easily. In those with inhuman blood, a higher dosage is required for the mixed herbs to take effect."

—From the collected documents of Prince Gerard Stillgrove, heir to Moldermouth

18 Midanae, in the Benevolent year 112 A.E.

Gerard stood with his hands folded in front of him, blinking against the early-afternoon sunlight, while he awaited the arrival of the Dux Doctrina. With his siblings beside him in their finery, he felt confident enough to receive them without his parents there to oversee. In fact, he was elated that they showed such confidence in his abilities to task him with something so important in the first place.

The Stillgrove family Doctrina stood on the other side of Roman, her eyes forward as she sought out her peers. Doctrina Ophelia was only in her mid-thirties if Gerard remembered correctly. Young for a Doctrina of her distinction. She'd grown up on the mainland and had been educated in their schools, making her intimately familiar with all of their exports. His father was right to have elected her his Doctrina. Should she still be with the family once Gerard Ascended, he thought it would be an honor to have her.

Though that didn't stop him from eyeing the group of black and gray cloaked figures that approached from the northern border. A Father Superior led their parade, signaling to his peer. Doctrina Ophelia raised her hand in greeting before bowing respectfully.

"Honored Dux Doctrina," Gerard called out, stepping forward. "We are thankful that you've brought your newest class of Progenies to observe our work. Please, come inside."

On cue, Galilea and Roman dutifully headed toward the house, leading the group of Doctrinas inside. Meanwhile, Gerard hung back and smiled, greeting as many of them as he could as they passed.

At first, the smiles and waves came easily. It was part of his job as the heir. But he had to fight to maintain that smile as he got a closer look at the Progenies. This close, he could see how unwell they looked. There were only a few among the fully devoted Doctrinas, but they stuck out starkly to Gerard's trained eye.

He knew about the potions. His house was the one that supplied the mix of various herbs, after all. Individually, he was familiar with the effects of each of them. But mixed together, they clearly wreaked havoc on the body. The Progenies had dull hair and wan skin, and there were concerning bags beneath their yellowed eyes.

Poison was, generally, unkind to the body. But the Order of the Dux Doctrina could be trusted to mix the herbs carefully so as to avoid any fatal effects. And the Doctrinas that had been around for longer seemed mostly fine, aside from the off coloring of their eyes. But still, something about this felt *off*.

Towards the back of the group, one of the gray-cloaked ones caught his eye. She stood taller than most, and her skin retained a healthy flush. Her eyes, however, were swollen and dark. Familiarity nagged at him, but the answer did not reveal itself to him easily.

How did he know her?

The answer struck him with the weight of brutal clarity. *Of course* it was her.

Rhaella of House Veservus turned to meet his eye before hastily looking away. Gerard chuckled to himself. The Hawk seemed to have found her place in the world after all, no thanks to her brother. She appeared to be almost completely unaffected aside from the obvious exhaustion. It didn't surprise him that she had adapted to the potions and poisons far better than her peers. Perhaps her vampire genes had prevented her from being changed in the same way, or perhaps she was already so far ahead of her peers that the poison needed to catch up to her.

Though there were plenty of other methods to avoid the effects of the potions.

If the Hawk knew what mithridatism was, he wouldn't be the least bit surprised. From the conversations his father and his advisors had,

Gerard knew that not everyone who entered the Order could withstand it. And from the few brief letters he and Rhaella had exchanged over the years, she seemed too devoted to her family to willingly leave them behind. Whatever she was doing with the Order, it seemed a calculated choice. He commended her for holding her own.

Still, there was a nagging voice in the back of his mind that warned him to keep an eye on her during this visit. If her appearance had caught his attention, the superiors had most definitely taken notice. Depending on how long she had been in the Order, they would undoubtedly expect her appearance to have changed more drastically. And if she didn't adhere to their expectations, it was sure to cause trouble for her.

Gerard and Rhaella were not close enough that he could ask her outright about the circumstances that had led her to the Silent Keep, but he had never shied away from the challenge of getting to know his fellow nobles either. He decided he would forge a relationship between the two of them, and he decided to start now.

Gerard knew how to use his charm to do such a thing, and as he entered the house, he vowed to do just that with the Veservus spare. He would get his questions answered one way or another.

CHAPTER SEVENTEEN

"The damage is substantial. Upon first sight, I feared the hand would never be of use again. However, we are implementing an experimental technique to see if we can ease the tearing. If that works, we may be able to repair the tendons."
—*Medical records of Asriel Veservus, from the collected documents of*
High Lord Isaiah Oberon

20 Midanae, in the Benevolent year 112 A.E.

When the summons arrived on an unremarkable morning, Asriel wasn't surprised. He'd been waiting for his father to call him home since abandoning him on the docks. There was no sense of urgency in his father's writing, but the message was clear. It was time to return to Briarhall.

A few extra Veservus guards emerged from the shadows and corners they'd been lurking in for the past weeks to load Asriel's things onto the awaiting ship. In the meantime, Asriel lugged Barrett two doors down to the archives. With the archivists' permission, they descended the dim stairs. Duty was first; he would have to contend with the little inconsistencies he'd left unattended to until now.

"Not that I'm opposed to watching you perform errands all morning," Barrett remarked. "But I would like to ask what you're doing."

"What *we're* doing," Asriel corrected. He flipped another page. "What we *have* to do."

"Which is…?"

Glancing at him out of the corner of his eye, Asriel said, "I need to show my face around the Palace. So that when I disappear for a bit, no one will think anything of it."

His guard shifted uncomfortably. It was cramped between the shelves, and with his armor on it seemed even moreso. Shoulder brushed against shoulder, and Asriel pretended that it didn't send chills through him to be this close to Barrett. The summons mentioned that House Lancor would be waiting for them at Briarhall, and he didn't want to start anything he couldn't finish before it came time to leave.

"There," he said, slamming a book shut. Placing it carefully back on the shelf, Asriel gestured for Barrett to lead the way out of the archives. Once they had emerged back into the light, Asriel directed them to the library. Barrett did a cursory sweep of the room, finding it empty, and decided to walk toward the secret door.

For a brief moment, Asriel fiddled with the key. He had a terrible feeling that his father was going to make him return it once they got to the house. Selfishly, he didn't want to give it back. It would be terrible if he happened to forget it before getting on the ship. If somehow, it accidentally ended up tucked away with his things in the suite. Inexcusable, really.

He unlocked the door and dipped inside with Barrett on his heels.

There was still a lantern on the desk from their last excursion. The flame had long since gone out, but wax had dripped through onto the documents beneath. Asriel swore and removed the metal thing, setting it on the ground. As Barrett shut the door, cutting off the light, Asriel stood still and waited for his eyes to catch up to him.

They hadn't done much to tidy the mess left by Asriel's father. The papers hadn't been moved since they had been here last, still out of order and strewn about the surface of the desk. With the indefinite promise of time ahead of them at the Palace, Asriel hadn't felt the need to. Only now, that time had run out.

As Asriel took a seat at the desk, Barrett finally lit the lantern. A soft glow illuminated the room, but it was still dim. It was almost a comforting sort of darkness, though. One that could be settled into. But Asriel held no such desires for this place. Despite the trust his father placed in him by even allowing him to know of its existence, this library was a frightening place with the knowledge of the hidden tunnels hidden far beneath.

Not to mention the wyrm Asriel hadn't been able to stop thinking about.

It had come so close to him and Barrett. With its sense of smell and hearing, it should have found them with no difficulty, especially since Asriel was coated in the same dirt the thing wriggled around in. He had practically immersed himself in its domain and come out unscathed. His instincts screamed at him that there was no way it was mere coincidence that had afforded him and his guard their lives.

"Do me a favor, would you?" Asriel pointed to the shelves near the door that led to the hidden tunnel. "Find me a book on blood. Anything to do with blood."

"That is a highly unhelpful order," Barrett said. "Your family, hailing from a house founded by *vampires*, likely has dozens of books on the subject."

"You're very funny," Asriel said. "Now if you could find one, please."

"I think that's the most earnest you've sounded in your whole life," Barrett teased, trailing his fingers along the shelves. He read the titles on the spines aloud, muttering them under his breath. Asriel listened for anything that might be of use to him. In the meanwhile, he pulled open the bottom drawer with the false bottom.

The certificate for the mysterious Doctrina was on top of the pile, just as Asriel had left it. Hastily, he placed another sheet of parchment atop it and made a copy with his charcoal. Then, he began the task of sorting through the rest of the papers. Many of them were pointless confirmations of confirmations of appointments. Letters affirming that more letters had been received. Lists of expenses. The other houses might have viewed House Veservus as a strange, foreboding house due to its secrecy and knowledge of many things, but the reality was that they thrived on logistics, numbers, and tedious, repetitive things.

Maybe he was jealous of the other heirs, though maybe not all of them. Asriel certainly didn't envy Hiram Lightpike, who spoke numbers as a first language. Money was a fickle thing. It came and went, and the scales of value tipped every which way depending on the season. It did not seem appealing to be the one to balance those scales. The one who kept track of the minutiae of *cost*.

Asriel's hand stilled. The sigil of the Order stared back at him from the page. Beneath it, there was a copy of the history as it had been told in their schoolbooks. The little that was allowed to be documented about the Dux Doctrina. Details about the process of applying, of the levels of Doctrinas, of the rich years of them and the Lords working in communion. He knew these things already. He had spent hours researching the Dux before condemning his sister to her fate. And so none of this information was new, nor was it a surprise.

But the documents were aged. The lettering was faded and the edges of the page were wrinkled by years of constant touch. Peering closer, Asriel could see that the sigil was an older version of the one he knew they used now. It was a drawing done decades prior, if he remembered correctly. It was the same tower, but with small details changed. The current sigil was crisper. Simpler to the eye. This one had been done with a thicker pointed pen.

Wheels were turning in Asriel's head. From what he knew of his father, he would have been educated in the ways of the Dux Doctrina from childhood, not needing to be reminded of things well into his adulthood. There should have been no place for this paper in his drawers in the first place, let alone for it to show the kinds of wear and tear that it did. His father had always been cluttered. But he rarely kept documents that were this severely out of date or no longer relevant. And there was something about the placement of these documents that felt purposeful. Staged, even.

"Perhaps another thing I was meant to find," Asriel murmured. He looked up at Barrett. "I don't have time to copy these." Then, he shoved the documents into his pocket.

Standing from the desk, Asriel strode for the door. It was a gamble to exit the hidden library, as there was always the chance that a patron could be strolling the shelves, but Asriel honed in his listening and heard nothing. Deeming it safe, he nudged open the door and, upon finding the nearest shelves empty, he walked out.

"Let's head to the ship," he said darkly.

Isle Verdale wasn't far from Kingsgrave. They departed from the Palace docks in the early afternoon, and they neared the port of Briarhall before dinnertime. Red-cloaked guards helped them disembark before waving them toward the house.

Briarhall sat at the peak of one of the many hills on the island and the entrance veered off of any paved road to deter rogue carriages from driving too close. The trees that lined the path along the hill did an excellent job of obscuring the castle's midnight-black peaks. Several species of birds flew around the towers—some of them Asriel's own falcons.

In the distance, he saw his father approaching with a pair of guards.

Despite himself—despite the strangeness of everything he had found in the Palace—Asriel's mouth curled up into a smile as he jogged to meet his father.

"My son," his father said, opening his arms. Asriel fell into them with ease. "It's good to see you."

"It's good to see you too, Father," Asriel said into his father's shoulder.

His father pulled back to look at him. He traced a thumb along Asriel's cheekbone, and he couldn't help but think of how similar the shapes of their faces were. Asriel found himself leaning into the touch.

"Come," his father said. "The Lancors are here. You'll have time to bathe yourself and change, if you must. But make haste. We have mass, and then dinner."

Asriel rolled his head back to stare at the sky as he let out a guttural groan. So many weeks gone by without attending mass had made him indolent. Still, knowing Freya was inside, waiting for him, made his stomach flip in eagerness. The thought of sitting through mass with her at his side didn't sound like such a bad prospect after all.

He took advantage of his father's offer and shut himself into his rooms to freshen up. The ride on the ship hadn't roughened him up, but the day drew long and Asriel wanted to look his best for the Lancors. After bathing, he pulled on a deep red that matched his house's colors. He belted on high-waisted trousers before slipping into black boots with gold embroidery along the sides, and, to appease his father, he braided back the front pieces of his hair. Though his small act of rebellion was to leave the rest loose to fall down his back.

By the time Asriel was seated in a pew with his father at his left and Freya his right, it was late. Beside Freya, her father and her younger brother, Ledger, sat comfortably. They'd arrived early, of course. There was a priestess cloaked in shining silver on the altar singing an ancient hymn. The church was awash in candlelight from every available surface of the room, and as he glanced out of the corner of his eye, he could see it shining softly on Freya. The sight of it made Asriel smile.

As each priestess filed into the chapel, they bowed their heads. Once they reached the altar, one of them opened the holy tome and began preaching from the Good Book. Asriel only half-listened, having heard these scriptures hundreds of times throughout his life.

He leaned in close to Freya and whispered, "Are you entertained?"

"Quite," she whispered back, a conspiratorial smile on her face.

Asriel's father leaned over and shushed the both of them. This only caused them to giggle, which Asriel did little to stifle. What were a few dirty looks from his father when he had put that look on Freya's face?

When the priestesses prompted them, they all rose to their feet and walked toward the little altars around the edges of the room. The guards remained at their posts. Asriel eyed Freya and jerked his head toward the wall.

"Would you like to light a candle with me?"

She nodded. "I would."

They went over to one of the empty altars, kneeling before the stand of candles in various stages of melting. Asriel took one of the wooden sticks and caught the flame of one candle, bringing it over to one of the unlit ones. Its flame flickered briefly before rising brilliantly.

In a quiet voice, Freya asked, "What are you praying for?"

Asriel shot her a look before turning back to the candle. "I don't really believe in this. But my father likes me to look the part, so I light the candles with a solemn expression on my face."

Freya huffed a quiet laugh. "I think it's sort of… nice. To have something to believe in. I don't believe in it the way my father does, or the way your father does, but I like to think that there's some force guiding us to where we're meant to be."

"That's a lovely thought," Asriel said. "And where would you like to be?"

She grinned at him. "I think I'm in the right place."

The words sent a thrill through him. To know that she was as happy to be here as he was to receive her calmed him. It assured him that this betrothal was not lost yet. He may not have had the confidence of her father, but he had her heart at the moment. And that mattered to him so much more.

"Come," High Lord Lancor said. He raised a hand to the priestesses. "I'd like to read the wax, if we may."

"Certainly, my Lord," a priestess replied, smiling from beneath her hood. "Right this way."

"I guess we'd better heed him," Asriel said, rising to his feet. He extended a hand to Freya and was pleased when she took it.

They followed the priestesses to the far wall, where a stoup full of water waited. On a countertop behind it, chunks of completely melted wax all melded together into one misshapen blob. A priestess tore off a handful and held it up for all to see.

"What does my Lord require an answer to?"

High Lord Ewan Lancor lifted his chin. "My house would like to know if the betrothal between my firstborn daughter, Freya Lancor, and the heir to House Veservus, Asriel Veservus, is meant to pass."

The priestess held the wick to another flame until it caught. Then, she looked between Asriel and Freya before deciding to hand the chunk of wax to him. He accepted it carefully and began to lower it into the water. It was heavy, and he wanted to be sure to place the hollow part of it on top so that the tiny wick within could remain lit.

He'd performed ceromancy before, though not often. Rhaella had always had steadier hands. But he hated how the water was always so *cold*. So, his brow furrowed in confusion as he placed the wax in the water, dunking his hands in with it, and he found that the water was hot where it touched the wax. Asriel flinched, yanking his hands out of the bowl. But the hunk of it toppled. If the flame went out, the judgment would be called and his betrothal would be over. Without thinking, he dunked his right hand back in the water to keep it upright. His skin met where the wax had started to melt, and because the water was already so hot, the wax molded to the curve below his thumb. Hissing, he drew his hand back, and the wax followed, clinging to his skin.

"Gods, this burns," he said through his teeth.

"*Asriel,*" his father snapped. "Mind your tongue. We're in the house of the gods!"

"It's alright," the priestess assured him, taking Asriel's hand to remove the now-dried wax. As she did, she inclined her head toward the bowl to observe the wax floating in it. "The flame is strong. The gods look upon this match with favor."

Freya's father frowned. "And the burn?"

224

"Human error," she said, unconcerned. With the last bits of wax removed from Asriel's skin, she placed his hand against his own chest. "Feel your heartbeat, my Lord. It's strong. Just like the flame."

It was strong from the rush of anxiety at almost ruining the ceremony, he thought to himself. But Asriel simply nodded. He wasn't about to correct the priestess and cause more strife than he already had. And especially not when Freya was trying to catch his eye. There was such a look of hope in hers. He blinked, hoping he could match it even if he didn't quite feel it for himself just yet.

High Lord Alden took both of their hands, joining them together. Noting the tattoo that covered his father's throat, signifying his short-lived marriage with Asriel's mother, Asriel felt a swell of emotion. With a carefully constructed beaming smile on his face, his father lifted their hands and said, "The gods have shown their favor. Let us continue with the betrothal as planned."

With a tight-lipped smile, High Lord Ewan nodded his head and placed his hand atop their joined ones, essentially adorning them with his blessing.

"Let's have dinner, shall we?" Asriel's father said.

They reconvened in the dining hall, thoroughly starved after such a lengthy mass. Asriel and his house were used to eating so late. And knowing that the Lancors were, arguably, even more devout than they were, they seemed right at home.

Asriel loaded a plate full of roast chicken and mashed potatoes topped with a savory sauce. After adding a few extra vegetables, he handed the plate to Freya.

"My Lady," he said, bowing his chin.

"So," High Lord Ewan cut in, filling his own plate. "We paid a visit to House Midar a few weeks ago. There, we learned a little about your excursion to see Prince Midar at his camp."

Asriel stiffened. He eyed his father for help, but found the High Lord's eyes fixed firmly on his own plate. Gulping, Asriel scrambled to conjure memories of how Rhaella had described her time in the Midar camp.

"He had only complimentary things to say about you, Prince Asriel," High Lord Ewan continued. "It seems you've made a friend in the Eighth

House. The relations between your houses seem solid."

"It is," Asriel agreed. "Prince Virgil and I did what we could to further the war effort."

"So I heard. The rumors swirling on Segsiege are that you and your half-sister are becoming quite the formidable pair of strategists."

"Speaking of which," Freya said, her fork halfway toward her mouth, "where is your half-sister?"

"Sister," Asriel corrected automatically. "She's furthering her education at the moment."

"Where." The tone in the First High Lord's voice assured him that it was not a question.

Asriel's eyes darted toward his father. Blinking rapidly, Asriel tapped out the pattern to spell out, *He knows.*

Subtly, so that it looked as though he were just setting his fork down oddly, Asriel's father signed, *I will handle it.*

Asriel's father cleared his throat. "My daughter is with the Dux Doctrina now. We're very proud of her."

High Lord Ewan seemed to stew on this new bit of information. Nodding slowly, he continued eating his dinner. Between bites, he said, "So she serves her nation in more ways than one. Well done, Alden."

That seemed to quell whatever tension existed between the two High Lords. Whether the leader of the First House wanted to lord over the fact that he knew something about his compatriot before being told directly, Asriel couldn't be sure. It did assure him, though, of the core principle of House Veservus: It was valuable to know things others didn't.

What one did with that knowledge mattered more, in some ways. But ultimately, it was *knowledge* that afforded the ability to steer conversations. Asriel desired such a power greatly. His talents at making conversation lied in what charm he could muster for his peers. And it was a skill he was still learning to temper with the rest of the High Lords.

High Lord Ewan Lancor didn't know where all of the secret doors were in the Palace. Asriel did. Further, Asriel had spent these past weeks memorizing every inch of the maps he'd found. He could navigate the catacombs with his eyes closed, if necessary. He *would* find a way to make such information useful.

It was the middle of the night by the time they finished dinner. Everyone had been escorted back to their rooms. Even Barrett had been relieved of his duties thanks to the impregnable nature of the house. Asriel didn't want to sleep. He was restless—anxious, thanks to the presence of House Lancor—and embarrassed to be witnessed by his father. Frustrated, he made his way to the aviary, where his falcons waited.

They squawked as he entered, flapping their wings furiously. Asriel bent his forearm and one immediately flew to him, perching there. He rubbed its feathered head with a finger, laughing softly to himself. He had missed these wretched birds dearly.

In the quiet, Asriel's mind tallied up all the key players who were now on the board. And when he did the math, he felt wholly unequal to them. With a Lady Wife at his side, the looming truth of his Ascension felt even closer, and he felt unprepared in that regard as well. It would not become his fate until his father passed, but it would happen eventually. The future would only ever come closer at this point. It overwhelmed him to think that it would *never* be as far as it had been before.

Roughly a month ago, the Concilium had sent out notices informing every heir to begin pursuing spouses. They were strongly-worded suggestions, nothing more than what Asriel's father already wanted him to accomplish, but they felt foreboding nonetheless. The current generation of current High Lords had all married young—and had children young—so they were young as High Lords. Even Asriel's own father hadn't yet reached fifty. Try as he might, though, Asriel couldn't picture himself with multiple fully grown children by that age. Could Freya? He shuddered to consider the prospect and pointedly vowed to avoid asking her that question.

Asriel sent the falcon back to its perch before taking a seat on one of the stone benches. The name of his grandsire had been carved into it long ago, and it looked weather-worn in the dim light. Generations of names of Veservus men had been carved into these benches by Lancor hands. Their families were intrinsically tied, just as each stronghold house was. Asriel knew there were connections to the other houses that he couldn't remember at the moment. Memories that were not his own.

Thanks to those centuries of trust before the war, the tension caused by House Veservus's deserters hadn't severed the connection between his house and the other stronghold house's entirely, but damage had been done. That bond would need careful tending and mending before it was as strong as it had once been. And Asriel couldn't quiet the voice at the back of his mind that suggested he might not have steady enough hands for such careful work. Not when the incident with the wax was still so fresh in his mind.

The Lancors were traditional in the ways of the old world. They had carried out and maintained so many of the traditions that the stronghold houses had left behind. They were, in Asriel's political opinion, the most conservative when it came to Lucerianism, heeding its roots in the religions of old. They picked their marriage-matches carefully, and the value House Veservus held nearly twenty-six years ago was vastly different from what it was now. Which meant House Lancor would most value loyalty and transparency if this betrothal were to come to fruition.

Asriel would be hard-pressed to describe himself as noble, but he thought he could become that for Freya. Not only was she an enviable match, she had shown him kindness when she didn't have to. She'd definitely been warned to be wary of him, and yet she'd walked with him and sat beside him and spoken in his defense. She had done more than he could ever ask for, and it was certainly more than he deserved.

Footsteps sounded at the door and Asriel rose to his feet as Freya approached in a silk robe. And *beneath* that silk robe, she had on an obscenely delicate nightdress. She was statuesque, just shy of matching him in height. Her long, delicate neck melted down into burly shoulders and muscular arms that spoke to her fierce dedication to her craft. She had a slender waist, and round hips that swayed side to side as she approached. And her long legs, equally muscular, were bare to the aviary's chill air.

When Asriel finally managed to drag his eyes back up the expanse of her body, he saw that her hands were clasped behind her back and that that damning smile was still spread across her face.

"They told me I might find you here," she said. "Your guard is *very* familiar with your habits."

"What are you doing here?" Asriel said, stepping closer. He began to make a small circle around her.

Giggling, Freya said, "It's part of our courtship that I should gift you something. While my house specializes in material goods, I thought you would appreciate an experience more." She paused. "That, and my cousins in House Redspire warned me that I should know how to ride a horse before claiming it."

"Did they now," Asriel murmured, stopping directly behind her and leaning down to speak directly in her ear. "Am I to be the one to teach you?"

"You'll find that I am quite learned, my Lord," Freya said sweetly, tilting her head to expose her neck to him.

"I intend to find out if that's true," he said, running his lips along the length of her neck. "You must not be very shy, if you came all this way so exposed."

"Quite the opposite," she said. "I thought it might please you to be amongst the things that make you happiest when I called on you. The ghostly halls of Briarhall kept me well-hidden."

Asriel's hands caught her waist, and he dragged her to the nearest tree, pressing her back against it. One of his knees nudged hers apart, keeping his thigh between hers. Freya arched against him, her hands sliding up his chest.

"You're tense," she said. "You have been since you arrived here. You weren't like this at the Palace."

"My father wasn't at the Palace," Asriel said, sighing. "And neither was *yours*. The burdens placed upon me make it hard to stand tall. I'm sure you're no stranger to the feeling."

"Let me help you carry them, then" she said, pressing her body against his. One of his hands went to her hip, massaging there with his thumb. "If we are to marry, I want to be worthy of it."

"You won't like hearing about it," Asriel said. "I've had to take on duties that are distasteful. I've done things a brother should *never* do to his sister."

Freya studied Asriel's face and, slowly, clarity washed over her. "You were the one who sent your sister to the Order. Not your father."

He nodded. "I did. It's not so bad. Rhaella is talented in that way. It suits her to be there. Though I think she would've preferred broaching the idea herself."

"She'll come around," Freya said, sounding more sure than he felt. "I did, when duty required that my brother hurt my feelings."

"What do you mean?" Asriel furrowed his brow.

She traced her fingers over it, smoothing out the tension. "I'm five years older than my brother, Ezra. When I turned five, just before he was born, my father promised me the world. And when Ezra came along and he turned out to be a boy, my father promised it to him instead. It's not Ezra's fault that he's the heir instead of me, but it doesn't make it hurt less that he is."

"Gods, I'm so sorry," Asriel said. He recalled the fact that Ezra had only just come of age, and therefore had only just been *formally* declared the heir. This wound was fresh. "That's terrible."

She blinked, looking away. "I've made my peace with it. Besides, I'm useful in other ways. Ways my brother can never be." She punctuated that sentence with a long graze of her knuckles along his jaw. Equal parts gentle and intentional.

The words made Asriel's stomach turn. They reeked of political intentions that had no place in a father's love, nor in this moment when it was just the two of them. Her words reminded him that all of the High Lords could—and would—use their daughters as bargaining tools. It disgusted him when he thought of Rhaella and it disgusted him when he thought of Freya.

His sister, he could do nothing for at the moment. For Freya, however, he had the opportunity to *do something*. He could offer her the promise of a better future. A *different* one than the one she had made herself settle for.

Every prophecy bestowed upon him told him he was meant for greater things. Perhaps this was what they meant.

Surety covered him in its warmth. Maybe he did believe in fate. In a greater plan for things beyond his control. He walked a dangerous path, so unprepared for his role as the heir. But his time at the Palace and this new courtship with Freya could be a new start. Asriel could be better—and he *would* be better—as long as she would have him.

There was still the matter of studying and improving his swordplay and learning the ever-shifting politics of Adristan. But all Asriel could focus on was how good Freya felt as she ground against him, the thin fabric of her nightdress and his cursed trousers the only barriers.

In mere moments, Asriel had torn those barriers down with his bare hands. Cocooned in the aviary, beneath so many trees and the flapping of wings, Asriel dug his teeth into the soft skin of Freya's neck. The air sang with the sound of her hitched breaths as he peppered each small hurt with kisses. The rest of the world fell away, and when she fell over the edge—dizzy with pleasure—he followed her willingly.

CHAPTER EIGHTEEN

"You shouldn't place your bets on the fates of men. It rarely works out in your favor."
—Common House Lightpike saying

4 Luceriary, in the Benevolent year 112 A.E.

Rhaella was beginning to grow sick of traveling on ships. Doing so had never bothered her before, but after traveling to the fourth island in a matter of weeks, she was growing tired of the constant rocking of the boat. She and the other Dux selected for this trip had already visited the first half of the stronghold houses, and, despite herself, she had learned a lot from shadowing the Doctrinas of each one.

Initially, meeting with each of the heirs and watching their faces shift between shock and then confusion at the fact that she was now a Doctrina had been overwhelming. Now, she just felt numb to it. They were headed for Trimount, which meant they'd be meeting with House Lightpike soon. Rhaella would rather crawl beneath the floorboards of the ship and hide out until it was time to depart than face them down, but she had once again been robbed of such a choice.

The Lightpike brothers knew her too well, which—unfortunately for her—meant that they would be able to recall their shared childhood memories with as much clarity as she could. Any time she had been sent to their house as punishment, she fell apart. No matter how much it tore her to pieces, her father had frequently thrown her to those preening peacocks as though he had no need for her at all.

Ramsey and Hiram Lightpike had seen her cry, and that was a death sentence in her eyes.

None of the members of House Lightpike's court stood on the steps of Castle Fallcrest to receive them. And Rhaella thought it was just as well. Instead, a group of Ladies in waiting stood to greet them and usher them inside. Begrudgingly, Rhaella let out a gasp as they walked inside and she caught a glimpse of House Lightpike's splendor. They had clearly taken inspiration from ancient, haunted architecture—for the gods' sake there was a *gargoyle* up in the rafters—and the effect was gorgeous.

As they walked further into the house proper, the rich, vibrant greens of their house surrounded her and her fellow Doctrinas on all sides. Peacocks, the sigil of their house, were *everywhere*. Hidden in the minor details of the crown moulding and prominently displayed in paintings and tapestries. There was so much opulence on display, and yet the whole thing still managed to feel understated. She couldn't wrap her head around the artistic choices, and yet it still *worked*.

With a pang, Rhaella wondered what Aida would think about all of this.

Neither the High Lord nor his heir waited for them inside. Instead, it was Ramsey who stood on the bottom step of the grand staircase at the end of the room. Rhaella resisted the urge to roll her eyes. He stood with Sage Oberon—the heir to their house—whom she had met on a previous island visit.

"Welcome," Ramsey said briskly. "My fathers are occupied, as is my brother—the heir. I'm supposed to direct you to our guest wing."

Beside him, Sage remained silent, which only made them look more intimidating with their tattoos. Draped in white robes that covered all but their bald head, their piercing blue eyes met Rhaella's, and they nodded a polite greeting. It was a greeting meant for a Princess—something she had never been.

Ramsey directed groups of Doctrinas and Progenies to follow various Ladies in waiting, splitting them up into different bedrooms on the second floor. Their party dwindled until Rhaella was the last one left without a room, and she almost couldn't believe her luck. But then again, that meant that she now had no other choice than to stare directly at House Lightpike's spare while she awaited instruction.

"As I live and breathe," he said, swaggering toward her. "The Hawk of House Veservus. I didn't expect to see you walking the halls like a normal person. I figured you kept to the rafters, I hear they make for better eavesdropping."

"Very funny," Rhaella said drily. "Where am I staying?"

He held up his hands. "Not so fast. We've only just gotten reacquainted, why don't you tell me what you're doing with the Order?"

She glanced at the hall of closed doors. "My superiors won't appreciate my talking to you."

"They can't say anything if I demand it," he replied coolly. "You've already met Sage, now it's my turn. Fair's fair."

Fair, she scoffed to herself. What did that even mean here?

She pressed her tongue into her cheek, biting back annoyance. "Fine," she said. "Can we talk somewhere less… obvious?"

Ramsey gestured toward the only open door behind her, which she could only assume was her room for the duration of her stay. The three of them entered and shut the door. Sage leaned against the wall next to it, clearly just as uncomfortable as she was.

"Good to see you again, Sage," she said politely.

"You as well," they finally said. Those were the first words they'd spoken this entire time. "Apologies for Ramsey's persistence."

"I had an inkling he would be that way," Rhaella said, ignoring the Seventh Prince entirely. "I'm not put off, it's simply his nature."

Ramsey barked out a laugh. "Did your brother warn you about me? I had a great time talking to him at our last meeting."

"So I heard," she lied, blinking up at him from the desk chair she sank into. "Word is you're always as pleasant as you were with him."

"He is," Sage answered for him. A small smile played on their face.

"Traitor," Ramsey said, rubbing his hand along Sage's head.

After spending almost a week of rounds in House Oberon, Rhaella was fairly familiar with the tattoos covering most of Sage's head. There were illustrations from medical textbooks trailing down their temple, and various tools crossed over one another behind their ear and across the crown of their head. Across the base of their skull, Rhaella knew the word *devotion* was inked in all capital letters. When she'd asked Sage what they were devoted to, their answer had been one simple word: *People*.

"What are you doing in the Order?" Ramsey asked again.

"You don't have to answer that," Sage tacked on.

She flickered sympathetic eyes toward Sage before glaring at Ramsey. "I'm serving my house. I figured you'd know plenty about what it means to do such a thing."

His eyes darkened. "*I do*. It's just a wonder to me that High Lord Alden would let go of his only daughter so easily."

Rhaella tilted her head. "Just as I'm surprised that High Lord Galahad would send his second son to greet political officials."

Ramsey blinked, and Rhaella wondered if she'd taken things a step too far. The Prince said nothing for several long moments. Sage watched him with concern, reaching out a hand that Ramsey waved away. Taking deep breaths through his nose, he shook his head.

"Whatever you think you know, Veservus, it clouds your vision."

With that, Ramsey stormed out of the room, slamming the door behind him. Sage watched the closed door for a few seconds before taking in a sharp breath through the nose.

"Don't mind him," they said, turning toward her. "He carries burdens beyond his strength. It has nothing to do with you."

Rhaella rested an arm on the back of her chair. "You know something about those?"

They huffed a quiet laugh. "You can't poach secrets out of me, winged one. That was a valiant effort, though."

"I had to try," she shrugged. "You didn't tell me you'd be here."

"Neither did you," they pointed out.

She wiggled her brows. "The Dux haven't been very forthcoming with where they're taking us next. I can only guess."

"Oh, but you're usually very good at that."

"I am," Rhaella conceded before making to unpack her things. "I should get ready for whatever it is the Lightpike Doctrina has planned."

Sage nodded with an uncomfortable amount of understanding. "I'll let you prepare yourself. Should you find the rest of the house inhospitable, however, I'll be around."

Sage had partially stepped through the door when Rhaella called out, "You never told me *why* you're visiting."

They looked back at her. "House call—forgive the funny wording. Even nobles require a check-up on occasion."

Sage stepped out, shutting the door once more, and leaving Rhaella alone in the silence. She bathed and redressed in fresh robes first, before taking a moment to collect herself in the mirror. Her hair had grown a little more, which meant she could plait two small braids along the top of her head while leaving the rest loose.

The ritual of braiding her hair settled the nerves that crawled up her throat every time she readied herself to meet with another practicing Doctrina, allowing her an indulgent moment to herself and no one else. She knew it had been another stroke of sheer luck that she had avoided having to share a bedroom again, and she couldn't help but wonder when that luck would begin to run out. She had needed to bunk with a few other Progenies at the Hutch and at Airsoft, but had been left to her own devices in Moldermouth and Pearlscape.

The only houses left were going to be the hardest. Soon, they'd have to visit Castle Darsor—Aida's home—and then they'd pay a visit to Castle Silverfort—Virgil's home.

They, they'd visit Briarhall. Her home.

She shook off the thought before the thread could unravel and send her into a full-blown spiral. Pushing away from the desk, Rhaella exited the bedroom and made her way back to the foyer to attend to her duties. One of the Mothers Superior who had accompanied them from the Silent Keep was already there, and an unfamiliar face stood beside her—Rhaella could only assume they were the Lightpike Doctrina. All around her, her peers gathered, eagerly awaiting their first assignment.

"Progenies," the Mother Superior said. "Today, I leave you in the very capable hands of Doctrina Cadmus. You could learn a lot from him. Don't waste him."

"Thank you, Mother Superior," Doctrina Cadmus said, bowing slightly. "It's an honor to serve the next class of advisors."

Rhaella did not like self-important Doctrinas, and she had a feeling this afternoon was going to be a long one. She found the Doctrinas who held to their vows—who did not speak unless spoken to—were more tolerable.

And Doctrina Cadmus was the opposite of that. In fact, he almost reminded Rhaella of Dogan with all of his preening. It made her face twitch while she tried desperately to hold onto the emotionless mask the Reverend Mother insisted upon. The one that never wavered until she remembered she'd been sent here against her will. Then, bitterness slipped into the cracks of her soul and poured out of anywhere it could reach—which was most frequently her expression.

Although Rhaella's mind slipped further and further away with every step her and her peers took, her stride never faltered. Cadmus led her and the rest of the Progenies to a conference room, and they sat around the square table, waiting for instruction. What Rhaella didn't expect was for every noble in the house to follow them into the room. The High Lord and his family, as well as Sage and their guards, came in and took their respective seats. Before silence could fall, Doctrina Cadmus shut the heavy door, and the meeting began.

"We have to deal with the expenses of the war," the High Lord said, wasting no time. "It cost us more than just lives to defeat the traitors."

Rhaella stiffened. It was an open secret among the Order that a noble had joined their ranks, let alone a daughter of a disgraced house. If she had to sit through this meeting and listen to officials disparage her house, she thought might truly fail at the Reverend Mother's task.

Out of the corner of her eye, Rhaella spotted Sage watching her carefully. Ever so slightly, she shook her head. It was embarrassing that even they anticipated this to be difficult for her. She did not need witnesses to the defamation of her family's name.

When she glanced to her left, she saw that Ramsey was watching her as well. His lip curled up into a sneer, but she looked the other way, avoiding his eye. She followed the lead of Doctrina Cadmus and produced a small pad of paper from her robes, meaning to take notes.

"Word from Greenisle?"

Rhaella stiffened, and her pen hovered above the page as she listened to Doctrina Cadmus. "According to Doctrina Nicholas, our men are still estimating the total number of casualties. High Lord Vincent will be sending a fresh supply of troops to every island once they can solidify how many are needed."

"Every house?" A nobleman draped in green scoffed. "Do the traitors of the Third House *deserve* to replenish their forces from our people?"

"House Veservus shed just as much blood as any other," Sage offered quietly but firmly. "My kin and I patched up many that were wounded, and buried those that were killed."

"Even those that abdicated in favor of the royalists held the banners of House Veservus," another nobleman said.

Doctrina Cadmus shook his head. "I have it on good authority from Doctrinas of several houses that we need not fear nor abandon House Veservus. They will receive the troops they ask for."

Rhaella loosed a breath. Carefully, she observed the reactions of her fellow Progenies, searching for signs of displeasure. Finding none, she settled into her seat.

High Lord Galahad continued, "We will, however, hold our pursestrings tighter in their case. The other six houses will receive their allotted amount of guards at no extra cost. The Third House will owe us information, as is their trade."

The nobles surrounding the High Lord nodded as though this was the most logical outcome. It wasn't fair. It wasn't *right*. Her and her house had faced just as many casualties at the hands of the traitors. Her father's inner circle, once loyal, had betrayed *his* trust as much as the nation's. Their house had been left with limited resources because so many of their working people were gone. Those early weeks of the war were dark times. Ones she did not wish to revisit any time soon.

They *needed* the replenished troops these men talked about so casually.

If the Seventh House knew of her deal with Virgil—if they knew that she had his approval—they would change their minds. People trusted House Midar implicitly, but Rhaella knew in her bones that what people *really* trusted was Virgil. The swirling rumors of his attempts at abdication in his teen years meant little when he had come to the nation's defense the moment they needed it. In their letters, he said he didn't want this burden of leadership. It was a cruel irony that he was so well-suited to bear it.

Under other circumstances, she would have thought it folly on Virgil's part to extend such a generous deal to Rhaella and her house. She couldn't be sure if it was thanks to the vulnerability she'd shown him that he had granted such a kindness, or if it was his own judgment. Perhaps it was a combination of the two.

She couldn't speak of the deal now that she was sworn to hold her tongue until someone asked for her counsel. For now, she could only hope that Virgil would vouch for her house and hold up his end of their deal.

"Any word from Segsiege?"

"House Lancor says they are content with their supplies as is, my Lord," Doctrina Cadmus said. "They ask for nothing more. Not from the mainland, and not from us."

"Very well," High Lord Galahad said. "And the Order? What news?"

A Father Superior from the Silent Keep spoke up. "We suffered few casualties in the war, my Lord. Additionally, the incoming class of Progenies is four dozen strong. The Order thrives, even now."

"Good," the High Lord nodded. "House Lightpike will do its part to keep it that way. Upon your departure, should you find the need, write to us immediately detailing anything that would serve your cause better."

Rhaella resisted the thought to write *H.L. Lightpike: A suck-up to the Order*, as that did not seem wise. Instead she scratched out a hasty transcript of everything the High Lord and Doctrinas were saying. The High Lord's trusted circle of nobles did not pitch in with much to say aside from the odd comment about things that had already been dealt with. The councilmen were less like political advisors and more like Lords of validation for their leader. It seemed to Rhaella that there were far too many people sitting at this table, if any real business was to get done.

A few hours later, and with little of real importance accomplished, Doctrina Cadmus dismissed the Progenies for the evening. As they were clearing out of the room, Ramsey sidled up to Rhaella's side to whisper in her ear.

"Did you like that?" He smiled smugly. "Did you like hearing how the nobles of Adristan scorn your house?"

She could feel the skin on the inside of her cheek tear as she chewed at it, but submissively she said, "Yes, my Lord."

Ramsey patted her shoulder. "That's what I thought you'd say."

Rhaella shrugged off the touch and followed her peers to the dining hall. She ate her dinner alone. The Progenies had free reign for the evening, and she knew Castle Fallcrest housed a small library that she desperately wanted to see. Though she was sure to run into plenty of her peers there, and would be forced to make conversation. Better to be alone instead, while she could.

She lay in bed later that night, cranky and restless and full of wandering thoughts. Her mind swam with visions and images that were near-perfect recollections. She saw her brother staying behind at the Palace of Many Rooms with their father beside him. She saw Virgil leaning in, close enough to touch, in the library at the Silent Keep. And she saw Ramsey, taunting her. Even though he only stood as tall as her chin, he had made her feel so small in that moment. It was thanks to a lifetime of self-control that she hadn't backhanded him instantly.

Sleep would be no friend to her tonight. She gave up pretending and sat up in bed, reaching for a match to light the candle. With her hand outstretched toward the nightstand, Rhaella decided to visit the library now, in hopes that it would be empty by this hour. The Lightpikes practiced Lucerianism, and though mass was definitely over for the night, discretion would still be imperative. Donning her robes, Rhaella tied the fabric tightly at the waist so the hemline wouldn't brush against the floor. She pulled on a thick pair of socks so as to forgo shoes, and, finally, she tightly braided her hair back out of her face.

Though her father and her brother and the Order—and even Ramsey—might have clipped her wings, it felt good to stretch them out once more.

Her footsteps were silent against the plush rugs that lined the floors of Castle Fallcrest. The library took up two floors of the house, and there was an entrance on both levels. Making her way down the hall toward the upper entrance, Rhaella let herself in and shut the door behind her as silently as she could.

The second floor was a rounded balcony that overlooked the first level. Shelves that were taller than her circled the entire room, and spines of every color greeted her. There were no signifiers of genre or subject matter, and she felt like she could look through the shelves for hours and find something new at every step. It would take some work to locate any books relating to royalists, but Rhaella thought she might like to chip away at such a monumental task.

And she very well might have, had she not picked up on the sounds of conversation coming from the first floor. She flinched at having been startled, but they were too far away and too immersed in their conversation to have noticed her. Rhaella stuck to the shadows, waiting and listening to what they had to say.

She recognized the voice of a Mother Superior who had been traveling with them, as well as the voice of Doctrina Cadmus. She hesitated when she heard the voice of the High Lord, though. Whatever information she was hearing sounded like delicate business. But they hadn't shut themselves in the privacy of a conference room, which told Rhaella that they were either careless or too comfortable in their own home. Maybe both.

The library was open to the entire house, and there was no guarantee that Rhaella was the only patron, at least from their perspective. The nobles were taking a risk. And judging by the urgency of their voices, it was an unavoidable one.

"Where is Ramsey?" The High Lord snapped.

"We sent for him already, my Lord," Doctrina Cadmus said. "They should be waking him now. He'll be down any moment."

No more than a few seconds later, she heard footsteps in the hall behind her. They were distant, but they sounded closer with every heartbeat. Rhaella's eyes widened. She pushed herself deeper between the shelves without so much as a sound. Ramsey burst through the doors, followed by guards. He descended the stairs in a fury, taking no notice of his surroundings. When the sleep-wrecked Prince sidled up to his father, they resumed speaking.

Mincing no words, the High Lord said, "My fellow High Lords and I have agreed to hold a congress."

Rhaella's eyes widened. Meetings came and went, but a congress was a serious matter. Especially on such short notice. Every High Lord, every heir apparent, and every Doctrina had to be in attendance in order for a congress to commence. There was no room for excuses once the date had been solidified. In her memory, there hadn't been a congress in *years*…

Perhaps it had been more like a decade.

"Alright," Ramsey said, sounding impatient and put out. "Did you wake me just for that?"

"There's been an update on your brother."

There was a pause, and when Ramsey spoke again, his voice sounded quite small. "What news?"

"He still has not awoken," the High Lord said. "You'll have to keep up his duties for the foreseeable future. Which, at this point, may mean attending the congress in his stead."

"I can't do that," Ramsey said, aghast. "I'm not your heir. The others won't see me as their equal."

Another voice sighed, different from those who had spoken so far. Sage stood at the edge of the group, a grave look on their face. With hands folded into their white robes, they said, "He didn't respond to our latest treatment. That's never happened before."

Ramsey shuffled on his feet. "So try a different treatment."

"It's not that simple," Sage said.

"Then *make it* simple." Rhaella almost felt a pang of sympathy at the note of panic he tried to keep from creeping in at the edges of his words.

"Son," High Lord Galahad snapped. "This moment is crucial. You must embrace duty."

"I embrace *nothing*," Ramsey said sharply. "This is Hiram's fate, not mine. When he wakes up, he'll take up his duties as he had before."

"We have to contend with the fact that he might not wake up—"

"Don't speak such things out loud," Ramsey snapped. "You'll attract ill will that way."

"Ramsey, I need you to be realistic," the High Lord said. "Should Hiram fall away, you *will* become my heir."

"I don't want to be the heir," Ramsey said, and the pitch of his voice grew consistently higher as he spoke. Gods, was he *crying?* Rhaella suddenly felt a sense of disgust with herself for eavesdropping.

"And you think *I* want this?" High Lord Galahad's voice was shaking, though he somehow managed to remain just as unyielding.

"Alright," Doctrina Cadmus said. "That's enough. This matter will not resolve itself tonight. We should retire."

There was a bout of murmured agreements. Footsteps departed through the lower level doors. Pushing herself deeper into the shadows, Rhaella listened as Ramsey passed back the way he came, slamming the door shut behind him. Cautiously, she stepped out from between the shelves, peeking over the balcony. Would it be worth perusing the books now?

"You're not as careful as you like to think," a voice said from the darkness.

Rhaella yelped and fell away from the balcony. Sage stood on the first floor, looking up at her with a carefully blank expression on their face. Righting herself, she fiddled with her robes.

"You scared me," she said breathily.

They tilted their head. "They've all gone. You don't have to worry. And before you ask how I knew you were there, I didn't. You simply didn't wait long enough to ensure you were alone."

"What do you want?" Rhaella crossed her arms over her chest. Then, remembering she was speaking to a Prince—in the most technical of terms—she said, "My liege."

"You can say Lord," they said. "I'll be High Lord someday. Have to grow accustomed to it eventually."

"That doesn't seem very fair to you," she noted. "Nor is it the point of this conversation."

"You and I are both capable of multitasking," Sage said. "I am neither Lord nor Lady, but I will be High Lord. Just as Allison Redspire and Zerin Aviatis are High Lords, though they are not men. And, to answer your question, I came to ask a favor."

"I'm not in a position to deny you," she said, laughing despite herself. "What can I do for you?"

They looked so genuine that it tugged at Rhaella's heartstrings. They said, "It is not common knowledge that Ramsey's older brother is not well."

"And it will remain that way," Rhaella said immediately. "I do not answer to my father anymore."

They leveled her with a look. "So you skulk about, listening in on private conversations, for what? For your own sake?"

"Old habits are difficult to break," Rhaella said blithely. "It was wrong of me to listen. The Lightpikes' secrets will stay with me."

"I should hope so," Sage said, moving toward the door.

"Is that why you're here?" She called out. "Why you traveled all the way from Scalesound?"

They nodded. "I told you earlier. House call."

Rhaella chuckled. "Goodnight, my Lord."

"And you, Princess," they said, bowing slightly.

"I'm not a Princess."

Light twinkled in Sage's eye. "And I'm not a Lord."

They left her, the door softly clicking shut behind them. Rhaella immediately departed from the library. Lingering wouldn't be worth the added risk. Her time in the Order had dulled her skills. Her inability to control her emotions was making her clumsy. And although mistakes were not unheard of for her, it was embarrassing nonetheless. After all, she had earned the nickname *the Hawk* as a teenager. She just needed to lessen how frequently she slipped up, and sleep was key to that mission.

Though she doubted she would be able to sleep for very long, *some,* she decided, was better than *none.*

She awoke the next morning with the sunrise, as she always did. Blinking drearily, she stretched her limbs and donned her robes once more. Her hair was still neatly braided from the night before, so she left it alone. Before she left her room, Rhaella gathered whatever materials she imagined a day in Doctrina Cadmus's service might require, and she made her way down the same stairs as last night where her peers had gathered in the foyer.

This morning was like most every morning had been on their trip. The Progenies attended meetings alongside Doctrina Cadmus and took note of how he conducted himself in tandem with High Lord Galahad. Compared to her father and Dogan—or what she had observed of the relationship between Virgil's father and Doctrina Nicholas—the relationship between Doctrina Cadmus and the High Lord was a marvel. The best way to describe High Lord Galahad was *brisk.* He did not mince words, and his tone was rarely kind or gentle. She could absolutely see why Asriel and her father had described him as abrasive. Even so, every decision he made seemed to be in genuine service to Adristan.

He did not have to be nice to be a good High Lord.

When they were set free for the afternoon, Ramsey waved a taunting goodbye from his seat at the table. Rhaella wanted to have more sympathy for him, but she wasn't supposed to know what he was dealing with. So, she raised one hand and made a swooping motion, the Vessial gesture for *go fuck yourself.*

"Progeny Rhaella." A Mother Superior caught her in the hallway. "You're needed in the library."

Rhaella bowed before passing her superior, heading for the library's main doors. Upon entry, she was faced with the sight of several Superiors who had chaperoned this journey, blank stares on their faces. It made her stomach twist.

"Sit down, dear," one of them said.

Slowly, Rhaella took a seat as she had been prompted, and she stared up at her superiors as she waited for an explanation. Perhaps they knew about her eavesdropping. Doctrina Cadmus was competent; it made sense that he might have overheard her footsteps above his head. Or perhaps it was Ramsey who had complained. He could have spotted her in the darkness, after all.

"We wanted to ask you a few questions, to test the things you've seen and heard so far on your rounds," a Mother Superior said.

"Alright," Rhaella said, clenching and unclenching her fists.

"If your High Lord were to ask you to lead a status meeting without them present, what would be your first order of business?"

Her eyes flickered across the floor, avoiding her superiors altogether. "I would give an update as to where the High Lord is, based on what they instructed me to pass along."

"Eyes up, Progeny."

Sweat broke out along her temple. Unbidden, the words of a prayer of protection ran through her mind. *Caught.* Rhaella took a shuddering breath as she lifted her eyes, which were still blue, to meet her waiting superiors.

After a pregnant pause, one of the Fathers Superior cleared his throat. "We try to tailor the training experience to every particular Doctrina. But without ample medical records, we can't always ascertain that we are doing right by you. Seeing as the nature of your birth was, well, illegitimate, we don't have a complete medical history for you."

One of the Mothers Superior picked up where he left off. "Therefore, this is our mistake. We were unaware that your bloodline is somewhat resistant to our potions. It seems a higher dose will be necessary for you."

"I-" Rhaella stammered.

The same Father Superior held up his hand. "You aren't in trouble. The fault lies in us for not securing accurate data for you. We'll correct this now."

Rhaella broke out into a cold sweat as one of the Mothers Superior approached her with a tray of freshly brewed potions. She had no choice but to drink. When she downed the one meant to enhance her senses, a pounding started in her temple. The one that produced a protective force field made her cough. And when the last one touched her lips—the one that bound her to the Order for life—her vision swam. The Superiors excused her, but when she stood the room spun for several heartbeats before her body met the floor and her vision went black.

CHAPTER NINETEEN

"It is the duty of a Doctrina to observe. They are to be the watchful eye, never seen. The eye has no need for speaking, nor for taking action itself. Instead, it must relay information to the mind. From there, the mind determines how best to proceed, at the behest of its High Lord."
—Code of Conduct for the Dux Doctrina

15 Luceriary, in the Benevolent year 112 A.E.

Visiting the other islands of Adristan was a privilege, Virgil was aware of that. Some people lived their entire lives on one island without ever traveling for work or pleasure. The commoners weren't loyal to any one house—they could take turns living on every island if they wanted to—but ships were expensive and the cargo vessels rarely accepted civilian passengers. When he had been younger, Virgil wished he could have attended every school in Adristan so that he could explore each island and all they had to offer. In his adulthood, duty afforded him that same privilege, even if it was a different sort now.

Bianca stood beside him at the railing, looking out at the water. Virgil was glad his cousin had agreed to accompany him as he delivered a fresh set of guards to each of the houses. Mila was busy with the High Lord, sifting through a fresh batch of betrothal proposals. Virgil decided to leave well enough alone and not get involved with anything regarding marriage while his father was around.

Currently, they were circling the islands, depositing guards at various islands as they waited for confirmation of where to go next. Communication from House Lightpike and House Midar was slow, which vexed him endlessly. They could have made this trip in just a few short days had they been given a plan, but instead he was beholden to the whims of the Lords and ministers who did not frequent his braziers.

By now, the ship was rounding back toward Sandorne, home to

House Redspire. Virgil had only been to Sandorne in the context of the war, to ensure that their house was fully equipped for battle, so the idea of exploring it in relative peace seemed exciting. In passing, at meetings and parties, he'd met the Princess—Aida Redspire. Her four younger sisters were scattered about Adristan, indulging in every passing whim, and there might have been a bit of jealousy that cropped up on him at the thought of such freedom. Aida's aunts—the High Lord and her Lady Wife—were known to travel when they could manage it as well.

"I've been to some fun parties on Sandorne," Bianca remarked. "The fae know how to have a good time."

Virgil hummed. "I don't know that I trust your idea of a good time."

His cousin let out a hearty laugh. "You like drinking, you like dancing, you like girls. It's all very standard."

"I like more than just girls," Virgil muttered. "Not that it matters right now."

"You're still on that?" Bianca said flippantly, casting a glance at him. Once she caught the stoic look on his face, though, she sobered. "That was callous. Forgive me."

"It's fine," Virgil said, shaking his head. He hesitated before saying, "She wrote me a letter."

Bianca whipped her head toward Virgil. "I thought Doctrinas couldn't send or receive mail during their training."

"I bet Uncle told you that." When his cousin nodded, he scoffed humorlessly. "He told me that, too. She was able to, thanks to passing her exams, which shouldn't come as a surprise. And yet, it warmed me to open it and realize it was from her. Though I almost wish she hadn't sent it."

"Are you going to respond?"

"It's probably not a good idea," Virgil said. "But yes. I intend to."

Bianca chuckled softly. "If you had said no, I would've encouraged you to do it anyway."

"I would expect nothing less," he smiled. Then, he turned around so that his back was pressed to the railing. He crossed his arms over his chest and tilted his head back to stare at the sails. "Speaking of our uncle…"

"Here we go," Bianca groaned, resting her forehead on the railing.

"He's come up with a list of prospective nobles for me to pursue. All of them highborn, all of them with something to offer our house. All of them utterly insulting in their suggestions. Our uncle is most eager at the prospect of pursuing Galilea Stillgrove."

Bianca pulled her dark waves into a bun with the tie around her wrist. Neutrally, she said, "Princess Stillgrove is intelligent, dutiful, and witty. She's as desirable a match as any."

"She's also of no interest to me," Virgil said. "We have a solid relationship with the Fifth House as it is. I know Galilea as an *ally*, not a prospect. She is industrious to be sure. And I'd be a fool to deny her beauty. But our conversations stall once we get beyond matters of state. I can't be with someone I can't talk to. Uncle suggested her because of her family's wealth, not because of our compatibility."

"So disregard him," Bianca said. "Do what you always do and tell him to piss off."

Silently, Virgil considered the idea of a courtship with her. The money and prestige it could bring them, given the right circumstances. The idea of such a thing sounded so bleak he wasn't sure he could even manage to daydream about it. Suddenly, he said, "I wish I could talk to Aunt Velda about this."

Bianca huffed a laugh. "My mother is content with her duties in the north. She'd be wasted here, assuaging our fears for us."

"Is it not strange?" Virgil asked. "How Uncle Nicholas is as close as he can get to my father, whispering his counsel in his ear, while Aunt Velda is kept at arm's length."

"One of his highest-ranking generals is not what I would call *at arm's length.*"

A particularly strong wave rocked the boat then, and Virgil reached out a hand to steady his cousin as he caught his own footing. Righting themselves, he and his cousin stepped away from the railing and went to sit on some of the cargo that was on deck.

Virgil toyed with one of the many daggers holstered at his waist. "What if it's because my father knows he doesn't have to worry about his sister? What if he's worried about Uncle Nicholas?"

"Worried how?"

"Worried about what he's capable of."

Bianca shrugged. "Uncle Nicholas is a menace, but I don't know that I believe he's capable of anything truly terrible. His proximity is what your father wants, and he's grown quite accustomed to getting what he wants."

Was that true? Virgil leaned back against the cargo and rolled pipe weed into a joint with practiced ease. He considered what Bianca said and couldn't pinpoint an event where his father had been forced to concede to the whims of another house. Even among the nobles he allowed to participate in his decision-making, his father usually had the last word. Generations of service had established House Midar's goodwill within the rest of Adristan's subconscious. People seemed to *want* to give his father what he wanted. Never mind that in most cases his father's suggestions were generally the most logical course of action.

It seemed as though it was his father's personal life that suffered the most because of this, though. The detriment of his marriage, and now his relationship with his son, were the price his father paid for such sway. That was the cost of a successful lordship, it seemed.

Thus far, Virgil had only needed to sacrifice his dignity for the sake of his people. It was his burden to bear that he had saved the nation at the steep cost of his dignity. For such a cause, he had been nicknamed *The Shrike*. He was destined to kill for honor, but be deemed a butcher.

As he glanced to his left, Virgil saw his uncle far above them at the helm of the ship. Uncle Nicholas seemed focused on the ocean as his black robes billowed in the wind that had picked up. Autumn had brought a chill with it, and soon it would be too cold to travel without heavy coats. As for the Doctrinas, they'd be restricted to layering only what they could fit beneath their robes. That outer shell defined them at first glance, and it seemed the Doctrinas were unwilling to sacrifice their image even for the sake of comfort.

Uncle Nicholas must have felt Virgil's gaze on him, because he turned to meet his nephew's eye. Virgil held the man's stare for a moment before raising the joint to his lips and minding his own view of the ocean.

When they docked at Sandorne that afternoon, Declan and Eric approached, ready for Virgil's instruction. He waved them away.

"I'll handle everything," Virgil said. "Just make sure none of the new recruits make fools of themselves."

"Can do," Eric said at the same time Declan said, "Of course."

To Bianca, Virgil said, "You're in charge."

She laughed. "You give up your power so easily."

He rolled his eyes. "Keep them in line, please."

Virgil disembarked, and the captain of the Redspire army met him within moments. Khalil was an older man with a decorated history of service. Virgil had fuzzy memories of seeing him in his father's war room, back when the idea of going to battle on a daily basis was a faraway theory. Strategies they should consider and then save away for a rainy day, not things they would come to rely on for their own survival.

Virgil reached out a hand to the man. "Captain Khalil."

"Virgil, my boy," Khalil said, patting Virgil's shoulder as he shook his hand. "Honorifics have no place here. How was the journey?"

"Fair. The weather wasn't too bad. I can't speak to how it'll be in the coming weeks, though." He gestured behind him toward the ship, where the soldiers were disembarking. "We have your unit. They're young, but they're hearty and ready to work."

Khalil nodded. "I trust you. And if they misbehave, I know how to get them up to standard. Your grandfather was the one that taught me, you know."

"I do," Virgil said fondly. Then, "I'm going to need your signature on a few forms for our records. And I'll also need the High Lord's, if she's around."

"She isn't, actually," Khalil said. "But her heir is. I assume her signature will do?"

"It should," Virgil said, unsure. If it mattered that much to his father, *he* could sail all this way to correct the issue.

Castle Darsor really was a wonder. It was quite the hike to get from the docks to the house, but seeing it come into view on the horizon was worth the trek. The house glowed with the colors of a painted sunset, and it was a testament to the skill of the fae heritage of the main families. As they entered the foyer, Virgil was surrounded by sculptures of nude figures, paintings detailing the end of the world, and the distant sound of a lute. He craned his neck to take all of it in as the captain led him through the halls to find the Princess. She wasn't in the row of conference rooms near the front of the house, nor the study belonging to the High Lord.

When they passed a maid draped in nearly-sheer fabric with generous cutouts, Khalil asked, "Have you seen Princess Aida?"

Hoisting a basket of fabrics higher on her hip, the maid said, "I saw her last in the library. She has a guest, sir."

"Thank you, Katelyn. That'll be all." the captain said, sending her on her way. To Virgil, he said, "The library is on the second floor. I hope you don't mind a tall set of stairs after your long journey."

"Not at all," Virgil said, following Khalil.

The stairs were carved marble. Shades of orange mixed into browns and creams. They were so polished that, when Virgil looked down, he could faintly see his reflection swimming amidst the colors.

"I hope being captain is treating you well," Virgil said, keeping one hand on the railing. The stairs were growing higher and higher, and the slope was becoming steep. All around them, Virgil could see balconies at eye level, growing ever higher the more they climbed. There were hundreds of little alcoves for people to sit and read in—or perhaps they were meant for patrons to create something of their own.

"It is, but I'm getting tired," Khalil said. "I'm ready to train the next captain."

"Any prospects so far?"

"A few of my lieutenants," Khalil said. "But the most promising is the heir's second sister, Alora."

"A Princess leading the charge," Virgil said, smiling. "I like the sound of that."

At last, they reached the top of those damned stairs. If he weren't constantly pushing his physical limits, Virgil would have been winded by the time they reached the second floor. He felt a pang of sympathy for the servants, who likely had to walk up and down all four flights of stairs on a daily basis.

"It's just in here," Khalil said, pushing open the door to the library.

Princess Aida was hard to miss, stuffed into a ballgown with an enormous skirt that spread out around her. She was standing next to the first row of shelves, arguing with someone whose back was turned to the door. A Doctrina, Virgil realized. A gray-robed, tall Doctrina, with hair braided away from her face.

Rhaella's shoulders sank as she watched Virgil and Khalil approach. He had to remind himself to not stop short at the mere sight of her. At some point, he was going to have to see her again, he thought. Why not now?

The closer he came, the more he realized that her face was rife with tension, just as her shoulders were. She was swimming in her Doctrina robes—

Had she lost weight?

Frustration was clearly written across her body, and he had the urge to ask her what was wrong. If he could fix it for her.

There was a beat of silence before Virgil realized that Khalil was waiting for him to speak. He shook himself out of his stupor and bowed before the Fourth Princess.

"Princess Aida," he said, straightening. "It's nice to see you again. I hope you'll forgive my brusqueness, but I came for your signature on a few forms regarding your new unit of guards."

Aida's eyes flickered to Rhaella before turning back to him. She didn't look much happier than her friend did. "Very well. Captain Khalil, would you leave us, please?"

She offered no explanation, and she did not owe him one. The captain left the library without protest, shutting the door behind him.

"My, my," Aida said, glancing between the two of them. "Shall we take a seat?"

"Aida," Rhaella started.

"*Please.* The temperature of the room raised several notches the moment he walked in. You didn't tell me you two knew each other."

"Another thing we can add to the list of what we don't know about one another," Rhaella said bitterly, eyes on Aida.

The two had been fighting, then. That's what he and Khalil had walked in on.

With no more than a cursory glance toward Virgil, Rhaella continued.

"He and I worked together during the war."

"You wound me," Virgil said, placing a sarcastic hand on chest.

"Well, that's no surprise," Aida said, taking a seat at one of the prettily carved out tables. Light was coming in through the windows, beating down on them. "Anyone with information of note spoke to the Hawk during the war, or they know someone who did. That still doesn't explain how you two know each other so well."

Virgil eyed Rhaella. Clearly, she was in a terrible mood. He didn't want to push whatever invisible boundaries she had set around their… *familiarity*. Dipping his chin slightly, Virgil urged her to answer in his stead.

She blinked at his wordless gesture, perking one brow. She kept an eye on him as she said, "I have friends besides you, Aida."

"Now *I'm* wounded," she said drily, adjusting herself in her seat. She couldn't seem to get comfortable. "I thought your whole world revolved around me."

"Oh, you'd love that, wouldn't you," Rhaella muttered, and Virgil thought he detected some fondness there.

"I don't want to take up too much of your time," he said, drawing the documents out of his pocket. "It's just a few signatures."

"Don't worry about it," Aida said, forcing herself to sit up straighter. It seemed uncomfortable with her giant gown. "You wouldn't happen to have a pen, would you?"

Virgil produced one from his pocket, and they fell into silence as Aida read through the documents. He tried to remain professional, but he found himself stealing glances at Rhaella. She wasn't looking at him, but she was clearly *aware* that he was looking at her.

Leaning in slightly, he asked, "What are you doing here?"

Finally, she looked back at him with a carefully schooled expression. "I'm making my rounds as part of my training. The Order brings us to every island, where we shadow the Doctrinas to each High Lord." She paused, then. "I was on Greenisle only a few days ago."

She had been there. She had been there while he was away, busy delivering guards, and he had missed her. Silently, Virgil cursed himself before wondering if that mission was intentional. If his father—or, more likely, his uncle—had anticipated the arrival of the Order and sent him away.

"So you're here on duty," Virgil said. "Shouldn't you be with the House Doctrina, then?"

Aida answered for her. "Doctrina Xanthe is not as strict as some of the others might be. My aunts appointed her for that very reason. She gave the poor, exhausted Progenies the day off. So Rhaella is free. At least, as free as she *can* be. Your pen," she said smoothly, extending it back to him.

Virgil took the pen from Aida, pocketing it once again. With some difficulty, the Princess rose to her feet, and Rhaella offered her arm immediately. Virgil thought it might have been a peace offering between the two of them.

"Why don't I take these documents to Captain Khalil?" Aida offered. "I don't mind."

"You don't have to do that—" Virgil started, but Aida cut him off with a mere flick of her hand. As though she wasn't addressing a fellow heir. To Rhaella, she said briskly, "I can buy you twenty minutes. Use them wisely."

Rhaella looked puzzled. "I—"

"You're both so *eloquent*," Aida said, sweeping out through the library doors. She turned back only once more with her hands on the doorknobs. "Time is a gift. Don't waste it."

Then, she shut the library doors, sealing them inside.

"Forgive her, she's…" Rhaella's voice trailed off as she looked at him, fully this time. "Did you get my letter?"

"I did," he said. He swallowed down the things he really wanted to say. *Are you thinking of me the way I think of you?* Instead, he said, "Thank you for thinking of me."

"Will you write back?" Her brows pinched together, softening her features. "To the Silent Keep."

Thickly, he managed a gruff, "If that is what you wish."

"I want the same things as you," Rhaella said, unblinking.

"You can't know that," he said, voice dangerously low.

Her mouth pursed, the ghost of a smile fighting its way to the surface. "I thought you were under the impression that I knew everything."

"Ke bawp," he said fondly. "There is so much you don't know."

Her stare hardened, and Virgil wanted to laugh as he could *see* her brain working as she turned his words over in her head. It wasn't the first time he'd spoken Menmal in front of her, and it wasn't the first time she looked confused by it.

"You really don't understand, do you?" His smile grew bigger. "Lunw ma zcï."

"Don't tease me," Rhaella said, eyes narrowing. "I know you have a secret language within your house. I just don't speak it."

"And I wouldn't expect you to," he said, and his smile refused to dim even at her scowl. "It's just entertaining to see you frustrated by what you don't know."

"I'm a quick learner," she said, raising her chin in a beautiful show of defiance. "Say it again."

Foolishly, Virgil took a step closer. Menmal was a delicate thing. A language long-dead and meant to stay in the shadows. Though he trusted that Princess Aida had kept her word and bought them twenty minutes of privacy, he didn't want to risk anyone besides Rhaella overhearing.

That, and he just wanted to be closer to her.

"Say lunw."

"Lewn," she tried, her mouth tripping over the consonants.

"No," he said. "Lunw."

She licked her lips, pressing them tightly together before trying again. "Lunw."

"Good," he murmured. "Ma."

"Ma," she repeated, drawing the word out just a breath too long.

"Shorter. Make your words more clipped. Direct. Lunw ma."

"Lunw ma."

"*This is my…*" Virgil said slowly. "Zcï. Lunw ma zcï."

"Lunw ma zcï. What does it mean? This is your what?"

"*This is my language,*" Virgil said. "Lunw ma zcï."

Rhaella repeated the phrase under her breath a few times, honing in on her pronunciation. Her eyes went distant, her mind occupied with the words alone. After a few tries, she blinked, meeting Virgil's gaze with crisp clarity.

"It's a harsh way of speaking," she said. "It makes my mouth feel like it's full of cotton."

He chuckled. "I know precisely what you mean. I imagine your family's language is much simpler?"

It was a leading question, and they both knew it. Something sparked in Rhaella's eye at that. Perhaps it was the glittering realization of what he was attempting to do. At the challenge he had just laid at her feet.

"It's less direct," she answered. "The words don't exactly translate to the common tongue."

"Well, from the little I've heard, it's not just spoken. You have some other element to it."

She nodded slowly, considering how much to say. "There's two unspoken dialects. There's a sign language, and a code that's deciphered by blinking."

"Should you be telling me this?"

"No," she said breathily. "But I want to."

"Teach me something, then," he said, refusing to disguise the open wanting in his tone.

Rhaella silently ran through a few options before holding up her hands and making a few gestures. Her fingers were long and elegant, and he thought that the callouses that littered her palms were a beautiful thing. The sign of a life spent connected to something *tactile*. She repeated the gestures a few times, but Virgil lost track of where the words began and ended. After a minute, it looked like she was just dancing with her hands.

"Slower," he said. "Please."

She made one final gesture before pausing, nodding for him to mimic her. Once he did, she repeated the first one again before adding a second one. This process continued until she had made seven gestures.

Giggling, she held up her hands in pause. "No, no, I repeated that letter on purpose. You have to make this one twice. There's two Ls in my name."

He froze with his hands raised. "We're spelling your name?"

Eyes twinkling, she said coyly, "I thought you'd remember it better."

Stirring himself from his wonder, Virgil tried repeating the gestures in sequence without her help. "*R-H-A-E-L*.... How do you make the L twice without muddying it?"

"Here," she said, holding out one hand. He placed his hand in hers, palm upright and watched in fascinated awe as she traced the symbols across the surface of his skin. "*R-H-A-E-L-L-A*. Rhaella."

"I'll take care to remember it," he said. "Do all of your signed words need to be spelled out letter by letter? That seems inconvenient."

"The dialect of Vessial that my family speaks is an incomplete restructuring of what it once was. Some things are spoken. Or they can be signed. Or blinked. The name *Rhaella* doesn't exist in the spoken dialect. I have a different name for that. If I want to use my real name, it has to be spelled in sign. The more delicate things are rarely said aloud."

"That makes more sense. It certainly seems more in line with the secretive nature of your family."

When she laughed again, it was louder. Bolder. He didn't care to examine the warmth that bloomed in his stomach at the sound of such a thing. "Is that right? You made a deal with my secretive family not so long ago, if you'll remember."

"I do," Virgil said. "And it's thanks to my very own secret language that my father was willing to let me argue on your behalf."

"Your secret language that you've now let me in on," she pointed out. "Now that I have a taste, I can deconstruct it and figure out the rest. I spend a lot of time with my nose buried in books these days, you know."

Daring to lean in a fraction closer, a vicious smirk crept across Virgil's face. "There *are* no books left on Menmal."

Her face tightened in frustration, defiance still blazing in her eyes. "I've done much harder things than translating languages. I'll take my chances."

"I wish you luck," he said. "And I hope you find something worthwhile in your books."

"Thank you," she said tightly, but there was no real malice in it.

This ease that they had managed between the two of them set a fire in Virgil's bones. He had never experienced such a thing with any other person. He wanted to bottle this feeling and drench himself in it whenever shadows and fear lingered at the corners of his mind. She was a light, and he was unable to bask in it. He was jealous of his past self who still got to do so. Only three months ago, she'd been beside him at his camp, challenging him and pushing him to create better strategies to move them towards peace. How had things devolved so quickly?

"Our twenty minutes is drawing short," she said, drawing him back to the cold light of reality. "They're going to wonder where we are."

Virgil said, glancing toward the library doors. "I came with my cousin. And my uncle."

She made a face. "He wasn't altogether very kind to me during my short stay at your house."

Darkly, he said, "What did he do?"

She shrugged, trying to downplay whatever she really felt. "He was rude. He wasn't particularly sweet to my peers, either, but he showed a clear disdain for me. It seems my family's reputation hasn't improved much."

"That wouldn't have happened if I was there," Virgil said. "I'm sorry I wasn't."

"There's only so much you could've done," Rhaella said plainly. She perked up as though something had dawned on her—though she stubbornly refused to voice whatever it was just yet. Virgil watched as she chewed on her lip, weighing the consequences, before opening her mouth again. "There is something you *could* do for me, though."

"Anything," he said immediately.

"High Lord Galahad Lightpike is in charge of the expense involved with you sending out all of these new troops. He's intending to withhold guards from my family's house unless my father gives out sensitive information. It's no secret we're in desperate need of guards. Can you *please* make sure we get them? I don't want you to stray outside your duty, but I also don't want them to pick my father apart for scraps."

"Consider it done."

"Thank you," Rhaella said, visibly deflating in relief. She scrubbed her palms on her face just then, leaving angry pink streaks in their wake.

"I would ask something of *you* in return, though."

"Yes?"

Virgil's gaze bore into her, refusing to shy away. Not about this. "If my uncle ever gives you grief again, at any of these Order functions, you tell me right away."

"He's technically my superior, Virgil. I can't really complain—"

"You can, and you will," he said firmly. "To *me*."

It killed him inside that she looked so distressed. Her eyes kept flickering to the doors, anxiety wafting off of her.

"I don't trust that my privacy will be respected as long as I'm at the Silent Keep. Whatever I put in my letter to you, it was only what I didn't mind them knowing."

"We're both familiar with speaking in code," Virgil said. "If you tell me you had a lovely walk on the grounds of the Keep, I'll know that I owe my uncle a particularly harsh session on the mat."

She snorted. "I would never describe walking the grounds as lovely, so I think that makes for a perfect code."

"Excellent."

Virgil knew their time was coming to an end. She was going to return to her fellow Doctrinas, and he would board his ship once more and set sail for the next island. Still, he felt the bone-deep need to keep talking to her. To share all of the things he had been keeping inside. He wasn't sure when it had grown so insistent, but he also wasn't sure he minded.

"I've had issues with my uncle as of late. I don't trust him. I think he wants more than the sliver of power he's been allotted."

She tilted her head in thought. "That doesn't surprise me after what I saw. But tell me what it is you've noticed."

Virgil gnawed on his cheek. "I sense a desire for control in him that pushes him past the boundaries a Doctrina should adhere to. I'm beginning to fear the worst."

"What is the worst?"

"The royalists," he said bluntly. "It's been too quiet since we left the front. You said you're surrounded by your books all day. If you can, will you look up what resources the Order has on the royalists?"

"I already have been," she said. "At the Keep, as well as in the house libraries. I'll write with whatever I find."

"We should," Rhaella agreed. In the following silence, a flush crept across her cheeks, burning bright pink. "There's a farewell custom in House Redspire, and we *are* in their house right now."

"Show me," he said, not daring to move a muscle until she did.

She stepped closer now, only a breath away. Gently, she reached out a hand, cupped the back of his head, and drew his face toward hers. Rhaella was almost as tall as he was, which, thankfully, meant that all he had to do was lean into her strength. For a brief, dizzying moment, he wondered if she was about to kiss him, but then—in a flash—that moment was over. She simply pressed her forehead against his, and took a few deep breaths. If he wasn't mistaken, there was a slight hitch in her breath when she did it.

"Scì tha dled," she murmured, stepping away. "Have fun finding *that* in a book."

Virgil watched her walk away without protest; his feet felt rooted to the spot. His memory rarely failed him but, selfishly, he wanted to commit this moment to perfect detail. Pulling the pen from his pocket, he meant to make note of what she'd said. Only, when he pulled the cap off, a folded piece of paper fell out. He knelt to pick it up, unfolding it so he could read.

You owe me.

He snorted. Aida Redspire, the perfect friend for a hawk like Rhaella. Now indebted to her, Virgil considered all the ways in which he might pay her back.

CHAPTER TWENTY

"Double check that the [REDACTED] was left in its proper place. Relay [RE-DACTED] to Asriel before the last night of the congress. Remove [REDACTED] from the tunnel office."
—Note found in the collected documents of High Lord Alden Veservus

26 Luceriary, in the Benevolent year 112 A.E.

"Thank you," he said. Then, regretfully, "We should go."

For what it was worth, the congress was perfectly timed. It had taken an exhausting amount of back and forth between him and the other High Lords, but once they'd come to a decision on when to hold it, Alden wanted to laugh at the irony. It might as well happen now.

This timeline gave him a day to get his affairs in order, and another to travel. Then, for however long it took, he and the rest of the governing force of the nation would be detained within the Palace as they attempted to iron out the tangled state of their politics. It wasn't his favorite way to spend time, but it was inarguably necessary.

Never before had he encountered war to the extent they had seen this year. Despite that, he knew with absolute certainty that it could have been worse. A few of the minor houses revolted, drawing in support from lower-ranking members of the stronghold houses. They rallied a sizable amount of peasants. Still, none of it was a match for Adristan's armies. And yet, Alden couldn't shake the feeling that something should have happened between then and now. Rhaella was talented, there was no question about that. But her dealings with the Midar Prince couldn't have produced this sizable a victory.

Something was wrong. He could feel a storm brewing on the far-off horizon. It couldn't be seen yet, but he'd be damned if he was caught off his guard when it finally made landfall.

He would not be caught unaware like he had been at the celebratory feast the day they declared victory.

It might have been bad timing and good luck that Asriel had stumbled upon Rhaella's tryst with the Midar Prince. But Alden faced no similar fortune. His luck had run out years ago, and all he had left were his wits. His ears prickled from the moment his daughter had departed from the crowd for the trees. It hardly took any skill for him to mask his footsteps from his daughter as he followed them. And it took even less effort to stay hidden from his bumbling son.

The Midars were not part of his plan. Rhaella would see that someday, and she would understand.

Eventually.

When she made her rounds and came to House Veservus—not as a daughter, but as a Progeny—it broke his heart a little. He wondered how they were treating her, but he didn't dare ask. Although, he did want to know that they were keeping their word and giving Rhaella her own room whenever possible, and not just pocketing his money and doing no such thing. It was the smallest kindness he could afford her after orchestrating her departure.

He called for Dogan, and his Doctrina came right away like a loyal beast. The dark mesh mask covering his face looked intimidating in the shadowed evening dusk.

"Go find out if the others have started traveling to the Palace," Alden ordered.

It would take a few days for everyone to arrive, depending on how organized they wished to leave their houses behind. For those who showed up early, they took it upon themselves to explore each of the Many Rooms the Palace was named for in the name of staving off boredom.

Once he had a chance to sift through the backlog of information in the archives and elsewhere, he needed to speak to Galahad Lightpike. His old friend was cunning, trying to squeeze information out of him with the guards as leverage. As if he needed more of that. Galahad had more than he realized, and Alden would make good on his word without the need for threats.

According to Dogan, the Lightpikes had already arrived at the Palace,

263

and the Redspires weren't far behind. Alden called for his men to ready a ship, but there was no sense of urgency in his words. He wasn't about to hunt down his peers. The peacocks would make themselves known when they were ready to be seen.

He could hear Asriel moving around in the other room. Loudly, clumsily. He still hadn't grasped what it meant to move in silence. Alden debated giving him another lesson, but perhaps there was skill to be found in noise, too. Asriel certainly made plenty of it.

Rising to his feet, Alden abandoned his work at the desk. There would be plenty of work to be found in the Palace, and he was eager to get to it before prying eyes were around to witness it.

CHAPTER TWENTY-ONE

"Sing me the song of the Shrike / Leading with bloody fists and the like / He fights even when he knows it's not right / Then he disappears into the night"
—*Peasant song based on stories of the war*

28 Luceriary, in the Benevolent year 112 A.E.

Virgil felt most at home when there was sweat running down his face and when his practice swords batted away imagined-enemies. Sparring with his cousins had been more like a game when they were children, but it had become a necessary task as they grew into adults. Though the pleasure wasn't entirely lost. Now, the practice of it fell somewhere in between childhood joy and adult responsibility. He enjoyed it as long as it remained a contained activity. The training room at the Palace was not ideal, as it was on the third floor, but it would suffice for the few days that they'd be here for the congress.

"Is that your idea of a strike?" Bianca laughed, dodging with ease.

"He's getting lazy," Mila said airily. Rather than opting for a sword, she stuck to a chain whip. It wasn't metal, of course, but it stung nonetheless. It had been fashioned out of some sort of soft material—malleable enough that it could still be shaped into chains—but forceful enough to remind opponents to keep their wits about them.

Instead of quipping a reply, Virgil threw his body weight into his next strike, disarming Bianca and sending Mila flailing backwards. He chuckled darkly, pleased with himself.

"Better?"

Mila caught herself on her haunches, one hand pressed against the ground for leverage. Tossing her strawberry-blond hair back, she grinned up at Virgil fiercely. There was a defiant challenge in her eyes. She launched herself to her feet, sprinted at him with her full-force, and released a strangled battle cry as she ran.

Virgil made the tactical mistake of ducking, which allowed his cousin to latch onto his back. Arms around his neck, she wrestled with him to stay up there. She managed to bring him to his knees, where he laughed and raised his hands in a placating show of surrender. Only, as she dismounted, Virgil swept at her ankles and knocked her clean off her feet. And as he placed the dull point of the practice blade at the column of Mila's throat, he glanced up to address Bianca.

"Is that another point for me?"

"Alright, alright. We get it," Mila said from the floor. "You're the all-powerful heir. *You win.*"

Virgil extended a hand to help Mila up, which she took before dusting herself off. He couldn't understand how she enjoyed sparring with her hair loose. Even with his hair tied at the nape of his neck, the little bits of hair that clung to his sweat made his skin crawl.

"Do you want a haircut?" Mila asked, watching as he scratched at his nape.

"Mind your tattoo!" Bianca snapped.

"I am," he retorted. "And no, thank you. I like it this long normally, just not while I'm sparring."

"With any luck, it'll only bother you during practice sessions from here on out," Bianca said, placing their weapons back on the rack.

Virgil blew out a long breath. "That's what I'm hoping we'll settle."

Declan met them at the doorway and his eyes flitted briefly to Bianca—then Mila—before settling on Virgil. He cleared his throat, one hand tugging on his shirt collar, before seemingly deciding better of it.

Before Declan could back down, though, Bianca said, "Oh no. You don't get to dangle information in front of us like that and then act coy. What *news*?"

Declan rolled his neck, clearly uncomfortable. "I just thought you'd want to know that several of the other houses are starting to arrive. House Lightpike is here. House Aviatis just arrived." He paused, even more visibly uncomfortable than just a moment before. "Oh, and the Order of the Dux Doctrina…" He trailed off, letting the end of the sentence hang open.

The Order of the Dux Doctrina. There it was.

Mila snorted, but quieted when Virgil shot her a look.

"I haven't gone out of my way to greet the other houses yet," he said, wiping his hair with a towel. "It'll look odd if I do so now just because the Order is here."

"What about you?" Bianca said, leaning forward to stare at Mila. "Do you think any of your potential suitors are here?"

She rolled her eyes. "Don't get me started."

"Very well," Bianca said, too cheerfully. "I'm hungry."

Virgil was too, but if he went to the kitchens and Rhaella was there, he wasn't sure how he'd react. The last time he'd been near her had been too close a call. It had been all he could do lately to stop daydreaming about their foreheads pressed together, her mouth only a tip of the head away. And now that there were so many eyes on them at all times, Virgil couldn't help but regret not closing the distance when he had the chance.

"Virgil," Mila muttered in a sing-song voice, nudging him with her elbow.

"Sorry," he said, ducking his head. "I'm tired after all the sparring."

Bianca patted his shoulder, and it was a quiet sort of comfort. He took it, leaving the training room behind.

A bath did him good, as did a shave. He left a layer of stubble behind that he quite enjoyed.. It made him look aggressively similar to his father which, truly, he didn't dislike. As he looked in the mirror, Virgil thought he looked very much like a Midar.

He was dressed in the family colors, wearing a rich, deep blue shirt with silver accents along the waistline. He donned simple black pants, and he holstered daggers to himself wherever he could. Even if the Palace was technically neutral ground, he felt naked without at least a few weapons within close reach.

The final touch was the pin bearing his family's crest that he attached to his shirt, right above his heart. The wolf bayed at the sky, surrounded by foliage and thorns. A cursive *M* crawled over top of the image. Virgil ran his fingers over it, feeling the ridges of the decorated metal, and grounding himself in the heavy feel of the metal. He wore this family crest so rarely that the weight felt foreign to him—but also not unwelcome.

He needed a good meal before he could face the rest of the houses, that was for certain. If he really wanted to, Virgil knew he could call for a Mediator who would be happy to bring it straight to the suite. But there was a certain level of discomfort he felt around ordering people to serve his every whim. It bothered him at home, and he tried to avoid it when he could. The Palace was no different.

Virgil told himself that Rhaella would be tied up with her duties and that the likelihood of him running into her was too slim to warrant avoiding the kitchens. But in all honesty, a small part of him couldn't help but hope to see her. Before he could overthink it for one more second, he strode out of the suite and down the many sets of stairs.

There were various attendants working in the Stillgrove kitchens when Virgil got there. They were hard at work, preparing the food for the guests that were set to arrive throughout the day. He waved away anyone who tried to offer him food before pulling a carton of eggs out of the icebox, along with a handful of vegetables. With his free hand, Virgil grabbed a hunk of cheese and shut the icebox with his foot. It took him a moment to find an empty burner on the stovetop, but once he did, he set up shop.

He found a freshly sharpened knife first, and then he chopped onions and peppers before setting them over the flame. While those browned, he took a grater and shredded some of the cheese. Then, with careful precision, he cracked several eggs. The first one shattered in his fist, bits of the shell mixing in with the broken yolk. He cursed under his breath and tried again, managing to avoid ruining the rest of the carton. The amount of focus this required drew sweat on his brow, which was annoying.

Virgil whisked the eggs into submission and poured them over the charred onions and peppers. Once it was time, he flipped it and added the shredded cheese, watching it cook with hungry impatience. At some point, he'd need to grow out of the habit of letting the day grow long before eating a real meal. But today was not that day.

He found himself a quiet corner to eat and scarfed down his food with a vengeance. Maybe it was the best thing he'd ever eaten, or maybe he was hungrier than he let himself notice, but he didn't care to determine which was which. Every time the door to the kitchens opened, he felt every muscle stiffen as he waited with held breath while the person revealed themselves not to be Rhaella. Occasionally, a black-cloaked Doctrina would walk in, paying him no mind. Those were the moments that drove Virgil to near-insanity.

Congresses were more stressful than was warranted, he decided. To schedule one required such delicate balance between *all* of the houses, which meant compromising and deal-making. He'd rather hoped they would be able to avoid scheduling one altogether, but the consequences of the war had proven too much for each house to handle independently.

Perhaps he was simply put off by the amount of people it required to make seemingly simple decisions.

Virgil placed his dirty dishes with the rest that were in need of washing, and he left the kitchens in search of something to do. Nobody expected anything of him until the congress had officially commenced, and that couldn't happen until every house had arrived. The Palace of Many Rooms was full of the many wonders of Adristan, including its populus. In the meantime, Virgil decided, he could view the artifacts in the museum. Perhaps he could create something in the workshop. Or maybe he could even continue his training.

In the end, he decided that he might find some peace in the library.

Virgil was anything but surprised when he found Rhaella prowling the shelves. She was a few stacks deep, nearly hidden by the rows of books, but her gray robes were visible between the gaps. Her blonde hair was a stark contrast to the overall darkness of the room, almost blinding in its brightness. The windows may have been open and there might have been sunlight streaming through them, but the shelves were far removed enough from its light so that the books didn't age prematurely.

He watched her trail a hand along spines, her eyes flicking to him now and again. And after a moment, he jerked his chin toward an empty table and took a seat. For a horrifying second, he thought she might not follow him. Then, to his relief, she joined him shortly after.

"I thought I'd find you here," he said.

"We're in *my* family's room," she said, toying with the hem of her sleeve. "How was the journey from Greenisle?"

He chewed on his cheek. "The skies were strange today. I do a lot of sailing, but rarely do I see a red sunrise before a voyage."

She narrowed her eyes. "Are you normally so superstitious?"

"I wouldn't put it that way. You just learn to notice patterns when sailing. Not to mention the number of shrikes I've seen since docking. They'vebeen bothering me all day."

"Well," she said, leaning forward on her elbows. "We're in a contained space filled with every major house, several of whom are arguing at the moment. Then, we have their top guards, armed with enough weapons to fill a brand new armory. Not to mention the sheer number of political power-players roaming the halls at this exact moment… Danger isn't exactly an *impossibility*."

"What are the odds you've determined?"

She put on a face, pretending to consider it. "Not highly likely, though a drunken brawl or two are almost guaranteed."

He hummed. "I think it falls to me and my duty to break those up."

"Then you'd better get patrolling, Commander," she said, wiggling her brows.

Virgil snorted. "You're very funny. Did you find me any information?"

She hesitated, and from the faraway look in her eye, Virgil realized she was listening for any eavesdroppers. He was becoming familiar with the way she looked while listening. Her preternatural sense was otherworldly in its execution. It made him intimately aware of how little he knew her. And yet, he also couldn't deny how desperately he wished for the opportunity to grow more acquainted with this particular expression of hers.

Noting that the library was empty except for them, she blinked back to the present and nodded her head. "I didn't learn much, but there are a few things of note."

"Tell me."

"The remaining royalists have reached an almost religious zeal, but not for Lucerianism. It's more like a reverence for their so-called Trueborn.

There are quite a few aspects that cross over with Lucerians, though," she said. "They both seem to like fire very much."

"Does that matter?"

"No, but…" She trailed off, biting her lip. Virgil's gaze sharpened, then, watching her mouth in open fascination. Rhaella seemed suddenly insecure, not wanting to continue.

He pushed gently. "What is it?"

She turned her eyes toward the ceiling, watching the sunlight dance across it. "Do you believe in prophecies? You know, fortune tellers and the like?"

"I can't say I do," he answered honestly.

Tucking loose hair behind her ear did nothing when the braided strands continued to fall in her face. Virgil ached to reach out and tug on one of them, but he refrained, opting to cross his arms on the tabletop instead.

A Mediator entered the library then, and went to browse the shelves. Virgil and Rhaella stared at one another, an unspoken agreement written clearly on both of their faces. They had to be careful with what they said.

"When I was younger—ten, I think—a fortune teller was at a festival held on Isle Verdale. Asriel and I got our fortunes read. He got something befitting an heir and future High Lord. Mine, however, was strange. I've never really found any deeper meaning to it beyond the superficial, but I'm starting to wonder if there may have been at least *some* truth to what the fortune teller told me."

"Go on," Virgil prompted her. He was curious to hear where she was going with this.

"Everything had to do with fire in some form. Fire in my eyes, flame in my spirit, things like that. I hadn't thought about it much before, but the wording in all of the books on royalists brought it back to mind for some reason."

He watched the Mediator leave the room before speaking again. "Tell me the prophecy."

She shook her head. "It's been years. I don't recall the exact wording."

Virgil didn't entirely believe that she would have forgotten such a thing, but he didn't press the matter further. If she was misleading him, he trusted her enough not to pry. "Fire is a common motif in the histories," he noted. "Either that, or the fortune teller could have been a fraud."

Rhaella rolled her eyes, which drove him mildly insane. Not for its disrespect, but for the casualty of it. Again, it drove him out of his mind to find such ease with the imposing woman sitting across from him. She was so unguarded in this moment that he wanted to freeze time so it would never end.

"That's the superficial part," she said. "There could be a deeper meaning to it."

"And you think it has something to do with the royalists?"

"I don't know," she shrugged. "But why did I receive such a riddle only a few years before the royalists declared war, and I played a key part in ending it? All of this language surrounding fire just feels too coincidental to be an accident."

She had such an incredible mind. It almost took his breath away to watch it in action. Virgil turned her words over in his head. Arguably, he could draw similarities between the fire imagery present in Lucerianism, royalist dogma, and her fortune. But he couldn't be sure whether such musings would actually matter to the issue at hand.

"I feel silly," she said, breaking the silence. "I should stick to the facts. There are plenty of them to wade through without silly nonsense from holiday carnivals."

"You aren't silly," Virgil said. "It could matter. We don't know, and we likely won't for a good while."

"My patience wears thin," Rhaella groaned, dropping her head into her hands.

"I know, ke bawp," he said gently.

Rhaella stared at him unblinkingly. "You said that last time. What does it mean?"

He laughed softly. "I thought you would have deconstructed my language just from the little I taught you."

To his delight, her cheeks turned bright pink. "It wasn't enough to work with. I taught you how to sign seven letters. You taught me three words. *You owe me*."

"Is that right?" He leaned back in his chair, comfort settling over his body as he stretched out in the chair. "What have I always called you?"

As realization washed across her features, she turned an even deeper shade of pink.

"Oh," she said. "Little bird."

"Yes, ke bawp," he repeated.

Mastering herself, Rhaella said, "it's a shame we didn't get to make better use of that bird call."

"We still could," he said, blowing out an almost-musical whistle.

She smiled then, and it was bright and true. *Good.* That was how her face was meant to look. Broken open and split wide with happiness. He couldn't stand the exhaustion that had been washed across her features when he first found her here. She was still beautiful, but she was also beginning to bend under the weight of the Order. She was breaking and it was unacceptable.

"If we're counting letters," he said, "that puts me at fifteen total. You've only taught me seven. Now *you're* the one who *owes* me."

"I can give you seven right now," she said.

"Off the top of your head?" He chuckled. "Somebody's eager to pay their debts."

"Don't look so smug," she said. "My Vessial name is seven letters, too."

"You taught me your Vessial name."

"In sign, yes," she said. "I told you, I have a spoken name that's different."

Her language was endlessly fascinating to him. For each new thing she taught him, there was so much more to uncover. And he was thankful they could have a conversation like this at all. It was an incredible show of trust on both their parts that they could share a secret this delicate. His father would be furious if he found out, and he was certain hers would be, too. But this was something that existed only between the two of them. He would never betray this knowledge to his father or, gods forbid, his uncle. And he knew she would never reveal such a thing either.

"Do you want the common tongue translation first, or shall we go straight to the Vessial?"

Another Mediator walked in then, heading straight for the back row of shelves. Virgil watched them walk away raising a brow, allowing her the option of silence. She shrugged.

"It's fine," she answered aloud.

"Vessial, then."

"Vzoz cìr," she said.

"Vzoz cìr," he repeated, though his pronunciation was much clunkier than hers had been. Her voice sounded so elegant when she spoke in her own tongue. Her speech was almost musical in its perfection, and he wanted her to speak it again and again. "Now the common tongue."

She pursed her lips, holding in a laugh. "You don't want to try to pronounce it again?"

"No," he said swiftly. "What's it translate to?"

"Participles are complicated in Vessial," she said. "But, roughly, it means *seeing-daughter*."

"That you are," he said appreciatively. "So you weren't given your Vessial name until you got a little older, I imagine?"

She nodded. "Until I was about fifteen or sixteen, my father would just call me cìr. Daughter. Either that, or just Rhaella."

He wanted to ask her more questions. Anything to get her to speak more Vessial. He would even offer her more Menmal to get such a thing in return, but the library doors opened again. This time, though, instead of a faceless Mediator who made their way in, he spotted Prince Asriel.

Immediately, Virgil remembered how High Lord Veservus had sent Rhaella through the woods without even a single guard, meanwhile her brother had a seemingly-permanent shadow. The imbalance between the High Lord's two children sent fury straight to Virgil's head. He frowned, suddenly not in the mood to talk anymore.

Asriel's eyes flickered toward the shelves, then to his sister. "Rhae! I didn't know you'd arrived."

He came to their table and leaned down to hug his sister. Virgil noted how stiffly Rhaella returned the gesture. *That* was interesting.

"Is Father with you?" Her tone was sickly sweet. She was overdoing it, and she wasn't masking it well. This was unusual for her.

"Yes. He's already in the suite. It seemed like he wanted some privacy to work on a few things. What are you doing?"

For the first time, Asriel looked up and noticed Virgil sitting there. His throat bobbed, but he swept into a low bow.

"Prince Virgil," he said. "It's been a few weeks since we've seen one another."

"Even less time since I've written," Virgil said gruffly. "Mail seems slow-coming from your house."

Rhaella looked between him and her brother, quietly taking in the tension between them. Virgil cast her a glance, slightly perking one brow. She said nothing.

Asriel laughed nervously. "Am I interrupting something?"

"No," Rhaella said, managing to keep her tone even this time. "Virgil and I were just discussing strategy."

Incredulously, Asriel asked, "For *fun*?"

She rolled her eyes again in that endearing way. "No, you fool. In regards to all the work we did. Don't you remember?"

Her tone was light, edging on the playfulness Virgil would have expected between siblings. But he thought he detected a hint of real animosity beneath her words, too. If Asriel noticed it also, he played it off well.

Unshaken, he raised his hands in surrender. "My mistake. I was just going to call for tea, would you both care for some?"

"I'll take some, thank you," Rhaella said.

"Sure," Virgil said flatly.

"Barrett," Asriel said, turning over his shoulder. "Would you?"

Asriel's guard eyed Virgil warily, though recognition flared in his eyes. He'd completed a few years of training on Isle Verdale. It was a statistical impossibility for Virgil to not know who he was.

"You can relax," Virgil called out to him. "I'm not going to assassinate your charge while you're fetching tea."

"Of course, my Lord," Barrett said, bowing before he departed through the doors.

"I'll wait to do that until he gets back," Virgil muttered under his breath.

"Is that necessary?" Rhaella asked as Asriel took the empty seat beside her.

Virgil ignored her pleading. He wasn't going to soften himself for her brother's sake, even if she was attempting to. Instead, he fixed his gaze on Asriel, staring at him long enough to make the Prince squirm.

"How's duty treating you?"

"Well enough," Asriel said. "Same as you, I expect."

"Oh, I wouldn't know about your day to day duties," Virgil said, grinning. "Thank you for writing to me about how the trade meeting went all those weeks back."

"Of course," Asriel said, glaring. "Remind me why you weren't able to come?"

His guard returned with the tea then, tailed by both Declan and Eric. Once the tea had been set on the table, all of the guards posted against the wall, leaving each other a wide berth.

Virgil reached for the kettle, refusing to answer Asriel outright. To Rhaella, he asked, "How do you take your tea?"

"Is it black tea?" She peered at it, sniffing. "As it is, thank you."

He handed her a mug, and when her fingers brushed his as she took it, a shiver went down his spine. Even though they were calloused, her hands were still so soft. Only after pouring himself a mug did Virgil give the Third Prince his attention again.

"I had to attend to some duties for my father which, unfortunately, coincided with the trade meeting. I'm sure you understand the need to place certain duties above others."

"Quite." Asriel's words were clipped. He turned to Rhaella and blinked an unnatural amount of times. Virgil held in his scoff, knowing that he was actually *speaking* to his sister.

She blinked only a few times before turning back to Virgil. "I've been stuck with the Order since I arrived. I only saw five other ships in the harbor. Do you know who else is here?"

Virgil ticked the houses off on his fingers. "Lightpike, Aviatis, Redspire, myself, and yours. And the Order, obviously."

She frowned. "Are we early, or the others late?"

"Somewhere in between," he shrugged.

"House Lancor should be here any day now," Asriel said, sipping his tea. "Their ship docked at the ports at Isle Verdale to pick up Freya, and then they were set to make their way here."

"Do I finally get to meet her?" Rhaella shot her brother a look.

Asriel nodded even as his face twisted with annoyance. "Yes, Rhae, you can."

So Virgil's word *had* done them some good then. The Lancors were going through with the betrothal after all. Virgil didn't regret putting in a good word for House Veservus, but he did regret that only Asriel would reap the benefits of such a thing.

"I should get ready," Asriel said, downing the last of his tea. "I want to look my best for her. I'll come find you after she gets settled."

He enveloped Rhaella in another hug as he stood, which she accepted but did not return. Virgil watched her blank face, how dull she looked in her brother's arms. It would be inappropriate for him to ask what was wrong, but he could infer enough on his own. In all likelihood, she was finally sick of Asriel's shit.

Once Asriel and his watchdog left the library, Virgil asked, "Are you okay?"

She waved a hand. "It doesn't matter."

"It does," he replied sharply.

With a beseeching look, she asked him, "Can it not, just for a little longer?"

Virgil acquiesced, saying nothing more. He couldn't make himself refuse her when her voice had sounded so small. So *tired*.

Rhaella sighed. "We should mingle. That's what our families will be expecting."

"Mingling. My favorite," he said, not even sounding convincing to his own earst. Gesturing to the door, he said, "After you."

Rhaella stood and started following him out. Virgil's guards had already excused themselves to find something else to do, and he appreciated that their presence was merely a reaction to Ser Barrett's presence.

Then, Rhaella slowed until she came to a full stop. For a moment, the corners of her mouth twitched before she allowed herself a smirk. Looking up at him with a twinkle in her eye, she said, "So ke is little, isn't it?"

He nodded. "It is."

"So what would be the Menmal word for…" She waved a hand at his figure. "All of this?"

Virgil burst into laughter, clutching a hand to his stomach.

Rhaella remained unamused. "I'm nearly the same height as you. It isn't fair for you to call me little."

"It's the sentiment," he said, wiping his eyes.

"Alright. Then, sentimentally, if I wanted to call you *large*, what word would I use?"

Between laughter, he said, "Lesht."

She muttered the word to herself a few times, licking her lips between tries. Then, she said, "Very well, lesht bawp. I'll see you around."

As Virgil watched her walk away, a few realizations came crashing down on him at once. First, he saw that she practically floated on air as she walked away, her robes nearly touching the floor where they swished around her boots. Second, he could no longer deny how much he enjoyed her presence. He had never been able to, if he was being honest with himself, but this time felt different somehow. For the first time since first hearing of it, the idea of attending the upcoming congress seemed like less of a drag, all because of the mere possibility that he'd see her there.

As long as he had an excuse to be around Rhaella, he would deal with whatever political nonsense came his way. And damn him for the transgression, but he'd suffer years worth of this torture if it afforded him just one more moment to exist within her orbit. He'd accept whatever duty his father handed to him. As long as it meant he'd see a glimpse of her, he'd do it. For her, Virgil would become the thing he'd fought against at every step until now.

Feeling somehow entirely changed within the span of a mere moment, Virgil went to find his father, assured in the knowledge that even the worst of conversations couldn't shake the way he felt.

CHAPTER
TWENTY-TWO

"The Grand Introduction is a time-honored tradition, implemented to prevent an imbalance of power between the houses. In order for a congress to proceed, all eight major houses must be present with an equal number of official attendants. Parties must include the heir apparent, Dux Doctrina, and a pre-approved amount of attendants."
—Major & Minor Laws, *collected by High Lord Vincent Midar*

30 Luceriary, in the Benevolent year 112 A.E.

House Oberon arrived two days after the other houses. The nature of these congresses meant that the proceedings could not begin until every member of the Concilium had been accounted for, and so the aristocracy had stalled. Left to wait indefinitely until the last of them made their way to the Palace.

The rules of the congress required that every practicing Doctrina attend, as well as the Reverend Mother, the cardinal Superiors, and a few chosen Progenies. It also required that the majority of the councilmen were present, and that all eight High Lords *and* their heirs attended. If a house could not present an heir apparent, they needed to present an heir presumptive in their stead. Though from Rhaella's understanding, each High Lord brought all of their children, regardless of status.

Her father had not made the same choice. He never had.

There had never been an opportunity for her to attend congresses when she had been nothing more than a bastard and a ward. Her father typically sent her on reconnaissance missions whenever he and Asriel were tied up at the Palace. Without the presence of other high-ranking nobles on the islands, the rest of the aristocracy merely served as a treasure trove for her to pick gold out of.

She couldn't stop herself from wondering what things might look like if she were still a part of her father's house. If he would have let her come along this time. She thought she might have had a gown commissioned of the finest reds and blacks. She would don the family jewels and represent House Veservus in the quiet, subtle way she always had. She would openly mingle with the other children of the stronghold families. It would be whispered about, but she could allow herself to dance with Virgil for everyone to see. She could be courted, and go home to ride Egorion across the skies of Adristan and beyond.

But now, since she was a part of the Order, she would stand against the wall in gray robes and stay dutifully silent until someone approached her. She could neither dance nor drink… At least, not openly. Those privileges were reserved for practicing Doctrinas. For the ones in black robes who had paid their dues. Tonight, Rhaella would continue to watch from the sidelines. It was nothing new for her, but that didn't make it any less painful an obligation.

In the days it took for everyone to arrive, she spent her time in the library, drinking in every resource it had to offer on the royalists. The nature of waiting for the congress to commence meant that she and Virgil could meet at tables and talk without seeming suspicious. And as much as she hoped those conversations would be a reprieve for her, they were mostly full of frustration. There were so many questions and a distinct lack of answers.

If she had solely been seeking answers to her own questions, she might have given up by now. But she didn't want to disappoint Virgil. She couldn't tell when they'd reached this point that she now cared so much, but she didn't resent it either. If she was honest, she'd been racing towards that cliff as long as they'd been writing letters. And yet, that cliff's edge still seemed like it was so far off in the distance. It was impossible to ignore. She cared what Virgil thought about, and she cared what he thought about *her*.

She hadn't anticipated how painful it would be to know Virgil Midar and to be unable to touch him the way she wanted to. Talking to him was always a highlight of that day, even though the occasions were few and far between. If she could, she'd converse with him well into the night and into the next day. But that was coupled with the urge to run her fingers along his jawline and feel his stubble against her skin. To bear the weight of his considerable body against her own. To know him in such a way that a Doctrina never could.

There were so many vows between them. A vow of chastity. A vow of service to the Order. Potions to keep her bound to those vows, making them more than just words. Sure, other Doctrinas broke their vows all the time. They fucked who they pleased so long as the Superiors remained none the wiser. But how was she to handle this never ending *ache* in the pit of her stomach every time she thought of betraying her word?

She had never had a sensitive stomach before, but since being given the proper dosage of potions, she felt disgusted with herself every time she fantasized about giving in to her desires with Virgil. Every time she thought of abandoning her post. Whenever she wanted to open up to her brother. When she wanted things that were unbecoming of a member of the Order.

It was horribly inconvenient.

If she wanted to overcome the effect of the potions, she would need to continue pushing her tolerance, she decided. Her old methods were no longer going to work. As soon as she returned to the Silent Keep, she vowed to steal from the supplies. Inventory duty rotated between Progenies; Rhaella would have to wait until it was her turn. For now, she was going to have to suffer through the poison infiltrating her bloodstream.

Someday, she was going to be forced to take a potion that bound her in service to Asriel, as long as her father's money remained good to the Dux. She was already bound to him, and had been from birth. But this would be a legitimate tie between them. Something tangible that they would drink down to the dredges and that would remain in their systems. Regardless of any friction between her and her duty to the house she served, Rhaella would never be able to separate herself from it. She'd never again have any distance between her and her brother once she took that vow. No matter what, once she took that vow, she would no longer be acting in her own best interest.

The thought sent chills skittering across her skin.

She had rarely acted in her own best interest before, and certainly not now. But on the rare occasion she did manage such a thing, it felt empowering. When she thought back on the times she had stolen away into the night and drank herself stupid at taverns, kissing any willing mouths and taking home the most attractive bodies, she smiled with fondness. She missed how she had danced until her limbs were sore.

Those nights felt far away now, and they'd feel even farther away once she graduated from training.

House Oberon had arrived that morning, but that felt like years ago already. The nobles had been in meetings since then, and they'd barely come up for air. The doors to the large conference room they occupied had remained shut since the start. If she was honest with herself, she was feeling *bored* with no clear directive. She had exhausted the Palace's supply of books on royalists, leaving her to make friends with the other Progenies.

Or.

She gave herself no time to second guess the thought, she simply acted on it. Slipping into the hallway, Rhaella made for the conference rooms, looking for a quiet space to listen in.

The meeting spaces were as ornate as they had been when they were the king's spaces. Ordinarily, the congress would be held in the great hall just off of the foyer. But seeing as the Mediators were still hard at work readying it for the Grand Introduction, the High Lords and their heirs had been relegated to the next-largest space. It had once been an auditorium with a large stage for the king's entertainment, and it had since been converted into a versatile space befitting the needs of its user.

Today, it was a meeting room.

There were no guards lining the hall. The Palace of Many Rooms was a peaceful place. It was a neutral gathering space, with no need for guards or their weapons. Despite her ancestors' good intentions, though, Rhaella couldn't help but see it as an oversight. Especially when she considered how many other prying eyes were in attendance.

Rhaella made her way to the upper level of the auditorium, where a door with an ancient lock opened easily under her touch. It opened onto a thin walkway that was housed comfortably between a series of wires which raised and lowered the curtains onto the stage. It made for the perfect place to sit, since she had never been afraid of heights. Carefully, Rhaella walked out to the middle of the walkway and she sat, letting her legs dangle and hiding behind the swaths of fabric.

Voices argued below. She recognized her father's voice, alongside that of one of the Lightpike men.

"I'm not suggesting as much," her father said. "All I'm saying is that it would be worth keeping an eye on."

"And are you volunteering your own soldiers for such an effort?" Lord Regis, husband to the High Lord, said. "Because I'm not seeing any other volunteers."

"It is the duty of every noble at this table to contribute," her father argued. "A nationwide patrol is something we have been lacking."

"And why do you think that is?" One of the many masters of coin prompted.

Someone sighed. Maybe Asriel, from the cadence. "I think my father makes a fine point. We're leaving the waters surrounding each island up to chance. That is where we're being hit the hardest."

"Which would require reinforced ships," High Lord Lancor said. "That will take a substantial amount of time. Not to mention the expense."

"If it's what we agree is best," High Lord Aviatis said, "our coffers are abundant. We can supplement the cost."

"Now, I'm not saying we won't—"

Awareness tingled across the back of Rhaella's neck. *Someone was outside the door on the other end of the walkway.* Though their presence didn't unsettle her, and she made no efforts to hide when the door creaked open. Especially not when Virgil stepped onto the narrow path. She scoffed to herself at the irony.

Her attention remained fixed on the meeting below, but she felt it as Virgil settled himself on the edge of the rafter, letting his legs dangle. The two of them didn't speak for some time, and instead just listened. The High Lords were still entrenched in a vicious argument, and her father continued to play both offense and defense.

The conversation had moved from the topic of soldiers and ships to the state of the towns. In places as far out as Isle Verdale, the heavily-populated areas required substantial reconstruction. Rhaella knew that her father was painfully aware of this, and that he had been developing a plan to rebuild. In fact, she had been in charge of proofreading those very plans before everything had changed so drastically.

Nodding toward the sounds of the congress, Virgil whispered, "How much have you heard already? Do you need context?"

"A national guard. The need for reinforced ships. A lack of time." She ticked each topic of conversation off on her fingers. "I've drawn several conclusions so far, and none of them good."

"You'd be right," Virgil said. "There are delays on nearly every major export from multiple islands, and there's too much of a pattern to suspect it's simply due to bad weather. We can't continue to ignore the possibility that the royalists are laying out their next bit of strategy and we've failed to see the bigger picture just yet."

After a pause, Rhaella said, "Have you given any more thought to your uncle?"

"Of course I have," he said, not unkindly. "He's been a menace all day. He speaks out of turn, he talks over my father, and he talks over *me*. To make matters worse, my father won't do anything to put him in his place. He just lets him speak, because he's his brother. Maybe if he had worthwhile advice to offer, I could suffer through it. But his insight is *terrible*."

"People can want for power," she said. "But that doesn't make them suited for it."

"Spoken like a Doctrina," Virgil said, smiling sadly. "I don't think this will get resolved within the congress. They're going to send a wave of troops out to see if they can take care of it."

"Will you have to rejoin the effort?"

"No," he said on a shaky exhale. "Not for the first few waves, at least. If the fighting escalates, then I'll go."

She nodded, crossing her arms so she wouldn't reach out and touch him. "I didn't see you get up to leave."

"Then I was gone before you got here," he replied. "My father sent me to retrieve some documents from our suite, and I decided to take the scenic way back. I should have known you'd be up here too."

"Yes, you should have," Rhaella said, leaning over her knees to get a better view of below. Virgil's hand fisted in the back of her robe, eliminating the potential of her toppling forward. "This is a historic moment. I can't recall the last time we held a congress. I shouldn't keep you from this."

Virgil blew out a long huff of air. "My father is expecting me, true, but you should go too. I heard a Mediator in the halls mentioning the Reverend Mother. It seems her ship should be arriving any moment now."

Rhaella shuddered at the thought of seeing her again. "Great," she muttered.

She kept her head down, even as Virgil tried to catch her eye, but he was persistent. Carefully, he placed gentle fingers beneath her chin and lifted her face to look at him. His eyes bore into hers. They were a rich brown, soft and searching. She realized then that her first impression of him had been correct. There was nothing other than earnestness in those eyes of his.

"Are you going to be alright?"

In the placating way she always had, Rhaella put on a smile, knowing that it didn't reach her eyes. She nodded, and her skin rubbed against Virgil's calloused hand. "I always am."

His eyes flickered down to the congress, then back to her. "I'll fill you in on any details I learn. Go, before your Superiors start coming out of their hiding places."

Though it pained her to do so, Rhaella heeded Virgil's warning. He went back to the congress, and she went to the library. No sooner had she sat down before a Mediator came calling for her and several of the other Progenies in the room to make their way toward the foyer. She followed towards the back, lingering as long as she could. Something in her blood confirmed her suspicions before she knew for certain, but as the Reverend Mother stepped into view, her suspicions were confirmed. Reverend Mother Locasta waited for the Progenies with her hands folded, stern and proud as always. Rhaella bristled at the sight of her, the potion poisoning her blood urging her to show deference even as she trembled in fear.

A Father Superior cleared his throat. "The Order expects you all to look your best tonight. The Grand Introduction is not the largest ball you'll attend this week, but it is the most formal. We're going to hand out some veils to you now. Don't worry, they're gray, not black. These will still signify you as Progenies."

"Additionally," a Mother Superior continued, "you've been granted access to the jewelry supply in the Redspire wing. Each piece is artfully crafted, and a worthy representation of Adristan. You'll be able to loan them out for the evening. Don't get any ideas, they're enchanted so that they cannot leave the Palace grounds."

So she'd be veiled and bejeweled, just like a fully dedicated Doctrina. *Splendid.*

"Wicked," one of the Progenies beside her said under his breath.

Rhaella supposed it was generous of the Order to allow them this little bit of extravagance. And she *did* enjoy wearing jewelry.

Small pleasures like these would keep her afloat.

She took the gray veil handed to her by a Mother Superior before a Father Superior led them to the Redspire wing. He rhythmically tapped his fingers against an unassuming wall, which then opened to reveal shelves upon shelves of glittering necklaces, earrings, and rings. Rhaella grabbed as much red jewelry as she could, pocketing a heavy necklace and matching earrings. She managed to grab five rings before the Father Superior cut her off.

She was very aware of the Reverend Mother who kept watch over them all silently.

"Tonight," the Father Superior said, "we'll be seated in the hall before the introductions start. You will watch silently and respectfully, and you will not show any bias toward the island or houses you may have originated from. There will be a few speeches, after which the nobles will be free to mingle and such. When that time comes, secure a perimeter around the room wherever you find gaps between the guards. You won't be punished for standing next to one another, but we prefer that you spread out as much as you can. You'll be called back to the table once dinner is served. After dinner, you will return to your posts. Once midnight strikes, you are free to decide when to retire for the evening."

"Make yourselves presentable," the Reverend Mother said, finally deeming them worthy of speech. "Uphold the reputation of the Order. That means grooming yourselves. That means cosmetics. *Go,* you have finite time."

The Progenies dispersed back into the Palace, heading toward the halls lined with nothing but guest bedrooms. Rhaella considered readying herself in the Veservus suite, but she cast that thought off immediately. She went to the room the Order had assigned her to, locking herself in before sinking into the luxurious tub. The finest soaps and oils lined the rim of the tub, and as she massaged them into her hair, she felt like a noble again for the first time since being cast off.

And the feeling only took root the longer she fiddled with cosmetics in the mirror—not much, just enough to cover the dark circles and bring some color back to her cheeks. If anything, she felt more regal than she had since leaving House Veservus. After braiding the front pieces of her hair, she settled the gray veil atop her head. Once all of the jewelry was on, she thought she painted a fine picture of a Doctrina. Bitterly, she was halfway pleased with herself.

Bells rang somewhere in the distance and she cringed against the sound. It was so sudden and cacophonous compared to the cavernous quiet of her rooms. Rising to her feet, she left the strange, empty room and went to meet her company.

The other Progenies gathered outside of the hall, giggling amongst themselves. It occurred to her then that this was their first congress, too. In another life, she wondered if she would be as excited as them. It was a sad thought, that it couldn't be true for this life.

"Get inside," a Superior hissed, waving them through the double doors. Hurriedly, they obeyed. The table in the furthest corner was clothed in black. That would definitely be theirs, then. The Reverend Mother was already seated at the head of the table, surrounded by Superiors on either side. The Progenies filled in wherever there were available seats. With some maneuvering, Rhaella managed to grab a corner seat and place her back against the wall so that she could observe the entire room unencumbered.

At every other table, there were masters of coin, masters of ships, masters of trade, and so many more. There were relatives of the noble families, as well as those known to be trusted confidantes to the High Lords. At the table reserved for House Veservus sat a distant uncle of Asriel's. Rhaella recalled that he usually resided on the mainland, overseeing the Veservus-trained scholars who were employed by the nobles in Steephelm.

Musicians began to play a gallant tune. The doors were shut, and the lanterns drawn low.

It was time.

Rhaella felt a pit in her stomach, though this one felt different from simple nerves. She thought it might have been excitement. The nobles were in the alcove at the top of the wide staircase at the other end of the room, and she fixed her eyes on the landing while she waited with baited breath.

"High Lord Ewan Lancor of House Lancor, Keeper of Amenities, Fashioner of All Furnishings, and the Strong Bones of Adristan. And his Lady Wife, Laila Redspire. And their son and heir, Prince Ezra Lancor."

The giants made their way across the floor toward their table, which had been draped in the classic orange of their house. Their finery included plates fashioned like armor, only they were constructed out of wood, which had been sewn into the shoulders, elbows, knees, and torsos of their clothes. Even from a distance, Rhaella could tell that the carpenters had mastered their craft when creating them. When Rhaella glanced to her left, she saw Freya and her younger brother Ledger standing beside the table draped in a similar orange swath of fabric. They wore clothes just as grandiose as the rest of their party. Once their father arrived and took his seat at the head of the table, they followed suit.

"High Lord Isaiah Oberon of House Oberon, Keeper of Health, Healer of All Wounds, and the Rejuvenating Breath of Adristan. And his cousin and heir, Prince Sage Oberon."

The High Lord and his heir made their way to the white-clothed table to Rhaella's right. Brilliant white robes draped their bodies, swooping over one shoulder to leave the other bare, exposing the mass of tattoos that covered both of their arms and necks. Rhaella thought that she spotted a fresh tattoo on Sage's head and frowned. The Second's customs regarding tattoos were vast; they took just about any excuse to decorate their bodies. But to do so while keeping the rest of the nation waiting?

Straightening in her seat, Rhaella felt a rush of anticipation for her family's arrival. She wasn't sure why she suddenly felt nervous to watch them come down the steps, but she was. Helplessly, all she could do was dig her fingers into the black tablecloth and try to keep her racing pulse in check.

"High Lord Alden Veservus of House Veservus, Keeper of Intelligence, Knower of All Events, and the Vast Brain of Adristan. And his son and heir, Prince Asriel Veservus."

Dressed in the most brilliant red doublets, her father led the charge with Asriel only a step behind. She felt a stabbing ache in her heart then that she could only describe as a sudden, albeit sharp, swell of pride. This might have been the first time she truly saw her brother for what he was. He certainly looked the part of the heir. And someday, he would take their father's place. Hot tears threatened at the corners of her eyes, but she wiped them away before anyone could see.

They had been seated to the left of House Lancor, which was ironic. She watched Asriel turn his face to smile at Freya, and she thought there might be genuine adoration in his eyes. Briefly, his gaze floated over to meet hers, and she offered her brother a small smile. He returned it in kind.

"High Lord Allison Redspire of House Redspire, Keeper of the Arts, Master of All Styles, and the Beating Heart of Adristan. And her Lady Wife, Lilliana Ledova. And their niece and heir, Princess Aida Redspire."

Judging by the way Aida clung to her aunts, an elbow looped through each of their arms, something was different about her friend. And then, with clarity as sharp as an arrow, Rhaella realized what that change must have been. Aida looked exhausted, but she was undeniably glowing. She did not look upset about whatever circumstances had set dark circles beneath her eyes.

Aida had given birth to her baby.

The dress she wore hid her belly, which was undoubtedly still swollen. She had to have given birth *just* before arriving at the Palace. Concern and love warred within her. Had she known, she would have been at her friend's side in an instant. But the fact that she didn't know was by design; Aida had made herself scarce these past few days.

Aida's three younger sisters were standing beside the table to the right of House Oberon. As their eldest arrived, they helped her into a seat as the Mediator continued with the introductions.

"High Lord Geralt Stillgrove of House Stillgrove, Keeper of Nourishment, Refiner of All Tastes, and the Full Belly of Adristan. And his Lady Wife, Regina Normora. And their son and heir, Prince Gerard Stillgrove."

The purple-clad members of the Fifth House made their way through the hall with their heads held high, gold jewelry shining brightly against their dark skin. The High Lord and the Prince had matching headpieces modeled after their house sigil, a ram. Great golden horns rose up off of their crowns, stretching toward the painted ceilings. Lady Regina had a similarly designed tiara. Meeting their younger children at the table to the left of House Veservus, they took their seats in an organized dance of efficiency.

"High Lord Zerin Aviatis of House Aviatis, Keeper of the Veil, Seer of All Things, and the Triumphant Spirit of Adristan. And her niece and heir, Princess Raven Aviatis."

Wrapped in great cloaks like that of owl feathers, with trains that dragged behind them on the marble floors, the High Lord and the High Priestess made their entrance. Raven had feathers woven into her hair so precisely that they seemed to be growing out of her head. Some artificial, larger ones stuck out of the back of her head, extending the style nearly as long as the train.

Rhaella had shared some communication with Raven, even going as far as meeting with her a few times in person, but she was always struck by how beautiful the High Priestess was. She exuded the same alluring beauty that the rest of the Sixth House did—smoke that slipped through the fingers. Unabashedly, Rhaella let herself be captivated as they made their way to the table to the right of House Redspire. She was so distracted that she didn't turn her head when the Mediator called out the next house.

"High Lord Galahad Lightpike, Keeper of Wealth, Accountant of All Coins, and the Nimble Hands of Adristan. And his Lord Husband, Regis Aviatis. And their son and heir, Prince Ramsey Lightpike."

With the upsetting violence of a sudden storm, Rhaella's heart dropped to her feet as she looked up to watch the Seventh House descend. They were draped in mourning veils; the same brilliant green as their house color went all the way down to their ankles, and the hems were decorated with peacock feathers. Ramsey had been legitimized as the heir. Gasps went through the crowd, and she couldn't help but search for Aida in the crowd.

Her friend kept her chin high even as tears rolled down her face. Rhaella watched as her hands grasped her skirts, and she was shaking. *Violently.*

Gods, she was turning pale. Her sisters shielded her from prying eyes, but how odd would it look that an heir was crying for a fellow heir?

When Rhaella looked to the Seventh House again, she saw that Ramsey was crying, too. Bitterly, and through gritted teeth. At once, she felt nothing but sympathy for him where there had been only contempt just seconds before. How terrible, to lose his older brother and have to present himself as the new heir only days later.

Undeterred, the introductions continued to roll in. The congress would not stop on account of a death. Death had become commonplace to them amidst the horrors of war. The Lightpikes had chosen the next recipient of their mantle of power. As far as the powers that be were concerned, everything had been settled. No need for further action.

"High Lord Vincent Midar of House Midar, Keeper of the Peace, Bringer of All Justice, and the Unrelenting Muscle of Adristan. And his son and heir, Prince Virgil Midar."

Immediately, Rhaella could identify the concern on Virgil's face. In all likelihood, he hadn't known about Hiram's condition, and so his death had come as a complete and utter shock. She ached to comfort him, and to be comforted in return. That need felt instinctual, whereas with someone like Ramsey or Aida, she just felt common empathy.

Once the Midar family had been seated at the furthest right table, Rhaella tuned out of the speeches each of the High Lords rose to make. She couldn't even force herself to pay attention to her father's. Her focus was consumed by so many secrets she had no right to know, and yet knew anyway. She felt weighed down by them, like if she were thrown into a pond, she'd sink straight to the bottom with them. It was a burden, and it wasn't even her own.

At some predetermined point, a Mediator said something that had nobles rising to their feet and filling the dance floor. The Superiors stood as well, floating toward the practicing Doctrinas to catch up with their peers. That was the cue for the Progenies to take their places between the guards around the room.

Her eyes darted to Barrett with precision. He was near the table lined with drinks and finger foods. Typical for Asriel. She made her way over to him, standing a respectable distance away, but still close enough that they could still converse.

Barrett dipped his chin in greeting with his hands folded securely behind his back. "Enjoying the view?"

Before she could help herself, her eyes landed on Virgil at the fringes of the dance floor.

difficult. Rhaella mimicked Barrett's stance, folding her arms behind her back and separating her feet. She straightened her spine and did her best to avoid openly staring at anyone. Even as she yearned to be amongst the heirs and spares she had grown up around, Rhaella found a quiet comfort in not having to perform the same way they did, and the thought tickled her. Perhaps she could lie to herself a little longer. Perhaps she could tell herself that her circumstances didn't make her miserable.

It was a wishful thought, and it was one she felt the gods owed her at this point. That is, if any of the gods were still keeping score for her.

CHAPTER
TWENTY-THREE

"All of that said, I hope that you are able to find something to keep your mind occupied between your duties to your family and your house. I don't believe in the gods, but I think even they would agree that you deserve that time for yourself. I know I've found some reprieve in writing these letters, and in reading yours
—Except of a letter from Virgil Midar to Rhaella of House Veservus

30 Luceriary, in the Benevolent year 112 A.E.

"Trying to," she replied. "Does it get any easier, watching everyone?"

"Somewhat," he said. "All I've ever known is to stand on the sidelines."

If that was all she had to grow accustomed to, that wouldn't be too

This was not Virgil's idea of a good time.

His cousins seemed to be having fun, at least, but he was counting down the minutes until he could finally leave. They were on the dance floor with the Stillgrove brothers, perfectly executing the complicated partner dances they'd all been trained in. But he was content to stand on the edge of the floor and observe the others.

Declan and Eric lingered along the walls, spread out on opposite corners. Technically, they were watching Bianca and Mila too, even though his cousins had their own guards. And truth be told, if they encountered any overly-friendly hands while dancing, they could handle themselves just fine. Midars had no need for guards. He wished the powers that be would accept that.

Surveying the rest of the guards who were spread around the room, he counted two or three for every High Lord. Sometimes four if they'd brought a spouse. At least one per heir. One or two for every noble family member in attendance. And between every guard, there were Doctrinas scattered about.

The Order held a relatively peaceful reputation, but he knew they were trained in combat; his father had done workshops at the Silent Keep throughout the years. Not to mention that many in the Order had the blood of strongmen—either from the Midars or another family line—coursing through their veins.

Virgil wondered how much steel was in the room at the moment. Rhaella had spoken true when she quipped that there was enough to fill a second armory. He'd guess there were at least four hundred blades scattered across the bodies in the room. That was, if every guard held the standard four blades. But he was sure they were holstered with more.

He was busying himself with counting out imaginary daggers, swords, and chain whips when someone tapped him on the shoulder. Virgil turned to see Aida Redspire, red-eyed and stone-faced, blinking up at him.

"Dance with me." It was not a question.

As was customary, Virgil bowed at the waist and extended a hand, which she accepted. He wasn't in a position to refuse her—considering he owed her a debt—but given the look on her face, he wouldn't have denied her anyway.

The musicians' song slowed into a waltz. It took Virgil a few beats to get the footing right, but he and Aida quickly settled into the dance as if it was the most natural thing in the world. Aida clung to him fiercely, and judging by the way she dragged her feet, it was necessary for her. Virgil tightened the arm he had around her waist, appearing to lead her in the dance while also carrying most of her weight.

She wasted no time. "I'm calling in my favor."

"Alright," he said slowly. "If it's in my power to give—"

"It is," she said sharply. "Your power is in your strength. I need to borrow that."

Virgil nodded as he navigated them through a turn. "Fair enough. How may I be of service?"

She looked at him unblinking, and Virgil realized she had been crying. Weeping, even. But her tears had stalled and all that remained on her face was cold decision.

"You're the commander of the armies. You have access to the records of everything that happens to the people in your command. Living *and* dead, correct?"

"I am," Virgil said. "I do."

"Good." She sniffled, but forced down further tears before they could surface. "I need you to figure out who incapacitated Hiram Lightpike on the battlefield. If they're still alive, I need you to kill them."

He blinked once, twice, several times before formulating a response. "That is a very big ask."

"Can you do it, or shall I count you as owing me two favors instead?"

He considered the fact that she was fae, and that they took their favors with deadly seriousness. Then, he considered the fact that it would be near-impossible to prove beyond a doubt just *who* had so severely injured the Lightpike Prince. Virgil wanted to tell her that he, too, had only just learned of his death. But the vengeful look on her face told him he should hold his tongue. He decided there was no harm in simply checking the records, though there was no guarantee he'd find the answer she was seeking.

"I can *try*," he said at last. "That isn't a promise. Whoever killed Hiram could have been killed in return, and their name may not be listed in our records. I only have what my men have relayed to me."

"If you do your duty and check, and swear to me on your life that you did, I will count the debt as paid."

He dipped his chin solemnly. "I will do my very best."

"Thank you," Aida said. Then, she winced. "I need to sit down."

"Of course," he said, walking her to the edge of the dance floor. Two of her sisters met him there, taking Aida from his arms. One of the girls shot him a look full of the same fierceness he admired in her sister. Virgil resisted the urge to chuckle. The Redspire girls were unrelenting, and he respected that.

With nothing better to do at the moment, Virgil paced the perimeter of the dance floor. He clasped his hands behind his back, and he watched as the increasingly inebriated heirs pushed one another to the dance floor. He envied the way they all seemed to abandon their worries and duties so flawlessly.

Notably, most of the High Lords had forgone the dance floor in favor of remaining seated.. His father, for example, was now sitting with Uncle Nicholas at his right hand. Perhaps, he thought humorlessly, if his mother had attended as she was supposed to, his father might be enjoying the company of the dance floor at the moment instead of confining himself to the shadows. Surely the Order would see to it that she knew how disappointed they were with her lack of performance.

His mother might not have loved his father as she once had, but she was still a Lady Wife. She still had duties to attend to. And, childishly, Virgil couldn't help but wonder why it was that she would be allowed to shirk *her* duties when his father had never given him the same grace.

Virgil would never be afforded that same luxury again.

"Didn't expect to see you dancing, Midar," a slurred voice said from beside him.

He turned to see Ramsey Lightpike, his green mourning veil pushed back, smirking up at him. Virgil reined in the urge to ignore him. The man was grieving, and freshly thrust into being an heir. He was facing impossible tasks, all at the same time. Virgil could empathize with that, but he reasoned with himself that he still didn't have to like Ramsey.

"I'm not much of a dancer, but I'll make an exception here and there," he replied. "For the right partner."

Ramsey pointed toward the Redspire sisters who were all seated beside one another. "Are you very eager to fulfill the requirements the Order sent out? Which of those girls would you say yes to? You know, my fathers had a betrothal lined up for my brother. But now that he's dead, they called it off instead of passing it to me. What do you make of such a thing?"

Virgil bristled, reminding himself to breathe. "I'm sorry for your loss."

"Uh, uh, that's not an answer, Virgil." Ramsey hiccuped between his words. Ramsey had surpassed *drunk* hours ago, and was beginning to grow belligerent. "I want to know if you're going to bow down to the demands of the Order and the councils. Who even *wants* to get married?"

"I'm putting it off," Virgil said honestly. "I've got bigger things to worry about."

"Sage is going to—" He broke off mid-sentence, before continuing again. "You've met Sage Oberon, haven't you? Sage is going to sail to the Silent Keep after the congress to protest their decree."

"They can't call it a decree," Virgil said, slowly walking toward the drinks table. He was going to get the poor man a glass of water. "It's not a direct order. Technically, we don't have to obey it. It's merely a *suggestion*."

"A heavy-handed one," Ramsey grumbled. He accepted the glass without protest, chugging it down in only a few gulps. "This doesn't taste like liquor."

"That's because it's not," Virgil said, taking the empty glass from his hand and refilling it before Ramsey could protest. "Here. Have more."

"My Doctrina is watching us," Ramsey said, drinking as ordered. "He looks pleased that we're talking."

"They tend to do that," Virgil said. When Ramsey looked confused, he amended, "Watch, I mean."

"Am I ever going to get used to it?" The vulnerability in that question struck at something vital within Virgil.

Virgil wanted to tell Ramsey that yes, it would eventually get easier bearing the weight of everyone's attention. But he didn't want to lie. Virgil was constantly put off by the particular sort of attention his uncle paid him. Even now, Uncle Nicholas's eyes flitted over to him when he thought Virgil wouldn't notice, and it made him feel slimy to be observed like that. His uncle hadn't yet realized that Virgil was *always* paying attention. He wasn't the same reckless teenager he'd once been. Of course he still felt the same urges to forsake his family's lineage, but for the time being, he resisted them. He was nothing more than a leashed animal, content to hide in its cage. To wait for the moment he was unleashed to roam free.

"Sometimes," he finally admitted. Virgil patted Ramsey on the shoulder, trying to provide as much comfort as he could before walking away.

As he continued to walk around the room, Virgil counted off the rest of the heirs. There was Ezra, tall and frightened, who was dancing in one corner of the floor with his siblings. Asriel was mixed in with them, standing scandalously close to Freya. Sage chatted with the Redspires, which was interesting when he thought about Aida's condition. And as for the Stillgroves, they seemed to be walking the room together, making conversation with anyone who would have them.

Virgil should have been doing any number of those things, but his feet carried him in a much different direction. Before he quite understood what was happening, Virgil found himself along the side of the dance floor, drifting in and out of the lines of guards and Doctrinas. The whole time, his treacherous feet carried him closer and closer to one Doctrina in particular.

There were other nobles of various importance chatting with the Doctrinas. Which meant it didn't look out of place when he stood beside her and leaned down to speak in her ear. At least that's what he told himself as he worked up the courage to say something.

"Hello," he practically whispered.

Rhaella didn't turn her head toward him, but he saw the corners of her mouth twitch. "Hi."

"Is this a good time to fill you in on the meetings?" He gestured around the room. "Or are you very busy with your staring?"

"It's occupying a good amount of my focus," she said, standing taller. "You can try to steal some of it, though."

Virgil snorted, ducking his head. "I wish the news I had for you was as pleasant as you are. They're launching a national guard, and the duty of overseeing them technically falls to me."

"That sounds like a lot of traveling."

"It might be," he said. "A lot of sailing, in fact. We're going to try to communicate through the braziers first, to see if that's good enough. But if it proves inconvenient, I may have to invest in bonding to some winged beast."

"Well, if your reaction to Egorion proved anything," she replied blithely, "you might be better off with a gryphon."

"I pet the damn thing," he argued. "That counts for *something*."

As she fought back a smile, she said, "Is that the only news?"

"So far. Most of the meetings have just been to review the expenses of the war, and to establish some new laws to prevent further damage. It was all very technical. Uninteresting. Everything we talked about could have been handled through correspondence alone. And the High Lords have been taking turns making jabs at one another. Your father is not as unpopular as some of the rumors make him sound, but he's been on the defensive more often than not."

"Riveting," Rhaella said drily. "If only he had a strategist who could help smooth things out before he even arrived at this congress."

"He lost out," Virgil said bluntly. "Someday, he'll realize the error of his ways."

"I don't anticipate that day being anytime soon." She shot him a tired look. "I need to be entertained. Go find someone to dance with."

Virgil wasn't quite sure how to tell her he'd rather be here, whether they talked or they just stood in silence. Would it matter if he did? He wasn't sure.

As he stepped away, Virgil said, "If you want to watch me dance, ke bawp, then I'll dance."

Virgil forced himself to face the crowd and not her as he walked to the tables behind the floor. He pulled Raven Aviatis onto the floor for one dance, then two. And after that, he danced with both Galilea and Roman Stillgrove. He had several drinks, though they were weak and watered down. He assumed it was for the sake of decorum so that the drunkards couldn't reign supreme. But even so, he began to feel a buzz after the fifth one.

He went back to people watching after a while. Mila was dancing with what had to be the tenth man in line for her. If they still used dance cards, the way some other nations did, hers would be eternally full. Virgil watched his cousin with a protective fondness. He wanted her to find the love she was seeking, but he wasn't sure she would find it in the clammy hands of these social climbing nobles.

Bianca suddenly approached, taking his arm in an iron-tight grasp. In a hushed tone, she said, "Uncle is driving me mad. *Do something.*"

Incredulously, he asked, "What do you want me to do?"

She shrugged wildly. "I don't know, make him behave. Your father surely isn't."

Virgil looked over his shoulder to their table. Uncle Nicholas sat beside his father, draped in his absolute finest. He wore black robes that cinched together with a harness that went over his shoulders and around his waist, and a glittering mask that had to weigh at least five pounds perfectly obscured his features. He also wore a wolf charm that hung from his neck, and Virgil noted how much subtler it was than the family crest. Various people flitted to and from his side, and they all whispered in his ear before departing.

His father, meanwhile, looked half-out of it. Drooping sleepily, his eyes blinked shut before he startled awake again. Virgil frowned. His father didn't normally get overly drunk at a function. Tipsy, maybe, on the most riotous of occasions. But even that was a stretch.

"He keeps bringing up your mother," Bianca murmured.

Virgil groaned, pinching the bridge of his nose between two fingers. "I don't have the energy for this. Just leave them be. Go dance, or do something else to get away from them."

She rolled her eyes. "You dance with me. I don't want any of these men near me."

"As you say," Virgil said, bowing sarcastically, which earned him a good-natured punch in the shoulder.

He led Bianca onto the floor, and they stood opposite one another as another dance began. Virgil knew all of them by heart, and could have mentally checked out. But he kept his attention focused outward, aware of everyone who was or was not dancing. The drinks had dulled how nervous crowded rooms made him, but the effect was beginning to wear off.

A step forward, and then a step back. Several bouncing steps in a small figure eight, and then he waited for Bianca to do the same. As he made another pass, he became intertwined in the crowd, faced by different women. There were so many beautiful ones here. If he were more willing to bend to his father's will, he could have his pick of them. He should have been annoyed with himself that he didn't want any of them, but he couldn't seem to manage such a thing.

Taking Bianca's hand, he held their joined arms up so she could turn in a circle beneath them. Then, he ducked down to do the same.

Really, he could have anyone he wanted. Noblewomen, honorable men, genderless folk. Those distinctions had never mattered to him. The war had put so many of his priorities in check. He already knew that he didn't want to play the games that the rest of the nobles seemed content to play. There was a hollowness in doing so. But those who refused to were often hardened by it, even more calloused than he was. Virgil needed life. He needed air to be breathed back into his lungs. He needed the sun to finally emerge from behind the storm clouds.

He swore in Menmal when he stepped on Bianca's foot. "*Leïch*. I'm sorry."

"Your mind is somewhere else," she said, placing her palm against his as they stepped in a circle.

"Miles away," he said, eyes searching the far wall lined with guards.

"You've been like this for weeks," Bianca said, elegantly dipping into a lunge before rising back up.

Virgil repeated the move. "Goù ruhsh toj buð." *The rock grows heavy.* In other words, he had too much to handle at the moment.

As the music came to a stop, Virgil bowed to his cousin and she curtsied in return. Then, they applauded the musicians. He raised a brow at Bianca, silently offering another dance. She shook her head, so they made their way over to a quieter area of the hall, far enough away from the dance floor and the tables that they wouldn't be overheard. For a few minutes, Bianca gave him the grace of silence, not pushing him to speak. Both of them simply swayed to the music playing, keeping each other company as they had their entire lives.

Bianca said, "I have a guess as to what's been bothering you. Aside from the matter of taking up your birthright, of course."

"I'd love to hear it."

"I'm not going to say it for you," she said. "What do you want, Virgil?"

"Things I can't have," he answered plainly.

Bianca crossed her arms. "You want the Veservus girl, then go get her! Damn her vows. People make vows they don't intend to keep every damned day."

"It would be a slight against the Order."

"And? They've lived through worse. Your father has the influence to make that go away. He already broke his rules for Mila, his second favorite niece. What do you think he'll do for you?"

Virgil laughed despite the tension that thickened the air. "I can't ask that of him."

"Why? Because he doesn't ask anything of you?"

Even as Virgil rolled his neck in frustration, he had to admit to himself that Bianca had a point. Politics were just a game. A give and take. The reputation his house had spent centuries building was enough for them to take more than what they were owed. Perhaps it was time he cashed in on some of that goodwill.

"Keep an eye on my father," he said. "*And* our uncle."

Bianca groaned exaggeratedly but offered him a wink. Assured that those ends were tied, he stalked around the edge of the room in search of a more private space. He passed the dancing, which was growing more mature and less refined. The refreshments table had emptied of drinks and finger foods. Dinner drew closer than he realized. He would have to be precise, then. It was a damn good thing he'd had plenty of practice.

There were several alcoves just off of the hall, though many of them were curtained and very visible. But there was one that opened beneath the stairwell they'd first descended through before curving into what likely used to be a servant's tunnel. When he eyed the tables across the room, he found that they were nearly out of sight thanks to the dancing taking place between them.

Virgil ducked inside, but before turning the corner, he put his hands to his mouth and made the call of a mourning dove. He repeated it in short intervals before retreating as far as he dared with the lack of light.

And then he waited.

It didn't take Rhaella long to find him. She poked her head around the bend and furrowed her brow when she caught sight of him.

"What are you doing in here?"

"Come here," he murmured.

Though hesitation still wore heavily on her features, she obeyed. She stopped short just before him and wrought her fingers together. Her anxiety made him curious. It made him want to know the source so he could vanquish it before her sight. And if it turned out to be him that was making her nervous, he would do whatever he could to dispel that, too.

"I wanted to talk to you," he said.

"Alright…" she said leadingly. "About?"

"I don't think you ever made good on your end of our deal. I went around singing the praises of your house to anyone who would listen, and I have upheld that to this day. And all I asked in exchange was your counsel. Granted, you did try. You helped me in those first few weeks. And you've been searching for things that may be of use to me now that you have access to all of these different libraries. You asked me once if our deal was equal." He exhaled heavily. "I no longer think it is."

"Virgil," she said, nerves tightening her voice. "What are you—"

Her words trailed off as Virgil stepped off of the wall he had been leaning against. He took those precious few steps that closed the space between them, until there was nothing but a whisper of air separating their bodies.

"What can I say? I'm selfish." With featherlight pressure, he cupped his hands beneath her jaw, his thumbs lightly tracing over her cheeks. "I want more."

He watched her wet her lips before her teeth dug into the bottom one. A buried urge within him wanted to replicate that gesture with his own mouth. His own teeth. Rhaella opened and closed her mouth a few times, searching for the right words.

She settled on, "Ask for it, then."

"Be with me." Virgil forced his voice to remain steady. He thought he might die if he didn't get this out of his system at once. "I'll be a good husband. Whatever is within my power to give you, you'll get. Anything you desire. Just let me share in your brilliant mind. Everything you think, I want to hear it. I want to know you as I know myself. More than anything, I want you by my side. Not just politically, but in *life*." He broke off, breathing heavily with the weight of all he had just laid before her. "Please, allow me that privilege."

He dared to think that it was hope breaking across her face in the dark. Rhaella leaned into his touch, her eyes going in and out of focus as she thought. Beautiful, he thought to himself. She was so *beautiful*.

"But the Order—"

"Damn the Order," he said fiercely. "My father has enough influence to get them off our backs. And yours does too, I'd wager. We have the upper hand, Rhaella. We should use it."

Perhaps she finally realized the gravity of what he was saying. Of what he was offering her. Because, to his relief, she smiled as tears fell down her cheeks and she nodded emphatically.

"Yes," she said, and she couldn't keep the tears out of her voice as she spoke. "I'll talk to my father after the congress is over. He'll help me. He's got to." She sounded nearly desperate at this point, but the excitement there was undeniable. "It can't be too late to leave the Order, I haven't made any binding vows yet."

Virgil crushed her against him, enveloping her in a hug. Into her hair, he murmured, "Thank you. Thank you." Kissing the top of her head, he repeated, "Ma ke bawp." *My little bird.*

Over and over, like a prayer to long-forgotten gods, he held Rhaella as he murmured sweet things that only they could hear. When he pulled back, he took her face in his hands again. The temptation to lean in and press his lips to hers was so strong it weakened something in him, and he almost broke right in front of her. He almost kissed her just then, hovering a breath away. She tried to chase his mouth with hers, but he mustered every ounce of restraint he could and he pulled back, chuckling softly.

"Save that for when I get to taste you as a free woman." She made a low noise of disapproval in her throat that made him feel heady. "Trust me, Rhaella," he said, dipping lower to trace his lips against the length of her neck. "I intend to taste every inch of you. I'll devour you if you let me."

He was pleased to feel her shiver against him. Then, to his surprise, she placed a hand on his chest and pushed him back so she could look him in the face. There was nothing but glowing determination and immutable pride on her face.

She tugged on a strand of his hair, drawing his face closer. "You had better make good on that claim, Virgil Midar. Being raised among nobles has left my expectations *very* high, you know."

He grinned widely. Gripping her chin in one hand and minding his strength, he said, "It's a promise. Now go, before I do something foolish like take you right here in this passageway."

Rhaella took several steps away, glancing at him right before she reached the curve that would lead her back into the hall. With a wicked smile, she said, "Shlu twuh slìf dya shom." Then, she was gone.

Dizzy with happiness, he waited more than the cursory amount of time before reemerging into the revel. Once he did, he walked on lighter feet, sauntering back to his cousins who greeted him with drinks in hand. He wouldn't tell them, not yet. This good news was meant for the privacy of Castle Silverfort, once they had the logistics settled. Right now, he was in the mood to dance. Jokes seemed funnier, the music felt sweeter, and the weight on his shoulders lessened considerably.

As he glanced across the room, offering Rhaella a smile, something new broke open within him. It was utterly surprising how much more inviting the prospect of a life in this world seemed at that moment. Virgil didn't believe in the gods; his family never had. In this moment, though, he felt touched by the divine. Like he was finally worthy of goodness.

For the first time in Virgil's memory, he almost believed such a thing to be true.

CHAPTER TWENTY-FOUR

30 Luceriary, in the Benevolent year 112 A.E.

Asriel was having the time of his life.

He was on his eighth drink—or maybe his ninth—he'd lost count. But the wine was the finest Adristan had to offer, brought in from Sandorne. There were a dozen barrels full of it, and it was better than whatever swill they had back at home. Not that that stopped him from drinking, but it was more fun when it tasted this good.

And for every glass he finished, Freya readily offered him water or a bite to eat from the refreshments table to keep him standing. In exchange, he kept an arm wrapped around her waist, pulling her close despite the looks it earned them from the rest of the aristocracy.

Between dances, he stumbled off of the floor and went, full cup in hand, toward where his sister stood a few paces away from Barrett. Holding up his drink, he asked, "Want some?"

She glanced around the room before imperceptibly nodding her head. "Law shlu."

"You're welcome," he said.

Asriel blocked Rhaella's body with his own as she drank, praying his father or one of her superiors wouldn't catch her. The gods knew *that* would be problematic for her. She had never been much of a drinker, though, and he was surprised to see a flush spread across her cheeks.

"Are you alright? You're red."

Rhaella's face remained impassive as she shrugged. "It's warm in here. Are you not warm?"

"Actually, I am," he said, wiping sweat from his brow. "Want any more to drink?"

She shook her head. "I'm fine."

"Very well," he said, flipping the cup in the air before catching it. "Farewell, my fellow hawk."

He signed *Goodbye* in Vessial before turning on his heel. On his way back to the table bearing his family's color and sigil, he caught sight of Freya, who was flawlessly executing a dance with a nameless nobleman. She was laughing wildly, and it should have made him jealous. Instead, he felt a wave of pride to be attached to someone so... *alive.*

Freya was lightning in human form. If there was ever anyone that could match him step for step, it was her. He didn't know how he received such a blessing—it wasn't thanks to the gods, that was for certain. Whether it was his father's immeasurable intelligence or just genuine good fortune, he was thankful. Asriel wasn't sure if he could handle a spouse who didn't enjoy dancing and drinking as much as he did. He needed a partner who laughed at life just as much as he did.

When the music faded out and the dancers began to applaud, Asriel jumped in the fray and situated himself across from his betrothed. She smiled devilishly as she curtsied, and then the music was roaring again. Asriel thought he knew this dance, though he stumbled over the first few steps, hitting his shoulder against...

"You should watch your step," Virgil said with a grin, winking at him. If he wasn't mistaken, the man had just made a *joke.* With him.

Well, that was new.

Asriel failed to come up with a reply in time, so Virgil just chuckled and continued dancing. What business did he, of all people, have being so friendly? Maybe he was in good spirits thanks to the drinks. That would make the most sense. And Asriel chose to indulge in the feeling, counting himself as having won over the Eighth Prince for once.

"You're supposed to turn me here," Freya said, holding out her hand expectantly.

"Oh. Apologies," Asriel said, taking her hand so he could do as she said.

They caught up with the rest of the dancers, switching places before stepping to the side to meet their new partners. Suddenly, Asriel was faced with the largest woman he'd ever seen, all muscle and taller than even he was. She definitely wasn't as tall as a Lancor, but still very tall. He eyed the blue sash tied over her silver dress and realized that he was looking at a Midar noble.

"I don't believe we've met," he said, offering his hand to her. "I'm—"

"I know who you are," she interrupted, a knowing smirk on her face. "I've heard plenty about you, Prince Veservus. Are you enjoying the party?"

He swallowed, desperately curious to know what, exactly, Virgil had told this woman about him. He found himself at a loss for words, and he could only nod his head before using the dance as a means to circle her to study everything about her. When he was facing the Midar woman again, he found that she, too, was sizing him up.

"You're lankier than I thought you'd be," she said, crossing her arm with his. "What do they feed you on Isle Verdale?"

"Oh, you hadn't heard?" He raised an eyebrow. "We don't sustain ourselves on food. I find lone drunkards out in dark alleyways and drain them of their blood."

She snorted. "That's one way to get your fix. So you can hold your liquor?"

"Certainly," he said. "You should try it sometime."

"Virgil didn't say you were funny."

"Virgil doesn't know everything about me."

Curtsying, she said, "I'm Bianca Midar."

"Well, Bianca," Asriel said, taking another step in the formation so they were no longer facing one another. "It was a pleasure."

"Quite," she said. Then, she turned to face her next partner, as if their conversation had been but a blip.

It left Asriel feeling off-kilter. Bumbling and disorganized. He was aware people talked about him; he was no imbecile. But hearing such a thing from the mouth of a stranger made him feel exposed. He no longer felt like a hawk that could soar above the clouds. Instead, he felt like a bug beneath a magnifying glass.

Another turn and he was facing Freya again. She was bright as ever, and he thought she had every right to be. Every partner she met had the privilege of having her for just a moment. Without the responsibilities placed upon an heir, all she had to do was bask in the attention. For her, this dance was only that—a dance. She did not have to posture and she did not have to politick. She only had to smile.

"Asriel?" The skin between her brows pinched. "Are you well?"

"Of course I am," he said, executing the next turn perfectly. "Why wouldn't I be?"

One hand on his arm, she said, "You're tense."

"I'm focusing," he lied.

"Well, alright," Freya chortled, allowing him to dip her.

When they righted themselves, the song had ended and the people were clapping. Asriel kept his hands around Freya's waist, and she leaned her body into his, clapping with her arms around his shoulders.

Someone in the crowd called out to the musicians. "Play something from the Gallant Era!"

The violinist looked to his companions in confusion. They murmured to one another, trying to recall a timely piece that they all knew. Asriel wracked his brain for one. The era sounded familiar; he had to have come across it at some point in his studies.

"*Waltz in E Minor* is from the Gallant Era!" He called out. Snapping his fingers, he said, "Send for an archivist. They can bring sheet music!"

The people around him whooped their approval. A small horde of archivists excused themselves from the hall to see to Asriel's demands. Applause burst out at that. Freya squeezed Asriel's shoulder, delight evident on her face.

"I love a good waltz," she said.

"Then it's a good thing I've commanded they play one," he said, pressing a kiss to her lips. She tasted like wine and buttercream, and he chased her mouth for seconds.

"Asriel," she said between giggles. "Not here."

"Why not? No one's paying attention to us."

She glanced to the side. "As a matter of fact, *both* of our fathers are."

"Then they'll see how enamored we are with one another and know they did an excellent job planning the betrothal," he said, leaning in for another kiss.

"You are insatiable," she said gleefully. Though she did not deny him a small peck this time. "Can we break from dancing while they hunt down the sheet music?"

"Of course," he said, taking her hand and leading her off the floor.

No matter where they chose to sit, Asriel was sure it would make a statement. He wasn't overly eager to talk to his father while intoxicated, however, so he headed for the Lancor table instead of his own. It had been fitted to accommodate the height of Freya's father and brothers—even the chairs were taller—and everything sat just a few inches above that of any other table in the room.

Asriel noticed that the chair Freya's mother occupied had several extra prongs near the bottom so she could step up onto it. As a Redspire, she was still tall thanks to her fae blood, but she was nowhere near the same height as her husband and children. Had High Lord Lancor chosen to marry someone from another family that had giants' blood, his children would have been even taller.

Evidently, Lady Lancor's genetics had nothing to do with most everything about her children. All three of them had their father's bright red hair, each of their faces was dusted with freckles, and—with the exception of their youngest sibling, each of their eyes were a deep, rich green. The youngest sibling had eyes that were a mix of bright green and a dark, earthy brown; though the effect did not dim his resemblance to the rest of his family.

"Asriel," High Lord Lancor said, dipping his chin.

"Please, sit," Lady Lancor said, gesturing to the few empty chairs.

"Oh, we can't stay," Asriel said. "I owe your daughter another dance. We just wanted to greet you. And I wanted to personally thank you for raising such a becoming young woman."

He slipped an arm around her waist and pulled her close to his side, an easy smile blooming on their faces. Freya's mother offered a tight, polite smile. Her father, however, did no such thing.

"I didn't feel the need to use such crass overtness when courting *my* wife," High Lord Lancor said loftily.

"Blame it on my youth," Asriel shrugged coolly.

"I can find a number of other things to attribute to such a thing," High Lord Lancor said, eyes flicking over Asriel's shoulder.

Asriel's father came and placed a hand on his shoulder. "One thing we've always disagreed on, Ewan, is how to court women."

"You have more experience than I do," High Lord Lancor said.

Asriel's father shrugged, arm brushing against his. "What man can say he doesn't have an appetite?"

"I can," the First ruler said definitively.

"Now, I thought we put that business behind us when we settled the betrothal. You're not a man to double back on your word, are you?"

"We haven't settled it," the other man replied. "When I agreed to entertain the idea of marrying my daughter to your son twenty-some years ago, it was on the contingency that you were still acting in Adristan's best interest when the time came."

"And I am," Asriel's father said without pause. "We've just spent the entire day working toward that. *Together.* Unless that isn't a priority for you?"

"He has a point, my love," Lady Lancor chimed in. "Give the boy his chance."

Asriel bristled at being called *boy*. But he kept his chin high and stood before these presumptuous nobles.

The First High Lord hesitated, then nodded. "You're right. Forgive me."

"There is nothing to forgive," Asriel's father said, a placid smile on his face. "My son, come sit with me for a moment."

Asriel turned to Freya. "I'll be back for that waltz."

Then, he turned to follow his father back to their table. Asriel could already feel the walls closing in, narrowing on the silence between him and his father. Somehow, somewhere in that delicate dance of a conversation they had just had, he had upset his father. He had made some unknown misstep.

"You know how to court Freya," his father said as they arrived at their table. "Yet you still need to learn how to court her father."

"You told me to be courteous, and friendly, and complimentary,"

Asriel said.

"Yes, but you need to find the balance," his father argued. "There is a limit. Especially with the Lancors. You balk and groan at my own religious convictions, and yet you are wholly unprepared for just how prudent they are."

Asriel doubted the strength of Freya's religious convictions after all of the sinning they had partaken in together, but he wasn't about to say that to his father. Freya was religious, that was certain. She believed in Lucerianism in a way that Asriel had long ago given up trying to mirror. Playing at piety had gotten him nowhere so far, and he had long since stopped trying. The only reason he could see to give it another chance was if it would win him the good will of Freya's father.

"What was that argument about, anyways?"

His father waved a hand. "An old grudge. Nothing worth telling you during the festivities. Someday, I can sit you down and explain the intricacies of my relationships to the other High Lords."

If they had some feud, it seemed to run deep. High Lord Ewan sounded bitter, and his father sounded impatient. Neither of which came as a shock, but for both of them to still bicker like this in front of everyone spoke volumes.

"Listen," Asriel's father said. "I'm proud of you. You've truly come into your own these past months. I can see that you are more of a man now than you were when you first arrived at the Palace. Managing the archives, taking up your own studies, it is exactly what I wanted from you." Naively, Asrel could feel himself beginning to smile, thinking his father was finally beginning to praise his hard work. "But it is not enough." His smile faded instantly.

"You cannot set a ceiling on your growth, my son. A wife will help nourish that growth. Do what you must to earn Ewan's blessing."

"I'm trying," Asriel said, attempting to keep his voice level.

"I know," his father said. "But you must try *harder*."

Asriel flinched as if he had been struck. Despite the ache inside his chest, though, he bowed to his father and turned to walk away. If the High Lord made an attempt to call him back, he paid it no mind. Asriel grabbed Freya from her family, remembering to bow to the High Lord and Lady as well, before searching for a quiet place. Very suddenly, he found he couldn't stand the chatter and the music and the joviality.

"Let me show you something," Asriel murmured as they left the hall. The foyer of the Palace wasn't much quieter, and music still echoed through the room. "This way."

He could hear Barrett trailing behind. He gave Asriel an overly-generous berth, but the tinkling of his armor felt like it was right in Asriel's ear. He couldn't sneak his guard drinks and snacks the way he did his sister. He couldn't even offer him the opportunity to sit down. Only after they left the congress entirely could Barrett afford so much as a break. They were due more guards from House Midar upon their return to Isle Verdale. As long as his father paid on time, it should be no problem.

He led Freya through the foyer and into the Veservus wing, where they found that the doors to the library were already open. A few other rogue partygoers had made their way out of the great hall in search of quiet, and they were strolling through the shelves and thumbing through the books without a care in the world. As he recognized each noble from the different houses, he whispered better suggestions for them to read. Things that would further interest them based on their heritage or talents. Then, he lightly suggested that they'd be most comfortable reading at the plush sitting area on the other side of the library.

Once the shelves were free of any wandering nobles, Asriel led Freya to the deepest pocket with barely-lit sconces in the wall. He pulled the key from his pocket and reached through the books to unlock the door, silently pleased by Freya's soft gasp of surprise. Pressing a finger to his lips, he pushed the door open only wide enough for her to step inside before he and Barrett followed suit and shut the door with an airy *click*.

"What is this place?" Freya's voice was breathy, and her face was slack in astonishment as she turned around in a circle.

"My father's private study," Asriel said, moving to sit at the desk. Subtly, while Freya was occupied by the wonder of all the information that lined each shelf, he halfway opened the bottom drawer. Once he ensured that the false bottom was in place, he nudged it shut with his boot.

She ran her hands along the spines, thumbing open titles at random. "I've heard rumors of hidden rooms such as this throughout the Palace. Of course, we have our doors that lead to the catacombs beneath. I don't know if you've been down there."

"I have," Asriel said. "My sworn sword and I have a map of every hidden door in the Palace. Though I can't say we've explored much of it."

"A map?" Freya asked as she whirled around with eyes wide. "And you haven't gone exploring yet?"

Ah. Asriel supposed it was rather foolish for him to admit that. He swallowed thickly, eyeing Barrett. "I've memorized the contents of the map. And most of the doors are warded. There's no legend with the symbols either, so I haven't figured out how to unlock them."

She tutted. "The Hawk should do better than that. I'm sure there are records in here somewhere. And if not, isn't it your duty to figure such a thing out?"

"It is," Asriel said tightly. "But I've been tied up with other duties."

She leveled him with a stare. "I've never been able to make such excuses for slacking on my duties, and I'm only a *spare*."

Because he wanted to get angry, he laughed instead, rolling his neck. "I suppose I shouldn't expect you to understand."

"There's no need to be catty," she said lightly, leaning back against the shelves. "I'm doing my duty right now in offering you my counsel. I may only be a highborn girl from a neighboring house, but this is to be my role in your life. Aside from giving you lots of babies to carry on your family name, I am to be your right hand. It's part of my job as a Lady Wife to ensure that you are the best version of yourself. And, if you're not, that you're working towards it. Crafting a legend for this map—if one truly doesn't exist—would cement your position as a worthwhile heir, wouldn't it? Wouldn't it be nice to be the heir who unlocked generations worth of puzzles before he's even the High Lord proper?"

Asriel's eyes floated to Barrett again, but Freya called his attention back almost immediately.

"You're looking to him, but I'm the one who's telling you what you need to hear right now. And with the amount of people in the Palace who are occupied by the party upstairs, there's no better time to begin."

"The doors aren't secrets," Asriel pointed out.

"Open secrets are still secrets," Freya said. "How many other nobles do you think know about them, outside of each family? My youngest brother Ledger has never even bothered to see them for himself. Do you really think the others are asking their archivists for the records of where each door is hidden? At best, each house knows how to get to *their* family tombs. Not the entire system of tunnels itself. That map you hold in your hand? That's *power*. Hone it. Turn it into the weapon it is."

"And how do you propose I do that?"

She raised her brows, wild excitement on her face. "Let's go into the catacombs. Let's find the tunnels that lead elsewhere. Let's see how it's all connected. Let's do it *together*. If we get stuck, then we know what to look for once we come back up."

From where he stood next to the door, Barrett cleared his throat. "My Lord, might I remind you that we're expected at dinner at the top of the hour?"

"We have time," Asriel said, checking his pocket watch to be certain. "If we're quick, we should be back in time for the first course."

"Is that wise, Asriel?"

Asriel cocked his head at his guard. "Yes it is, Barrett."

Perhaps sensing the tension between them, Freya stood and said cheerfully, "We should get going then, if we want to have enough time."

"Agreed," Asriel said, shoving out of the desk chair. "There's too much of a risk if I take you to the door in my family's suite. And there are too many eyes if I take you to the one in the library proper. So the door in here will have to do."

He took the pot of clay from the shelf nearest the empty wall and drew the symbol on its surface. When the door revealed itself and moved out of the way, he turned to Barrett, waiting for his guard to hand him a lantern. Thankfully, Barrett followed with no more than a roll of his eyes. As they descended into the frightening blue darkness, the lamplight only barely improved the conditions of his sight. The three of them held close together, not daring to stray more than a step apart.

When they arrived at the bottom of the stairs, Asriel wrapped an arm around Freya's waist to herd her away from the room of documents just off of the landing. Knowing that the center tunnel did not offer access to any of the tombs, he guided them towards the furthest-right tunnel instead.

"I can hardly see more than a few steps in front of me," Freya said, her voice echoing.

"It's like that here," Asriel said. "I would assume it's the same in your—"

As it did every time he dared descend those cursed stairs, the rumbling stopped him mid-sentence. Barrett stopped them in their tracks. Placing the lantern on the ground, he unsheathed his sword and held it aloft.

"It's time I finally killed that thing."

"What thing?" Freya whimpered.

"Don't," Asriel said, placing his arm across Barrett's chest. He couldn't justify *why* he didn't want him to, only that some instinct screamed at him that this wasn't the way. "It's bigger than you."

"I've killed things bigger than me before," Barrett argued.

The rumbling grew closer, as did the hissing, and they could hear slithering echoing through one of the paths around them. Nearby, debris fell onto the floors, trickling down like hail in a storm.

Asriel began to turn them in the direction he thought would lead them back to the stairs. Only, where he thought they'd taken the right amount of steps back, instead they had only wound themselves deeper into the tunnel. Somehow, he'd gotten them all turned around, and he was afraid he could not outrun the consequences of this misstep.

The rumbling sounded like it was on the other side of them now, urging them further in the direction he thought was upwards. Powerless to move anywhere else, the trio obeyed, jogging through the empty hallway until more noise sent them hurtling down a corner and into a different tunnel. This pattern repeated itself multiple times until some of the walls—and the scribbling atop them—began to look familiar.

"I've been here before," Asriel breathed.

They came to a stop when the slithering quieted, and both Barrett and Freya stared at him as though he had grown a second head.

"My father used to bring us down to the tombs to pray. To honor our dead." Asriel wiped sweat from his brow. "Rhaella and I used to go exploring past where we were allowed and I recognize those markings written up there."

"What do they say?" Freya asked, clinging to his arm.

"It's a common saying in Lucerianism. You'll know it. *May the dead lie where the future leads.* Though it's written in Vessial, our family tongue. There's a direct translation for that phrase, but it's too mouthy in our language. So instead, we say Kwawf lav flì pwo lav ullù. *May the sleeping hide the path.*"

There was a sound, then. Though it might have been the normal sounds of underground tunnels and not the wyrm. All the same, Freya took a few steps deeper into the tunnel.

Cringing, she asked, "And what does it mean?"

"It means our family tombs are this way. And thus, a door that will take us out of here. Let's keep going."

Now certain that there was slithering behind them, they hurried down the path. The surroundings became more and more familiar to Asriel as they went. Brown and gray archways were carved into the rock and dirt structure of the tunnels, brooding and mournful. The perfect atmosphere for a crypt. Briefly, he had the foolish thought that the wyrm was herding them toward where they wanted to go. He didn't dare voice that fear aloud, though. He was tired of being regarded as foolish, even if it was true.

As they passed through yet another archway, they came upon the tomb that housed Asriel's grandfather. It was cast out of gold, with red jewels embedded into the metal in a linear design, and it laid upon a small altar that rose above the ground level. Their house sigil was inscribed onto the lid of the coffin. Grief hit Asriel's heart with a pang as he ran a hand along it.

"Vyef, chti," he said. *Hello, Grandfather.*

The sight of the tomb was somewhat a comfort, too. It meant that the staircase that would bring them back to the library proper wasn't far, and that settled his nerves some.

But his nerves came back in full force as he looked over his shoulder to see a glimpse of green scales glittering in the mage lights. Asriel didn't scream. He didn't shout to alert his company. He only put a hand on each of their backs and pushed them forward.

And they *ran.*

When the stairs were finally in sight, Asriel ushered his party upwards, ignoring Barrett's attempts to place himself at the back of the group. Asriel had only taken one step forward—attempting to trail both Barrett and Freya—when the *thing* hissed entirely too near to his back. And he did not need to turn around to know that it was there, sizing him up. He could feel its breath, hot and sticky, at the back of his neck.

Barrett screeched his name as Asriel turned to face the monster.

The wyrm was large, but nowhere as large as Egorion. Asriel told himself that this was just another kind of dragon. He had been around plenty of those in his life. So, holding out his hands, Asriel tried reasoning with the thing.

Footsteps sounded behind him as Barrett raced back down the stairs. There wouldn't be time, though. The wyrm was already before him and its tongue slithered out, forked and menacing.

Hot breath hit the palms of his hands and Asriel wanted to squeeze his eyes shut, hoping to open them to find himself safe. If he took his eyes off of it for one second, though, he feared the beast might take it as surrender. So instead he kept his eyes open and his hands raised, making himself a match for something as fearsome as a wild wyrm. Asriel's breath quickly enough that he was nearly panting. And yet he still maintained his ground.

By the time Barrett and Freya made it back down the stairs, Asriel convinced himself that the fever rush of danger had clouded his vision. Neither of them saw what he had just witnessed. He couldn't allow himself to believe that the beast had just winked at him before slithering into a different tunnel.

With that, Asriel took the interaction for the victory it should have been, and he ran back up the steep staircase, never once looking back to see if the wyrm still lingered in the dark.

CHAPTER TWENTY-FIVE

"Adristan runs on a rehabilitation-based system. If you commit a crime, you have to serve a punishment that is appropriately related. Serious crimes fall to the High Lord's discretion."
—*Policies of Justice: A Collected Reading, by High Lord Vincent Midar*

30 Luceriary, in the Benevolent year 112 A.E.

A Mediator rang a bell and the dancing ceased immediately. The music wound down to something more suited for the background of conversation, and the nobles filed towards their seats. Distantly, Virgil noted that as the sound of that bell echoed through the room, Rhaella flinched. If he hadn't already been staring, he wouldn't have noticed, but he was sure he was the only one who had.

That observation, coupled with the fact that she appeared to be arguing with her father, caught his attention. It was the most animated he'd ever seen her, even as her father's face remained carefully passive. Virgil looked to the right of the High Lord and saw that the seat beside him was empty. Asriel wasn't on the dance floor, and he wasn't next to the drinks table. If there was anything that could anger Rhaella like this, Virgil could safely assume it was the continued responsibility for her brother that had been placed upon her shoulders by her father.

None of that would matter soon. Virgil was going to secure her station away from the Dux, he was going to bring her to Greenisle, and then he was going to give her the world. She would only ever have to see her family on her terms. Only ever have to serve them when *she* decided to. He vowed right then and there to nothing of her, not even her input on war strategy. After all she had done to serve House Veservus—to serve *Adristan*—she could very well never lift a finger again and he'd be damn grateful.

Servers began to bring out trays of food from the kitchens. Virgil was summoned by the rough sound of his father's voice, and he went to take his place at his right hand. He glanced at his cousins, their faces drawn tight, before looking at his father.

"Where's Uncle Nicholas?"

His father coughed into a napkin before replying. "Doctrina Nicholas went to take care of something." The correction didn't slip his notice, but his father continued on. "He'll be back, don't worry."

"I'm not worried," Virgil grumbled. "You'd be asking after me if I was late."

Virgil's father ignored the snipe and began to load his plate. That broke the seal over the table, and the rest of them followed suit. Mila grabbed a fistful of rolls before Bianca slapped her hand.

"Save some for the rest of us," she snapped.

"I don't like roast chicken," Mila moaned. "I need to fill up on *something*."

"Take more roast potatoes," Virgil said, passing her the spoon.

As the entirety of the governing forces of Adristan filled their plates with food, a Mediator came to stand in the center of the dance floor and cleared their throat. Thanks to the strange magic of House Aviatis, Virgil heard them as though they were standing mere inches away.

"Thank you, great High Lords and ruling families of Adristan. With the Grand Introduction seen through, this congress has officially commenced. It will not conclude until we have covered every submitted order of business. Please, eat to your satisfaction and engage in the festivities, but be warned that we will reconvene on business first thing tomorrow morning. A special thanks to House Stillgrove for the food, and to House Redspire for planning the ball. Now, the High Priestess of the great tradition of Lucerianism will offer up this day in prayer."

Raven Aviatis rose from her seat and joined the Mediator on the floor. Beneath the owl-like cloak, she wore a shimmering silver gown that reminded him of spidersilk. Dark makeup lined her eyes and lips, giving her a fierce look that had made even Virgil nervous to ask her for a dance. She looked every bit the High Priestess, and somehow also every bit the heir to the High Lord.

Raising her hands above her head, she began to recite a prayer that Virgil didn't know. Some people in the crowd joined in until the prayer was a chorus, rising and falling rhythmically. He could appreciate the beauty of her religion, even if he didn't subscribe to it.

When the prayer concluded, Raven bowed her head and sauntered back to her seat, meeting the eyes of every heir she passed. Virgil dipped his chin in respect.

"It's going to be so sad when she has to leave the priesthood," Mila said fondly. "She seems to enjoy it so much."

Virgil chucked, furrowing his brows. "What do you know about Raven Aviatis?"

Blushing furiously, Mila refused to meet his eyes. "Not much."

He wanted to press his cousin for more information, but Bianca was shaking her head as she pushed down her own laughter.

"Don't bother," Bianca said. "I already tried."

They dug into their food eagerly. Virgil realized that he had let another day pass without so much as a bite. All at once, the dinner became the best meal he'd had in ages; perhaps because it felt like it had been that long since he'd last eaten. Around him, conversations had dwindled while the others focused on their food. Apparently, they had all let the day get away from them amidst the chaos of the congress.

Beside him, his father coughed again. Virgil nudged a carafe of water closer to him, though he did not make any move to drink from it.

When his father's coughing persisted, Virgil poured his father a glass and handed it directly to him. The High Lord drank it down quickly before handing it back, silently demanding another. Virgil obliged him, eyeing him with concern.

He was about to ask his father if he was alright when he heard the hacking on all sides. It sounded at the table immediately next to them. And the table next to that. At each and every table in the room, each High Lord was hacking. *Violently.*

When Virgil looked down at his father again, he saw blood on the napkin in his hand.

Virgil lurched from his seat, and his hand went to the pommel of his sword. Various other heirs and spares did the same. Bianca rose and immediately fell back into her seat, clutching her head.

"I'm dizzy," she said, her words slurred. Slinking lower in her seat, her head swung back and forth lazily, as if she was half-asleep and the weight had become too heavy.

Mila put her hands on her sister's shoulder, panic pitching up her voice. "Bianca?"

Bianca had fully fainted now, lax in her seat. Mila was shaking her and repeating her name, and her voice grew louder with each repetition. She looked to Virgil with wide eyes, but he was powerless to do anything but stare.

"I didn't have any chicken," she said fearfully. But her words, too, had grown slurred. She lowered herself back into her seat, waiting for whatever took Bianca to take her too. The calmness of the motion frightened Virgil more than anything else.

And then he realized his father had grown quiet.

The High Lord—*his father*— was no longer coughing, but he was still spitting up blood. His head drooped, and his forehead nearly rested on the table. Even as Virgil shook him and asked questions, his father did not respond. By this point, Virgil's stomach had twisted itself into knots, but he felt no urge to faint. *What was happening?*

As he looked around the room, he saw heirs of every house shaking their High Lords. Some of them began to scream and cry out for help. And at the rest of the tables, siblings and aunts and friends had fallen unconscious and were unresponsive.

Virgil's eyes widened. "It's in the food! Make yourselves throw up!"

Without hesitation, he stuck two fingers down his throat until he felt bile rise up. Retching onto the patterned tile floor, he briefly saw stars. Yet he remained upright. He felt no dizziness and he did not slur his words. Rushing to his cousins, he forced his fingers down their throats as well. They vomited but did not wake. He positioned their heads carefully on the table so they wouldn't choke, and then he left the table.

He called out to anyone who was still conscious, "You have to vomit!"

Where the fuck was the Dux Doctrina's table?

Virgil searched the sea of cloaks for a blonde head collapsed onto the table and found none. If it weren't for the terrifying alternative, he would have felt knee-shaking relief then.

A moment later, Virgil found his answer as Rhaella sprinted across the floor. Sobs wracked her body with each step. Virgil wanted to lunge for her, but she reached the red-clothed table within seconds. Diving onto the floor, she pulled her father's body onto her lap and wept openly, some of her cries turning into screams.

"Mbap, mìn," she screamed. "Mìn! Mbap, mbap!"

"It's poison," another voice cried out. Gerard Stillgrove was going around to every table, checking the pulses of everyone who had fallen unconscious. His siblings were doing the same, covering as much ground as quickly as they could.

Virgil stormed to Gerard and clutched the front of his shirt in his fists.

"What the fuck is happening? What do you know?"

Gerard's eyes went wide with barely-contained fire. "My sister is trying to figure that out!"

"How is she awake?"

"We're immune to poisons," Gerard said, trying to shove out of Virgil's grasp. Virgil only held on tighter. "For gods' sake, let me *go*!"

Virgil shoved the Prince aside before searching the room to see who else was awake. Sage Oberon was going from person to person, doing what they could for the unconscious masses of people. They caught Virgil staring and gestured with their hands.

"There are tonics upstairs in the apothecary," they said quickly. "If Galilea is right about the poisons, I should be able to mitigate the effects."

Virgil nodded. "We need to get everyone who is still conscious."

As he scoured the room, it became apparent that only the heirs from every house were completely unaffected. Plus the Stillgrove spares.

And Rhaella.

Good fortune, possibly. Or perhaps she hadn't eaten yet. Or perhaps he should thank whatever magic the Order put her through strengthened her. But then, why were the rest of her peers laying on the cold floor and she was still standing? And where the *fuck* was her brother?

When he couldn't stand not knowing any longer, Virgil rushed to her side and shook her out of the stupor she was in. She was still cradling her father's head in her lap. Blood trickled out of the mouth of High Lord Veservus, as well as his open eyes, though he no longer saw anything.

Virgil cupped her chin and tried to pull her face to his, attempting to force open her mouth with two fingers. She fought him rabidly, slapping his hands away.

"I'm fine," she said through tears. "I'm fine."

"You need to take the antidote Sage has," he said. "But you need to vomit first."

"Whatever they gave the rest of them" she hissed under her breath, "it won't work on me."

Virgil wanted to argue, but there was steel in Rhaella's eyes, daring him to challenge her further. He backed off, nearly convinced that she was alright. She wasn't alright, but she at least wasn't about to… About to *what*? He didn't want to think of the likely possibilities.

His father and cousins were asleep. Rhaella's father was only asleep. They were all going to wake up, and this would be sorted as a grand misunderstanding.

The guards were in a frenzy, breaking formation to run to their respective charges. All around, people were screaming. Bodies continued to hit the floor, and the ruckus reached a fever pitch before finally beginning to quiet down.

When he tried to find the cause of the eventual quiet, Virgil realized that it was because there were so few people left who *could* cry out.

And then, he realized there were only ten of them left standing, aside from the guards.

Aida Redspire hiccupped loudly, her panic resulting in full-body tremors. Sage attempted to offer her a vial of some kind of sedative, but she refused. Ezra stood frozen with his eyes wide open in terror. Raven muttered something to herself, and Virgil realized she was praying. Even now. And, *gods*, Ramsey was pacing in a circle, wringing his hands through his hair.

Galilea Stillgrove approached Virgil. "I need to touch your lips."

"Excuse me?"

She closed her eyes, steeling herself through the frustration. "Questions later. Let me touch. I'm safe, I promise."

Seeing no reason to deny her, he nodded his head. Her fingertips brushed across his top and bottom lip before hissing and drawing back her hand.

"As I suspected," she said sharply. "Each of the heirs have been fed poison. Something slow-acting, though I can't place it. It won't kill you yet. And, if you take the antidote, it won't harm you at all."

"And you?" Ramsey asked, his tone sharper than any blade. "You aren't an heir. What happened to you and your brother?"

As calmly as she could, Galilea said, "Roman and I were given some kind of tranquilizer. Stronger than a sedative, not as deadly as poison. I believe that's what the other, lower-ranking nobles were given."

"You believe?" Aida asked, her tone hitching toward hysterical. "Or you *know*?"

Galilea stood her ground. "I believe. Because if I'm wrong, I'll never forgive myself, and neither will you. But I'm almost certain they were given something non-fatal."

That should have come as a relief. No one relished in the revelation. Each of them seemed stuck in some stage of shock, and Virgil thought he might be, too. The buzzing of the guards' voices around him faded as they attended to their fallen charges.

Beside him, Rhaella finally rose to her feet. Her face was streaked with tears and her eyes were bloodshot and red. "We have to help the rest of them. They..." She trailed off, unable to finish the sentence.

"I know," Virgil said, wrapping his arms around her. Even though he knew *nothing*. Even though this was the most bizarre moment of his life. "We need to get to the apothecary before any more of us fall."

"All of us should go together," Galilea said firmly.

"Please," Ezra begged shakily.

They all joined hands, walking in a tight cluster out of the hall and up the stairs to the Oberon wing. Sage led them through a set of doors and began to hunt through the drawers, pulling out vials and handing them to each person there. They handed him a vial, which Virgil considered hesitantly before taking and drinking entirely. If it truly was an antidote, he would act before doubt could cloud his judgment. If it was more poison, it was too late for him anyway.

"As I said, this tonic should only mitigate the effects, not erase them entirely," Sage explained. "You may still feel sick for a few days."

"What about the people downstairs?" Aida asked weepily.

"Roman and I need something else," Galilea said, waving away the vial Sage held out to her. "We were given something different."

"I thought you said you were immune," Virgil said, accusation coloring his tone.

Roman glared at him. "The body can only handle so much. We'll be in for a tortuous night if we don't take something."

Sage handed the two of them vials, which they took down with ease. Virgil kept one arm firmly wrapped around Rhaella's waist. Partially for his own comfort, and partially because she had started to sway on her feet.

"I won't faint," she murmured. "But it's beginning to have some effect on me."

"Then take something," Virgil insisted.

She only glared. "I will not."

Virgil looked at Sage beseechingly, but they only shrugged. "I already tried. She won't take it."

The urge to argue stirred in his chest, but a commotion in the distance had them whirling their heads toward the door. Each of the heirs placed their hands in one anothers, until they were one united front. Cautiously, they made their way back to the main staircase, only to see that nothing was actually happening in the foyer.

The noise must have come from the great hall.

From the stair landing, Virgil and the heirs heard the commotion more clearly. And battle-instincts told him it was the sound of steel against steel. *The guards.*

The relief was only momentary, though, as he considered all of the possibilities for conflict. He didn't dare to think they were fighting each other, grief overcoming their good sense, but he couldn't rule it out either. If fortune favored them, they would have found the culprit behind this night and brought them to justice.

Virgil pushed his way to the front of the group. "Stay behind me. Are any of you armed?"

Ramsey, still sniffling, said, "I am."

"Come beside me. The rest of you, run upstairs to the armory on the third floor and take whatever you can wield. If you're not experienced with a weapon, take a dagger. Take *several* daggers."

The rest of their group dispersed, footsteps furiously ascending the stairs. Virgil waited a minute, then two, before peeking over the railing. He couldn't see anything spilling out from the hall. Whatever was going on was contained. He forced himself to hope that meant Adristan's forces were fending off whoever could be so bold to poison the nobles. Organized fighting was difficult, even more so with this many unconscious or worse. But this was the exact sort of scenario he'd been trained to lead. Suddenly, the months spent in camps pushing himself—and his men—seemed incredibly, horribly worthwhile.

The rest of their group returned down the stairs. A small wave of pride went through him when he saw Rhaella with a quiver of arrows strapped to her back and a bow in one hand, with a longsword holstered to her hip. Vengeance was in her eyes, and every line of her body pulled taut.

"Stay close," Virgil said, the voice of the commander taking over. "Watch each other's backs, but don't try to be a hero." Then, hesitantly, he added, "Try to avoid looking at anyone on the floor. We need to take care of ourselves first."

They descended the stairs quickly. Virgil shoved open the doors to the great hall, refusing to let fear stiffen his movement. As he caught sight of the room, relief flooded his body. Guards wearing Adristan's colors were still standing, many of them subduing people he couldn't yet identify. Though there were guards on the ground, they were in the minority, and he could see many of them still moving. They were *alive*.

"Virgil!" Declan barked. He had his sword at the neck of a man on his knees. "Over here!"

Their group moved in unison toward Declan. Eric was in front of him, punching the kneeling man in the stomach whenever he moved too much. The fact that there were so many bodies on the floor, bloody and beaten, while this man had been kept alive, told Virgil all he needed to know.

This was their source of information.

"Speak," Virgil said, holding out his sword. "And I will make your death quick and painless."

The man spit on the floor. "Your hounds weren't going to let me speak with you. I come with very sensitive information, *not* for the ears of common men."

"These are not common men," Virgil said. "They're mine. And now you speak to the collective heirs of Adristan. *Talk.*"

"I know who you are, Virgil Midar," the man laughed. "The Shrike of Adristan. Thank you for speaking with me."

"Mind your tongue," Declan said, pressing the flat of the blade in further.

Virgil flinched at the nickname, but continued. "You're wasting your breath. Say your piece or die."

The man leered up at him. "I come on behalf of the Trueborn. They have waited a long time to receive their birthright, and we will give it to them."

"So you're a royalist," Virgil said. "And therefore our enemy."

"The Trueborn is not your enemy. They want to bring peace and order back to the nation. Your leaders were not going to allow that. The High Lords called for war. They brought battle and bloodshed to the common people."

"And so you poisoned them," Rhaella said, her voice entirely flat.

The man inclined his head toward her. "That's right, bastard."

Eric grabbed the man's face, squeezing tight. "What did I say about minding your tongue?"

"It's alright, Eric," Rhaella said.

The guard dropped his hand, quiet violence written all over his face. Declan didn't waver, and Virgil got the sense that if Eric had tried to kill the man in that moment, Declan would have let him.

"As I was saying," the man continued, "my friends and I put poison in your High Lords' food. Yours, too. Though, as I'm sure you've noticed, it won't kill you right away. We will give you the antidote if—"

"We've already taken it," Aida Redspire said, attempting to push her way forward. Virgil held out an arm to keep her back.

The man chuckled. "I suspected as much. We timed this poorly, you see. We had enough time to manage the dead. But not the rest of you."

"You gave everyone who wasn't a High Lord or an heir a tranquilizer. That won't kill us," Galilea said. "And we have the antidote for that, too."

Impatiently, the man looked up at the ceiling and said, "I don't suppose I can use the antidote to bargain with you to surrender, then."

"Not unless you have an antidote for the High Lords," Virgil said.

"Is there an antidote for death, butcher?"

Virgil chose to ignore the snide comment. He turned to the rest of the heirs, feeling more weary than he had before.

"The royalists orchestrated this to get us to bow to them. I think I speak for all of us when I say we will not do any such thing. Sage, Gerard, go upstairs and gather the antidote for the lower nobility. The rest of you, stay with me so we may deal out justice."

The man only laughed. "You think killing a few of us will do anything? It won't, you warbling Shrike. There are more of us than you could *fathom*. We will continue trickling through the cracks in your rule. We will remove the barriers you set before us. We will—"

An arrow whizzed past Virgil's ear and lodged itself in the center of the man's throat. He gurgled, choking on blood as his words fizzled out into a rattling fight for air. Then, he went lax in Declan's grip and crumpled to the floor. Virgil whirled around to see Rhaella splitting the group, her bow still raised and aimed at the man.

"He talked too much." Her voice was still terrifyingly flat.

"Rhaella!" Aida cried, going to her side. She put her hands on her friend's face, trying to shake Rhaella out of her numb stupor.

"Kill the rest," Virgil roared. "Leave no one holding royalist sensitivities alive. Find the hands that prepared the food and *bring them to me.*"

The rest of the heirs moved into action, going to their loved ones to check for breathing or a pulse. Virgil wanted to go to his table and check on his cousins, but a trickle of fear went through him at the thought of finding their lifeless bodies. He sent Eric instead. In the meantime, he kept his focus about the room, making sure the guards were slaughtering the people who had taken credit for slaughtering their own. No amount of killing would bring any of the dead back. It wouldn't make him feel any better. It wouldn't change that—

Don't think about your father. Do not *think about your father.*

He repeated that to himself until he obeyed, beating himself into submission. He couldn't be a son right now. He had to be the commander.

Sage and Gerard returned with an armful of vials and began distributing them. The heirs brought them to their relatives and friends, easing them back as they slowly awoke. Once the grogginess faded, though, the screaming started. So much screaming. More begging and pleading with bodies that would never speak again.

It was almost worse than the eerie quiet that preceded it.

At last, Sage handed Virgil a few vials. He forced himself to walk to the Midar table, where he knelt on the ground beside Eric.

"Here," he said, handing Eric a vial. "Wake Mila. *Please.*" He hated how hard he had to fight to keep his voice from breaking at the plea.

Virgil pulled Bianca's body toward him and poured the vial into her open mouth. He held his breath, fearing that Sage and Galilea were wrong. Fearing that she, like his father, was dead. But then she began gasping. She swallowed mouthfuls of air. In Eric's arms, Mila did the same. Virgil's head lolled back to face the ceiling and he let tears stream freely down his face. He allowed the emotion he'd been so staunchly pushing down to rise back to the surface.

"What's going on?" Bianca attempted to turn her face. But if she did, then she would see the truth. And Virgil wasn't even ready to see that for himself.

Gently holding her gaze upwards, he said, "Don't look."

"Virgil," she said, sniffling as sobs wracked her body. "I feel sick."

"I know, cousin. We're bringing justice to the people who did this. It's almost over."

Eric whistled for his attention and nodded toward the doors leading out of the hall. "Virgil."

As the guards dragged the cooks into the great hall, the seconds felt as long as hours. Virgil hated to stand here and watch them struggle against the restraint, thrashing back and forth and crying out for mercy, but he would do what must be done. Just as he always had. No matter how hard their cries tugged at his sensitivities, he needed to remember that they had either poisoned the food themselves, or been negligent enough to allow someone else to do such a thing.

Neither of those sins could be forgiven.

Galilea Stillgrove stepped forward and took each of the cooks' hands in her own. She said nothing to them, ignoring the pleas they lobbied at her. Once she had laid hands on each of them, she calmly walked over to Virgil. Her face was blank, and there were no traces of the devastation in her face that he felt was written all over his.

"They have multiple poisons on their fingers."

He bowed his head. "Thank you."

Unsheathing Airslinger once more, Virgil crossed the dance floor to do what his duty required. He had only taken a few steps, though, before Bianca's voice stopped him in his tracks.

"Not with that, Virgil."

He watched in horror as Bianca dragged herself to his father's body and unsheathed the family sword. Veritas. The one that should have remained his father's for several more years. Until his father was ready to hand it over. He stared at Bianca with the sword in hand, a desperate look on her face. At once, Virgil understood that he no longer had a choice. The sword was his now. He *had* to accept it.

Virgil walked toward Bianca in a trance, took Veritas, and held it up to the light. He could tell, just by looking at it, that his father had sharpened it recently. Almost as though he knew this moment was on the horizon. It sent a chill through him to think about his father in such a way already. To have already acknowledged his father's now-permanent existence in the past-tense. Virgil gripped the sword tightly and crossed the room with it in hand, and adjusted his grip on it once. Then twice. No matter how he tried, the pommel felt foreign in his hand.

As he slew the cooks, one by one, they screamed. And though they were right in front of him, the sound felt far away in his head. As if they were actually a great distance away from him. But then his boot would slide in the blood that covered the floor and he was promptly reminded to return to the present. Every movement felt unknown and far-away, though. Or, perhaps, maybe he was somewhere else. Maybe his body truly had gone somewhere else and his mind hadn't caught up yet. He couldn't think through the haze in his mind, and it was *maddening*.

He felt sick, and it wasn't from any poison.

He would not allow himself a moment's rest until they'd ensured that everyone who had been given poison received an antidote. That all of the royalists were dead. That all of the High Lords were brought to the mortuary—though they all allowed the Mediators to oversee that particular task. None of them—not even the butcher of Adristan—had the stomach for such a thing.

Rhaella approached the gathered heirs, her face drawn. "I need help waking the Order."

Several of them grabbed vials and walked toward their table that had been swathed in black. Some of the Doctrinas were beginning to wake on their own, thanks to their raised tolerance to poisons. They were sluggish and confused, but seemed largely unaffected. Nowhere near as impacted as the rest of the room. Although it took more than one vial to wake the Reverend Mother. Whoever had organized this knew how high of a dose it would take to incapacitate the second most powerful force in Adristan and they had acted accordingly. Even he—without a spymaster's upbringing or a Hawk's shrewdness—knew how dangerous that information could be.

The Order took count of their own. A few of Rhaella's superiors had fallen victim to the deadly poison, and a few more to the violence that followed it. Her fellow gray-cloaked Progenies were fine, though. Thoroughly shaken, but alive.

In the chaos, Virgil hadn't gotten a good look at who had been slain when the guards rained down their vengeance. Apparently, the royalists had made the mistake of revealing themselves, and the guards had shown no mercy. Some were noblemen of middling rank, some were members of minor houses or relatives of those in the stronghold houses. Others were Doctrinas. And there were common people mixed in among them as well. Each and every one of them had been delusional enough to believe the promises of a supposed trueborn monarch. Virgil didn't recognize any of them from the battlefield, but he did know some of their surnames. As he kept a mental note of who hailed from which house, he added the task of following up with their families to his ever-growing list of responsibilities to take care of once the dust settled.

Uncle Nicholas made his reappearance at last, staggering out of the group of Doctrinas with one hand on his stomach. He was pale and wild-eyed, and there were veins bulging at his neck and forehead.

"Vincent," he said, rushing to Virgil. "Where is my brother? Where is my baby brother?"

Virgil hung his head and his shoulders stooped under the weight of finally stopping to breathe. "Royalists."

Uncle Nicholas's breathing turned ragged, and he dry-heaved off to the side. After a moment, he swallowed down his sobs before turning back to Virgil with fearful awe in his eyes. Slowly, Nicholas Midar lowered himself to his knees and bowed his head.

"My Lord," he said terribly. "The High Lord of House Midar."

CHAPTER TWENTY-SIX

30 Luceriary, in the Benevolent year 112 A.E.

As they emerged from the catacombs and back into the library, Asriel was surprised by the surrounding quiet. He took Freya's hand and led her through the doors, which had been thrown wide open. The long hallway in the Veservus wing was quiet too, which was not abnormal, but when he placed every small encounter side by side, his suspicions began to rise. Dinner should have started by now. His father might be angry with him for being late, but that was nothing new.

Though as the three of them walked out of the wing and into the foyer, Asriel found himself surprised at the sight of all the heirs gathered. He also hadn't expected his sister to run at him full-force, tears streaming down her face.

She crashed into him without mercy, beating her fists against his chest as she sobbed. Even Barrett didn't react right away, too shocked by the sight of Rhaella so undone to do anything other than stare.

"Where have you been?" Her voice neared hysterical as she cried, and she hiccuped between words. *"Where were you?"*

In the end, it wasn't Barrett who interceded but Virgil. With overt gentleness, he pried Rhaella off of Asriel before handing her off to one of his blue-cloaked guards.

Blue-cloaked and bloody, he noted.

Then, Virgil grabbed Asriel by the collar and pulled him close, nearly lifting him off his feet. With a burning hatred unmatched by anything experienced before, Virgil looked him straight in the eye and sneered.

"If I find out you had anything to do with this, I will fucking kill you where you stand," he said. "I hesitate for *her* sake, not yours."

"What are you talking about?" Asriel clawed at Virgil's hands, desperately trying to let himself down.

"Stop this!" Freya cried, daring to wrap a hand around Virgil's wrist in an attempt to separate the two.

Barrett had his sword at Virgil's neck in an instant, which had Virgil's other guard drawing on him in return. Rhaella pleaded with the guards to stand down, but she did not plead with the Prince. *Interesting.* For a moment, they all stood still. Then, Virgil shoved Asriel backward, straight into Freya's arms.

"Someone fill him in," he said, stalking into the crowd.

It was only then that Asriel noticed most of those gathered were in some state of disarray. Some of them crying, most of them bloody. He saw no wounds or outward signs of discomfort on any of them though, which merely confirmed that the blood was not their own.

Raven Aviatis stepped forward, her face disturbingly blank. Her cloak was tattered and she'd discarded her headpiece. Makeup ran in streaks down her face, but she had stopped crying as far as he could tell.

"Asriel, there's no easy way to say this…"

"You're all scaring me," Asriel snapped. "What's going on?"

"Don't," Ramsey Lightpike interjected. "Separate him and his company. Get their stories. If there are any discrepancies, Virgil can take care of them."

Virgil did not seem to need any convincing. Stepping forward, he clutched the loose fabric of Asriel's shirt in a fist and dragged him toward the library doors. Behind them, Barrett barked out in protest. He, too, had been taken by the arm by one of the Midar guards and dragged down the corridor. And, because the gods had a cruel sense of humor, Galilea Stillgrove grabbed Freya and walked her up the stairs.

Freya called out Asriel's name, each repetition more frightened than the last. But as Virgil shut the library doors, the voices faded into muffled noise.

"Speak," Virgil said, shoving him against the nearest shelf. "Quickly and precisely."

Though he didn't believe in prayer anymore, Asriel offered up the hope that the others intended to tell the full truth, too. He couldn't see a way to lie that wouldn't cost him his life. The look in Virgil's eyes was near-wild.

"I took Freya down to the catacombs," he said in a rush. "My guard, Barrett, went with us because he's my... He's my *guard*. That's his job."

"What were you doing in the catacombs?"

"Showing off," Asriel said, and sweat raced down his temple. "I wanted Freya to be impressed by me."

Virgil seemed to hesitate, his grip relaxing before he pressed Asriel harder against the shelf. "Your house gave in to the royalists during the war. How can I be certain your loyalties lie with Adristan?"

Incredulously, Asriel said, "I'm trying to prove exactly that to the Lancors. I'm trying to prove that I can be *trusted*. I want nothing more than to be good for the nation. Now will you *please* tell me what the fuck is going on?"

Slowly, Virgil backed off. Indecision filled his eyes. In a panic, Asriel realized that Virgil did not wholly believe him. Even so, he gestured toward the door.

"If your stories match, then I can tell you."

Virgil brought him back into the foyer then, dragging him toward Gerard Stillgrove.

"Hold him, would you?" Then, Virgil went to speak with his guard and Galilea a few paces away. Their heads bowed together in quiet discussion, and it was a short while before any of them looked up. When they finally did, Virgil's shoulders had visibly slackened.

"Royalists poisoned the dinner," the Midar Prince said. "All of the High Lords are dead. Their spouses and a few more nobles died alongside them."

Asriel paused for a moment before he broke into crazed laughter. He looked at his sister. "Rhae, tell your attack-dog his joke isn't funny."

Tears poured down her cheeks as she said, "He's not joking, Asriel."

He couldn't get over how *small* her voice sounded.

"That's— That's ridiculous. Father can't be dead, I just spoke with him." He pointed toward the hall doors, which were shut. "Take me to him."

"I can't," his sister said quietly.

"Take me to Father, Rhaella," Asriel demanded, command clear in his tone.

"She's telling the truth," Galilea said, stepping toward him. When she tried to touch his arm, he flinched away. "While you were down in the catacombs, they succumbed to the poison."

"I don't appreciate you playing along," Asriel growled, taking a step away from her. "All of you. Get a fucking *grip*. My father is not dead.."

"Sa," Rhaella said pitifully. *Brother*. "Please."

Asriel gasped for breath in short, almost spasmic bursts until his whole chest heaved and he hyperventilated. Then, in the blink of an eye, Barrett was at his side, supporting him before his legs could give out beneath him. And when the full weight of realization settled on him, and he realized that this was not some practical joke after all, the room spun so violently he felt his vision go black and fuzzy around the edges.

"My father is dead?"

The others nodded. He took in each of their faces, and it was impossible not to notice how grief-stricken everyone looked. Even Virgil Midar, whose exterior was usually hard as stone, looked hollowed.

"What do we—" Asriel's voice came out as nothing more than a soft squeak. He sucked in a breath. "Are they still *in there*?"

"Oh, gods," Freya said, and her voice trembled. She began to tear at her hair, messing up her curls and the headpiece placed there. "Oh, *gods!*"

Raven shook her head. "The Mediators brought them to the mortuary. A few of my acolytes will sail through the night to attend to them by morning."

"They're still cleaning the great hall," Aida said, and her voice shook too. "Once they're done, they want us in there."

"For what?" Asriel snapped dubiously.

The Fourth Princess looked at him as though he were an idiot. And then he realized he *was*. The biggest of them all, in fact.

Matter-of-factly, she said, "For the Ascension."

Of course. With no High Lords, there would need to be a ceremony to declare new ones. Asriel nodded his head in an attempt to compartmentalize, but it wasn't quite working. His head buzzed so loudly he could barely think, and he couldn't cut through the noise. All he could hear was his blood pulsing in his ears and his heartbeat racing as fast as could be.

"It has to happen in there?" Barrett asked, gesturing toward the shut doors. "There's nowhere else?"

"It's tradition," Raven said plainly.

"You're concerned with tradition right now?" Ramsey scoffed. "*That's rich.*"

"I don't see you offering any suggestions," Galilea said sternly.

The argument ceased as a huddle of Mediators came down the central staircase, their hands clasped tightly. One of them said, "We need you to follow us into the alcove to await your turns to Ascend."

"This is madness," Asriel said, wiping a hand across his face. "Can't we be afforded the evening? A *moment*, at the very least?"

"There are no High Lords in Adristan," the same Mediator said coolly. "That cannot stand."

Defeated in the face of duty, the heirs began to fall in line. What argument could they make that would justify leaving the country without a leader?

All of the spares followed the other Mediators back into the great hall, affording the heirs a few seconds to breathe. But there was nowhere else to go, and there were no more excuses to make. A Mediator waited patiently and directed them toward the alcove. Cautiously, they marched forward, each of them stepping into their shared destinies. Their new realities.

High above the rest of the room, in the alcove, they gathered at the top of the stairs to look down on the crowd waiting below. Asriel saw family, members of the various councils, members of the Dux Doctrina. The remainders of the Concilium, he realized with a sinking feeling.

The Reverend Mother and a Mediator had already taken their place atop the dais at one end of the room. There were books and the sacred texts—those containing both the laws and the scriptures that held Adristan together. Those laws and scriptures were the same ones Asriel would recite as he Ascended. As he took his father's title from him.

He looked around at the rest of the heirs, ashamed to realize that he still had not shed a single tear. He didn't feel the urge to. Where there should have been the gaping wound of grief, Asriel only felt only more of that odd buzzing that blocked out everything beneath it.

With magic bolstering their voice, the Mediator in charge of the Ascension began to call out names.

"Ezra Lancor of the First House."

The giant let out a shaky exhale, and then, he descended the stairs two at a time. He crossed the floor with his shoulders hunched but as he walked, straightened, rising to his full height. Once he rose up on the dais, he bowed to the Reverend Mother in respect.

Ezra recited the words that were sacred to both the Lucerians and to Adristan, and the Mediator declared him quickly and without fuss. Words were not the most important part of the ceremony.

A councilman who bore House Lancor colors stepped forward with a blade in hand. Even from this distance, Asriel could see that the handle had been fashioned out of wood. The Mediator accepted the blade, gesturing to Ezra with the tip. Ezra loosened the collar of his shirt, exposing the top of his sternum.

"Blood will have blood," the Mediator said, raising the knife. With a careful hand, she cut across Ezra's sternum. The blade was enchanted to soak up the blood, so that not even a drop poured down the front of his shirt. Holding it aloft, the Mediator held it so that it caught the light, shining with the blood of life and death and all that lay between.

Another councilman brought forth a basin filled with orange paint. The Mediator dipped the blade into it, swirling so that the red mixed into the orange. Asriel knew that the pigment had been crafted with the blood of all of the Lancor High Lords that had come before. Now that Ezra would Ascend and be anointed with the blood of his ancestors, he would need to give some of his own in return.

Every hand on the dais dipped into the basin. The Mediator, the councilman, and the Reverend Mother scooped paint into their cupped palms and colored Ezra with the pride of House Lancor. His face, neck, and hair dripped with paint as it fell in fat splotches onto his shirt and exposed chest.

Finally, the councilman produced a crown fashioned with stag horns and crafted from the finest materials that his house had to offer. Ezra leaned down far enough for the noble to place the crown upon his head, and when he rose, his gaze was clearer than before. More focused.

Reverend Mother Locasta stepped back, wiping her hand with a kerchief. "It is time to pick your right hand."

Without hesitation, Ezra said, "I name Doctrina Lucius as the Dux Doctrina of the First House."

His father's Doctrina. The man had survived the chaos and appeared alive and well. He stepped onto the dais to accept his position, and the Reverend Mother gave them both words to speak before handing each of them a potion. Then Ezra Lancor, having only just come of age at twenty, became High Lord of House Lancor.

Ezra stayed on the dais, moving to the side to make room for the next High Lord. He stood with his hands fidgeting and moving between his pockets and behind his back. Soon enough, the rest of them would join him.

"Sage Oberon of the Second House."

And the process repeated. Words were spoken and vows were made. There was magic in the things they said. Magic Asriel didn't really understand. It was nothing more life-altering than duty was, but the finality of it was breathtaking. Whatever they said on the dais bound a High Lord to service and a lifelong pursuit of fidelity to Adristan. Asriel had been preparing to do just that his entire life. He required no magic to seal his fate. And yet the thought of something so irreversible chafed.

An Oberon councilman brought forth a blade that looked medical in its purpose. Sage allowed the Mediator to cut along their wrist, and after their blood mixed into the basin, they were painted in the white of their house. Asriel could not understand how the blood didn't discolor the hue, but he assumed that must be due to some strange magic, too.

The councilman placed a crown bearing phoenix feathers on their head. The feathers draped down around Sage's temples, covering the tattoos there. Asriel thought they looked fearsome, for a healer.

When Sage was prompted to name their right hand, they chose a

Doctrina Asriel was unfamiliar with. Isaiah Oberon's Doctrina had been slaughtered in the conflict, he remembered too late. The Second House would receive a new High Lord and a new Dux Doctrina. So many changes in so little time, reflected tenfold across the entire nation.

"Asriel Veservus of the Third House." This time, the Mediator's voice sounded like a death knell.

Asriel flinched. He hadn't even realized he was next, he had been so lost in the ritual of the Ascension. He thought he would have had more time to prepare, but time was no longer on his side. Before he could think further, his feet carried him down the steps and across the floor. Face to face with the people who were about to alter the course of his life forever.

As Asriel stepped onto the dais, the Mediator held out the book to him. Taking it in his hands, his eyes glossed over the sacred words he needed to repeat out loud.

"Do you swear to entrench yourself in pursuit of the betterment of Adristan, for as long as you shall live?"

"I do," Asriel said. He felt the magic take hold then, seeping itself into his bones. Into his veins. His very life's blood.

"Do you swear to strive only for peace and prosperity, and to avoid violence wherever possible?"

"I do."

"Do you swear to work in tandem with your fellow High Lords, your Dux Doctrina, your advisors, and your chosen council?"

"I do. On the Martyr, on the gods, on the saints, I will be dutiful."

One of his father's councilmen—now *his* councilman, he realized—brought forth a blade with a handle shaped like the end of a quill. Asriel had seen the blade hanging in one of his father's studies. It was an unsuspecting thing. Completely at odds with the way it made him feel now, knowing it was about to be the very implement with which he wrote his fate in the history books.

The councilman had been a good friend to his father, and Asriel hoped he would pay his friend's son the same courtesy. He hailed from House Erestine, after all. His mother's house. He had always been loyal and polite, if condescending.

Asriel allowed the Mediator to cut him along the back of his neck, just below the hem of his shirt. Any enemy willing to slaughter him from behind was a worthwhile one. He would never rest with his back to the room again.

The noble, the Reverend Mother, and the Mediator coated their hands in a red so similar to the blood that had covered the floor that it made Asriel's stomach turn. But there was no time for such things. Their palms pressed against Asriel's cheeks and forehead, coating even his lips in the paint. It was thick and tasted metallic, and he tried not to linger on the thought that it was mostly blood. He was being painted with the life force of his father, and this would be the closest he'd get to having him back for the rest of his life.

They put a crown that bore hawk feathers on his head. It was heavy and uncomfortable, not quite fitted to his head. His father only ever wore this on special occasions, and Asriel couldn't imagine wearing it ever again after tonight.

"You may now name your Dux Doctrina."

Asriel's eyes scanned the faces gathered below the dais, frantically searching for anyone familiar. He latched onto Dogan. The man had survived, after all. That had to stand for *something*. With Dogan's help, Asriel could patch everything up that his father had been working toward. It would ease the transition. Even despite the man's many downfalls, he was a wealth of knowledge.

But when Asriel opened his mouth to speak, it was not Dogan's name that came out.

"I name Rhaella of House Veservus as my Dux Doctrina."

Gasps echoed throughout the hall. The Reverend Mother stiffened beside him. From the crowd, another Doctrina stepped forward. They did not rise fully up the dais, but they took a few cautious steps toward him.

"My Lord," he said gently. "Progeny Rhaella has not yet completed her training. She is not a Doctrina."

"I want her to serve as my Doctrina," Asriel said, surprising even himself with the conviction in his tone. "Do you deny that I have the right to name her?"

"Of course not, my Lord. But there is the matter of her training—"

"She'll be done within a few months," Asriel said, voice unwavering. "Doctrina Dogan will serve as the Interim Doctrina for House Veservus until then."

The Doctrina glanced to where Rhaella stood the crowd, and then back to him. He nodded his chin curtly before speaking again. "Of course, my Lord."

It was unorthodox. But then again, so was everything about this Ascension.

Dogan scaled the dais and faced the Reverend Mother at Asriel's side. He placed a hand on Asriel's back that was probably meant to be comforting, but it made his skin crawl instead.

The Reverend Mother looked between them stoically and Asriel considered that she, too, had been poisoned this night. Though, according to rumors of the Dux's training and practices, the poison likely hadn't affected her the same way it had everyone else.

"Do you swear to listen to one another with open ears, an open mind, and an open heart?"

"I do," Asriel and Dogan said in unison.

The Reverend Mother handed each of them a half-full goblet. Dogan drank it down without hesitation, meanwhile Asriel sniffed it suspiciously before raising the rim to his mouth. When the drink touched his lips, he fought the urge to gag and to spit it out. It was bitter and stale like a bad ale.

Magic coiled around him once more, and he groaned at the oil-slick feeling of it. It made him shudder and it sent chills down his spine.

Dogan, predictably, seemed unaffected.

And just like that, Asriel was officially named High Lord of House Veservus. In all of his childhood daydreams and adulthood nightmare, he had always thought it would feel more… Just, *more*. Aside from his disgust from the potion, and the strange tingle of the magic, he felt nothing.

He was utterly numb.

As he made his way off of the dais to stand with the crowd, he caught Rhaella's stare. She was pale, almost sickly so. Horror had widened her eyes, and she was trembling. Asriel was tempted to sign to her and ask what was wrong, but Virgil stood beside her, warning written clearly on his face.

Don't.

So he didn't.

Asriel joined the others at the far end of the dais, finding it difficult to stand and be watched by the whole of the crowd. To stop himself from balling his fists into his clothes, he shoved them in his pockets. Suddenly—horribly—he felt he understood Ezra's feelings perfectly.

Aida had risen for her turn by then, and she spoke the words with a clear voice. Confidence had never seemed in short supply in the Fourth House, and today was no exception. She made it through her Ascension with ease, and she seemed untouched by the tremor that had captured her voice earlier that night.

The Mediator cut her over her heart and painted her cream. Then, her councilman placed a crown atop her head with the hooves of a stallion cresting its band. She raised her chin, defiant to the grief that bore down on her shoulders.

After naming her Doctrina, Aida turned to the crowd, determination clear on her face.

"And I name my heir on this night, too. My son, Callias Redspire."

Outrage ensued. Even Asriel couldn't hold in the shock that took him as his jaw went slack. The Mediators did what they could to quell the rising upset, but Aida stood on the dais with her chin held high, refusing to allow the chaos to shake her conviction.

"My Lord," the Mediator said. "It is not required of you to name an heir at this time."

"I don't care," Aida said firmly. "My son will be my heir."

Hesitantly, the Mediator nodded. "As you say."

It took a moment for the room to collect itself before the Mediator could continue. They were only halfway through a mass Ascension, and there had been so much blowback. What would the future of Adristan look like if this was the first ceremony of many?

The Mediator gave them no time for reprieve. No time to process anything more than the most cursory emotions.

"Gerard Stillgrove of the Fifth House."

Between his vows to the nation and the cut the Mediator placed along his brow, Gerard was covered in purple paint and crowned with rams' horns. Proudly, he said, "I name Doctrina Ophelia as my Dux Doctrina."

The woman that rose from the crowd looked familiar, and it took Asriel a few extra seconds to realize that it was because she was the same Doctrina the Stillgroves had been working with for the past few years. He'd noticed her shadowing the High Lord during the meetings, offering her counsel when prompted.

"Raven Aviatis of the Sixth House."

There was no mistaking the disdain that rippled across Raven's features as she rose to her place at the front of the room. She practically spat out the sacred words, her lip curling as she spoke. She turned her face away as they cut the skin below her elbow. And when they painted her silver, the color settled into the lines around her mouth. The owl feathers in her crown matched the ones in her ceremonial headpiece. It was a perfect fit for the heir apparent. Still, it brought her no joy. Even as she named her Doctrina, neither pride nor accomplishment shone across her features. There wasn't even grief there. Just a burning, brimming anger.

"Ramsey Lightpike of the Seventh House."

When the Mediator called his name, Ramsey still looked as though he had not adjusted to this current reality. Without his father or his brother there for guidance, Ramsey simply looked *lost*.

A pang of sympathy went through Asriel. The boy had only just been made heir, and now was expected to Ascend to High Lord only days later. Who could blame him for feeling adrift? Who could blame *any* of them for however they handled this?

There was an underwhelming ceremony to being named heir, and yet Asriel assumed it must have come as a great shock to Ramsey. Not all of the houses participated in it, and Asriel imagined that the Lightpikes hadn't had to participate in a process like this since doing so for their second son.

Ramsey flinched when they cut one of his shoulders, as well as when they covered him in emerald green paint. The crown that was placed on his head bore the pattern of a peacock's feathers and it was a gaudy, ugly thing. Surely, it was heavier than any other sigil Ramsey had worn previously.

He named his father's Doctrina swiftly and without pretense, and then his Ascension was over. As Ramsey came to join the others on the dais, he practically stared a hole through the floor. His usual swagger and pride were nowhere to be seen.

"Virgil Midar of the Eighth House."

It sent a wave of fury through Asriel to see Virgil stride forward when the Mediator called his name. It seemed like he had been waiting for this moment his entire life. Like even tonight, when he was in the midst of so much grief and action and anger, he had been prepared for the sudden, heavy weight of duty to slam down on his shoulders.

And yet he looked entirely unshaken.

Asriel's gaze shifted to his sister once more, and he watched her as she watched Virgil say the words. There was an odd look in her eyes. She was still crying, and there was obvious pain there, but there was something else on her face too. Something he couldn't name. Something he had never seen there before.

Her eyes widened when Virgil lifted his shirt and he allowed the Mediator to cut along his abdomen. The blood didn't even drip, thanks to the blade's ancient magic, but the shock registered on her face nonetheless. His blood mixed into the basin with the rest of his forefathers', and so Virgil Midar's Ascension began.

Bitterly, covered in blue paint and wearing a wolf-crown on his head, Virgil spoke. "I name Nicholas Midar as my Dux Doctrina."

Virgil and his uncle spoke the words, and the ceremony was over. With Virgil declared, there was an entirely new set of High Lords. People clapped, slowly and awkwardly at first, before bursting into full applause at the sight of all eight of them lined up. It was a terrible and beautiful sight, each of them standing in the room where their forebears had just been killed. They were all bloody, with their clothes torn, and they were covered in gunk and paint that caked their faces and hair. Standing beside them all, Asriel looked too clean for his own good. He hadn't witnessed any of the massacre. And yet, he felt everything as it radiated off of his peers. Though he still couldn't manage to find any of it within himself, aside from that low-level static buzz he couldn't quite seem to shake

More Mediators stepped forward, unease still written on their faces. One of them—the one who had partaken in the Ascension—spoke carefully.

"My Lords," they said. "We think it would be best if we maintained a proper headcount for the evening, before anyone retires. In the morning, we'd like to do the same."

Looking amongst one another for a spokesperson, the heirs grappled over who would speak for them. At first, several of them tried, talking over one another. After a long moment, it was Aida's voice that cut through the other noise.

"That's fine," she said, nodding her head. "Have the guards set a rotation so some of them can sleep. The rest of us will go to our rooms and wait to be retrieved in the morning. No one leaves the island until we reconvene at breakfast."

With those orders, the Mediators began to take count of the members of each house before sending them to their suites. Asriel watched Freya's figure retreat along with her brothers and she shot him an apologetic glance over her shoulder before exiting the hall.

Anyone present without loyalties to one specific house was sent to one of the numerous guest rooms around the Palace, but not before their names were taken. And not without a strict reminder that they, too, were to attend the headcount at breakfast. It felt so militaristic of an order. So frightening in its rigidity.

When House Veservus was sent to bed, it was only Asriel, Dogan, and the guards that hadn't gone down in the fray that were left. Rhaella would remain with the Dux in whatever room she had been assigned to. It was a small party for their small house. And their High Lord, who currently felt very, very small.

They went down the hall, back to the Veservus suite. In hushed voices, the guards set up a rotation for the evening. All of them had to be nearing the brink of exhaustion, but there was no one else to watch over them in the night. In the end, they decided Barrett would take the first break.

Dogan pushed into the suite, wishing Asriel well as he shut himself into his room. Asriel realized with a start that the largest room—the room his father had occupied—was now empty. The thought of sleeping in there disgusted him. All of his father's things would still be in there. What if the sheets were still warm?

He didn't realize he'd started sobbing until Barrett put a hand on his shoulder, pulling him into a tight embrace. Asriel buried his face in the space between Barrett's neck and shoulder, fingers clutching the little bit of shirt that peeked out from beneath his armor.

"I don't want to go in there," he cried.

"You don't have to," Barrett assured him. "You still have your room."

The tears fell harder. Now that he had started, Asriel wasn't sure he could stop. "*Stay with me.*"

Barrett stiffened even as he continued to rub circles across Asriel's back. "I don't want to make you feel worse, but I have to ask. Do you want me in there with you because you want *me*, or is it because Freya isn't here?"

Despite the tears that fell down his face and the horror that wracked his body, Asriel traced his nose up Barrett's neck. "I want *you*," he said.

As he'd hoped, Barrett shivered. "Fine. Let's go to bed."

Asriel let Barrett take his hand and pull him into the bedroom. No candles were lit, and neither of them moved to change that. With a tenderness Asriel did not deserve, Barrett pressed his lips against his. He reciprocated in kind, helping his guard remove his armor. It was a tedious process, but at the moment, Asriel was thankful for it. He needed the familiar routine to clear his mind. And when Barrett pulled at his clothes, Asriel gave in without a fight.

Barrett was not often this patient or gentle with him. Normally, fucking between them was full of gnashing teeth and pushing and pulling and breaking skin. The way Asriel preferred. But tonight he felt content to let himself relax and to let Barrett maneuver him however he decided. He gave himself over to pleasure entirely as Barrett rode him.

That wasn't to say Asriel did nothing. He wrapped a hand around the back of Barrett's neck and pulled him in for a kiss every time his head rolled back as he moaned. Swallowing the sounds, tasting their sweetness, drinking them in greedily.

As he felt Barrett tighten around him, Asriel took his hips in hand and increased their pace, guiding them both toward release. It happened fast—faster than Asriel had intended. He swore as he came, endlessly grateful that it was Barrett in his bed tonight and nobody else. Barrett always knew what Asriel needed. He never had to explain himself, and he never needed to justify anything. And so it cost Asriel nothing to get up and offer to clean Barrett when they were through.

Afterwards, the two of them lay on their sides and whispered into the dark. Asriel reached out and traced his fingertips across the scars lining the skin beneath Barrett's chest. He'd been considering covering them with tattoos, and, selfishly, Asriel was glad that he hadn't gone through with it.

"Everything will be different when we get back to Isle Verdale," Barrett said quietly.

"Wildly," Asriel said, splaying his palm across Barrett's chest. There were other scars there too. And their origins ranged from training mishaps or simply small scraps. But none fascinated him as much as the affirming ones beneath each pectoral. "The world changed while we were in those tunnels."

"I'm surprised by how well you're bearing it," Barrett said, placing his hand over Asriel's.

Asriel had given up crying. He felt empty of tears, as if the grief lingered in a strange, faraway place where it could no longer touch him. It disturbed him that he wasn't more outwardly upset. Internally, he was devastated. The thought of never speaking to his father again was unfathomable. And yet, it was also unchangeable.

"It's going to hit me later. *Really* hit me. You're probably going to find me on the floor of a conference room in Briarhall, curled into a ball in utter shambles." Even as he said it, though, Asriel doubted its truthfulness.

"Don't make fun," Barrett scolded. "It hurts me enough that you're in any pain at all."

"At least I didn't consume any of the poison the others did." Asriel stiffened, burying his face into the pillow. "That was a terrible thing to say. I shouldn't have said it."

Barrett ran his fingers through Asriel's hair, tangling his fingers in the long locks. "It's alright to say that. I won't judge you."

"Am I a terrible person?" Asriel asked. "Am I grieving incorrectly? I know I should be more upset. I should be downright *inconsolable*. And yet I find it hard to feel anything at all."

"When I learned that my parents had died while I was away at training," Barrett said, "I thought the world had ended. Time stood still for a few moments, but I didn't cry. My body kept moving, and I went about my life in much of the same way. My mind was still there, stuck in that

349

moment when my commanding officer handed me the letter. The version of me that existed in that moment had tears to spare. The version of me that had to keep going didn't."

"Did you ever?" Asriel asked. "Cry, I mean."

"I shed a few tears on their birthdays. Or when I accomplished something and wished I could tell them about it." Barrett sat up, letting the blanket fall away. "They'll come. Maybe not right now, but they will."

Asriel sat with Barrett's words in silence, watching as his guard pulled himself from bed and put his armor back on. The second watch would be starting soon, and desire couldn't keep Barrett away from duty.

"I'll come wake you in the morning," his guard said as he leaned down to press one final kiss to Asriel's lips.

"Fine," Asriel said, sinking into the blankets.

Once Barrett left, sleep came for him quickly. The morning woke him too soon, chasing away vivid nightmares of people screaming as bodies fell to the ground. Asriel sat up abruptly in bed, awoken by the sound of footsteps approaching. When Barrett opened the door as promised, they offered one another soft smiles.

Asriel dressed in his finest clothes. He braided his hair back entirely, and he smudged red shadow beneath his eyes so no one would see the real shadows there. He took a step back to admire himself in the vanity mirror, and he thought he looked very much like his father.

"Ready?" Barrett asked gently.

With a nod, Asriel stalked out of the room. He threw open the doors to the suite, and he began ordering the guards about.

"After the headcount, return to the suite and gather all of our belongings. Load everything onto the ship and prepare to set sail. We're returning to Isle Verdale before dinnertime."

Asriel left no room for questions or misdirections. Only clear, calculated decisions.

"Yes, my Lord," the guards said in unison.

Asriel kept his spine straight as he walked the halls of the Palace. He felt different than he had yesterday. Changed, but not in the physical way of the Ascension. His father's voice played on loop in the back of his mind, reminding Asriel of how he should carry himself. How he should address his fellow nobles. How to be the High Lord.

All of the lessons he had not yet finished learning had suddenly become so very real, and Asriel wasn't sure whether or not he'd pass them given the test. Nevertheless, questions like that no longer mattered. As he pushed open the doors to the great hall, all that mattered was that he felt as though he had been changed. Altered on some catastrophic level.

Asriel rolled his neck as he approached the Mediators and the gathered crowd of nobles, and he saw that his sister was already among them. They turned to stare at him, and he saw that they were all changed, too. Even the common folk who were among their numbers. This was not the Adristan he had woken up in yesterday, and it was not the Adristan he would likely face tomorrow. This was the face of an Adristan who was only beginning to reform its identity amidst tumult and uncertainty.

This was the face of an Adristan whose future he would now have a direct hand in shaping.

With a clear voice, Asriel addressed the crowd and said, "House Veservus is here."

CHAPTER TWENTY-SEVEN

"It was difficult to contain your wondrous existence into a simple moniker. But I have done it, and I deem that you are to be called vzoz cìr - my seeing daughter. You are the very best of me, so much so that I think myself wretched now."
—*Letter from High Lord Alden Veservus to his daughter, Rhaella, on her naming day*

31 Luceriary, in the Benevolent year 112 A.E.

The sun rose as though nothing was different, even though everything was different. Birds continued chirping. Waves continued to roll against the rocks at the base of the island. And Rhaella's life was still dictated by the rules of her training. And yet, her father was dead and her brother was now the High Lord House Veservus.

It was the final day of the holy month—a holiday to those who practiced. The Feast of Saints had never stuck out to Rhaella as anything but an excuse to slip away to the taverns and blur the evening. Now, though, it had taken on an irrevocable new weight.

Rhaella stood on a balcony off of the great hall, looking out at the sea. Virgil was a few paces away, and he leaned against the railing. His arms were crossed, and he hadn't stopped looking at the ground. A soft breeze had picked up into an annoying wind, tossing loose strands of hair into her face. She resisted the urge to brush them back, waiting for Virgil to do it for her.

When at last he looked up, Virgil said, "So this is it, then?"

A rogue tear ran down her cheek. "Don't say it like that."

Just last night they had been in one another's arms. Rhaella played the fool and snuck into his room, and he had let her. They hadn't slept much, if at all, though they hadn't gone further than holding and comforting one another. Yet it was incredibly selfish nonetheless. Though she didn't regret it, either. Most of the night, they simply laid there in darkness, limbs tangled as they took turns crying. Sometimes they talked, but there was nothing that could be said to ease the ache of their new circumstances.

"It doesn't have to be this way," he said as he pushed away from the railing. "You can come with me to Greenisle."

She wiped at her face roughly with the inside of her wrist. "I want to. You know I do."

"Then do it," he pressed as he stood by her side.

They didn't touch. People milled about on the other balconies and it was too visible. Too vulnerable. But that didn't stop Virgil from resting his hand on the balcony railing, right beside hers. If she stretched out her pinky, it would rub against his. She wanted to feel his skin one more time.

"If I stay with the Dux," she said shakily, "I'll have access to information I wouldn't otherwise have as a Lady. I can find more on the royalists to send to you. I can make all of this death mean something."

"It does mean something," he said. "It means the royalists are malicious but clumsy. We don't have to fight to make it mean anything more than that."

Rhaella shook her head. "It's not that simple. It can't be. There's too many details that don't add up. I could go to Greenisle with you and be your wife and spend my days wondering what went wrong here."

"Or?" Virgil prompted.

She looked at him straight on, which hurt her more than she had the words to say. "Or I could acquire enough information on why and how last night happened, and then I could use that as leverage to ease my transition out of the Dux. Now that we don't have the protection of our fathers, I need that. You know that as well as I do."

Virgil let out a heavy sigh, sounding miserable. "You're right."

For the first time since last night, Rhaella smiled softly. "Don't pretend that you hate to admit such a thing," she teased lightly.

He eyed her, fighting back a smile of his own. "You know I don't. I should be used to such a thing by now."

She scoffed, then said, "It's for the better. In the future, when I can return to you, it'll be with peace backing our borders." She stared out over the horizon as she spoke. "Not this fearful uncertainty."

Virgil turned his body so he was facing her entirely. Minding the people milling about, he reached out a hand and tugged on one of the tiny braids framing her face. He tangled it around his finger before letting it fall limp again and pulling away.

"I'm going to wait for you," he said sternly.

Rhaella's face softened. "You can try."

Suddenly straightening, Virgil took on a more serious tone. "When we exchange letters, keep anything compromising hidden. If you find anything to do with the royalists, give me the cursory details and leave the rest to discuss in person. I have a feeling we'll be attending more of these congresses in the coming months."

"It would help if you knew more Vessial," she said with a sigh. She cast her gaze out toward Isle Verdale in the west as she leaned against the railing. "Or if I knew more Menmal."

After a pause, Virgil said, "Bei kaw. Chi lolv mag nelk."

"One more time," Rhaella said, keeping her eyes outward.

"Bei kaw. Chi lolv mag nelk," he said. "Something is wrong. We need to talk."

Rhaella repeated the phrase to herself under her breath. She made a frustrated sound in the back of her throat when she couldn't quite manage to fit her mouth around each of the intricate words. And even if she managed such a thing, she wasn't sure she could say them with any sort of clarity. Word by word, she translated the phrase into its Vessial counterpart.

"I'll understand you if you say that. So hear me when I say ngkûsluh mogzhe. Yo os dya bai."

Virgil mimicked the sounds of her words until he could stumble through the phrase with enough nearness to its true pronunciation. And then, satisfied with their secret code, Rhaella glanced toward the open balcony doors. The silence stretched between them, growing impossibly larger and somehow also just as impossible to close.

"When does your ship leave?"

"When I say we're leaving," Virgil answered, matter of factly. Then he asked, "The Dux isn't granting you leave to mourn with your brother?"

She sighed. "I didn't ask."

"You know you're entitled to it," Virgil said.

"The other Progenies don't get to go home to their families," Rhaella said. "I'm not looking for special treatment. I'm no longer a member of a noble house. Not yet, at least."

Virgil's mouth was a hard line. "Swear that you won't push yourself right when you get back to your training."

She arched a brow. "Only if you swear the same."

"Unsheathe your dagger," he said, and he held out his palm.

Rhaella did as he said, drawing a blade from beneath her robes. She thought that she might never be unarmed again in her entire life if she could manage it. Virgil extended his palm to her, gesturing for her to do the honor. Carefully, she split open his palm before doing the same to her own. Then, they shook on it, blood smearing against their skin. And when they pulled apart, Virgil took out a handkerchief and wiped the blood from her hand.

"Next time we meet, Rhaella, vzoz cìr," he said clumsily. "We will be on opposite ends of the meeting table. I will look at you across it with fondness, and I hope you will do the same for me."

"Of course I will," she said on a breathless whisper.

"One more time." He shivered at the promise of what they were both admitting to. "I want to hear you say my name one more time before we leave."

She tickled her fingers against the arm that held hers, still attempting to wipe her skin clean. "Virgil."

Momentarily, he shut his eyes. When he reopened them, there was a wall up between them that hadn't been there before. Rhaella understood the need for it. Even with the threat of prying eyes, she might very well have thrown herself at him on this balcony.

He let her go.

"Safe travels," he said, heading back inside.

"Vyef." *Goodbye.*

And then she was alone on the balcony. She stayed there for some time, letting the sea air hit her face. She let it calm her. If she was good, like her father had taught her to be, she would have headed out to the foyer to find Asriel before he left for home. She would have assured him that he'd

355

made the right choice and that she was ready to expedite her training to return to his side.

But Rhaella wasn't sure she was good anymore.

After a long bout of consideration, she went inside. There were still red-cloaked guards milling about, which meant that Asriel hadn't departed yet. She approached one and asked where their High Lord—her *brother*—was. Pulling rank over the guards wasn't always necessary, but she felt so distanced from them now that she'd been gone for almost four months. It was the only leverage she had left.

They directed her to the library, which should have come as no surprise. She made her way there, nodding to Barrett who guarded the doors. But, to her surprise, he moved in front of her, blocking her path.

"It's not a good time, Rhae."

She frowned. "Obviously. Let me talk to my brother, Barrett."

Barrett shifted uncomfortably. "He's in really bad shape."

"And what shape do you imagine I'm in?"

He didn't budge for a few breaths, and Rhaella thought she was going to have to fight him to get in the door. But he sighed and stepped out of the way, muttering an apology under his breath. Rhaella ignored the urge to shoulder him as she stepped past, slamming the library doors shut behind her.

"Asriel?" She called out.

Red curtains had been draped across the windows, casting the room in an eerie glow. It felt as though the entire library itself was mourning. Conversely, Rhaella wasn't even permitted to wear her own mourning garments. Dux mourning practices were different from the rest of Adristan, and, after all, she was Dux before anything else now. While her peers would wear veils with their house colors for the foreseeable future, Rhaella would have to carry her grief inwardly, as she did everything else.

Once Asriel arrived back at Briarhall, he would be fitted with a blood red veil that went to his feet, similar to the one Ramsey had worn to the Grand Introduction. As the months went on and the grief became a bearable thing, the veil would be cut shorter and shorter until, at last, there were only scraps of fabric left. When their grandmother passed, their father started carrying around his veil scraps in his pockets. She wondered if that's what Asriel would do to honor their father someday.

The idea of the grief ever waning seemed inconceivable. And yet, Rhaella had managed to get out of bed today. She hadn't broken down in sobs over the thought of never seeing her father again. The pain clung to her like a second skin, but it did not weigh her down. Somewhere in her mind, she thought she had said her permanent goodbye to her father on the docks of Isle Verdale, all those months ago.

"I'm over here," Asriel called from between the shelves.

She followed the sound of his voice and found him sitting on the floor, his back against a heavy stack of tomes. He was dressed as nicely as he had been the evening prior, with his hair braided and makeup done. The red beneath his eyes was artificial, but Rhaella could see through the cosmetics down to the true dark circles beneath. When he looked up at her, the exhaustion he carried was palpable. He offered her a sad smile and patted the space beside him.

Rhaella sank to the floor and rested her head on Asriel's shoulder. In return, he rested his cheek on her head.

"What are we going to do?" His voice rumbled against her skull.

"You'll have to organize a funeral," she said. "And if I'm lucky, the Order will grant me leave to attend."

"I don't know how to do this," Asriel said miserably.

"I know," Rhaella said, equally as miserable, though she didn't allow it to leak into her tone.

"How many funerals have we attended back home? A handful, if that. I don't know if he left behind any particular desires for that sort of thing. And if I plan it and miss something he would have wanted, or if I include something he *wouldn't* have wanted, I'm going to feel terrible."

Gently, Rhaella said, "Asriel, I can't plan it for you."

"I'm not asking you to."

"No," she said, exhaling. But he was framing it in such a way that would compel her to offer. Only now, she had to keep to her training. It was less of a choice than it felt like, but she would stick firm to it all the same. Strange, that she would be thankful to the Order for something.

Asriel's voice trembled as he said, "I'm really gonna miss you, Rhae."

Silently, Rhaella thought that Asriel now held the authority to order her to come back home. He did not *have* to condemn her to a life among the Dux Doctrina, now that he could no longer disappoint their father. And no matter how badly she wanted to simply resent her brother for the way he had acted—the plans he had set in motion—she understood him too. She knew that he had acted out of fear of disappointing their father. Though that didn't make the knowledge sting any less.

But Asriel would never opt to bring her home if there was even the slightest possibility for something to go wrong. That had never been her brother's style. He had only ever acted when he knew there was no possibility for failure. No opportunity to truly learn from such experiences. Nothing truly at stake.

This was Asriel's decision alone, and she wasn't sure he'd make the correct one. But she silently vowed to let him learn nonetheless.

She made herself say, "I'm going to miss you too."

And she would. The loss of their father was something that only the two of them were ever going to understand in the same way. They had a decent amount of family back home, but half of them did not belong to Rhaella. And even those related to her through her father's blood held her at an arm's length. Some of them regarded her as a pariah. A stain on her father's reputation. And thus, she had never been a child. Not to them. She had never been deserving of innocence. Even the family that was kind to her only did so out of obligation to her father. With him gone, she couldn't anticipate they would continue with that kindness.

"Are you going to take over Father's rooms?"

Asriel scoffed. "No. Those will either stay empty, or I'll have them turned into very lavish guest rooms. I can't imagine sleeping there. It already feels disrespectful to do so here."

"Everything at home is going to remind me of him," Rhaella said. "It's going to feel like a museum for him."

Hesitantly, Asriel said, "Do you want me to get anything out of the way? I can keep some things in his room for at least the first few months when you get back."

"That's very kind of you, but no," she said. "It's not that I don't want to be reminded. I just don't want…" She paused for a long moment, and she took a deep breath before speaking again. "None of this should have happened this way."

"I know," Asriel said as tremors wracked his body. Rhaella gripped his arm tightly, trying to ground him.

They were quiet for a long time, sitting there holding one another. Rhaella felt like a child again, hiding from duty in favor of spending time with her brother.

As long as they were in the library, hidden between shelves, the reality of their situation did not have to exist. And so it could not hurt them. These pages were the same as they had been when they were younger. They remained unchanged—constants for them to cling to in an ever-changing world.

Asriel sniffled. "I feel like I'm going to get up and walk out that door and he'll be on the other side of it, ready to tell me everything I'm doing wrong. Those were his last words to me, you know. That I wasn't doing enough."

Rhaella sucked in a breath. "I'm sorry."

Suddenly, she couldn't recall the last thing her father said to her. It had been something unimportant. Nothing worth committing to memory. Rhaella remembered everything without trying, and yet this escaped her.

Her breath came quicker, in more rapid bursts. *She couldn't recall.* Had she told her father she loved him in the past few days? Did he know that she didn't hate him for sending her away? Would he have cared if not?

Asriel put his arm around her. He didn't try to offer words of comfort and she was glad for that, because they would have done nothing for her. Her brother had a way of saying the wrong thing at the wrong time. There was a chance it would make her laugh. But all she could do right now was ache.

"I have to get to the ship," he said after a long silence. "They've already loaded everything. It's just me they're waiting on."

"Alright," Rhaella said, pushing to her feet. "I hope I'll see you at the funeral."

"I hope so too." Asriel chewed on his lip thoughtfully, then said, "You're missing all of the other funerals."

Rhaella nodded. "If the Order gives me leave at all, it'll only be for

Father. You have to attend all of them in good faith so that you can tell me about them when I get home."

"I would've gone regardless," Asriel said, shooting her a look.

"I'm sure," she said, heading for the door.

When Asriel caught her arm, she stared back at him in anticipation. A pressing look was on his face, his brow furrowed and his mouth drawn tight.

"When are you going to be able to write?"

Rhaella counted the weeks in her head. "Another few weeks. Maybe a month, at most. I was able to send a letter out before I made my rounds, though. Did you receive that one?"

Cheeks flushing, Asriel looked guilty. He nodded his head. "There was so much going on at the time, I hadn't been able to send anything to you. But I'm making it a priority now. Do you know if they read your mail?"

She shrugged. "I assume they do, though I'm not sure."

In a voice just above a whisper, Asriel said, "Does everything about this feel... bigger to you than a few disgruntled Lords and peasants?"

"Of course it does," she hissed.

"Then write to me with your concerns," he said, unfazed. "Speak in code. Put it in Vessial if you must. Just let me know your thoughts. If there's any way we're going to figure things out, Rhae, it has to be together."

"I can manage that," she agreed. "Anticipate my letters. And don't be afraid to send anything before I'm able to write."

Her brother looked solemn, even as he affirmed what she'd said. As they made their way out of the library, Barrett broke protocol to envelop her in a hug. She returned it, letting him rub his hands up and down her back. When he let her go, Asriel pulled her in. She gripped his back like he was the only solid ground for miles. When they let go, she was a buoy in open water. Drifting and somehow also tethered to the same spot.

"Scì khlash shlu, ðoz." *I love you, sister.*

"Tuf shlu, sa." *And you, brother.*

Rhaella watched him walk away. Once he was out of sight, she ran back through the great hall and out onto the balcony to watch him board his ship. She saw more of her friends doing the same, and a few ships were out on the water already. The Palace was emptying. Gutting itself of all this grief.

Doctrinas lingered all over the Palace grounds, inside and out. The Reverend Mother hadn't issued any orders, and the Superiors made no move to organize their departure. If they were meant to stay on Kingsgrave for the time being, she would've liked some warning. Though she couldn't very well demand one.

Once the rest of the ships departed from the harbor, a Progeny came and found her, urging her to the foyer. Rhaella followed, not knowing what to expect. The rest of the Progenies were there too, along with all of the Superiors who had accompanied them on their rounds. Each of them had fallen unconscious thanks to the tranquilizers. It would have taken an unimaginably specific dose to incapacitate the Reverend Mother without killing her. Whoever had drugged the food knew poison just as well as the Order did.

Judging by appearances, only a few Doctrinas who were assigned to High Lords had been killed in the chaos last night. If not by a stronger dose of poison, then by the blades the royalists and guards had pulled on one another. It was all unnecessary death, but she thought that when they returned to the Silent Keep, she would feel those absences cut deeper. She could only imagine what the Order would do to refill their ranks. Whether she would meet any familiar faces after the next round of Progenies were brought in.

"We will spend the day helping the Mediators put the Palace back in order," a Superior said. "And once the sun goes down, we will accompany the Reverend Mother back to the mainland."

The Superiors began handing out assignments to each of the Progenies. There were the less desirable tasks, such as scrubbing the floors of the great hall. Seemingly pointless tasks, like surveying the floors of every guest room for belongings left behind. Rhaella silently willed the Superiors to give her a task of *use*. Something that would give her free reign to go back to the Veservus suite if only so she could be alone for a moment.

"Progeny Rhaella," a Superior said. "Go up to the Aviatis wing and put the church and the sacristy back in order for the priestesses for when they return."

Rhaella bowed and headed up the stairs to the second floor. All of the priestesses in residence at the Palace had returned to Pearlscape to select their new High Priestess now that Raven Aviatis was otherwise occupied. There wouldn't have been any time for them to tidy up before boarding their ship. And when she pushed open the door to the sacristy, she saw candles half melted and stuck to the wooden altars they sat on. Holy books that had been thrown open and left behind without a second thought. Shawls and cinctures rested on the pews.

The routine of cleaning was mindless. Blow out candles, clean the wax, check for scorched wood, relight the candles, put the books back on the lectern, repeat at every other altar scattered around the room. In the sacristy, Rhaella hung robes back in the closet and folded any spare clothes into the drawers. Then, she swept the floors of both rooms before mopping them with soapy water.

Rhaella nudged open one of the many closed doors in the sacristy, meaning to return the cleaning supplies to their proper place. She swore under her breath when she found it was the wrong room, and she moved to shut the door. But as she raised her eyes, she froze with one hand on the knob and the other on the threshold to steady her.

Past it was the mortuary. And on many tables, covered by many white cloths, were bodies.

There was another door on the other side of the room, which she knew led to the Oberon wing. They must have shared this as a meeting point, she realized morbidly.

Shakily, without thinking, she went further inside. She had no strong desire to see her father's lifeless body again, but the thought hit her that she might not be able to attend the funeral. If this was her last chance, she was going to take it.

Rhaella assumed that the bodies were organized by house, and, as it turned out, she was right. The bodies closest to the Oberons' side of the room were taller. The Lancors. First House. Rhaella counted off in her head how many bodies had fallen the night before. It matched the first row. The next row must have been the Oberons, then. And the one after that belonged to House Veservus.

Rhaella crossed the room in a few short strides. Aside from her father, they had only lost a few guards. No friends or extended family had been invited since they already could not afford the spare men. She cast her senses out in front of her, and she tried to pick out which slab held her father. She didn't want to disrespect the other dead by needlessly gazing upon them.

At her furthest left, she felt him. She felt the same blood that ran in her veins. The same essence that made them members of the Veservus family. Slowly, she stepped up to the table, and with shaking hands she drew back the cloth. Her father's shut eyes were the first thing she saw. With a sob, she dropped the cloth and clutched her hands to her chest. A drawn out whine escaped her, and she called out for her father in Vessial. *Mìn. Mìn. Mìn.*

She had to wonder if she was still a daughter if she no longer had a father. She had never had a mother to begin with. By all accounts, she was an orphan now. A lonely child of House Veservus and Isle Verdale. Her strongest thread tying her to nobility was now severed, and any remnants of it were being hacked away at every day she spent with the Order. Soon, the version of herself that had existed for the first twenty-five years of her life would be gone. All thanks to her father. This was his orchestration. His design. His hand.

The same hands that were now cold and still.

Rhaella moved to stand at the end of the slab, gripping the corners of it so she wouldn't collapse completely. She allowed herself to openly weep for a few minutes, perhaps longer. And when she was empty of tears, she raised her head and looked at her father's unresponsive face.

"Scì dvesh dya smoû zmû fsaût shlu. Scì jaì."

I'm going to do right by you. I swear it.

She felt her blood simmer beyond average mortal fury. This was divine anger. The sort her ancestors had felt. The kind that bolstered them to bring about the great house that became House Veservus. To do right by the people of Adristan and collect their shared histories. Better people had come before her and had been through worse. They survived it, and she decided that she would, too.

Rhaella turned her blood to steel. She fortified her skin and all of the layers of muscle and tissue and bone beneath it. To the wandering eye, she was the same sullen girl she had always been. But pieces of her had died along with her father, and the rest was sure to follow soon. Once she was entirely gone, all that would be left was the steel. She would be something stronger, then. Something that could withstand this agony.

Distantly, Rhaella let herself wallow in the fact that she wanted the life where she got to marry Virgil Midar and live as a pampered Lady. But that possibility belonged to a now-foreign version of herself. One that had started dying the moment her father had stopped breathing and her reality had shifted irrevocably. She reminded herself that soon, she would be stronger.

She would be reborn.

Rhaella clutched the fabric between her fists and then she covered her father's body again, all the while willing this new version of herself to surface sooner. For now, all she could do was wait.

"Vyef, mìn," Rhaella said, stepping back from the slab. *Goodbye, Father.*

She left the mortuary, shutting the door behind her with a soft *click*.

EPILOGUE

"Friends! Oh, horror! The High Lord has been killed!"
—*A herald on the city streets*

31 Luceriary, in the Benevolent year 112 A.E.

The heavy veil of mourning fell over Adristan, casting a shadow across the islands that did not let up even as the sun continued to rise and set. Shops closed, festivities ceased, and people hid in their homes. It was impossible to go outside without feeling it. The majority of Adristan's citizens had never even met their High Lords, but death was death, and the mourners followed.

This was true everywhere except for the night markets, which would never stop for something as simple as grief. Here, death was as common as the changing of the seasons. The transition from one High Lord to the next. Plumes of smoke rose up toward the low ceilings and they coated the room in the scent of tobacco. Somewhere in there, the herbal tang of experimental drinks wafted from a nearby stall. When they looked to where the smell came from, there was a line that backed up all the way to the door. Clearly, everyone understood that—thanks to the current state of things—it might be a while before another shipment came in.

At each of the food stalls, the lines were less intense. There, people conversed loudly, their voices bolstered by impatient hunger. Each patron barked out complaint after complaint about the changes to their daily lives. Nothing felt certain, but then again, none of them had ever lived through the assassination of a political figure before. Uncertainty was now a given, and discontentment was its loyal companion.

"We can expect every necessary expense to increase," one voice grumbled. "Who was the High Lord to me? I'm not mourning him. Why should I have to pay?"

"Prices've been low lately," another said. "That was bound to change eventually."

The new High Lords had not announced any such changes, but rumors tended to find their way to the masses regardless. The people were scared. Wary to see what they would need to do to stay afloat. Stability had not been a guarantee for a long time, and it did not seem like it would be on the horizon anytime soon.

Outside, under the light of the full moon, people walked to the next market. They never stayed in the same place for an entire evening. Not with the watchful eyes of the off-duty guards who milled about. Never mind the fact that they inhabited the same unsavory places and partook in the same unsavory substances as the rest of the masses.

Gravel crunched beneath boots and coins jingled from inside pockets. The march from one market to the next continued just as the politics of their world did. The world would continue to spin on, and so would their lives. Maybe it was cruel, but it was just how things worked. Change was their only constant. It was something that politics and the landscape of their world would never be. There was no fairness in death.

The night grew long, waiting in the food line at the next stall over. Soon, it would be morning. It meant nothing. It meant everything.

THE PRINCE &
THE SOLDIER

Humiliation was no stranger to Asriel, and the certainty of that had only grown once he'd reached his twelfth year. This was supposed to be the year he gained a dragon. Outside in the Veservus gardens, nobles were gathered for the happy occasion. Every person of note from his father's council. Cousins Asriel hadn't seen in years. Officials from neighboring nations. It was a larger party than his actual birthday had been.

And yet, he was sitting inside Briarhall in one of the many studies his father wouldn't think to check, crying into his balled fists. Egorion hadn't bonded with him; wanted nothing to do with him, in fact.

He chose Rhaella.

It wasn't supposed to be this way. Egorion was *his* dragon, promised since Asriel's birth. Even though they were boring and repetitive, Asriel had attended the dragon's trainings, watching as the dragon masters made him fit to be ridden by the heir of the house. He took meals inside the dragonpit, trying to form a connection with the damned beast. According to his father, who had bonded with his own dragon by the age of twelve, Egorion was showing all of the signs that they were a proper match.

Either everyone around him had lied, or Asriel had fallen short in some unmeasurable way.

Often, it was the latter.

Asriel did not wish to place blame on his sister. She had only just returned from a summer on the mainland, taking etiquette lessons at the Silent Keep with the Dux Doctrina. Since her return, she had been quiet. Less quick to laugh. Asriel had monopolized her attention, pulling her into his antics around the castle, but it hadn't seemed to help. But Rhaella had always been reluctant to swim in the depths of her feelings. When tossed into the current, she preferred to drown.

Much like he was doing now, he realized. If that made him a hypocrite, he didn't care.

Outside of the study, Asriel could hear servants walking past in intervals. None of them would be searching for him. They were too preoccupied with the festivities, getting the guests drunk on his father's good wine. Rhaella was probably being paraded around on their father's arm, being introduced to dignitaries and optioned off for a prospective match. A bastard with a dragon was better than most.

It was a wicked thing to call her that, *bastard*. Perhaps Egorion would make up for the sting of it. She deserved that much. But what of Asriel's pain? Would he be left to lick his own wounds for all his life? That wasn't fair either.

Asriel rose to his feet, dusting off his ceremonial trousers. He had to be mindful of his wrist, wrapped in a stiff bandage. The healer said he couldn't remove it for another few weeks. Around his neck, the family sigil hung on a heavy brooch. He clutched it in his good palm, felt the ridges of the metal press into his skin. Veservus men rode dragons. His father, the High Lord of the greatest of great houses, rode the fiercest one in all the land. Lesser men trembled before the sight of it. Someday, they would tremble before Asriel, too. Whether or not he became a rider, he was still of his father's blood. He still deserved that awe.

But Rhaella would have the glory. She had Egorion. It was a compromise that benefited neither of them. She had the dragon, and Asriel would get the respect. He would someday be High Lord, and she would still have Egorion. That wouldn't change, but it wouldn't improve anything else, either.

He pushed open the door to the study and stepped into the dimly lit hall. The windows were covered by thick curtains, red as blood. For a normal boy, it would be difficult to tell what the time of day was. But for Asriel, he could tell by the shadows crawling along the edges of the curtain that it was nearing sunset. The party would only be growing more raucous. The visiting vampire clans were just like his family—nocturnal. For people like them, the festivities were only beginning. Once it neared midnight, they might break to pray and give thanks to the Martyr for the good fortune bestowed on Rhaella. And then they would resume drinking and dancing and debasing the prayers they had just offered up.

Asriel heard the people rounding the corner before he saw them.

369

There were two, to be precise. One older, closer to his father's age. And one young. Right around Asriel's age.

Lieutenant Rune rounded the corner with a boy in soft fighting clothes. The boy startled, halted mid-step when he spotted Asriel. But Lieutenant Rune pulled him along, coming toward Asriel with a smile on his face.

"Ah, it's good we found you," the lieutenant said. "You might as well meet this young man now. Prince Asriel, this is Barrett. He's going to be educated in our school for a few years before he heads off to be trained for the guard."

Asriel dipped his chin politely. He prayed the redness had faded from his under eyes. "Welcome to Briarhall."

"Welcome, indeed," Lieutenant Rune said. "He's going to become a proper scholar, and then he's going to train his hardest. For you, my Prince. He's to be your sworn sword once you both come of age."

"Oh." Asriel had guards, though they were sworn to his father. They were his by proxy, and only that. A sworn sword was a luxury, something houses with larger staff could afford. The High Lord needed to be heavily guarded. The rest of them rationed off however many remained.

It wasn't often that they received new guards, especially ones who weren't shipped directly from House Midar's boarding schools. Judging by the boy's ill-fitting training clothes and the frightened look on his face, he had been recruited off of this very island. Perhaps from one of the smaller, more rural villages.

In a mousy voice, the boy—Barrett—said, "Pleased to meet your acquaintance." Then, hastily, he added, "M-my Prince."

Lieutenant Rune chuckled. "Why don't we make our way toward the gardens? They seem to be having such fun out there."

That was the last thing Asriel wanted to do, but he couldn't very well say that to his father's man. Dutifully, Asriel nodded and followed the two toward the main staircase. Asriel mumbled passable responses to the things Lieutenant Rune said as his eyes darted toward Barrett, who walked silently beside them. He was skinny, too skinny. His hair was cut shabbily, and though he had done it himself. And he habitually tugged on the chest of his uniform. It was far from snug, but his fingers grasped at the fabric, pulling it off of his skin.

When they made it out into the garden, Asriel's father was there, laughing boisterously with visiting nobles from Steephelm. He spotted their party as they approached, and he smiled to see them all together.

"I see my son has met his new sword," the High Lord said. "Very well, very well. Rune, find yourself some liquor and join us. Asriel, show Barrett the grounds."

Asriel nodded, fearful of disappointing his father further. "As you say."

There was no palpable disappointment in his father's expression, but that was just because his father knew how to mask it. Asriel would be able to see it later, when his father didn't think he was looking.

"You've been crying," Barrett said quietly once they were a good distance away from the nobility.

Asriel frowned. "I have not."

Barrett shot him a knowing look. "Your eyes are red."

"And your clothes don't fit," Asriel spat out. "But I am *polite*, and so I didn't say it first."

For a moment, Barrett was quiet. They continued walking the expanse of the garden, passing all of the drunken aristocracy who paid them no mind. Asriel's eyes caught onto the topiaries and the fruitful trees. The season would be over soon, and their richness would shrivel up as winter took over. There would be no strong chill or snow, like there was on the mainland, but the earth seemed to know that not everything was meant to bloom year round.

After another stretch of silence, Barrett said, "Is it your wrist that's making you cry?"

Asriel looked down at the bandage. He tugged at a fraying thread and said, "No, it doesn't hurt when it's in this. I'm sad over something else."

"What?"

He hesitated. If this boy was supposed to be his sworn sword, he'd learn all of Asriel's secrets over time. Perhaps it would be easier to just tell him. To deny Barrett the opportunity of being disappointed by anyone else over Asriel's own faults.

"The dragon my father picked for me bonded with my sister instead."

Barrett did not react with pity, as the rest of the nobles had. To Asriel's surprise, the boy shrugged. "Dragons are scary."

"Yes, dragons are *scary*," Asriel said, exasperated. "That's why I wanted him."

"I thought High Lords always rode in carriages or on horses."

"They do. But some of them ride dragons, and the people love them for it."

Barrett tilted his head. "Then be one of the ones the people love on a horse or a carriage."

Asriel scoffed. This boy had to be from the furthest reaches of Isle Verdale. He simply did not understand how things were done. It could not be that simple.

Then again, *why* couldn't it be?

There was another pause, and then Barrett said, "They didn't have clothes that would fit me. They told me the recruits are usually bigger by my age."

"Yes, they are," Asriel confirmed.

"But it's also to hide the bandages."

"Bandages?" Asriel frowned. He stared at Barrett. "I don't see any bandages."

As if propelled by Asriel's words, Barrett tugged on the chest of his shirt, loosening the fabric from his body. Slowly, information worked its way through Asriel's brain. And then, after a too-long thought, he said, "*Oh.*"

Barrett nodded. "Oh."

Well, that was that. Secrets had been shared in the garden, and neither of them were worse off for it. Asriel had no dragon, and he was no disappointment to Barrett. Barrett had been plucked from his village and given chest bandages and a fresh uniform, and Asriel thought nothing of it. Perhaps that would be a nice thing to have, someone who thought nothing of the things that felt large.

Unsure of what else to offer, Asriel said, "The grounds are boring. Do you want to see our secret tunnels?"

When Barrett smiled, Asriel could see that he was missing a front tooth. He nodded cheekily.

Without cue, the two of them began running toward the castle, laughing wildly as they did. The members of the party paid them no attention. Because it was nothing that the two boys were sprinting in the grass in their nice clothes. Nothing mattered at all. And in the midst of Asriel's despair, that meant more than anything else. More than a dragon, even.

LANGUAGE APPENDIX

Two invented languages appear in The Crownkiller Saga. In context, Vessial and Menmal are dead languages that have been reconstructed for House Veservus and House Midar, respectively. This is to maintain secrecy within the noble families, especially in sensitive political situations.

In the interest of transparency, words that appear in Heirs of Destruction are listed below. Some are not exact translations, and require the context of the story in order to be understood. If you wish to continue the story spoiler-free, feel free to skip these translations.

MENMAL

Menmal is solely a spoken language. It is described as harsh-sounding, throaty, and difficult to say. There are no surviving written resources on the language, so it is passed down verbally by the Midar family.

Iyd	You
Heke	Need (lack)
Chai	Become (begin to be)
Pcibe	Appearance (act of appearing)
Tuy	Like
Koh	He, it (masc.)
Op	Cousin
Manw	Yes
Dawich	Why

Leïch	Fuck (slang)
Aiyy	Off
Lunw	This
Ma	My
zcï	Language
Ke	Small; little
Bawp	Bird
Lesht	Big; great (very large); huge
Goù	The
ruhsh	rock; stone; metal; granite
toj	grow; evolve
buð	heavy
Bei	Something
kaw	wrong
Chi	we
lolv	need (require); require
mag	to: towards
nelk	talk; speak

VESSIAL

Vessial is a more incomplete reconstruction. The spoken aspect lacks translations for many words, so a sign language dialect was created to supplement it. There is also a nonspeaking code deciphered through blinking.

ðoz	sister
Siu	Remember

ŭ	you
afnaw	bird
swa	of
zyisha	prey
Ep	Yes
min	Father
Scì	my
cir	daughter
Yo	we
kù	all
ki	too; so; very; really
law	thank; bless
ðeìb	of
shlu	you
Scì	My
af	dragon
Zlaû	His, it (masc.)
yoûb	careful
dfuhj	information
Yo	We
me	have; take; grab; seize; esort; own; possess; include; clutch; grip
frish	more
vwen	than
vya	one
chtai lyo	library
Law	thank
shlu	you

Scì	I
joû	feel (perceive; sense); appreciate
vyuhs	fear
Shwosh	But
ki	too; so; very; really
slù	much
pfa	like
scì	my
min	father
Scì	I
twu	want; crave; desire; lack; choose
huht	he; it (masc.)
yap	say; tell; declare; confess; notify; inform; instruct
chei	no
Swosh	But
scì	I
smoû	do
mpùz	not
twon	know (a fact); know (be acquainted with)
a	that
scì	I
vyad	would
eswiffong	work (function); work (have desired result)
lav	the
mij	same
Scì	I
tha	must; have to
dled	go; leave (depart); continue

Jaw	be (exist); be (permanent state)
aw	good; excellent; great (excellent); moral
Vye	No
Kwaw	Maybe
Ep	Yes
Vzoz cir	Seeing-daughter
Shlu	Your
twuh	heart
slif	fit; belong
dya	to; towards
shom	me
Kwawf lav ùnzɔìshìvuhpi znû aìj li awn magrì zhuhfpuhgrɔìw	May the dead lie where the future leads
Kwawf lav flì pwo lav ullù	May the sleeping hide the path
Vyef	Hello
chti	Grandfather
Sa	Brother
ngkûsluh	something
mogzhe	wrong
Yo	we
os	need (require); need (lack)
dya	to; towards
baì	talk; speak; chat
Scì	I
khlash	love

shlu	you
Tuf	And
Scì	I
dvesh	come; go; become (change into); ge; reach
dya	to; towards
smoû	do
zmû	right; correct; valid; moral
fsaût	by (using the means of); by (using a route)
shlu	you
Scì	I
jaì	promise; assure

ACKNOWLEDGMENTS

In many ways, it feels surreal to be writing this section of the book again. After I published my first novel, I feared for a brief period of time that I would never be able to replicate that process again. And, for a while, my fears were aggravated. The next novel I attempted to write was a blunder—I failed to complete it three times. It was only after I returned to my old pile of ideas, and the one I knew was the book of my dreams, that I felt able to write again. Heirs of Destruction is the book I have always wanted to write. It contains every theme, every trope, every thread of ideas that I have ever wanted to put to page. From the beginning of my professional career, I knew that my writing process could never be a solitary one. I am humbled by the love and dedication shown to me as I put this book together. I was never alone. Allow me to thank those people now.

Cat, beloved, we did it again. You are every good idea that I have been unable to voice. The unconditional support you always show me continues to astound me. I am a better writer because of you. Thank you.

Camille, you are too generous to trifle with me. Your mind amazes me every single day, and I'm honored that you care about my words as much as I do. You remind me that I matter in this. Thank you.

Morgan, look at where we ended up. Your enthusiasm for life is an absolute gift, and so very necessary. Because of you, I feel not only heard but seen. Thank you.

Sarah, your patience and resiliency never fails to wow me. Your artistic gifts combined with your generosity have given me far more than I deserve (though you'll yell at me for saying so). Thank you.

B., your endless enthusiasm is something I will never be able to match but am always appreciative of. You are always a light in the dark, even when I insist on blowing out the candles. Thank you.

Joya, thank you for noticing that the doors were closed. Your laughter is infectious, and the uninhibited reactions you had to this story reminded me not to drown myself in the details. Thank you.

Leon, your commitment to making sure I put the best version of myself on page is so needed. You are always there to tell me when I may be in over my head, or can't see the forest for the trees. Thank you.

To the rest of my beta readers, Jakes, Alx, Clanky, Gabby, you made me want to make this the best it could be. You made my day with your commentary and excitement for this book. Thank you for making this feel like a story worth being told.

To the Congregation, thank you for being a beacon of community. I am so glad to share space with you all. You humble me and build me up every single day, and I will never get over the fact that you like me enough to stick around. Thank you.

To my sister, for drawing the map, and all of the other stuff, I guess. I'm so glad we've only gotten closer as we've aged. Hm.

To my readers, I'm astounded that I get to call you mine. You make me feel like I have a voice, and that I am someone who is worth the work I put into this craft. Thank you for wanting to read, thank you for reading, thank you for telling me that you want to, thank you.

Lastly, to my husband. This is my first book where I get to call you that!! Isaac, your support has never wavered. Thank you for your honesty, even when it meant telling me something needed work. Thank you for the takeout when I was tired and the encouragement to keep going when I needed it. You are the great love of my life and I am lucky to know you and call you mine. I love you.

ABOUT THE AUTHOR

T.N. Vitus is an award-winning author, specializing in the macabre and sacrilegious. They love writing anything under the fantasy umbrella, so long as there is rhythmic prose and complex characters. When not writing (which is rare), she is a voracious reader and consumer of media. If asked, they will gladly info-dump about Lord of the Rings or whichever fantasy they are currently fixated on. She lives in California with her loving husband.

You can find T.N. on most socials as vitusvital_ or evenstarsss. Her debut novel, SACRILEGE is available everywhere.